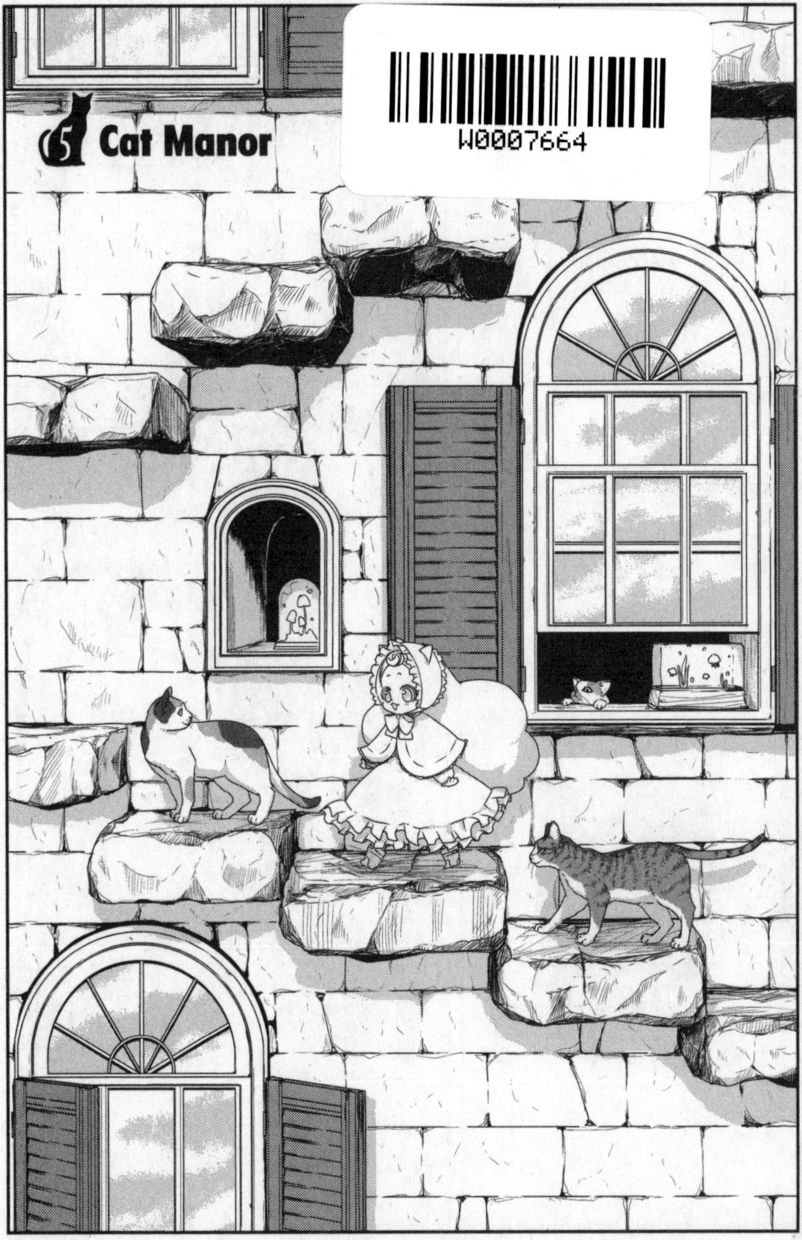
5 Cat Manor

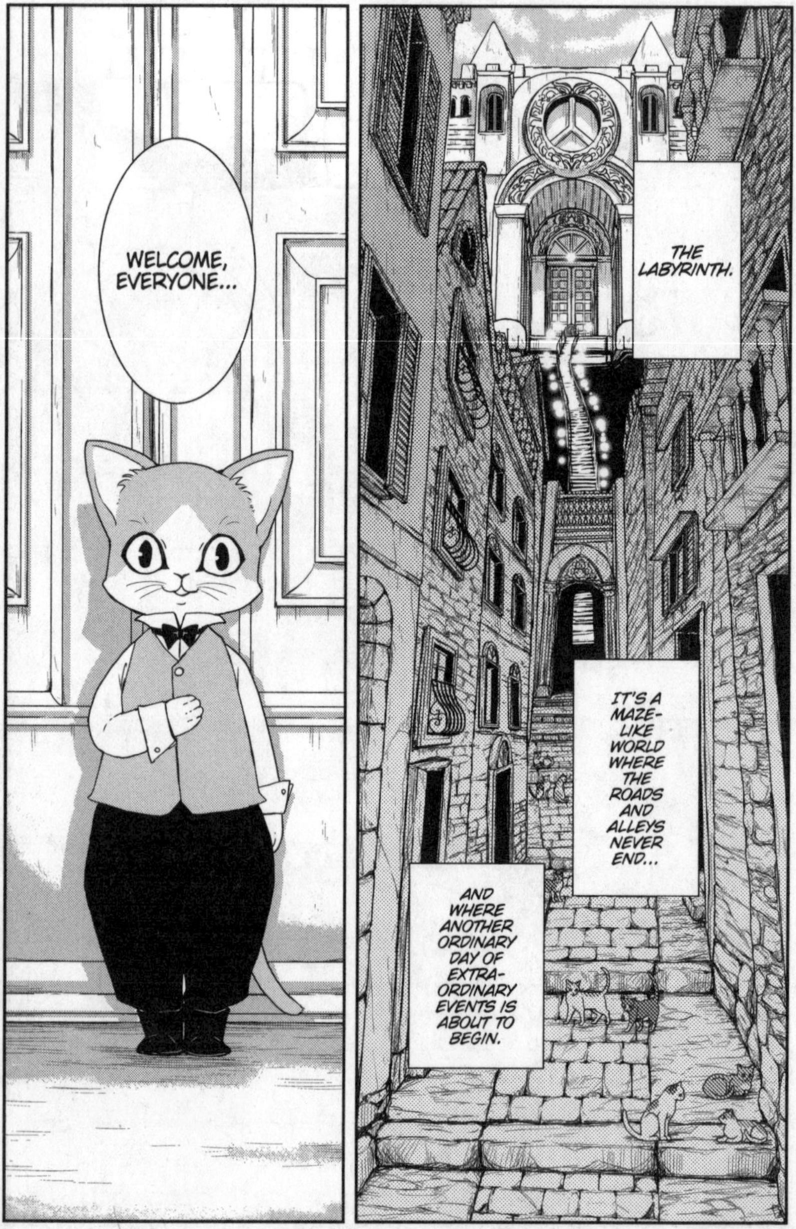
THE LABYRINTH.
IT'S A MAZE-LIKE WORLD WHERE THE ROADS AND ALLEYS NEVER END...
AND WHERE ANOTHER ORDINARY DAY OF EXTRA-ORDINARY EVENTS IS ABOUT TO BEGIN.
WELCOME, EVERYONE...

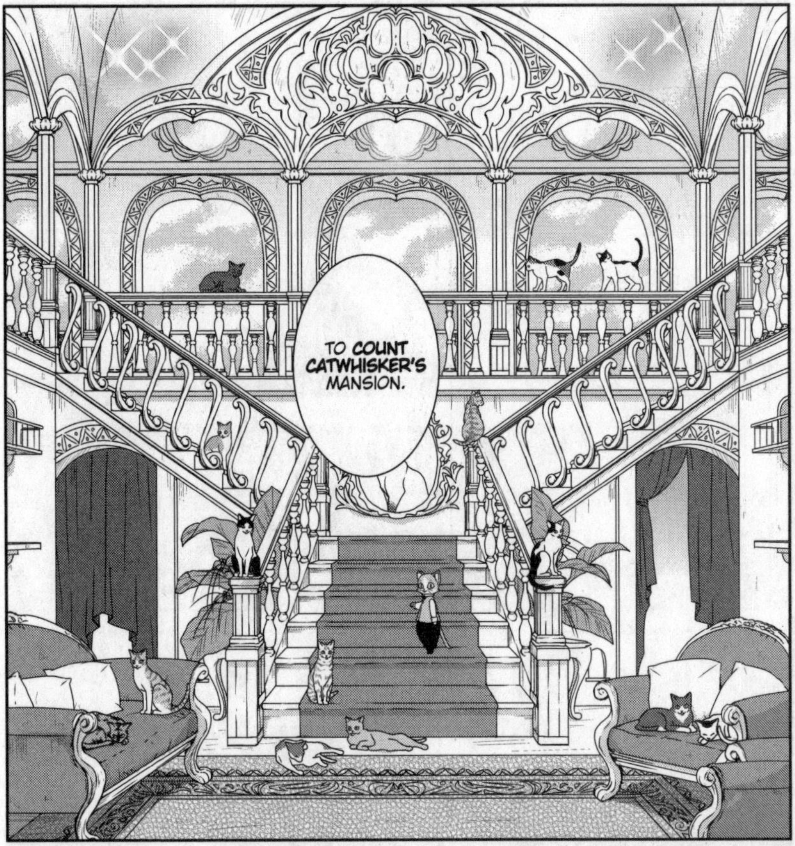
TO COUNT CATWHISKER'S MANSION.

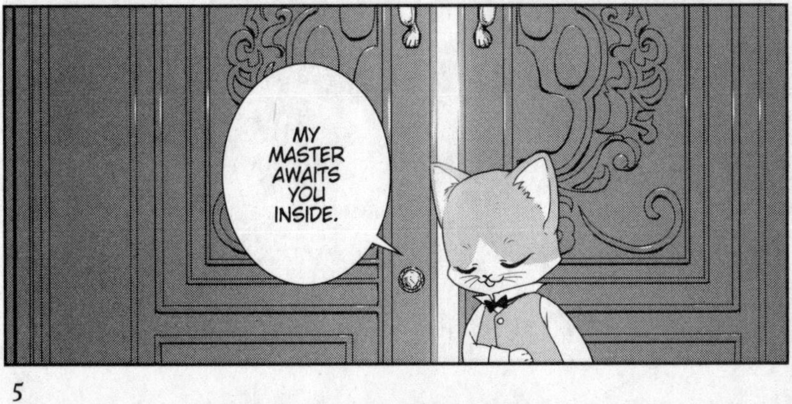
MY MASTER AWAITS YOU INSIDE.

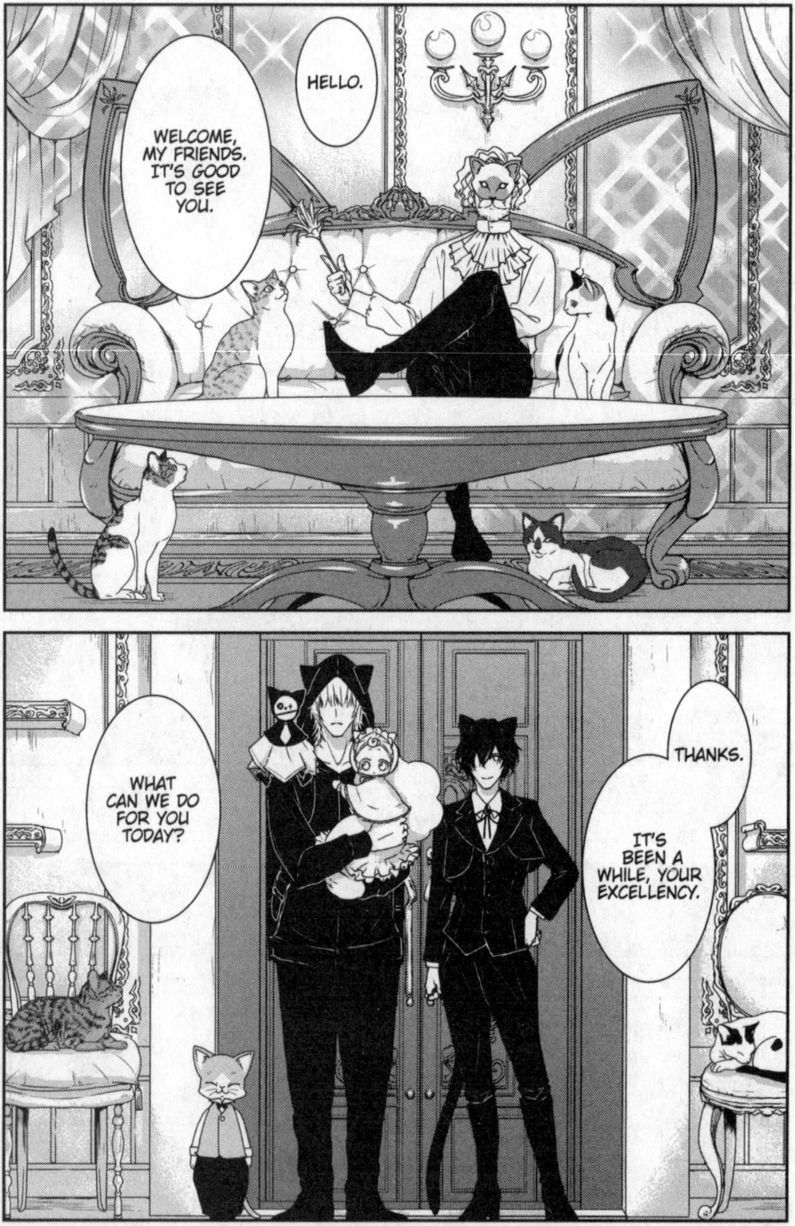
HELLO.
WELCOME, MY FRIENDS. IT'S GOOD TO SEE YOU.
THANKS.
IT'S BEEN A WHILE, YOUR EXCELLENCY.
WHAT CAN WE DO FOR YOU TODAY?

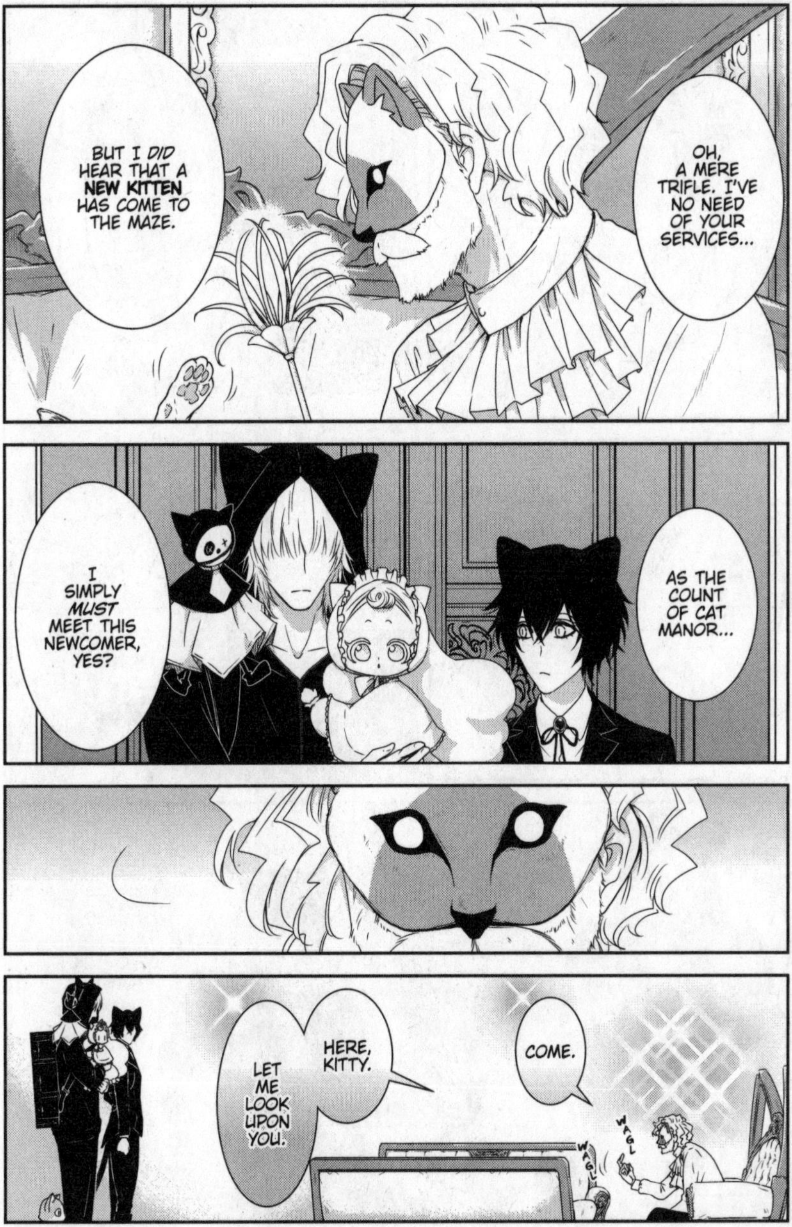
OH, A MERE TRIFLE. I'VE NO NEED OF YOUR SERVICES...
BUT I *DID* HEAR THAT A **NEW KITTEN** HAS COME TO THE MAZE.
AS THE COUNT OF CAT MANOR...
I SIMPLY *MUST* MEET THIS NEWCOMER, YES?
COME.
HERE, KITTY.
LET ME LOOK UPON YOU.
WAGL
WAGL

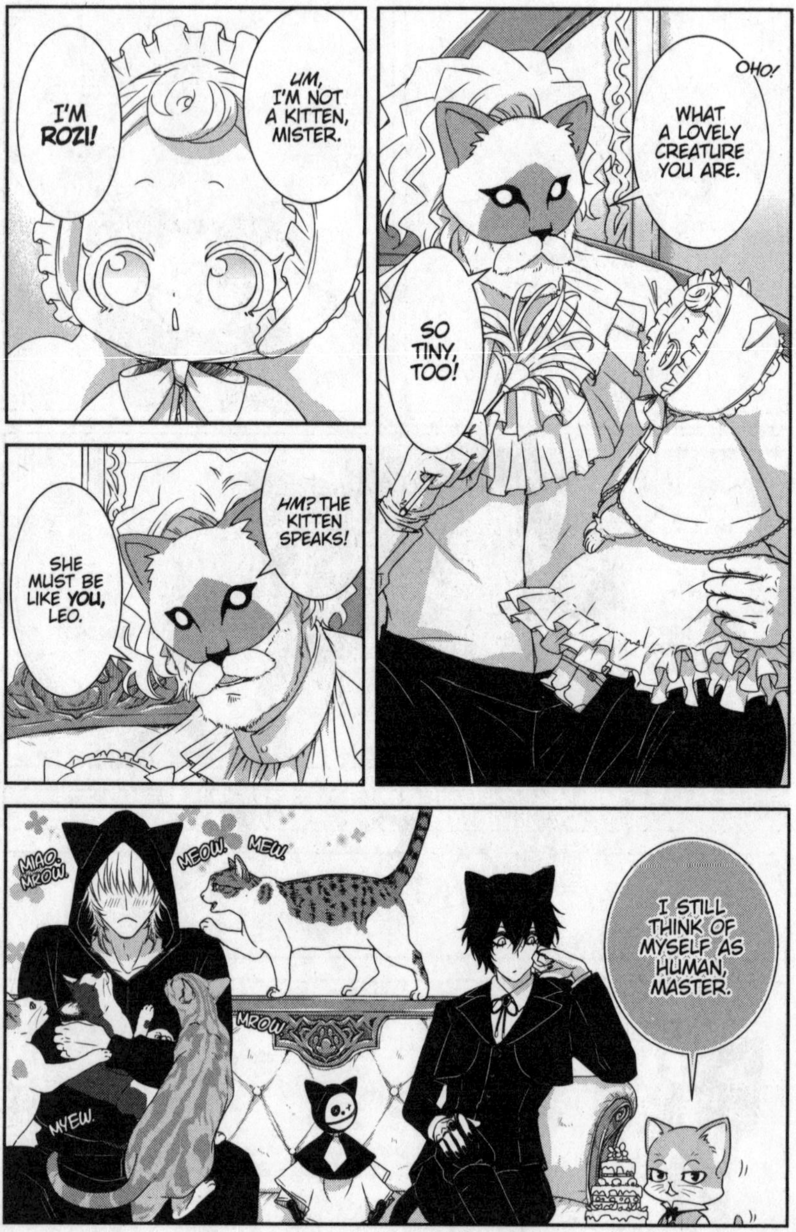
OHO!
WHAT A LOVELY CREATURE YOU ARE.
SO TINY, TOO!
UM, I'M NOT A KITTEN, MISTER.
I'M ROZI!
HM? THE KITTEN SPEAKS!
SHE MUST BE LIKE YOU, LEO.
I STILL THINK OF MYSELF AS HUMAN, MASTER.
MEW.
MEOW.
MIAO. MROW.
MROW.
MYEW.

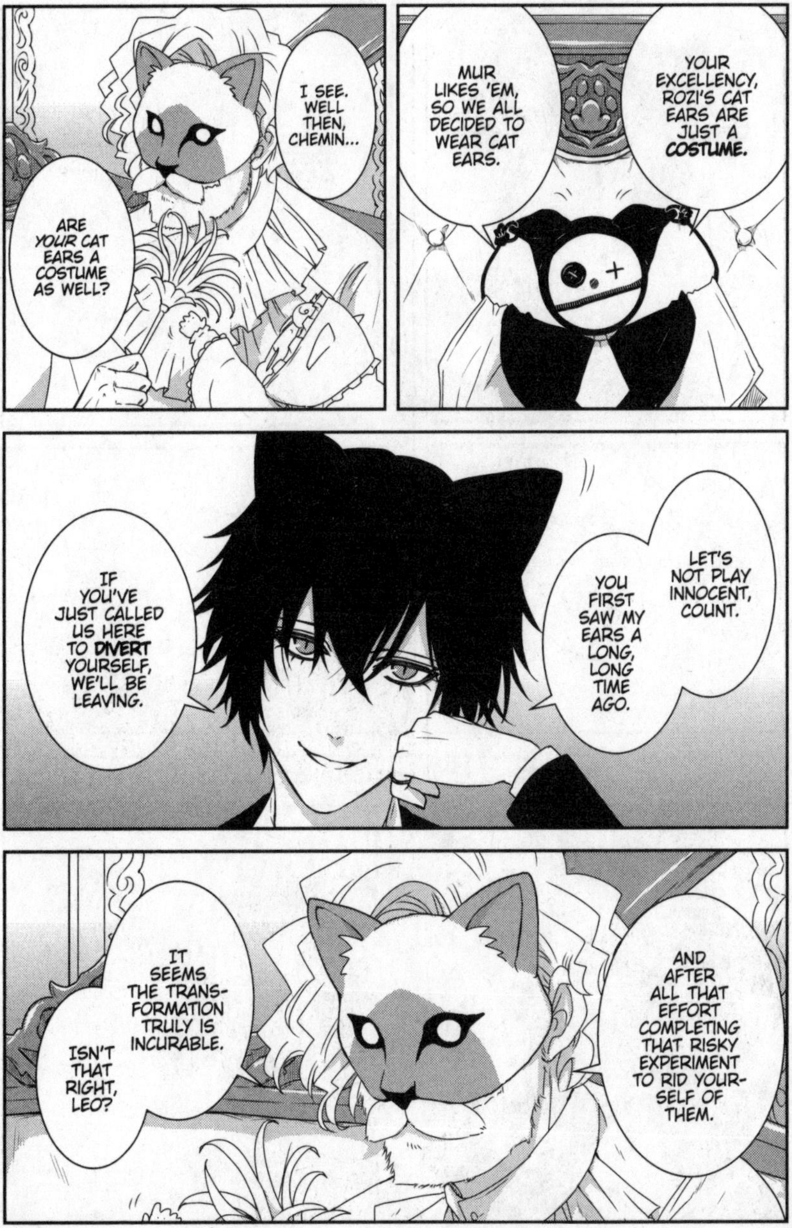
YOUR EXCELLENCY, ROZI'S CAT EARS ARE JUST A **COSTUME.**
MUR LIKES 'EM, SO WE ALL DECIDED TO WEAR CAT EARS.
I SEE. WELL THEN, CHEMIN...
ARE *YOUR* CAT EARS A COSTUME AS WELL?
LET'S NOT PLAY INNOCENT, COUNT.
YOU FIRST SAW MY EARS A LONG, LONG TIME AGO.
IF YOU'VE JUST CALLED US HERE TO **DIVERT** YOURSELF, WE'LL BE LEAVING.
AND AFTER ALL THAT EFFORT COMPLETING THAT RISKY EXPERIMENT TO RID YOURSELF OF THEM.
IT SEEMS THE TRANSFORMATION TRULY IS INCURABLE.
ISN'T THAT RIGHT, LEO?

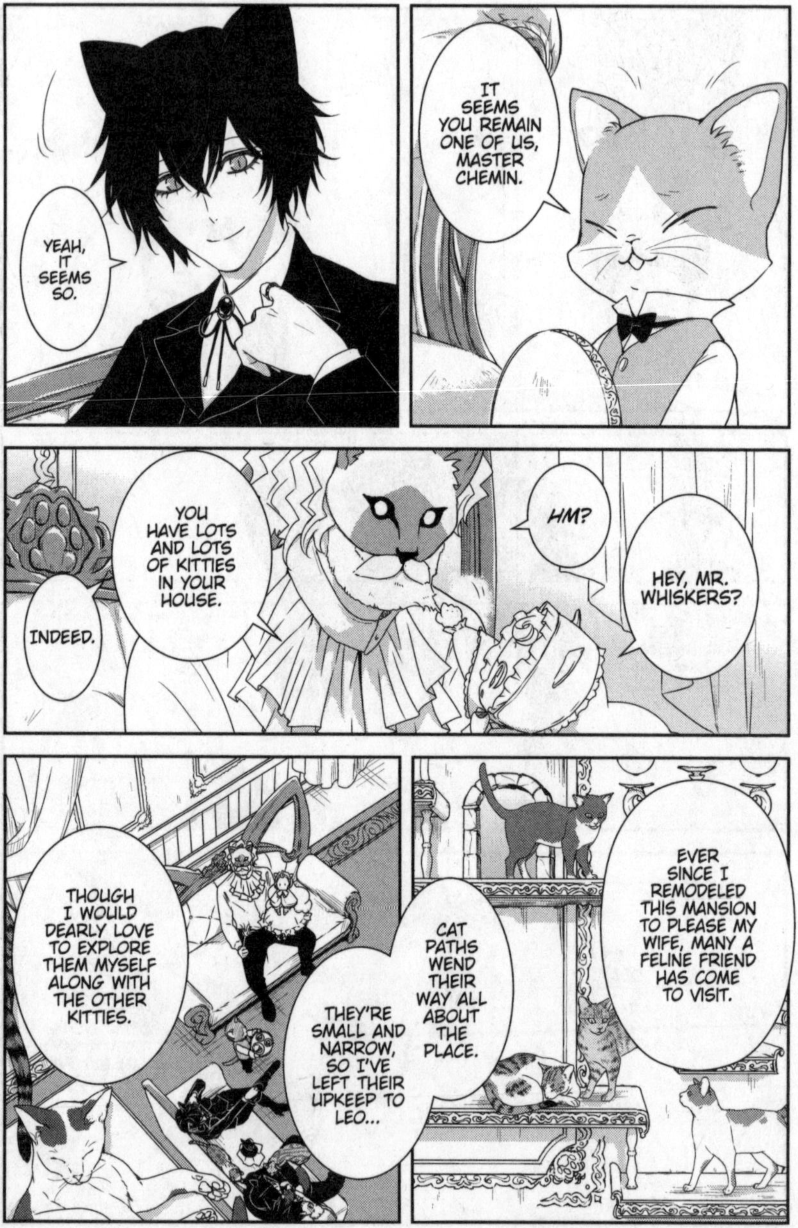
IT SEEMS YOU REMAIN ONE OF US, MASTER CHEMIN.
YEAH, IT SEEMS SO.
HEY, MR. WHISKERS?
HM?
YOU HAVE LOTS AND LOTS OF KITTIES IN YOUR HOUSE.
INDEED.
EVER SINCE I REMODELED THIS MANSION TO PLEASE MY WIFE, MANY A FELINE FRIEND HAS COME TO VISIT.
CAT PATHS WEND THEIR WAY ALL ABOUT THE PLACE.
THEY'RE SMALL AND NARROW, SO I'VE LEFT THEIR UPKEEP TO LEO...
THOUGH I WOULD DEARLY LOVE TO EXPLORE THEM MYSELF ALONG WITH THE OTHER KITTIES.

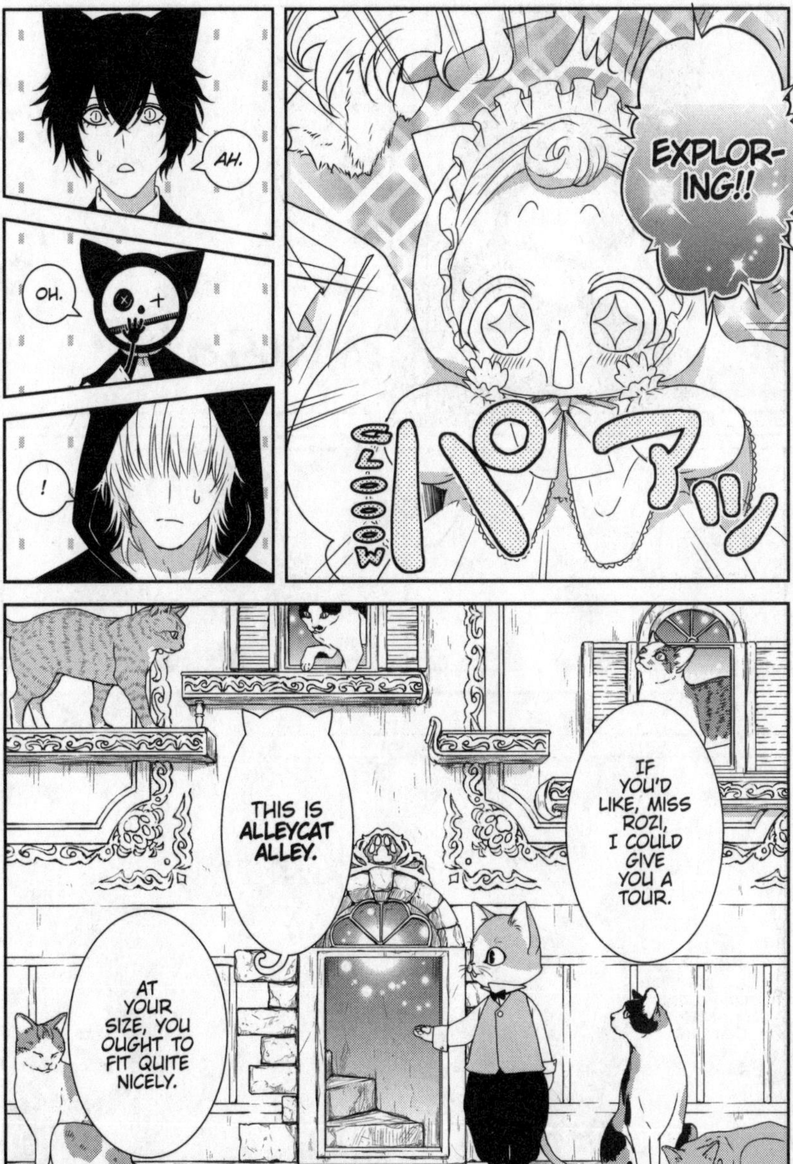
EXPLORING!!
GLOOOOW
パアッ
AH.
OH.
!
IF YOU'D LIKE, MISS ROZI, I COULD GIVE YOU A TOUR.
THIS IS **ALLEYCAT ALLEY.**
AT YOUR SIZE, YOU OUGHT TO FIT QUITE NICELY.

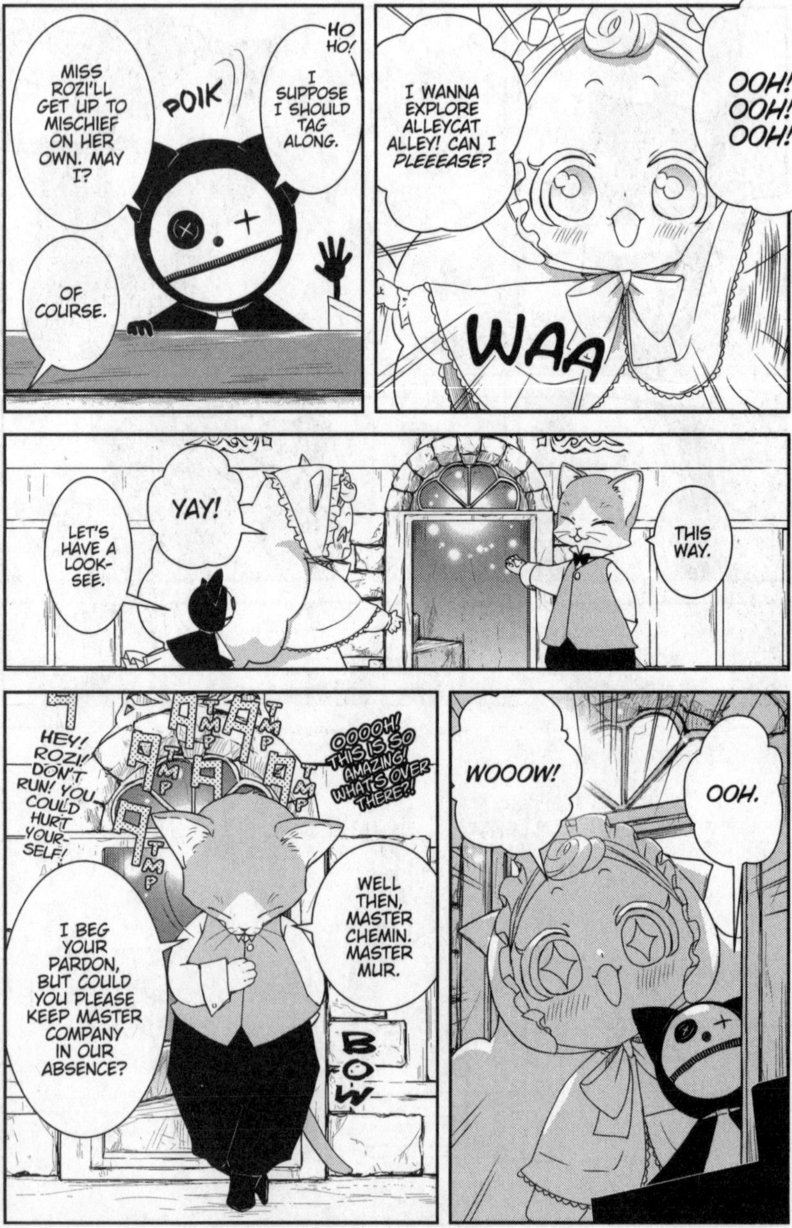
OOH! OOH! OOH!
I WANNA EXPLORE ALLEYCAT ALLEY! CAN I PLEEEASE?
WAA
HO HO!
I SUPPOSE I SHOULD TAG ALONG.
POIK
MISS ROZI'LL GET UP TO MISCHIEF ON HER OWN. MAY I?
OF COURSE.
THIS WAY.
YAY!
LET'S HAVE A LOOK-SEE.
OOH.
WOOOW!
OOOOH! THIS IS SO AMAZING! WHAT'S OVER THERE?!
TMP TMP TMP TMP TMP
HEY! ROZI! DON'T RUN! YOU COULD HURT YOURSELF!
WELL THEN, MASTER CHEMIN. MASTER MUR.
I BEG YOUR PARDON, BUT COULD YOU PLEASE KEEP MASTER COMPANY IN OUR ABSENCE?
BOW

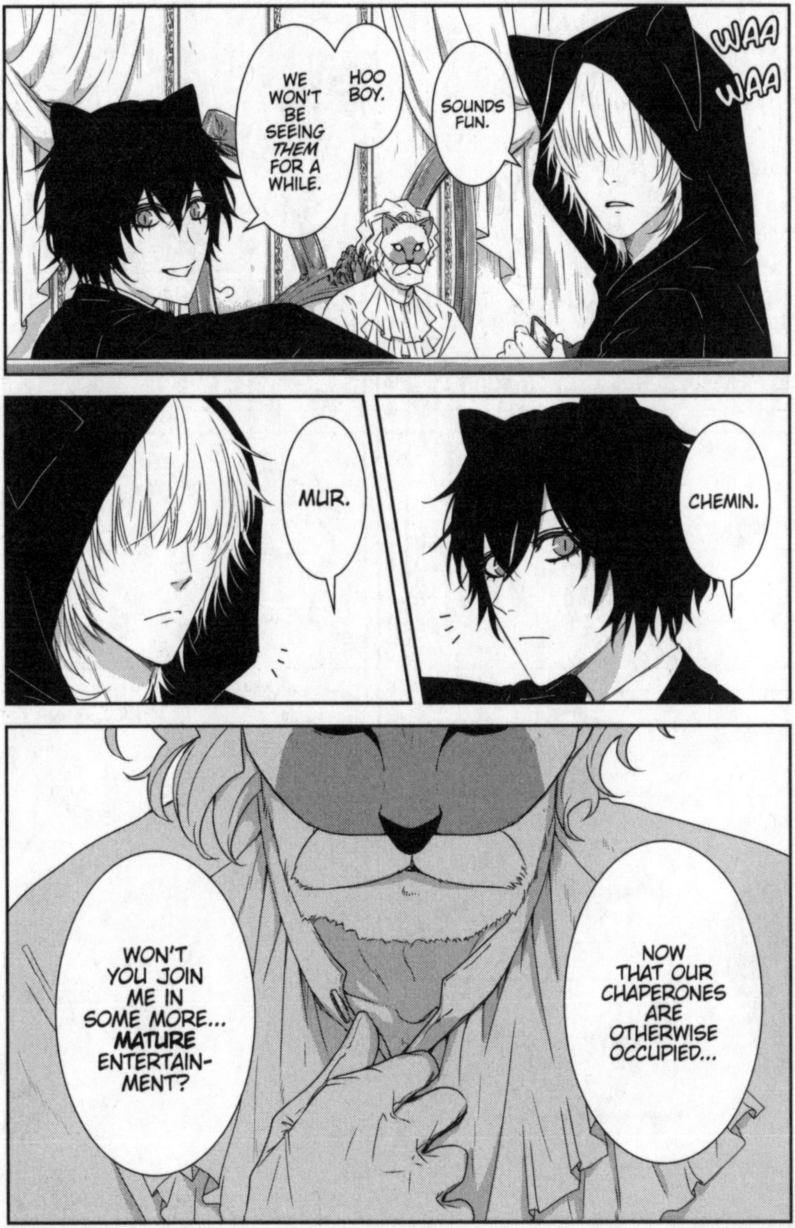
WAA WAA
SOUNDS FUN.
HOO BOY.
WE WON'T BE SEEING *THEM* FOR A WHILE.
CHEMIN.
MUR.
NOW THAT OUR CHAPERONES ARE OTHERWISE OCCUPIED...
WON'T YOU JOIN ME IN SOME MORE... **MATURE** ENTERTAINMENT?

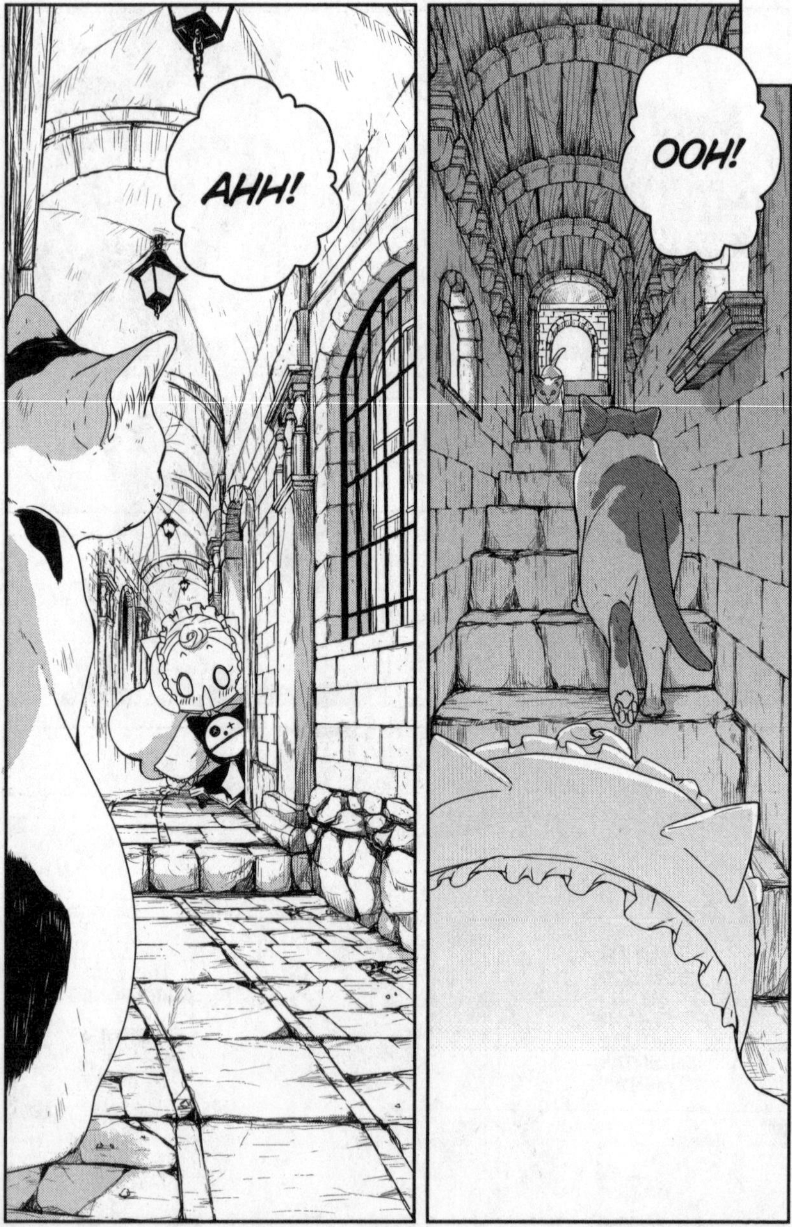
OOH!
AHH!

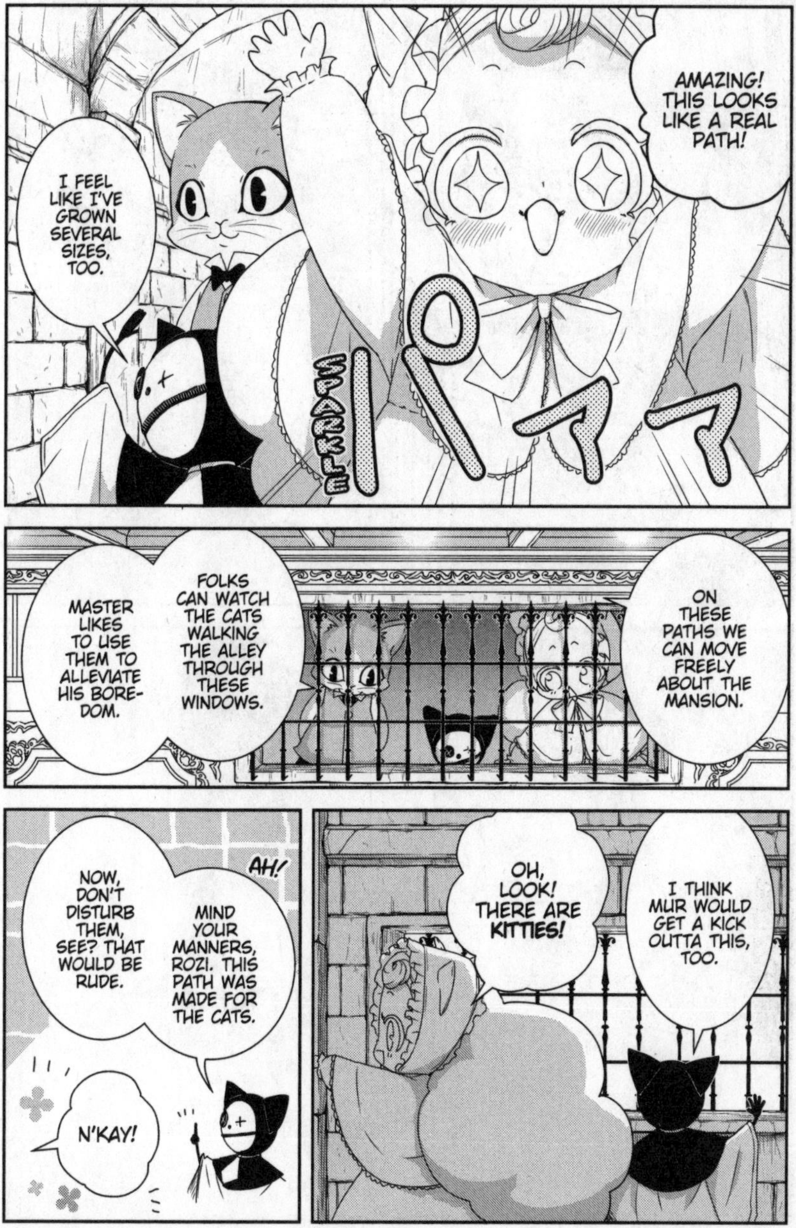
AMAZING! THIS LOOKS LIKE A REAL PATH!
SPARKLE
I FEEL LIKE I'VE GROWN SEVERAL SIZES, TOO.
ON THESE PATHS WE CAN MOVE FREELY ABOUT THE MANSION.
FOLKS CAN WATCH THE CATS WALKING THE ALLEY THROUGH THESE WINDOWS.
MASTER LIKES TO USE THEM TO ALLEVIATE HIS BORE-DOM.
I THINK MUR WOULD GET A KICK OUTTA THIS, TOO.
OH, LOOK! THERE ARE KITTIES!
AH!
MIND YOUR MANNERS, ROZI. THIS PATH WAS MADE FOR THE CATS.
NOW, DON'T DISTURB THEM, SEE? THAT WOULD BE RUDE.
N'KAY!

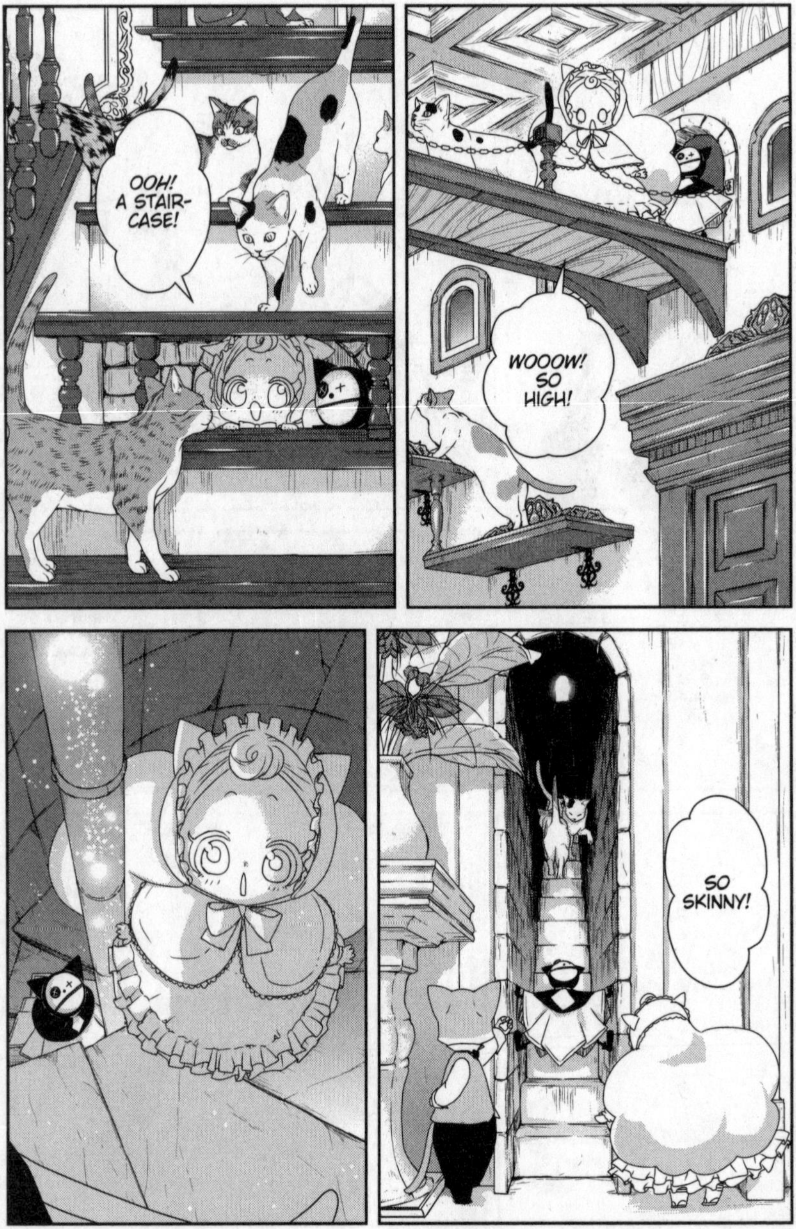
WOOOW! SO HIGH!
OOH! A STAIR-CASE!
SO SKINNY!

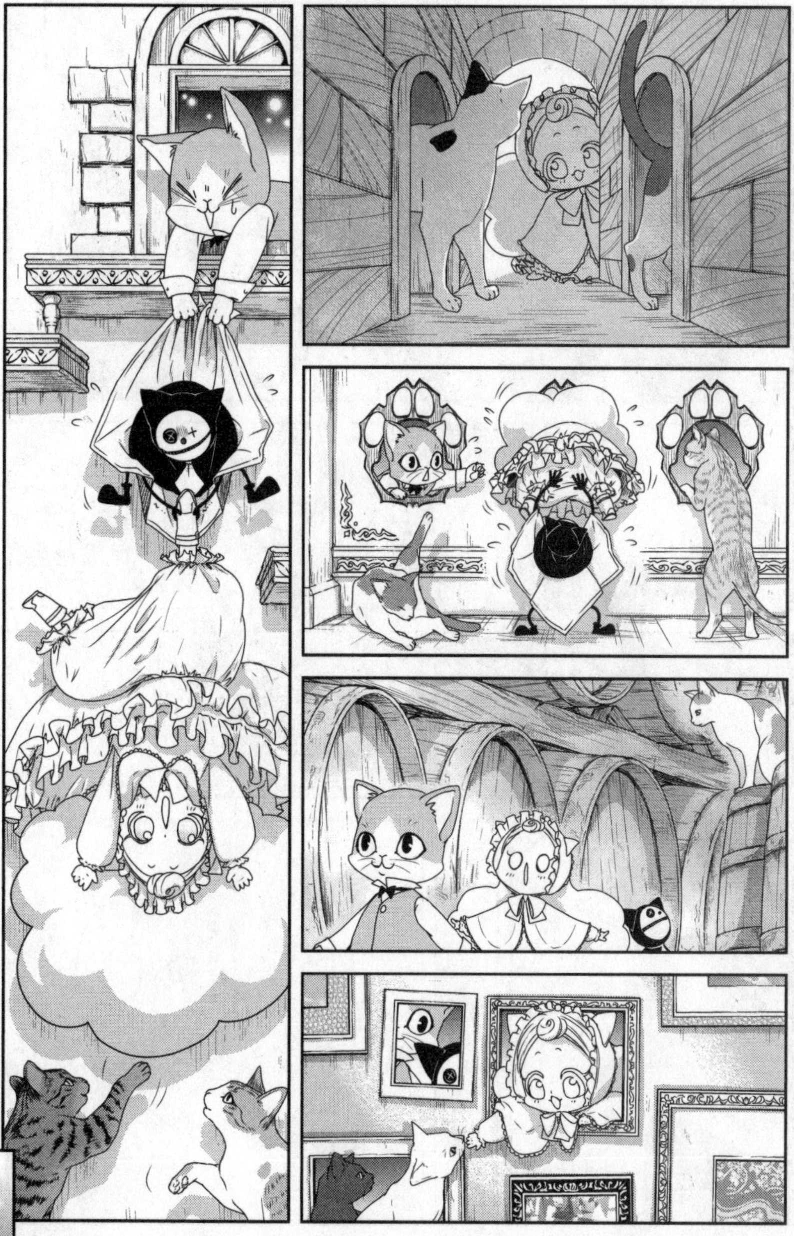

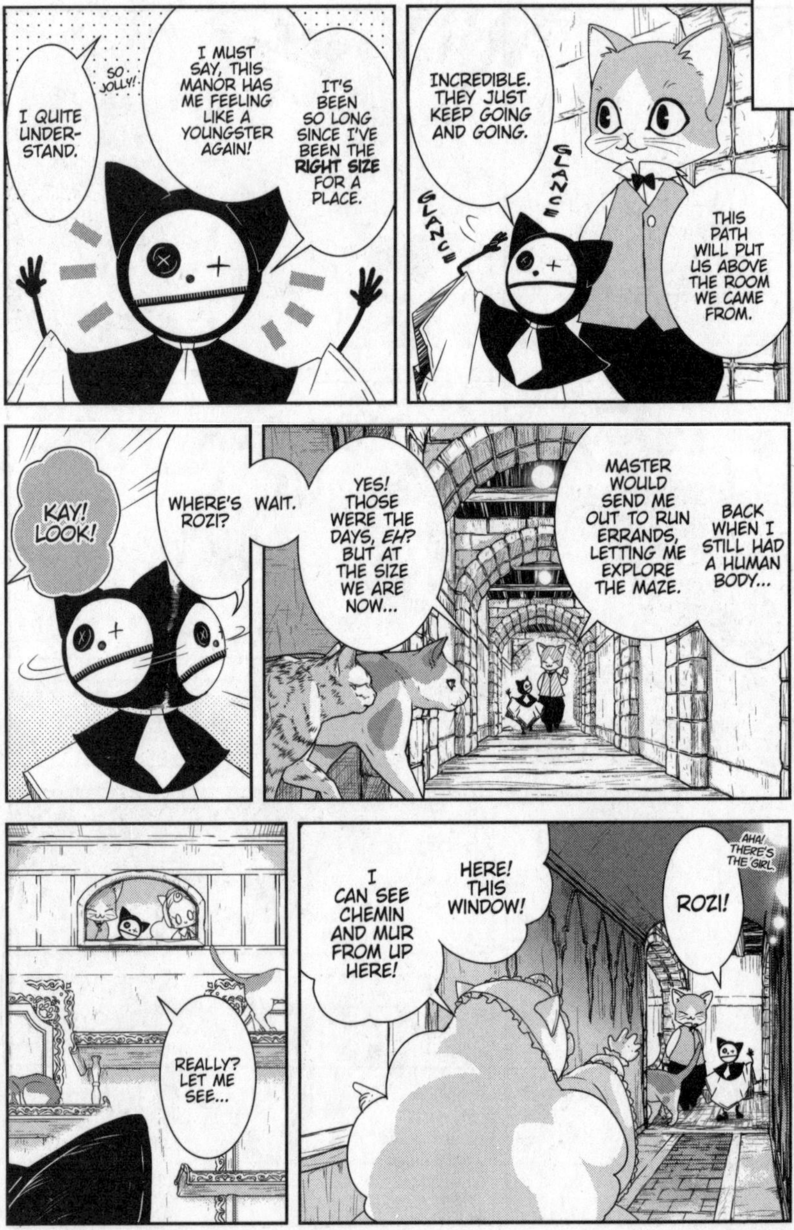
INCREDIBLE. THEY JUST KEEP GOING AND GOING.
GLANCE
GLANCE
THIS PATH WILL PUT US ABOVE THE ROOM WE CAME FROM.
IT'S BEEN SO LONG SINCE I'VE BEEN THE **RIGHT SIZE** FOR A PLACE.
I MUST SAY, THIS MANOR HAS ME FEELING LIKE A YOUNGSTER AGAIN!
SO JOLLY!
I QUITE UNDER-STAND.
BACK WHEN I STILL HAD A HUMAN BODY...
MASTER WOULD SEND ME OUT TO RUN ERRANDS, LETTING ME EXPLORE THE MAZE.
YES! THOSE WERE THE DAYS, *EH?* BUT AT THE SIZE WE ARE NOW...
WAIT.
WHERE'S ROZI?
KAY! LOOK!
AHA! THERE'S THE GIRL.
ROZI!
HERE! THIS WINDOW!
I CAN SEE CHEMIN AND MUR FROM UP HERE!
REALLY? LET ME SEE...

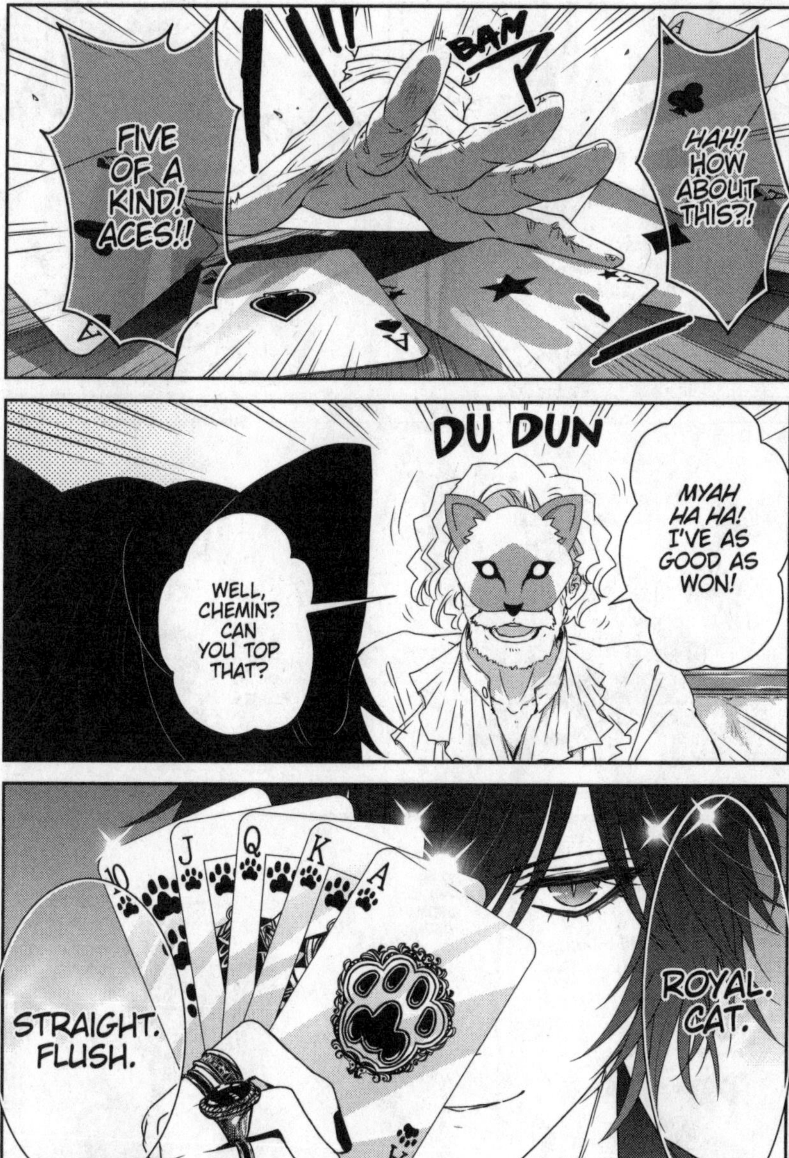
HAH! HOW ABOUT THIS?!
BAM
FIVE OF A KIND! ACES!!
MYAH HA HA! I'VE AS GOOD AS WON!
DU DUN
WELL, CHEMIN? CAN YOU TOP THAT?
ROYAL. CAT.
STRAIGHT. FLUSH.

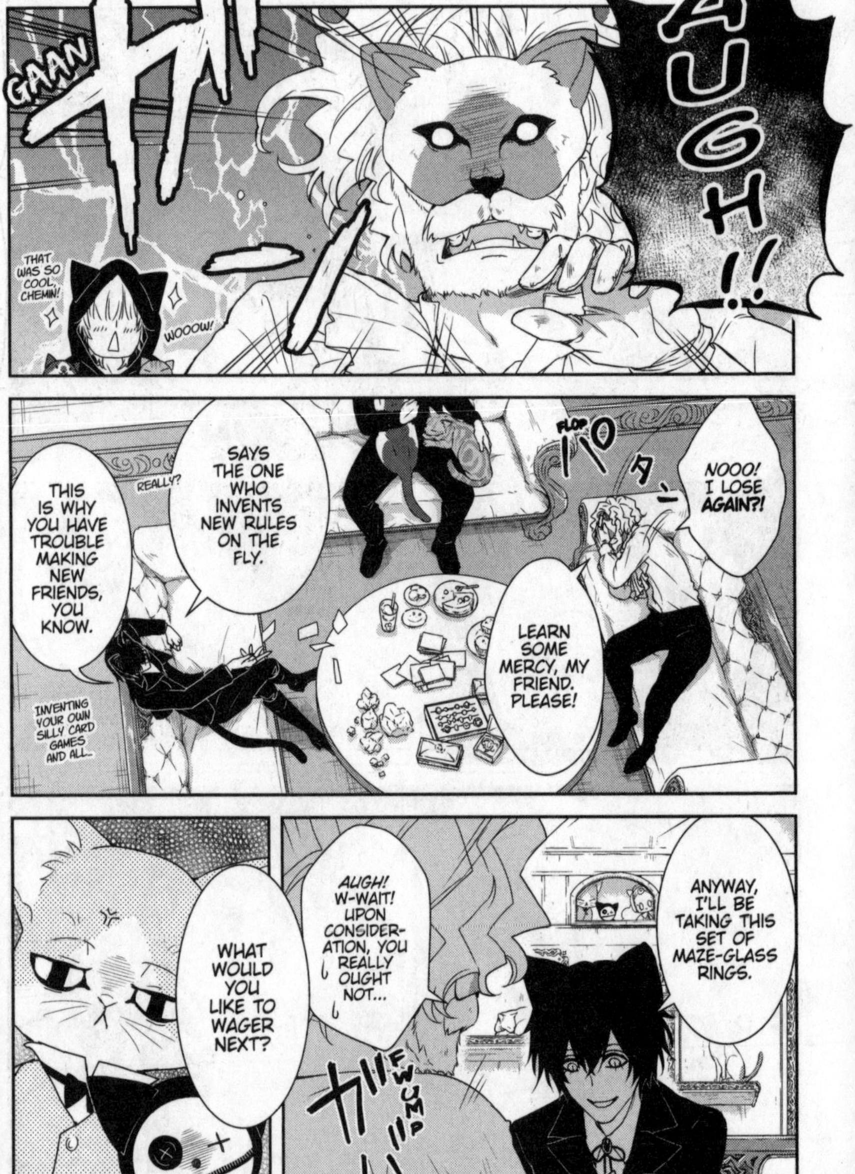
AUGH!!
GAAN
THAT WAS SO COOL, CHEMIN!
WOOOW!
NOOO! I LOSE AGAIN?!
FLOP
LEARN SOME MERCY, MY FRIEND. PLEASE!
SAYS THE ONE WHO INVENTS NEW RULES ON THE FLY.
REALLY?
THIS IS WHY YOU HAVE TROUBLE MAKING NEW FRIENDS, YOU KNOW.
INVENTING YOUR OWN SILLY CARD GAMES AND ALL...
ANYWAY, I'LL BE TAKING THIS SET OF MAZE-GLASS RINGS.
AUGH! W-WAIT! UPON CONSIDERATION, YOU REALLY OUGHT NOT...
FWUMP
WHAT WOULD YOU LIKE TO WAGER NEXT?

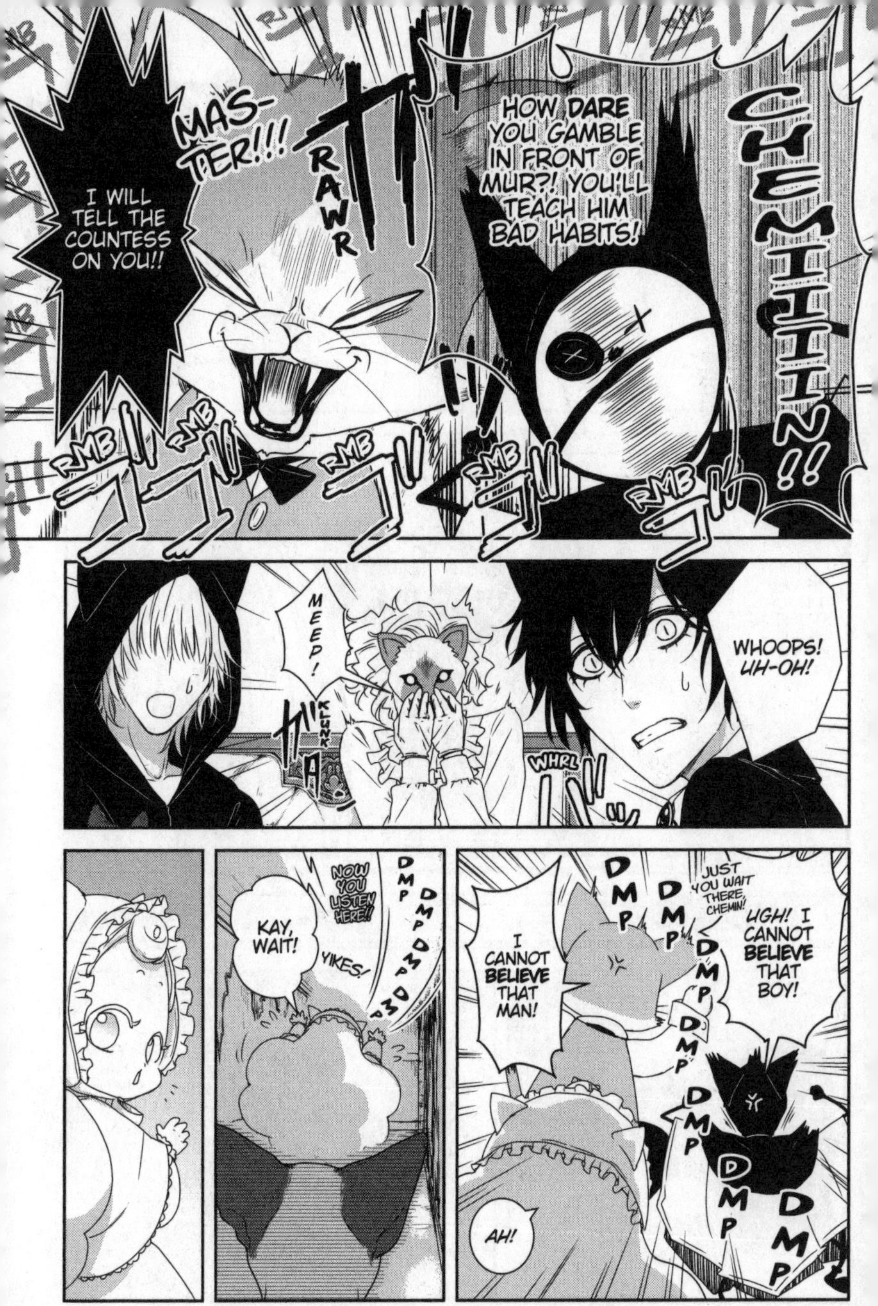
CHEMIIIIN!!
HOW DARE YOU GAMBLE IN FRONT OF MUR?! YOU'LL TEACH HIM BAD HABITS!
RAWR
MAS-TER!!!
I WILL TELL THE COUNTESS ON YOU!!
RMB
RMB
RMB
RMB
RMB
WHOOPS! UH-OH!
WHRL
MEEP!
KLUNK
UGH! I CANNOT BELIEVE THAT BOY!
JUST YOU WAIT THERE, CHEMIN!
DMP DMP DMP DMP DMP DMP DMP DMP
I CANNOT BELIEVE THAT MAN!
AH!
NOW YOU LISTEN HERE!!
DMP DMP DMP DMP DMP
KAY, WAIT!
YIKES!

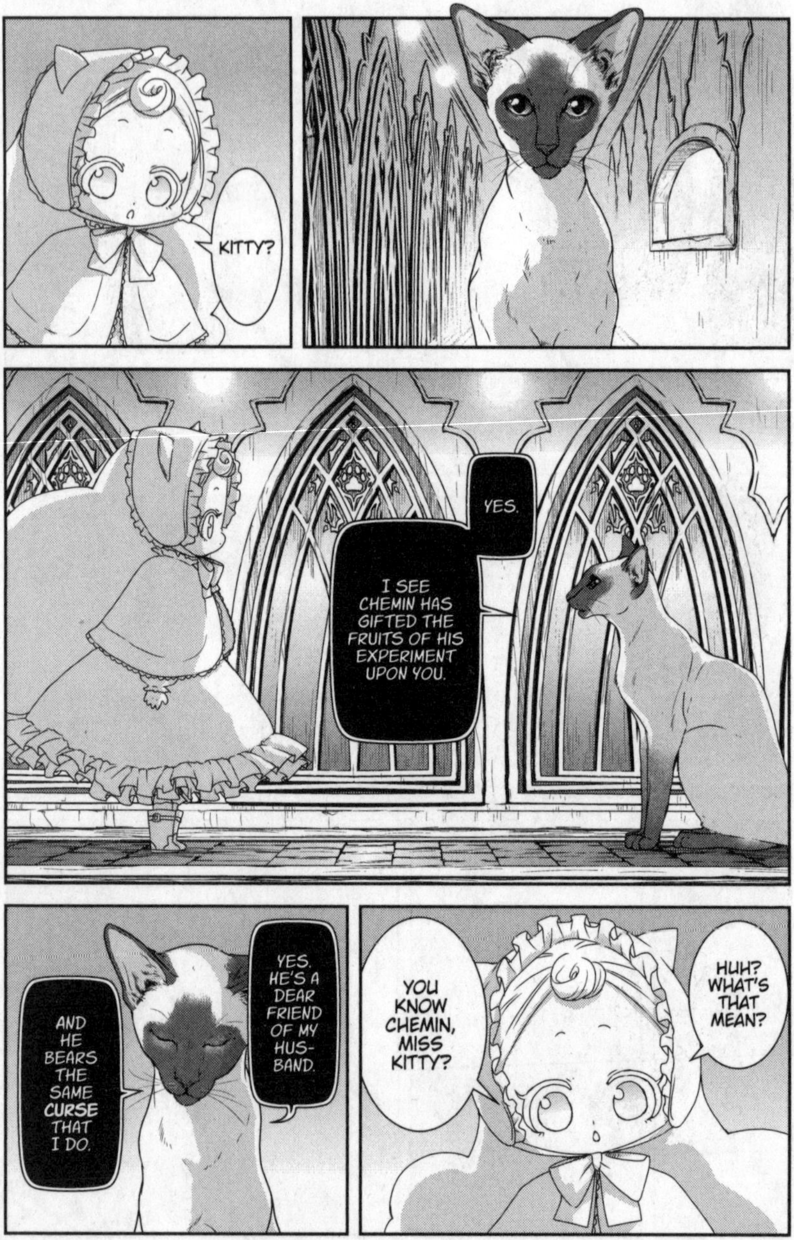
KITTY?
YES.
I SEE CHEMIN HAS GIFTED THE FRUITS OF HIS EXPERIMENT UPON YOU.
HUH? WHAT'S THAT MEAN?
YOU KNOW CHEMIN, MISS KITTY?
YES. HE'S A DEAR FRIEND OF MY HUS-BAND.
AND HE BEARS THE SAME **CURSE** THAT I DO.

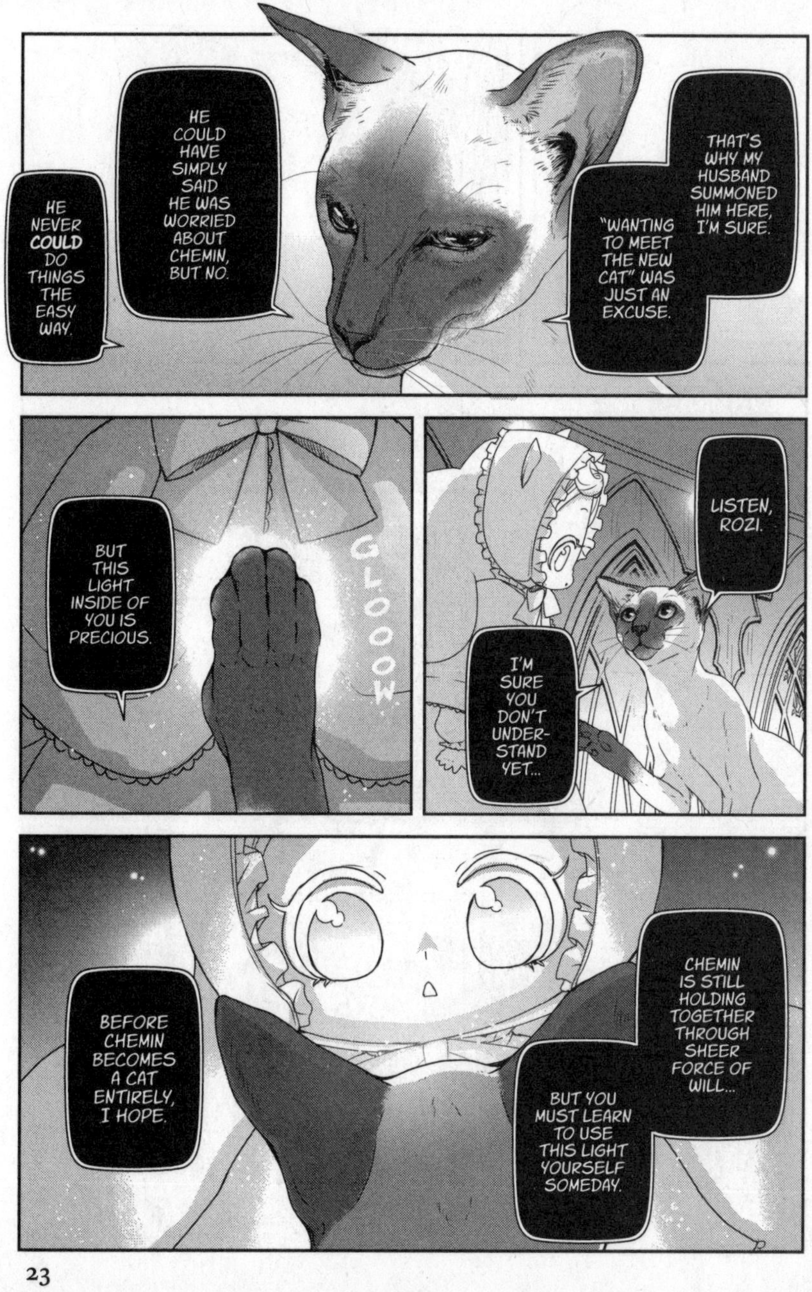
THAT'S WHY MY HUSBAND SUMMONED HIM HERE, I'M SURE.
"WANTING TO MEET THE NEW CAT" WAS JUST AN EXCUSE.
HE COULD HAVE SIMPLY SAID HE WAS WORRIED ABOUT CHEMIN, BUT NO.
HE NEVER **COULD** DO THINGS THE EASY WAY.
LISTEN, ROZI.
I'M SURE YOU DON'T UNDER-STAND YET...
BUT THIS LIGHT INSIDE OF YOU IS PRECIOUS.
GLOOOOW
CHEMIN IS STILL HOLDING TOGETHER THROUGH SHEER FORCE OF WILL...
BUT YOU MUST LEARN TO USE THIS LIGHT YOURSELF SOMEDAY.
BEFORE CHEMIN BECOMES A CAT ENTIRELY, I HOPE.

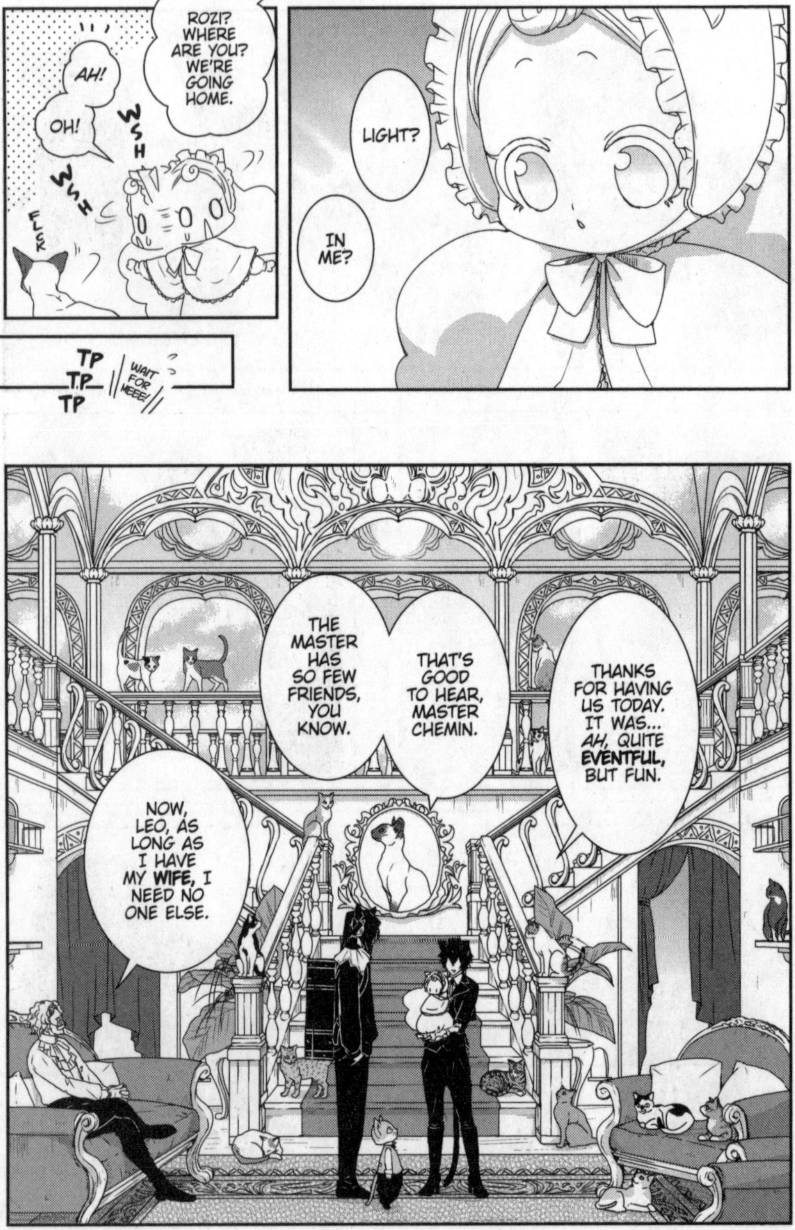
LIGHT?
IN ME?
ROZI? WHERE ARE YOU? WE'RE GOING HOME.
AH!
OH!
WSH
WSH
FLICK
TP TP TP
WAIT FOR MEEE!
THANKS FOR HAVING US TODAY. IT WAS... *AH*, QUITE **EVENTFUL**, BUT FUN.
THAT'S GOOD TO HEAR, MASTER CHEMIN.
THE MASTER HAS SO FEW FRIENDS, YOU KNOW.
NOW, LEO, AS LONG AS I HAVE MY **WIFE**, I NEED NO ONE ELSE.

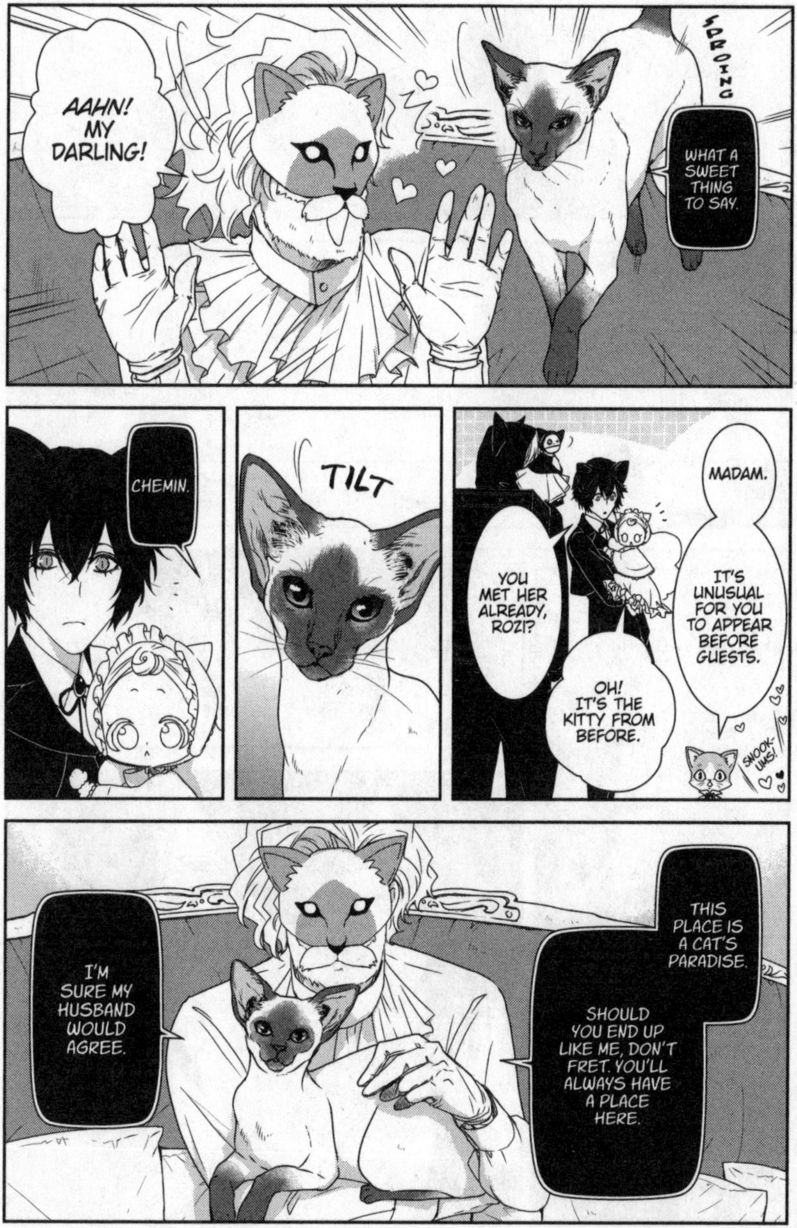
SPROING
WHAT A SWEET THING TO SAY.
AAHN! MY DARLING!
MADAM.
IT'S UNUSUAL FOR YOU TO APPEAR BEFORE GUESTS.
YOU MET HER ALREADY, ROZI?
OH! IT'S THE KITTY FROM BEFORE.
SNOOK-UMS!
TILT
CHEMIN.
THIS PLACE IS A CAT'S PARADISE.
SHOULD YOU END UP LIKE ME, DON'T FRET. YOU'LL ALWAYS HAVE A PLACE HERE.
I'M SURE MY HUSBAND WOULD AGREE.

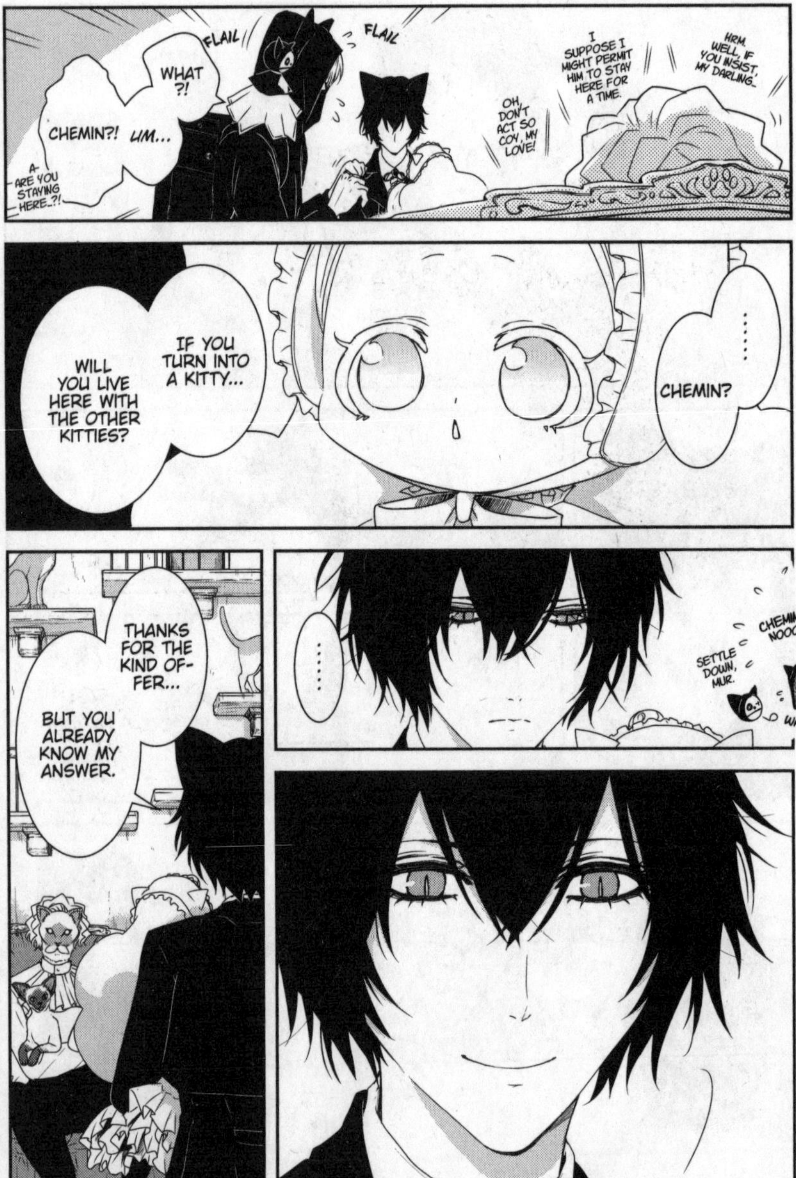
HRM. WELL, IF YOU INSIST, MY DARLING...
I SUPPOSE I MIGHT PERMIT HIM TO STAY HERE FOR A TIME.
OH, DON'T ACT SO COY, MY LOVE!
FLAIL
FLAIL
WHAT?!
CHEMIN?! UM...
A-ARE YOU STAYING HERE..?!
......
CHEMIN?
IF YOU TURN INTO A KITTY...
WILL YOU LIVE HERE WITH THE OTHER KITTIES?
CHEMIN?! NOOO!!
SETTLE DOWN, MUR.
WAAH!
......
THANKS FOR THE KIND OF-FER...
BUT YOU ALREADY KNOW MY ANSWER.

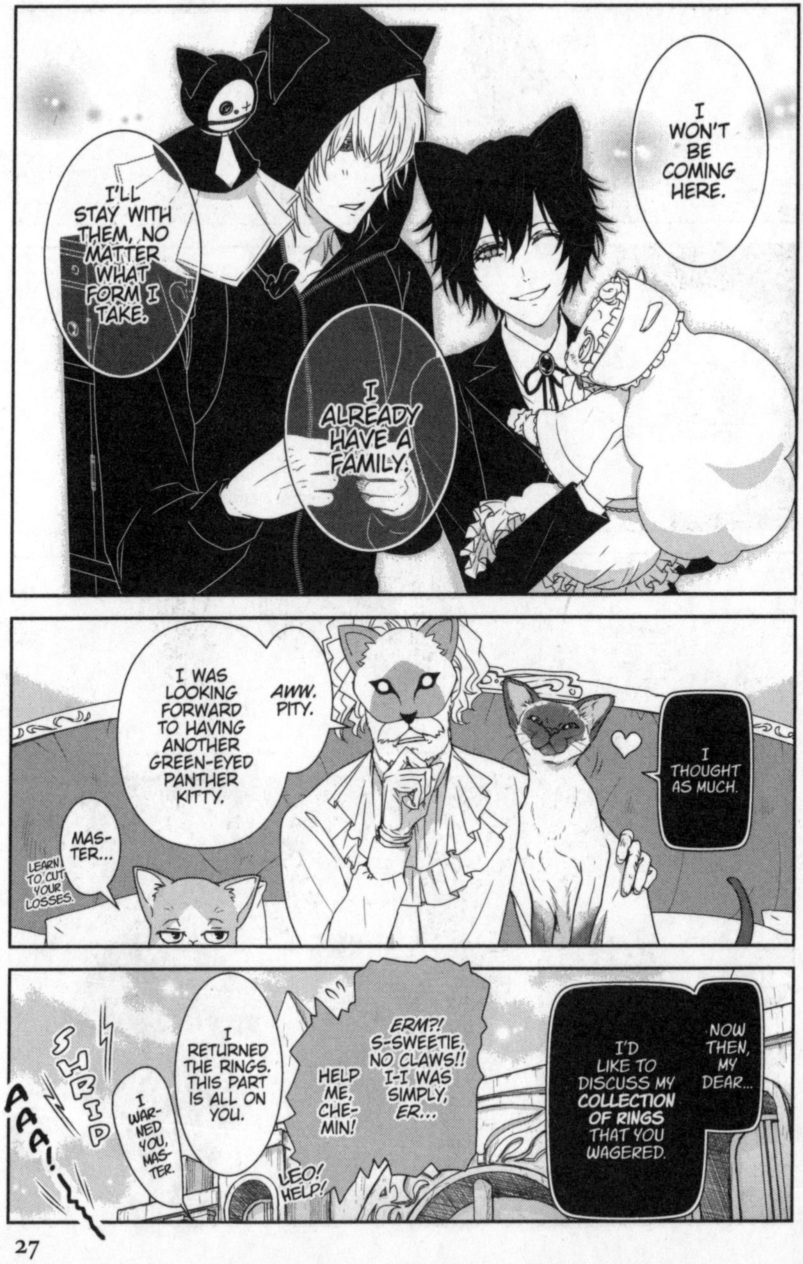
I WON'T BE COMING HERE.
I ALREADY HAVE A FAMILY.
I'LL STAY WITH THEM, NO MATTER WHAT FORM I TAKE.
I THOUGHT AS MUCH.
AWW. PITY.
I WAS LOOKING FORWARD TO HAVING ANOTHER GREEN-EYED PANTHER KITTY.
MAS-TER...
LEARN TO CUT YOUR LOSSES.
NOW THEN, MY DEAR...
I'D LIKE TO DISCUSS MY **COLLECTION OF RINGS** THAT YOU WAGERED.
ERM?! S-SWEETIE, NO CLAWS!! I-I WAS SIMPLY, ER...
HELP ME, CHE-MIN!
LEO! HELP!
I RETURNED THE RINGS. THIS PART IS ALL ON YOU.
I WAR-NED YOU, MAS-TER.
SHRIP
AAA!

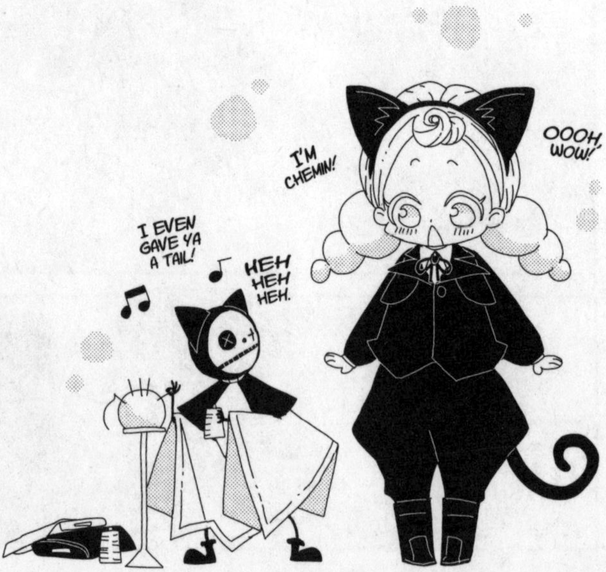
OOOH, WOW!
I'M CHEMIN!
HEH HEH HEH.
I EVEN GAVE YA A TAIL!

6 The Wooded Way

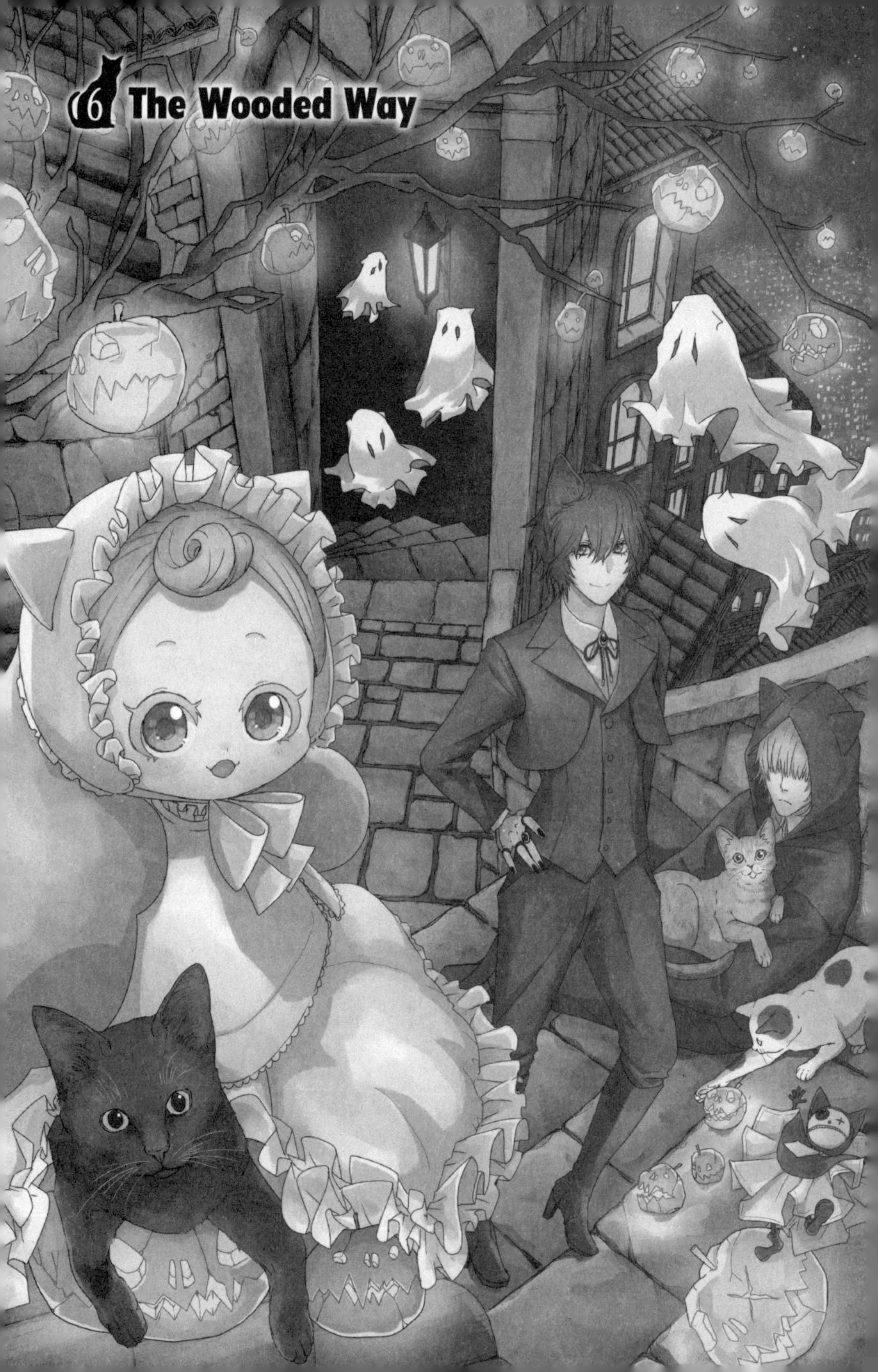

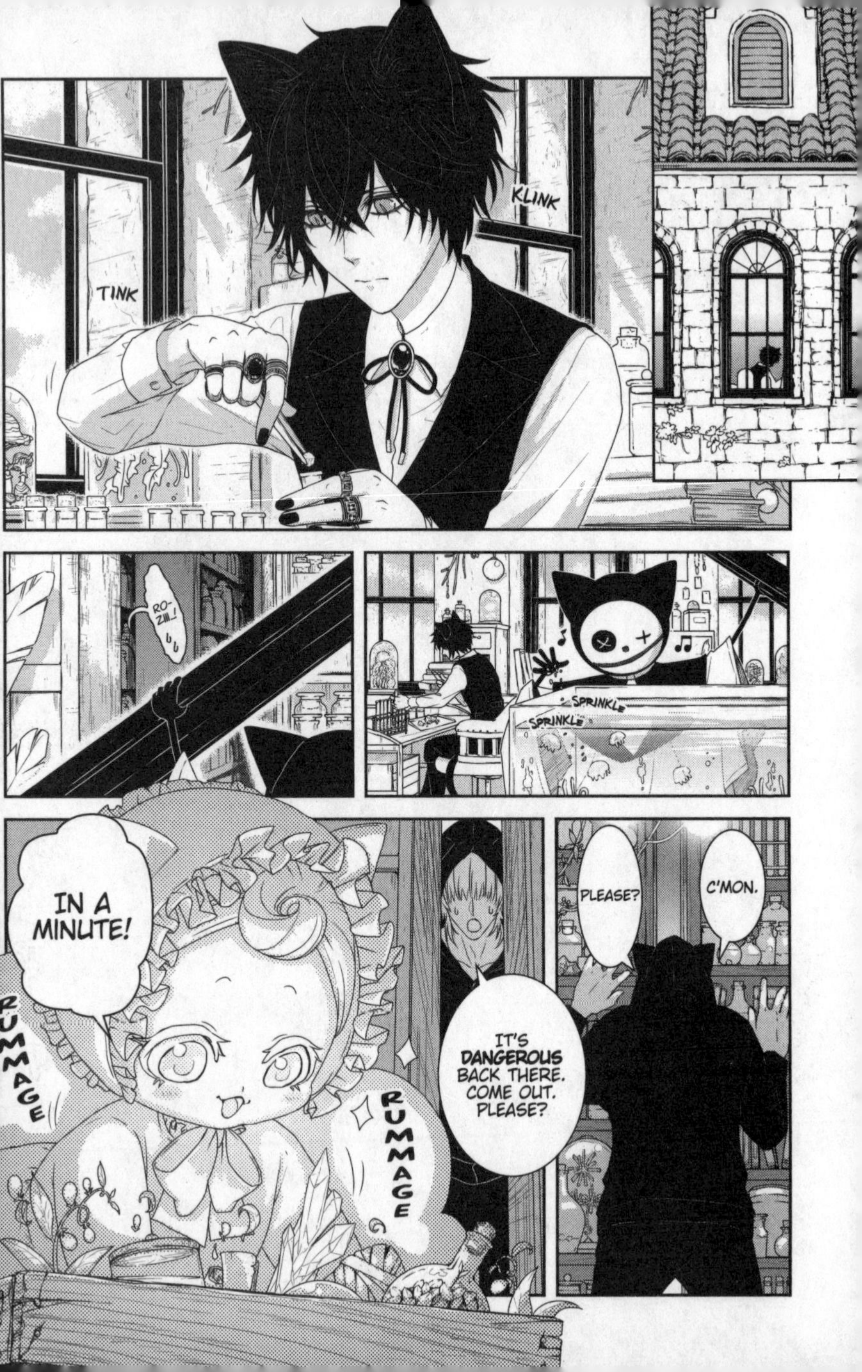
KLINK
TINK
SPRINKLE
SPRINKLE
RO-ZIII_!
C'MON.
PLEASE?
IT'S **DANGEROUS** BACK THERE. COME OUT. PLEASE?
IN A MINUTE!
RUMMAGE
RUMMAGE

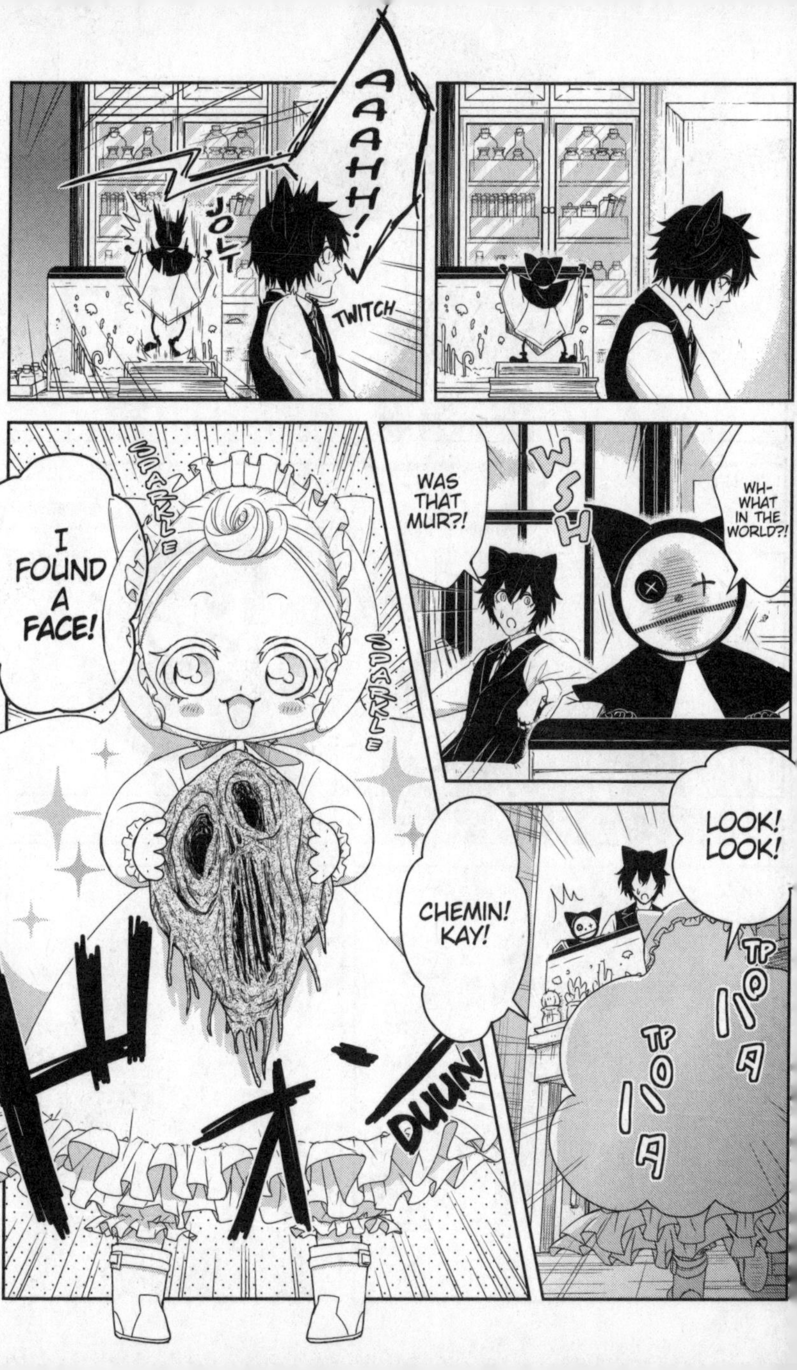
AAAHH!
JOLT
TWITCH
WH-WHAT IN THE WORLD?!
WSH
WAS THAT MUR?!
LOOK! LOOK!
CHEMIN! KAY!
I FOUND A FACE!
SPARKLE
SPARKLE
DUUN

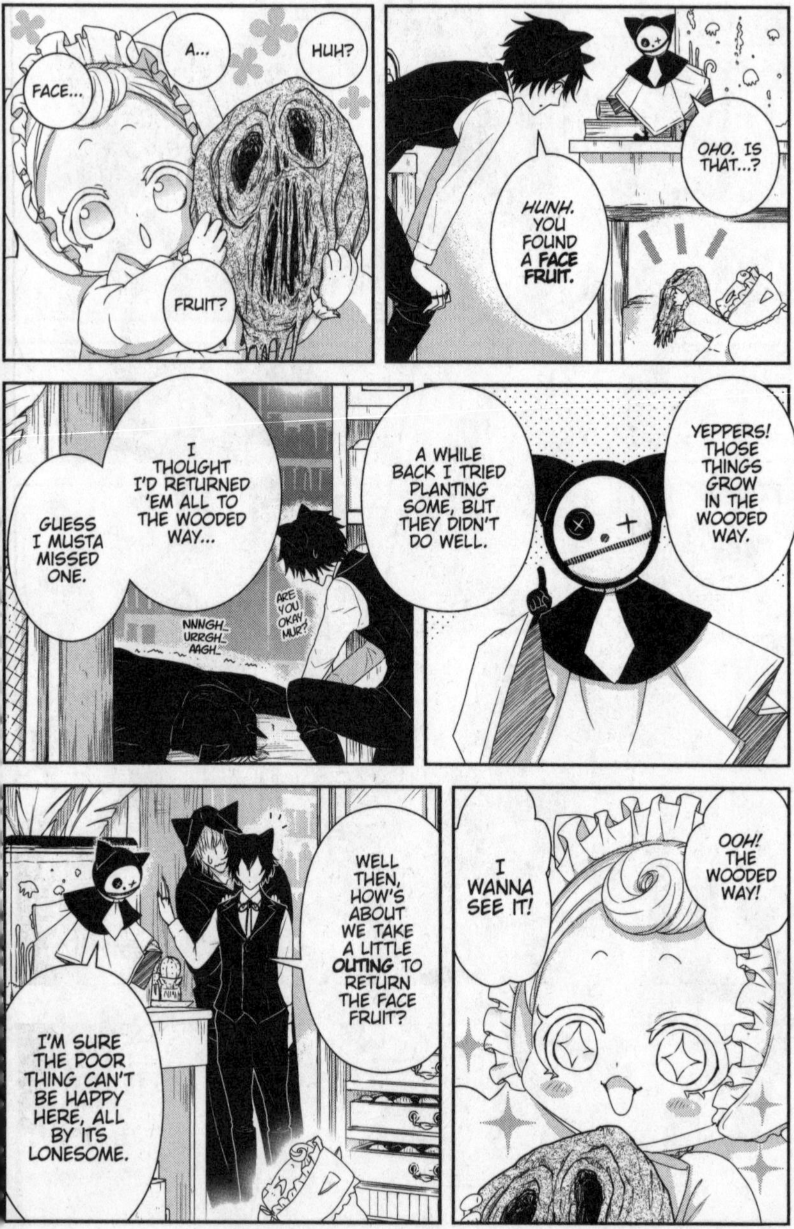
OHO. IS THAT...?
HUNH. YOU FOUND A FACE FRUIT.
HUH?
A...
FACE...
FRUIT?
YEPPERS! THOSE THINGS GROW IN THE WOODED WAY.
A WHILE BACK I TRIED PLANTING SOME, BUT THEY DIDN'T DO WELL.
I THOUGHT I'D RETURNED 'EM ALL TO THE WOODED WAY...
GUESS I MUSTA MISSED ONE.
ARE YOU OKAY, MUR?
NNNGH... URRGH... AAGH...
OOH! THE WOODED WAY!
I WANNA SEE IT!
WELL THEN, HOW'S ABOUT WE TAKE A LITTLE OUTING TO RETURN THE FACE FRUIT?
I'M SURE THE POOR THING CAN'T BE HAPPY HERE, ALL BY ITS LONESOME.

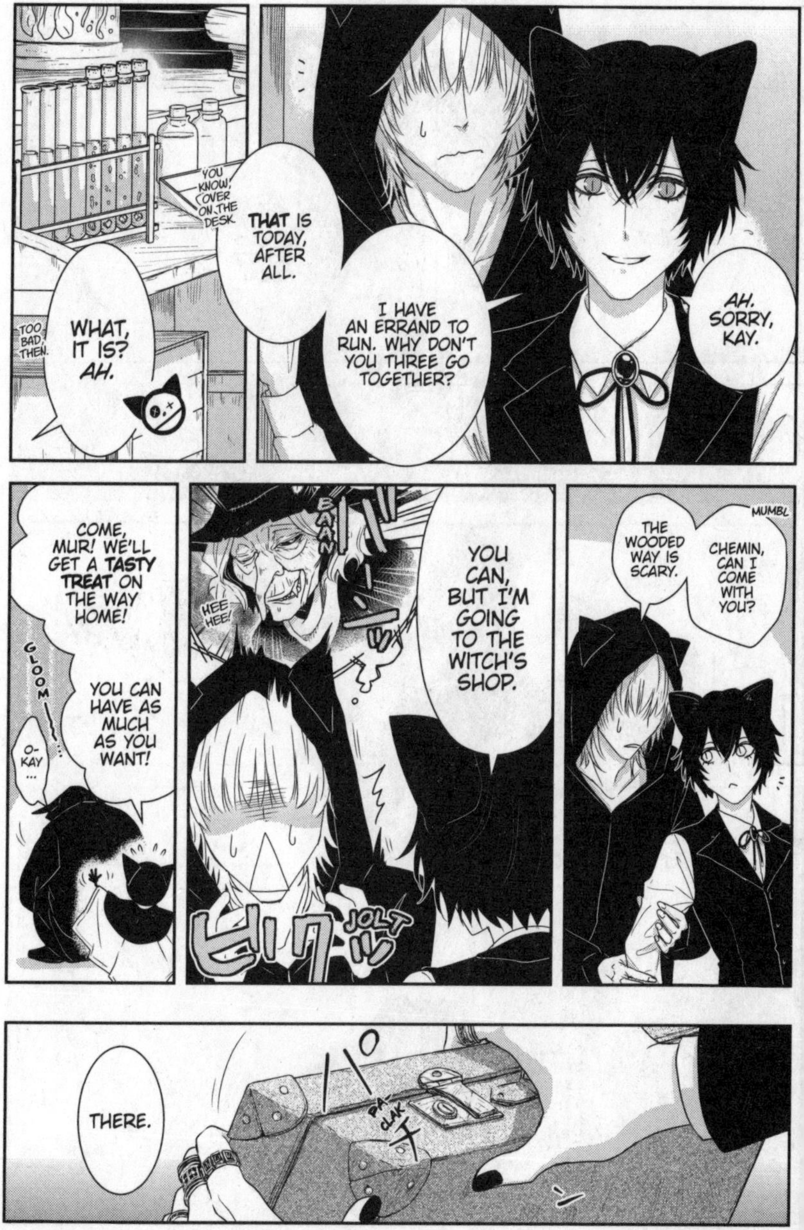
AH. SORRY, KAY.
I HAVE AN ERRAND TO RUN. WHY DON'T YOU THREE GO TOGETHER?
THAT IS TODAY, AFTER ALL.
YOU KNOW, OVER ON THE DESK.
WHAT, IT IS? AH.
TOO BAD, THEN.
MUMBL
CHEMIN, CAN I COME WITH YOU?
THE WOODED WAY IS SCARY.
BAAN
YOU CAN, BUT I'M GOING TO THE WITCH'S SHOP.
HEE HEE!
JOLT
COME, MUR! WE'LL GET A TASTY TREAT ON THE WAY HOME!
YOU CAN HAVE AS MUCH AS YOU WANT!
GLOOM
O-KAY ...
PA-CLAK
THERE.

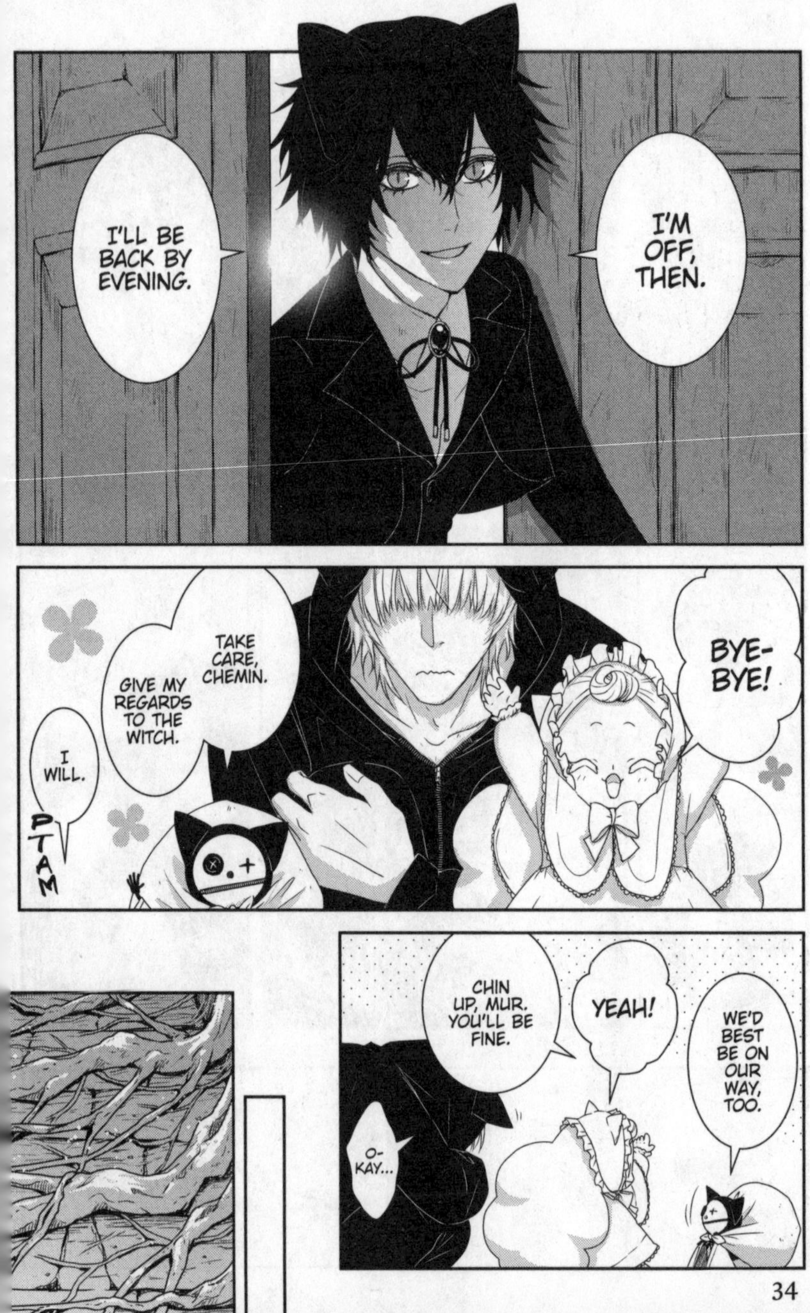
I'M OFF, THEN.
I'LL BE BACK BY EVENING.
BYE-BYE!
TAKE CARE, CHEMIN.
GIVE MY REGARDS TO THE WITCH.
I WILL.
PTAM
WE'D BEST BE ON OUR WAY, TOO.
YEAH!
CHIN UP, MUR. YOU'LL BE FINE.
O-KAY...

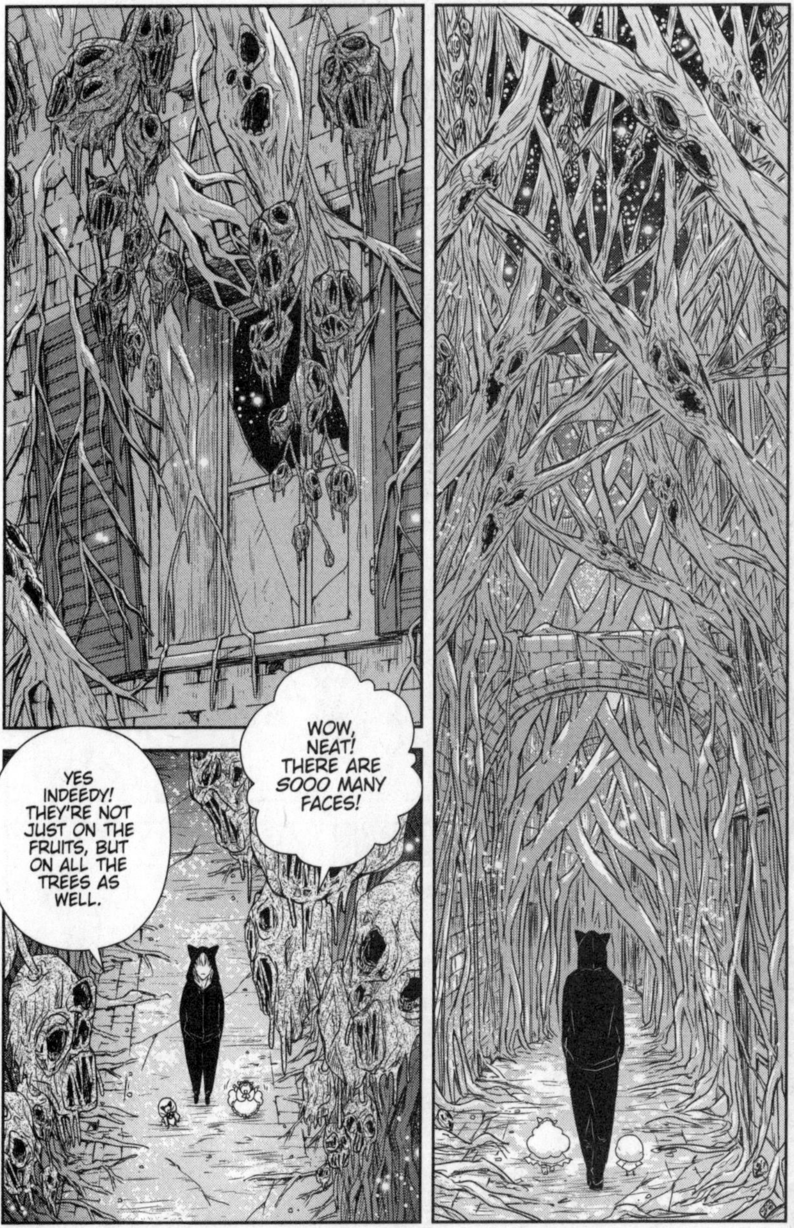
WOW, NEAT! THERE ARE SOOO MANY FACES!
YES INDEEDY! THEY'RE NOT JUST ON THE FRUITS, BUT ON ALL THE TREES AS WELL.

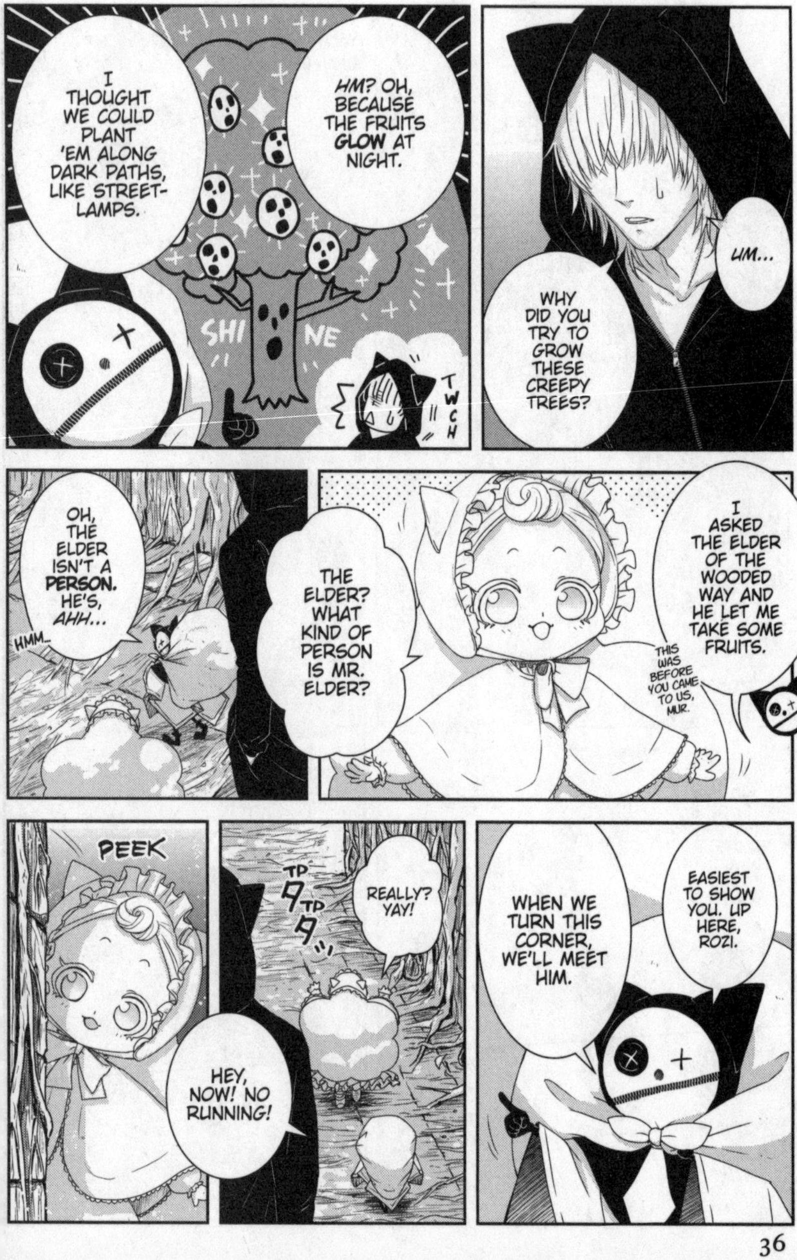
UM...
WHY DID YOU TRY TO GROW THESE CREEPY TREES?
HM? OH, BECAUSE THE FRUITS GLOW AT NIGHT.
I THOUGHT WE COULD PLANT 'EM ALONG DARK PATHS, LIKE STREET-LAMPS.
SHINE
TWCH
I ASKED THE ELDER OF THE WOODED WAY AND HE LET ME TAKE SOME FRUITS.
THIS WAS BEFORE YOU CAME TO US, MUR.
THE ELDER? WHAT KIND OF PERSON IS MR. ELDER?
OH, THE ELDER ISN'T A PERSON. HE'S, AHH...
HMM...
EASIEST TO SHOW YOU. UP HERE, ROZI.
WHEN WE TURN THIS CORNER, WE'LL MEET HIM.
REALLY? YAY!
TP TP
PEEK
HEY, NOW! NO RUNNING!

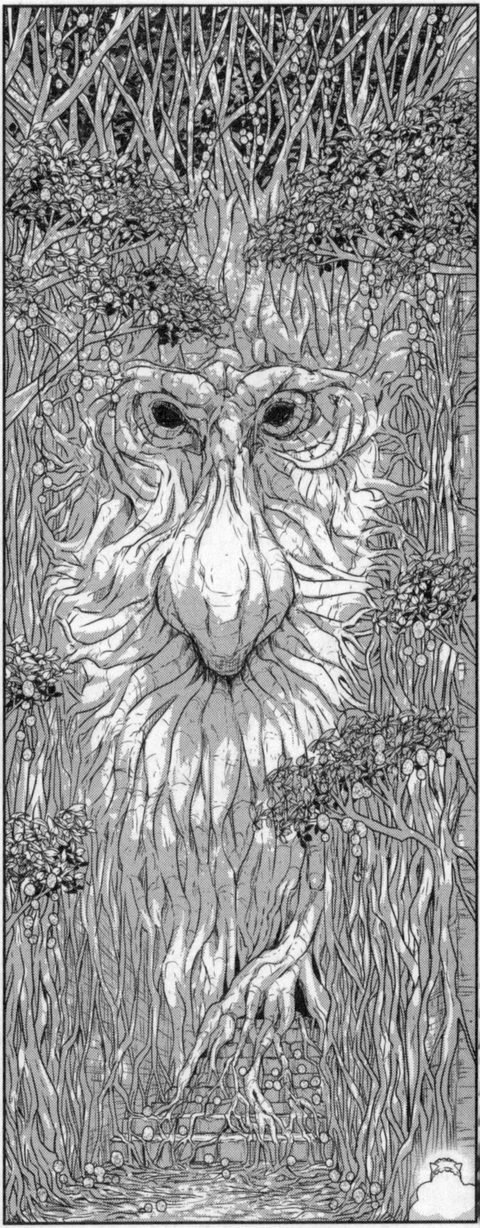
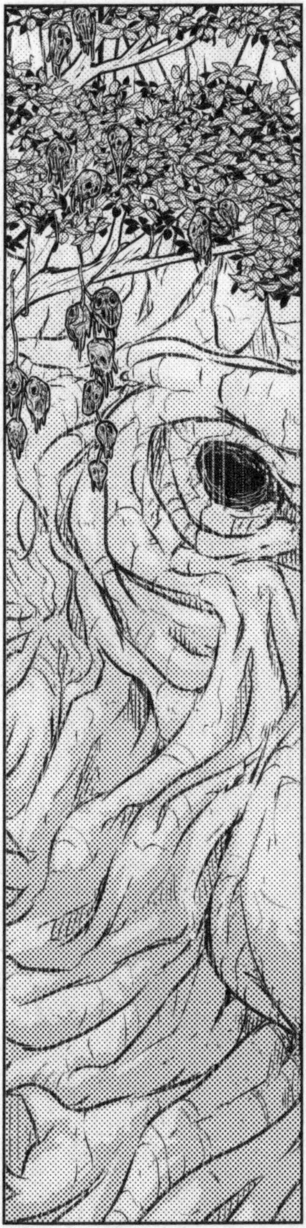

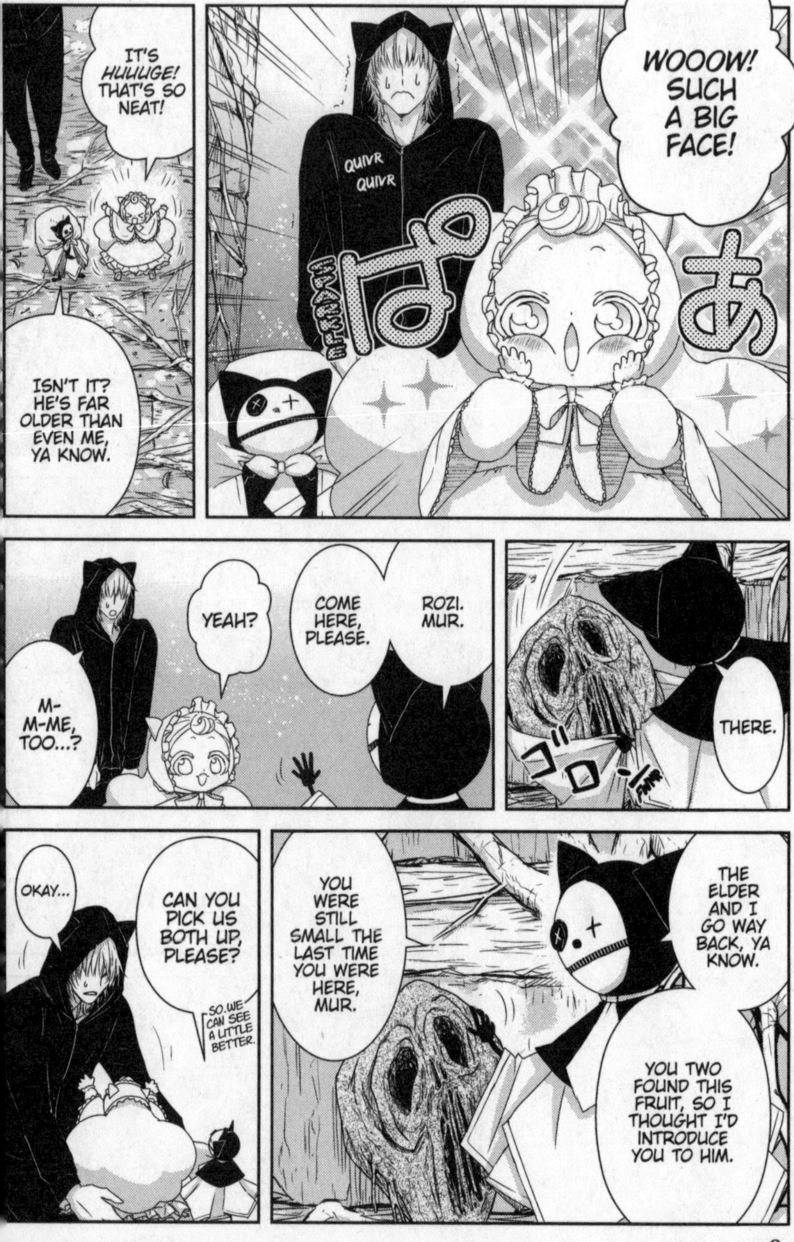
WOOOW! SUCH A BIG FACE!
QUIVR QUIVR
ぱあ
IT'S HUUUGE! THAT'S SO NEAT!
ISN'T IT? HE'S FAR OLDER THAN EVEN ME, YA KNOW.
THERE.
ゴロー
ROZI. MUR.
COME HERE, PLEASE.
YEAH?
M-M-ME, TOO...?
THE ELDER AND I GO WAY BACK, YA KNOW.
YOU WERE STILL SMALL THE LAST TIME YOU WERE HERE, MUR.
YOU TWO FOUND THIS FRUIT, SO I THOUGHT I'D INTRODUCE YOU TO HIM.
CAN YOU PICK US BOTH UP, PLEASE?
SO WE CAN SEE A LITTLE BETTER.
OKAY...

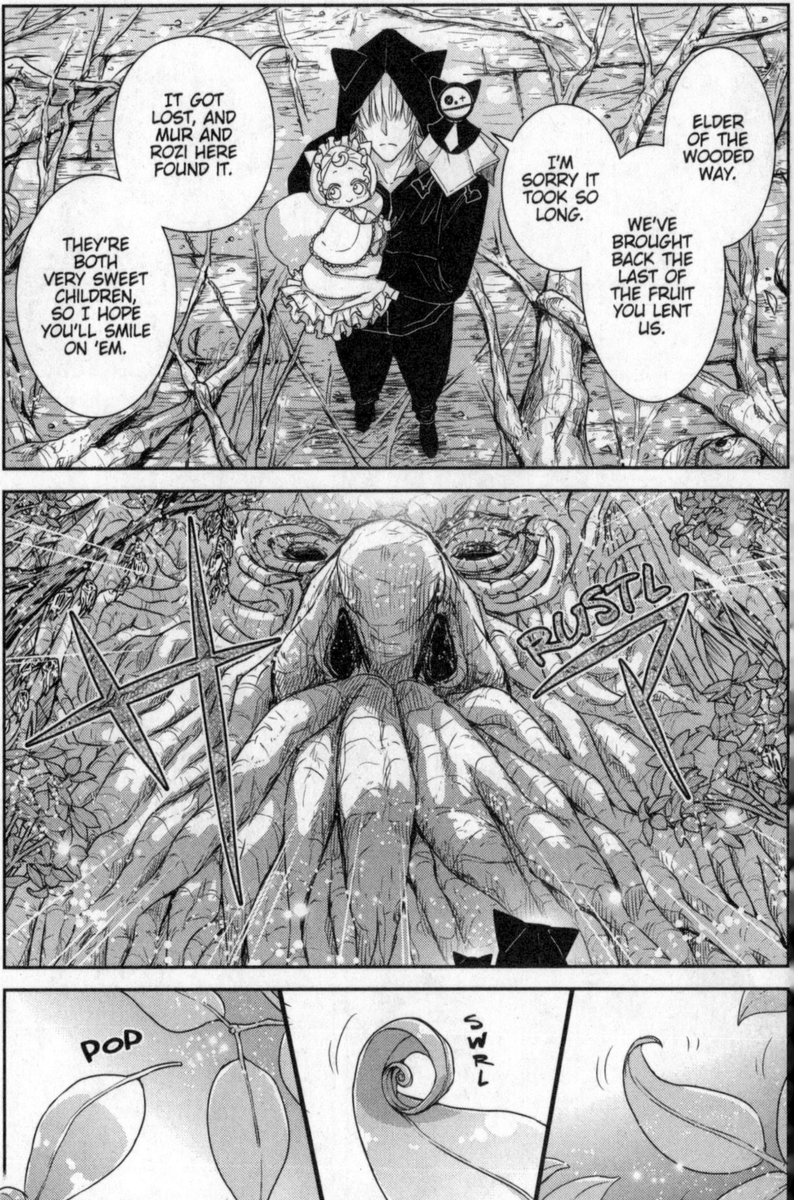
ELDER OF THE WOODED WAY.
I'M SORRY IT TOOK SO LONG.
WE'VE BROUGHT BACK THE LAST OF THE FRUIT YOU LENT US.
IT GOT LOST, AND MUR AND ROZI HERE FOUND IT.
THEY'RE BOTH VERY SWEET CHILDREN, SO I HOPE YOU'LL SMILE ON 'EM.
RUSTL
SWRL
POP

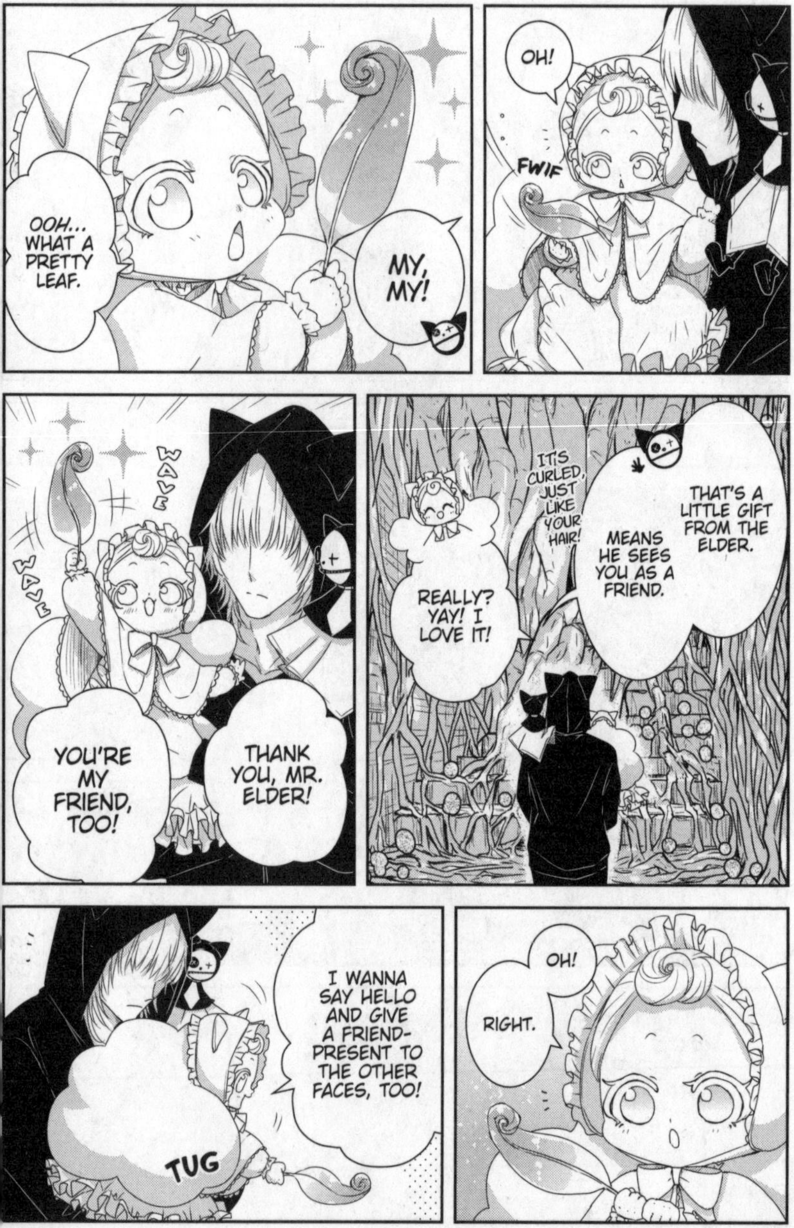
OH!
FWIF
MY, MY!
OOH... WHAT A PRETTY LEAF.
THAT'S A LITTLE GIFT FROM THE ELDER.
MEANS HE SEES YOU AS A FRIEND.
IT'S CURLED, JUST LIKE YOUR HAIR!
REALLY? YAY! I LOVE IT!
WAVE
WAVE
THANK YOU, MR. ELDER!
YOU'RE MY FRIEND, TOO!
OH!
RIGHT.
I WANNA SAY HELLO AND GIVE A FRIEND-PRESENT TO THE OTHER FACES, TOO!
TUG

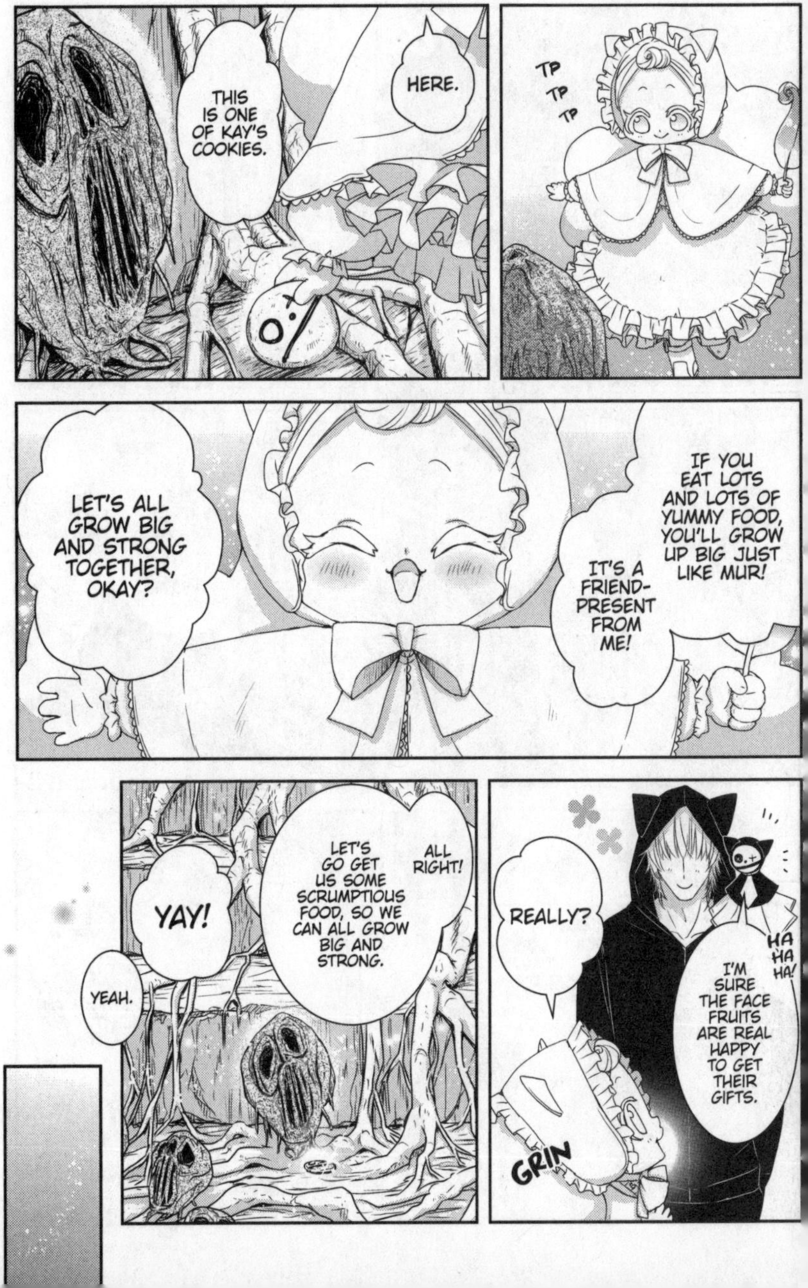
TP
TP
TP
HERE.
THIS IS ONE OF KAY'S COOKIES.
IF YOU EAT LOTS AND LOTS OF YUMMY FOOD, YOU'LL GROW UP BIG JUST LIKE MUR!
IT'S A FRIEND-PRESENT FROM ME!
LET'S ALL GROW BIG AND STRONG TOGETHER, OKAY?
REALLY?
HA HA HA!
I'M SURE THE FACE FRUITS ARE REAL HAPPY TO GET THEIR GIFTS.
GRIN
ALL RIGHT!
LET'S GO GET US SOME SCRUMPTIOUS FOOD, SO WE CAN ALL GROW BIG AND STRONG.
YAY!
YEAH.

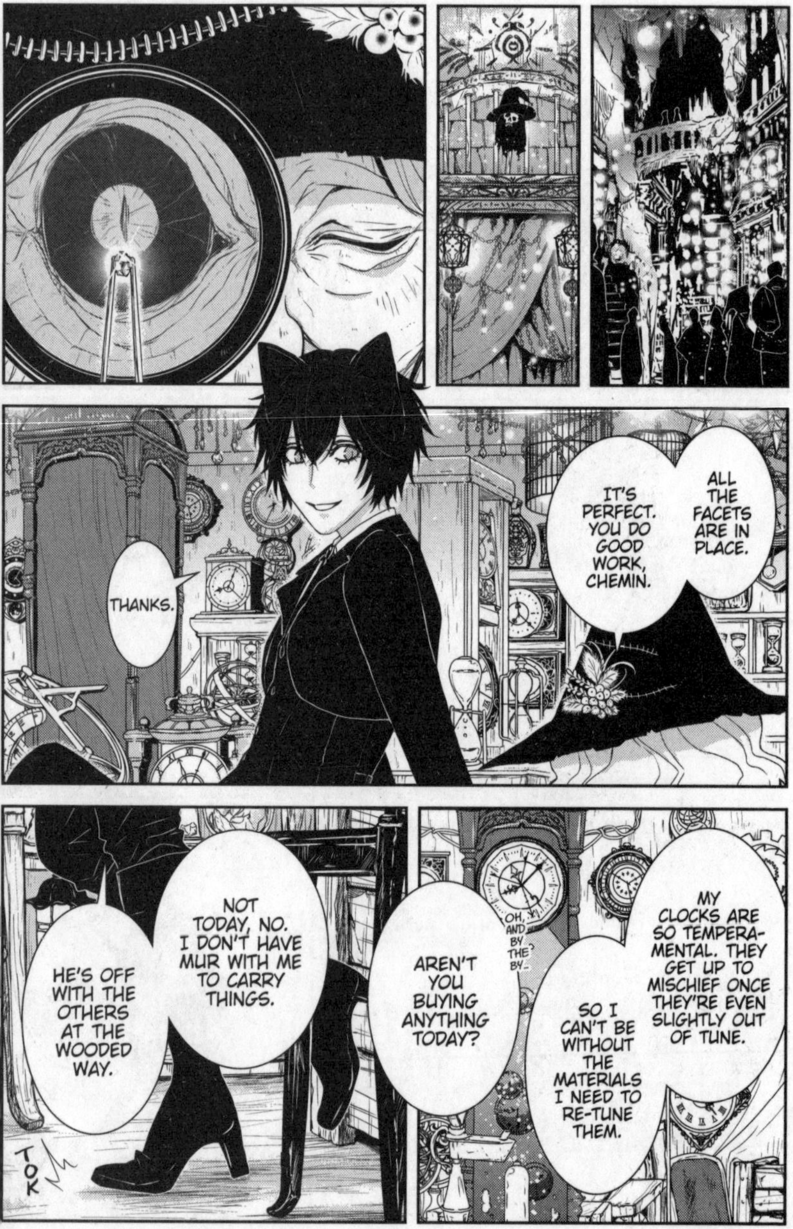
ALL THE FACETS ARE IN PLACE.
IT'S PERFECT. YOU DO GOOD WORK, CHEMIN.
THANKS.
MY CLOCKS ARE SO TEMPERA-MENTAL. THEY GET UP TO MISCHIEF ONCE THEY'RE EVEN SLIGHTLY OUT OF TUNE.
SO I CAN'T BE WITHOUT THE MATERIALS I NEED TO RE-TUNE THEM.
OH, AND BY THE BY...
AREN'T YOU BUYING ANYTHING TODAY?
NOT TODAY, NO. I DON'T HAVE MUR WITH ME TO CARRY THINGS.
HE'S OFF WITH THE OTHERS AT THE WOODED WAY.
TOK

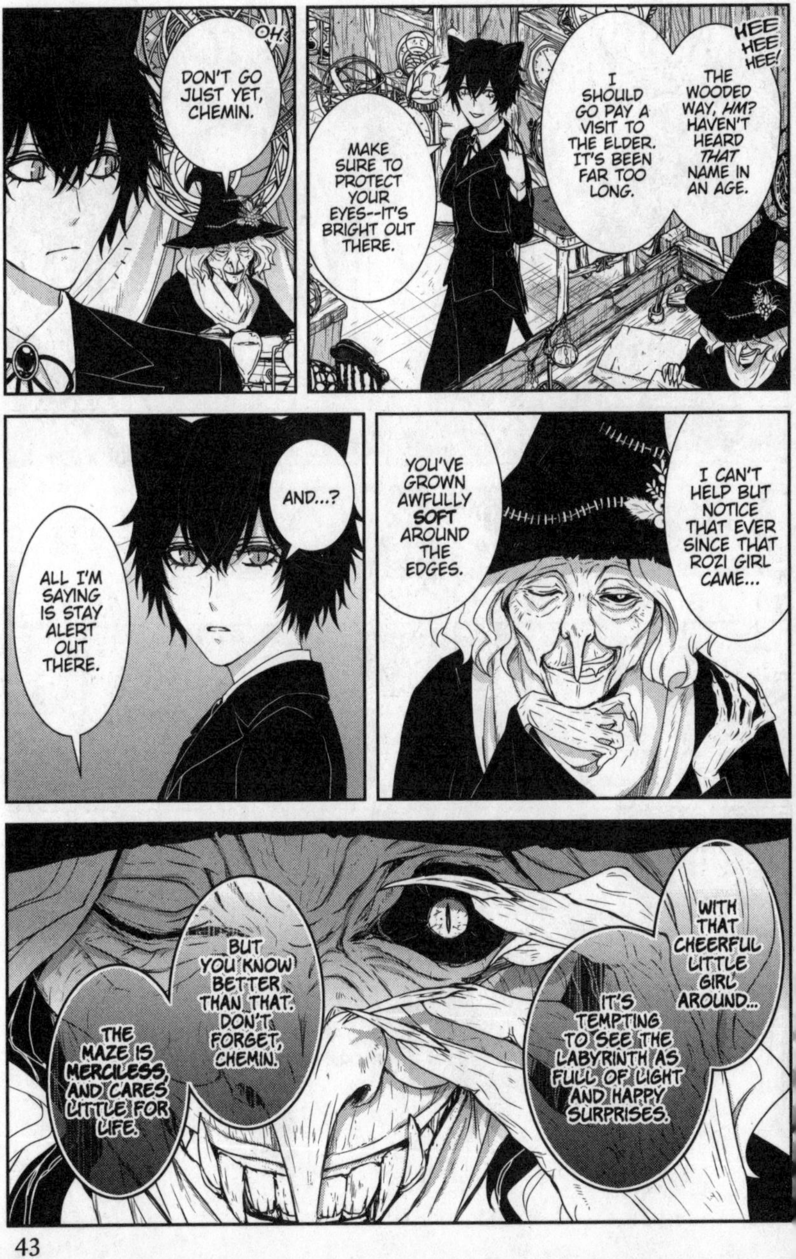
HEE HEE HEE!
THE WOODED WAY, *HM?* HAVEN'T HEARD *THAT* NAME IN AN AGE.
I SHOULD GO PAY A VISIT TO THE ELDER. IT'S BEEN FAR TOO LONG.
MAKE SURE TO PROTECT YOUR EYES--IT'S BRIGHT OUT THERE.
OH.
DON'T GO JUST YET, CHEMIN.
I CAN'T HELP BUT NOTICE THAT EVER SINCE THAT ROZI GIRL CAME...
YOU'VE GROWN AWFULLY **SOFT** AROUND THE EDGES.
AND...?
ALL I'M SAYING IS STAY ALERT OUT THERE.
WITH THAT CHEERFUL LITTLE GIRL AROUND...
IT'S TEMPTING TO SEE THE LABYRINTH AS FULL OF LIGHT AND HAPPY SURPRISES.
BUT YOU KNOW BETTER THAN THAT. DON'T FORGET, CHEMIN.
THE MAZE IS MERCILESS, AND CARES LITTLE FOR LIFE.

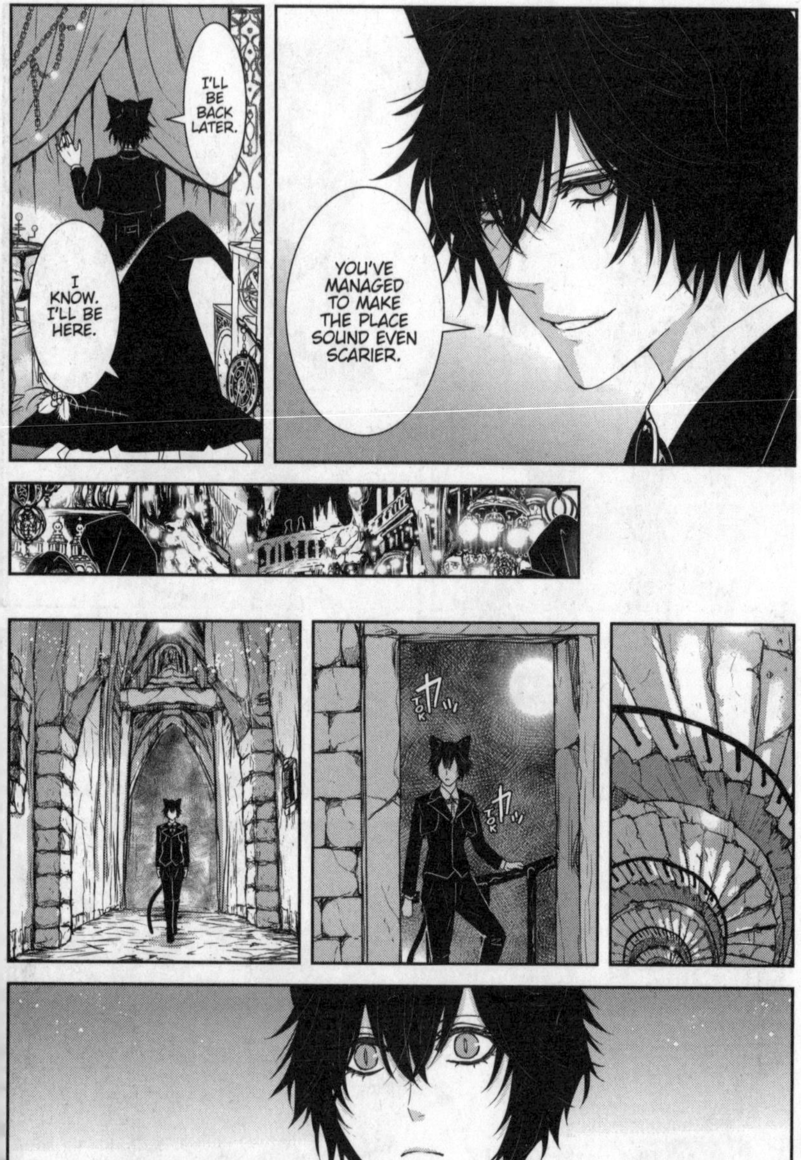
YOU'VE MANAGED TO MAKE THE PLACE SOUND EVEN SCARIER.
I'LL BE BACK LATER.
I KNOW. I'LL BE HERE.
TOK
TOK

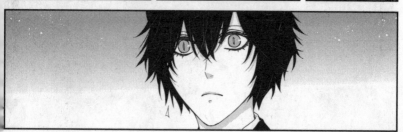

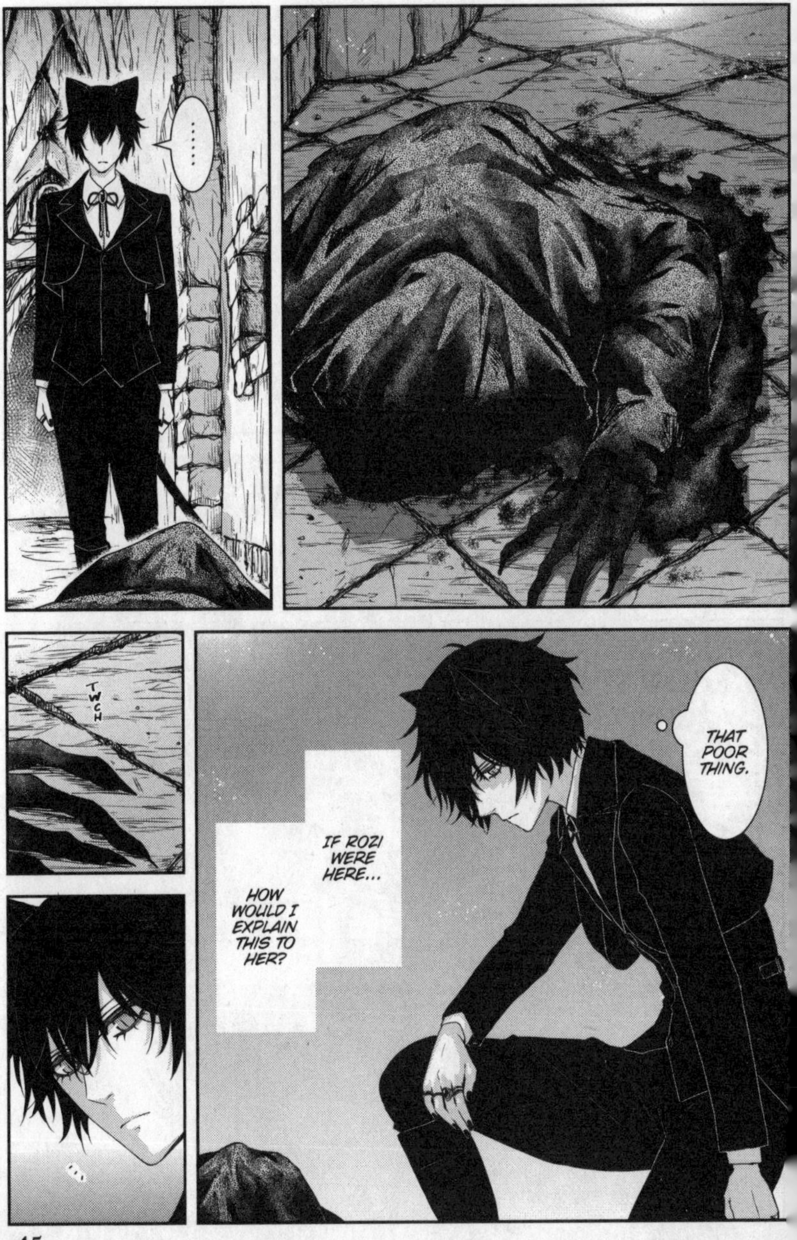
......
THAT POOR THING.
IF ROZI WERE HERE...
HOW WOULD I EXPLAIN THIS TO HER?
TWCH
...

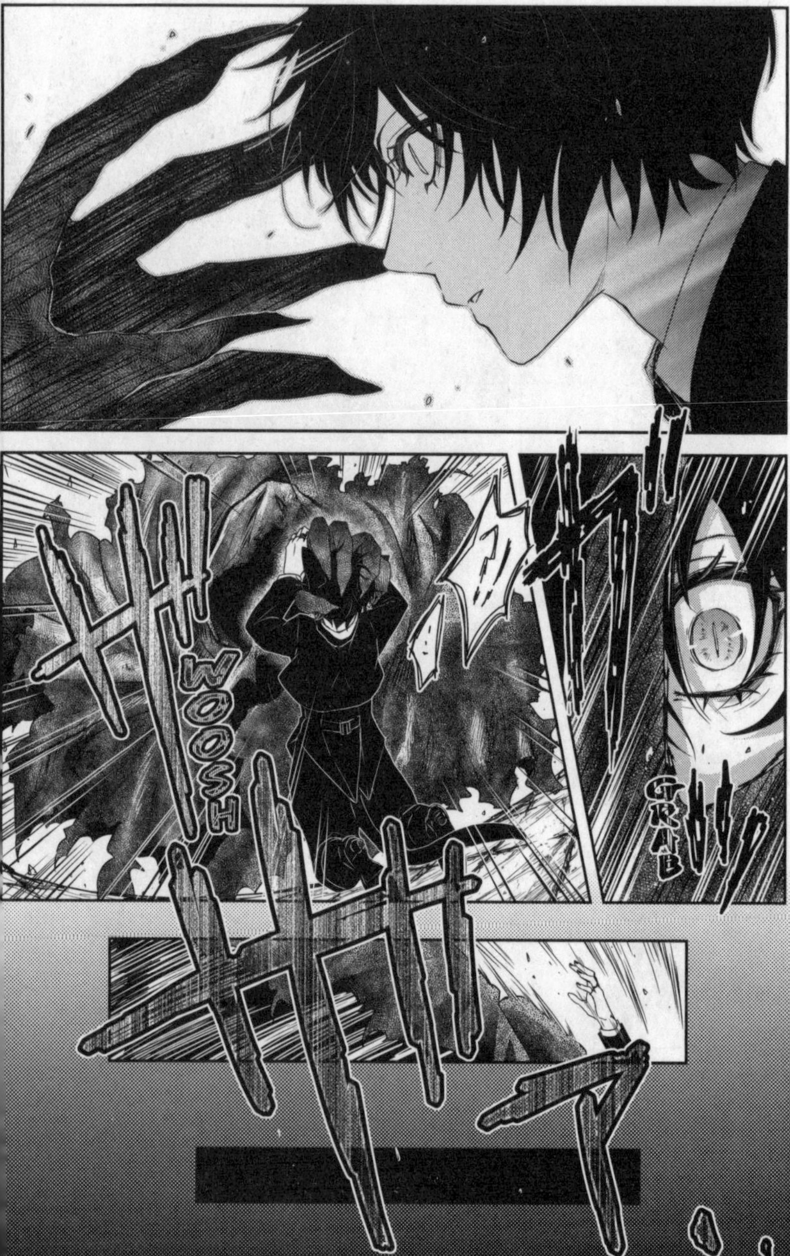
GRAB
WOOSH

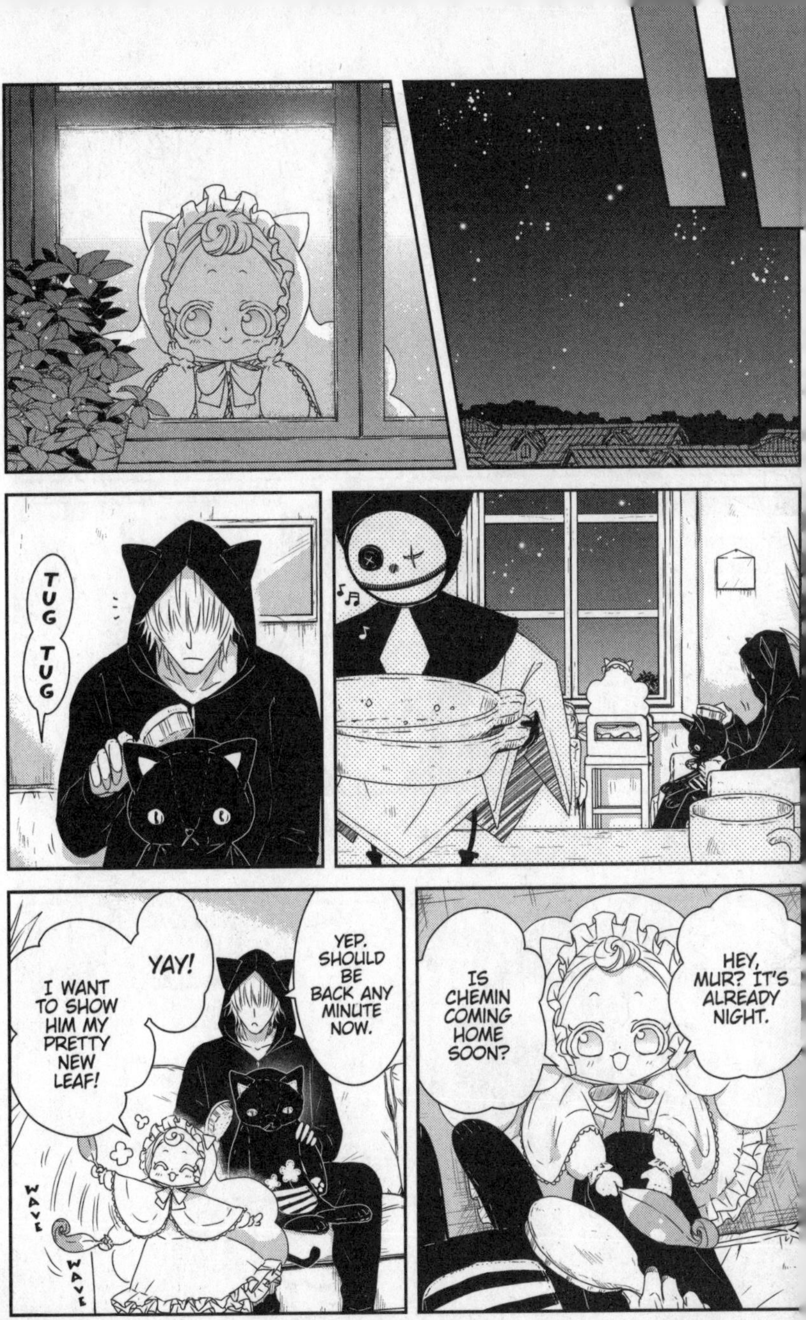
TUG TUG
HEY, MUR? IT'S ALREADY NIGHT.
IS CHEMIN COMING HOME SOON?
YEP. SHOULD BE BACK ANY MINUTE NOW.
YAY!
I WANT TO SHOW HIM MY PRETTY NEW LEAF!
WAVE WAVE

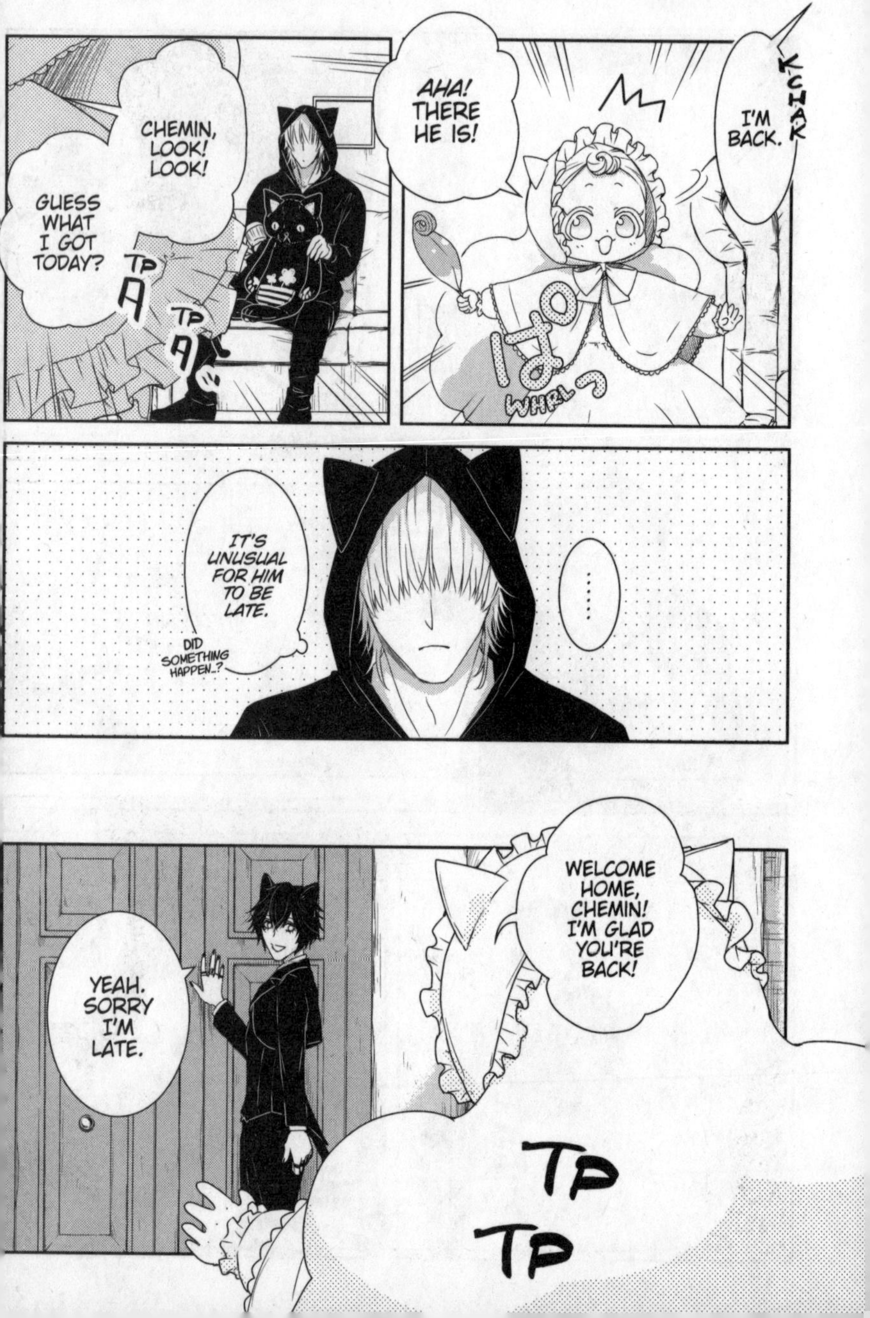
K-CHAK
I'M BACK.
AHA! THERE HE IS!
はっ
WHRL
CHEMIN, LOOK! LOOK!
GUESS WHAT I GOT TODAY?
TP A
TP A
......
IT'S UNUSUAL FOR HIM TO BE LATE.
DID SOMETHING HAPPEN..?
WELCOME HOME, CHEMIN! I'M GLAD YOU'RE BACK!
YEAH. SORRY I'M LATE.
TP
TP

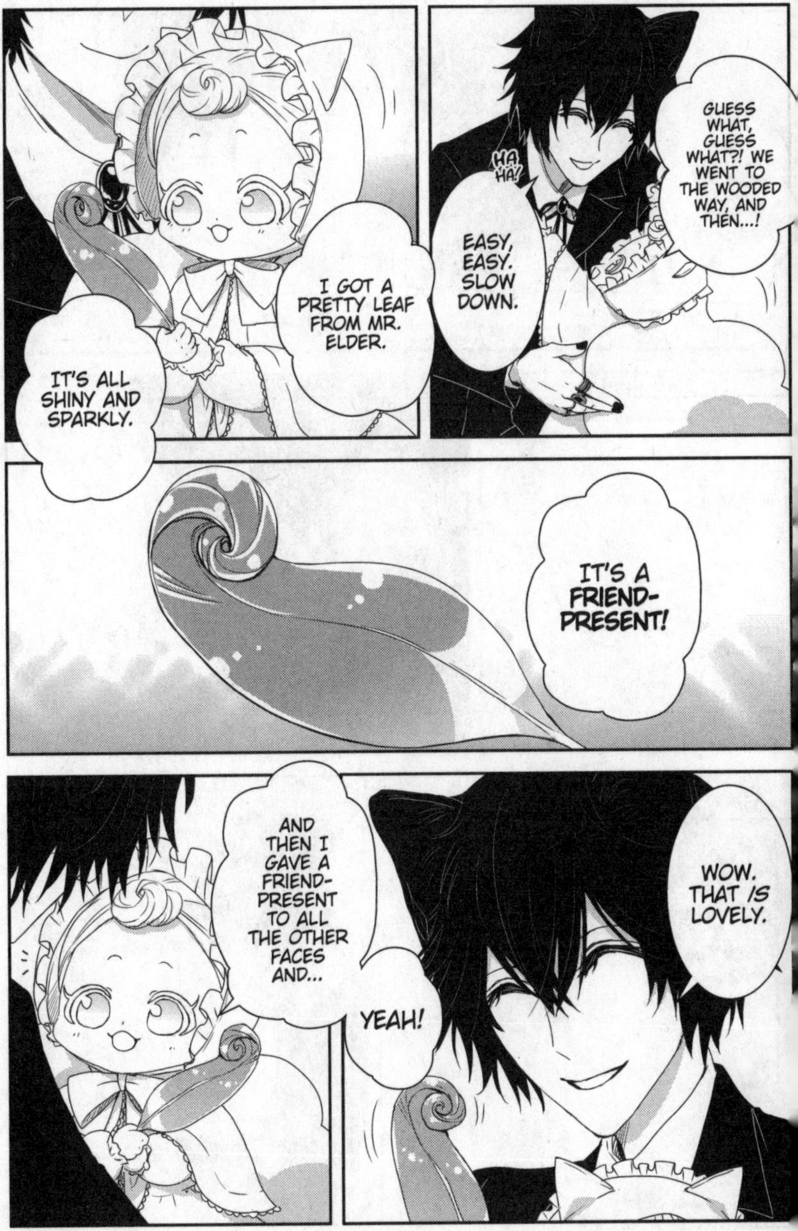

GUESS WHAT, GUESS WHAT?! WE WENT TO THE WOODED WAY, AND THEN...!
HA HA!
EASY, EASY. SLOW DOWN.
I GOT A PRETTY LEAF FROM MR. ELDER.
IT'S ALL SHINY AND SPARKLY.
IT'S A FRIEND-PRESENT!
WOW. THAT *IS* LOVELY.
YEAH!
AND THEN I GAVE A FRIEND-PRESENT TO ALL THE OTHER FACES AND...

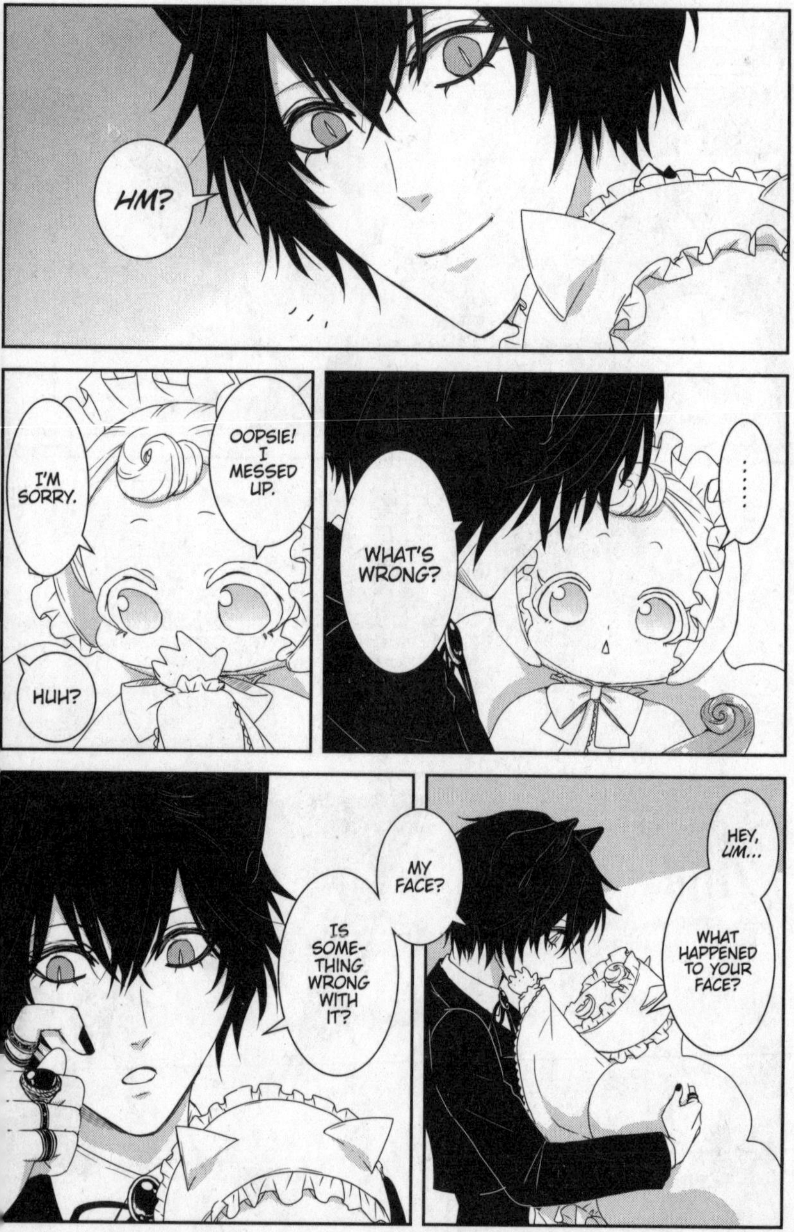
HM?
......
WHAT'S WRONG?
OOPSIE! I MESSED UP.
I'M SORRY.
HUH?
HEY, UM...
WHAT HAPPENED TO YOUR FACE?
MY FACE?
IS SOME-THING WRONG WITH IT?

KINDA.
SEE, THAT'S CHEMIN'S FACE.
WHO ARE YOU?

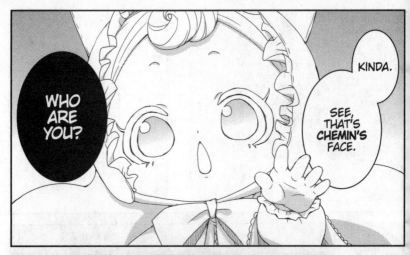

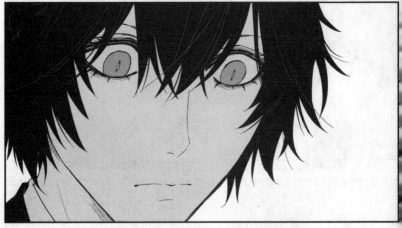

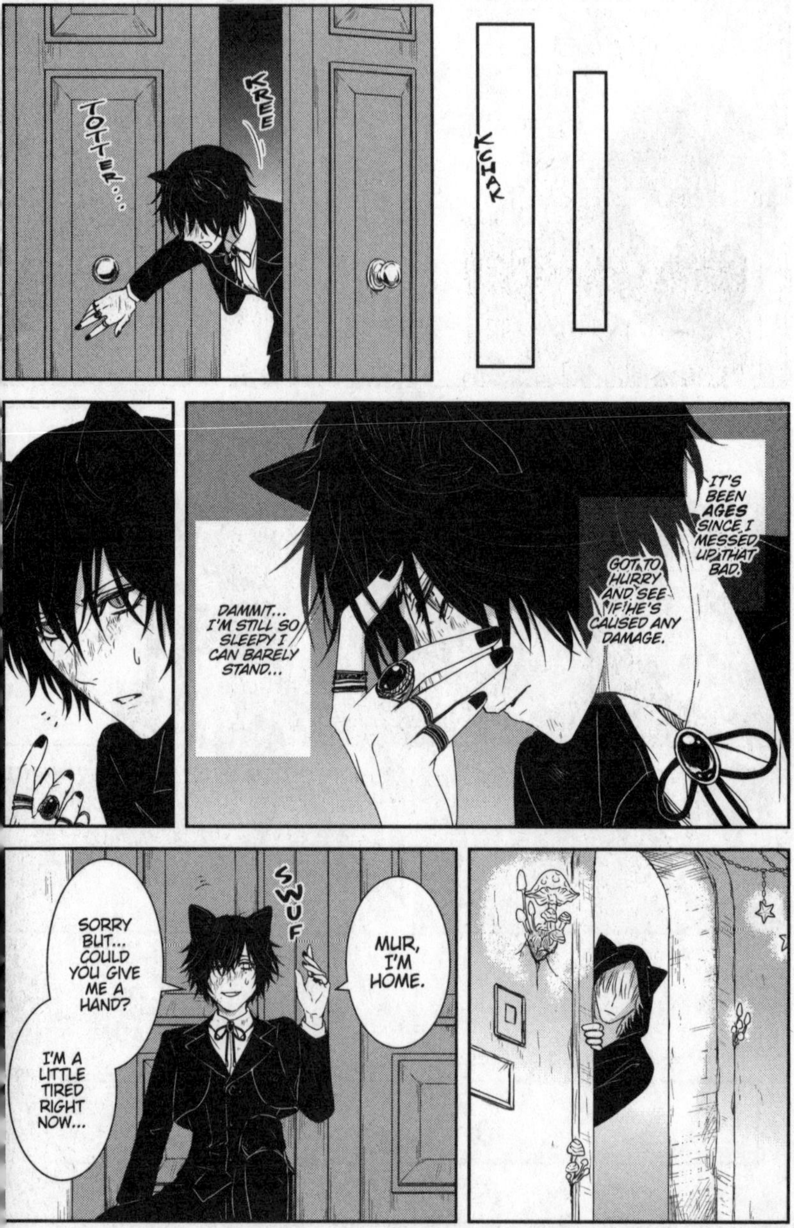
KCHAK
KREE
TOTTER...
IT'S BEEN AGES SINCE I MESSED UP THAT BAD.
GOT TO HURRY AND SEE IF HE'S CAUSED ANY DAMAGE.
DAMMIT... I'M STILL SO SLEEPY I CAN BARELY STAND...
MUR, I'M HOME.
SWUF
SORRY BUT... COULD YOU GIVE ME A HAND?
I'M A LITTLE TIRED RIGHT NOW...

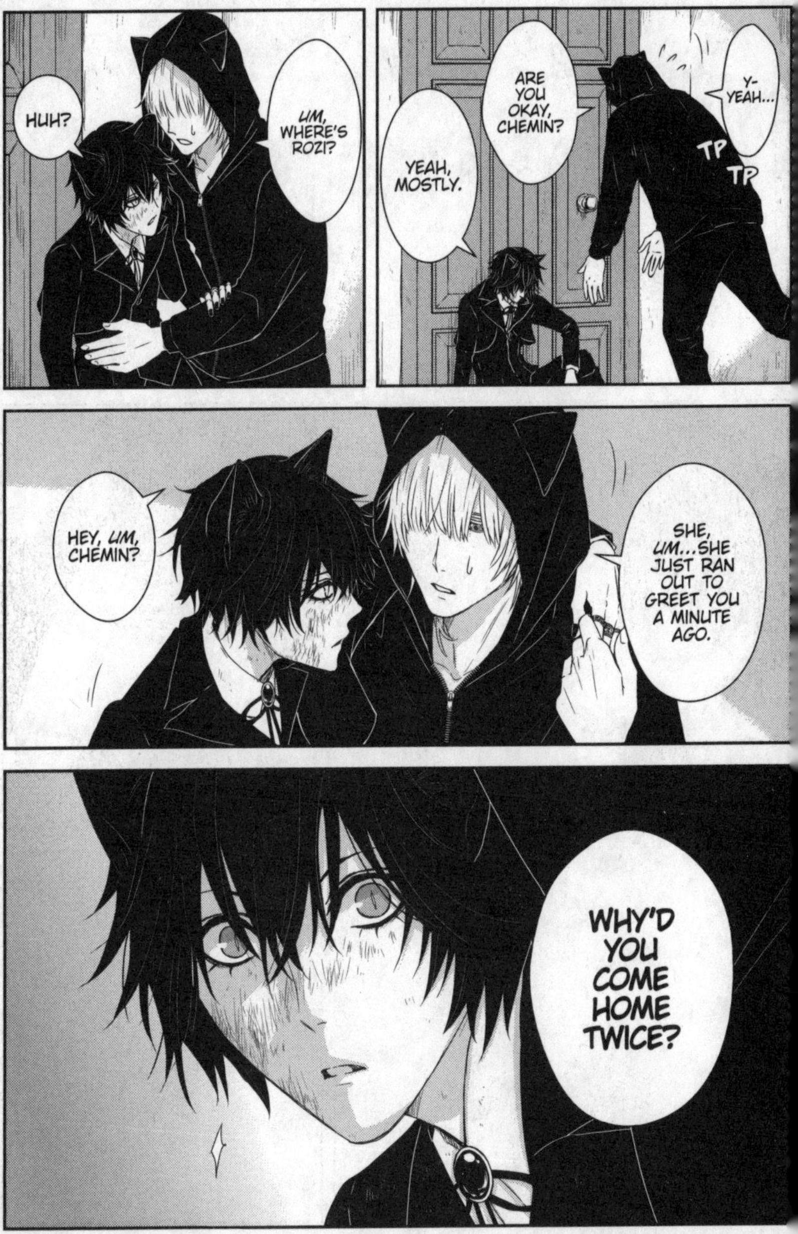
Y-YEAH...
TP TP
ARE YOU OKAY, CHEMIN?
YEAH, MOSTLY.
UM, WHERE'S ROZI?
HUH?
SHE, UM...SHE JUST RAN OUT TO GREET YOU A MINUTE AGO.
HEY, UM, CHEMIN?
WHY'D YOU COME HOME TWICE?

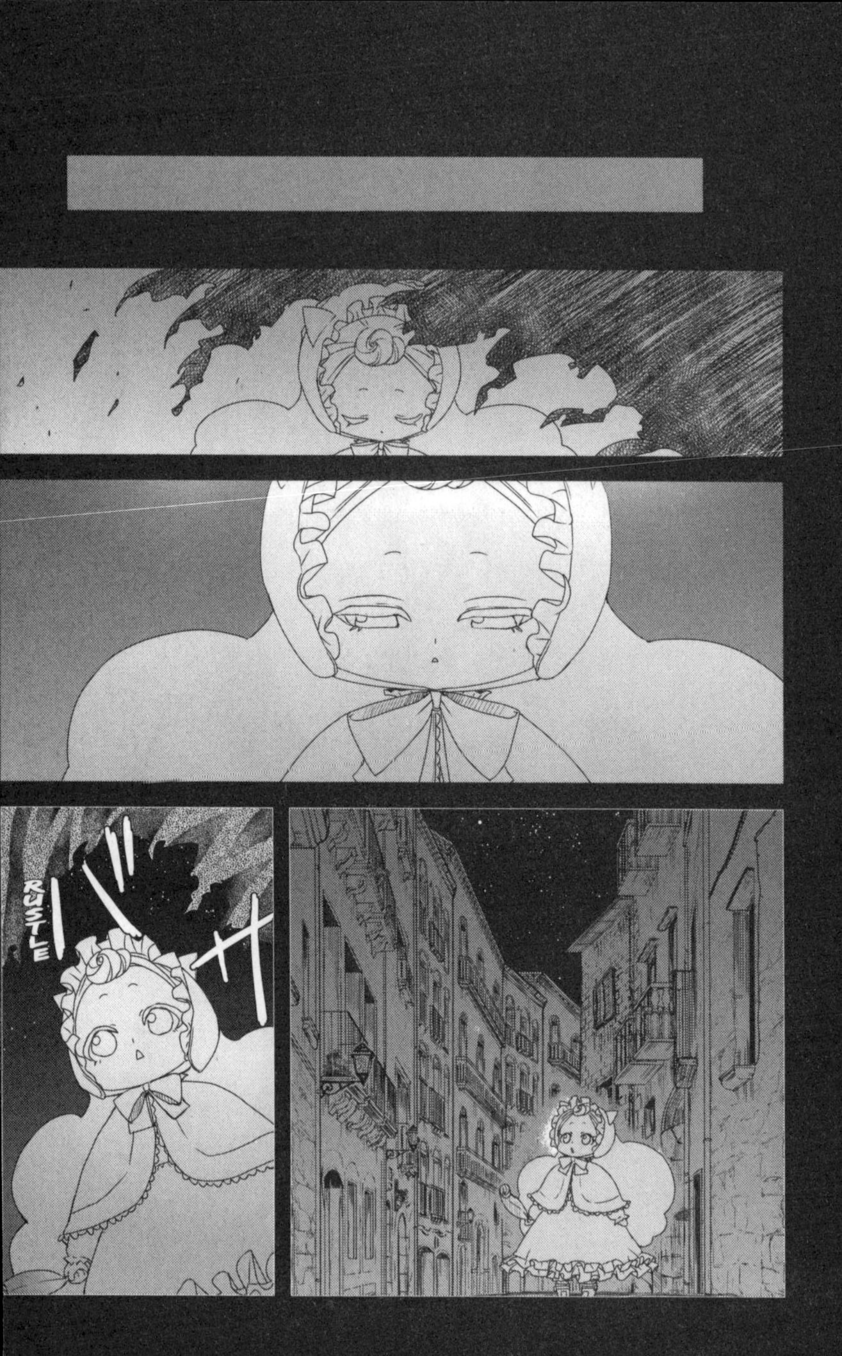
RUSTLE

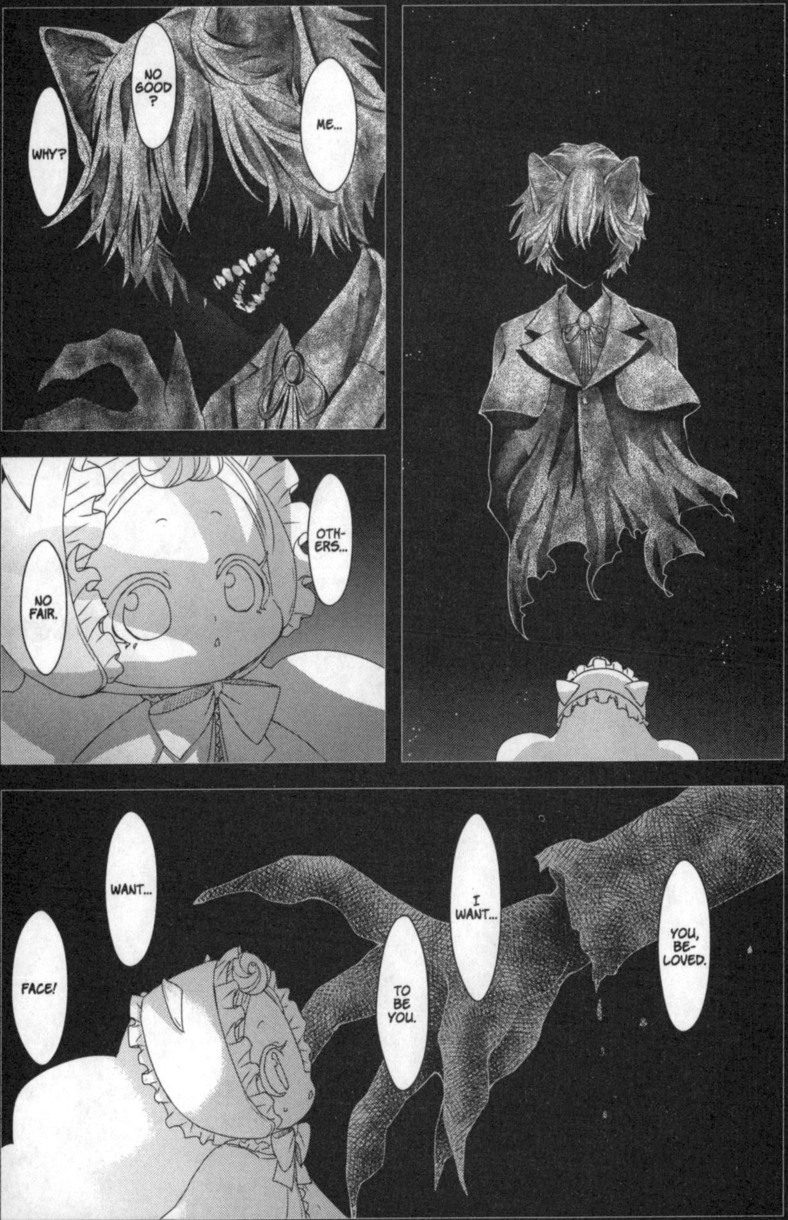
ME...
NO GOOD?
WHY?
OTHERS...
NO FAIR.
YOU, BELOVED.
I WANT...
TO BE YOU.
WANT...
FACE!

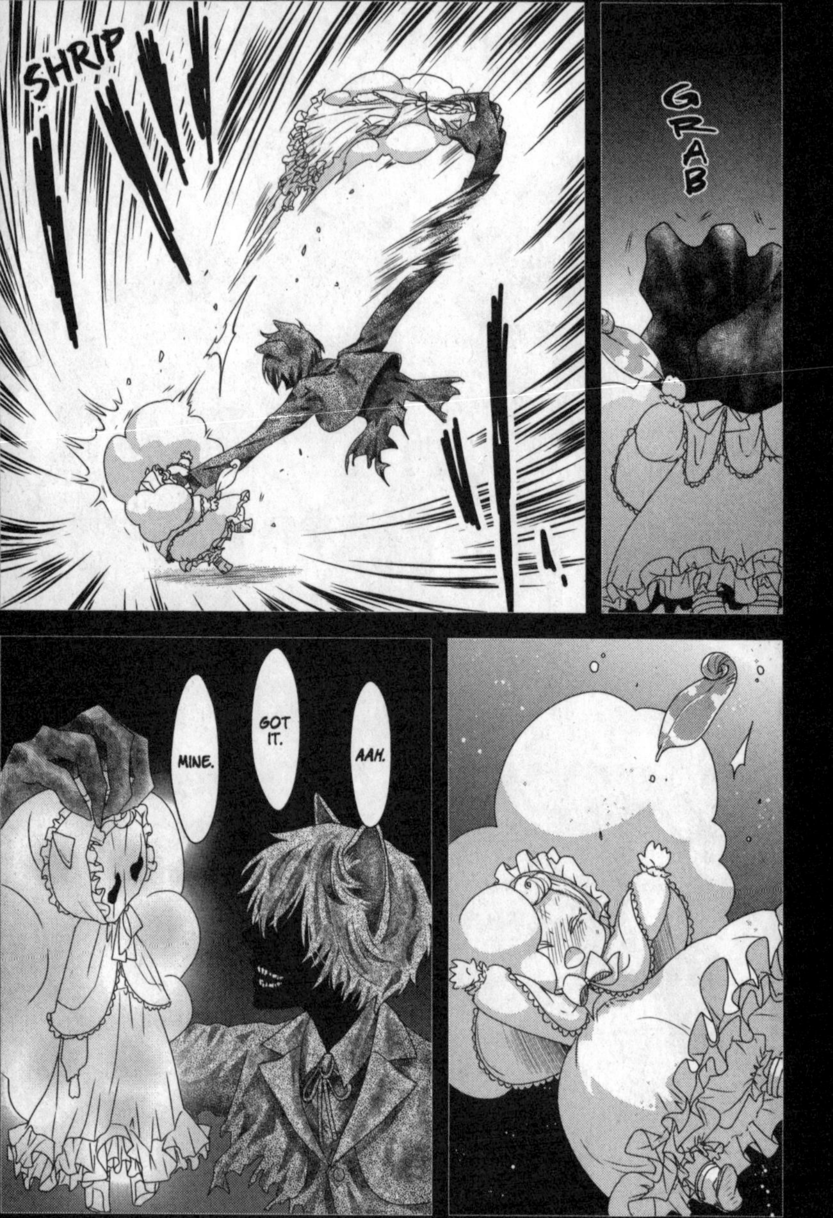
GRAB
SHRIP
AAH.
GOT IT.
MINE.

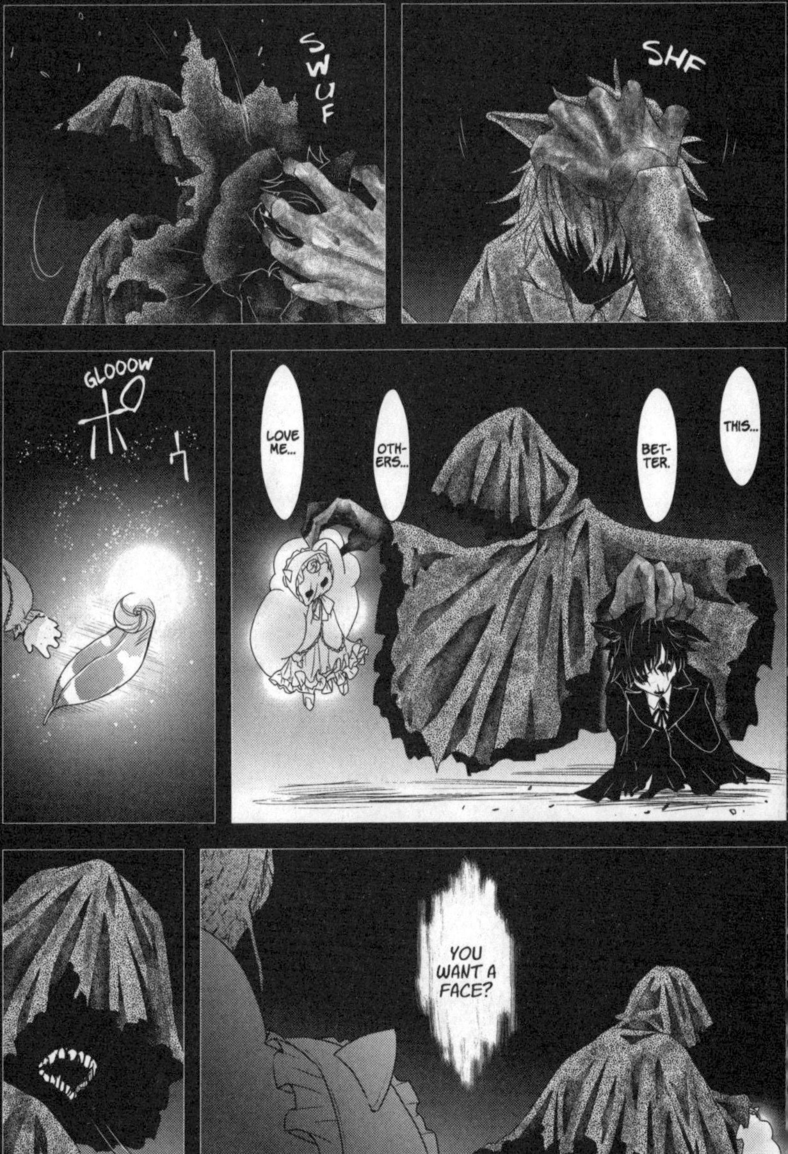
SHF
SWUF
THIS...
BET-TER.
OTH-ERS...
LOVE ME...
GLOOOW
YOU WANT A FACE?

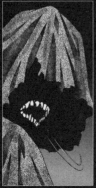

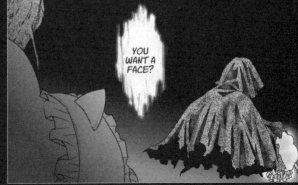

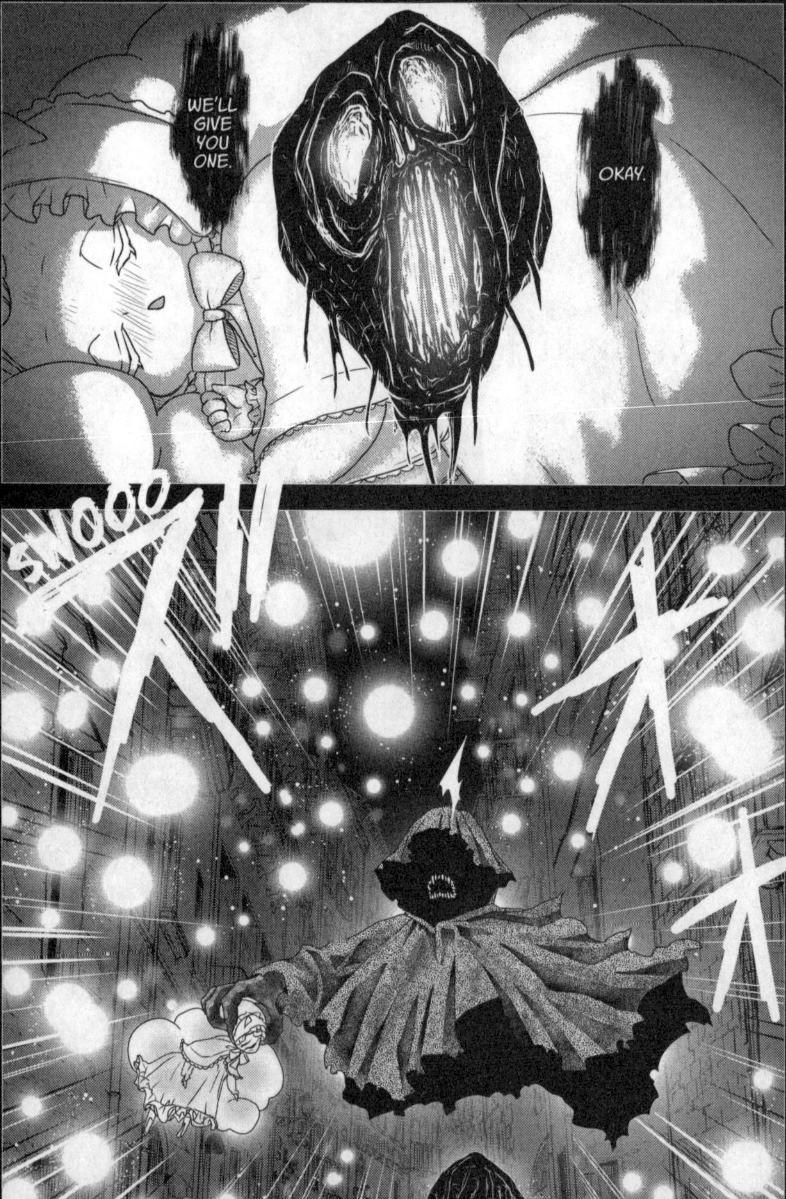
OKAY.
WE'LL GIVE YOU ONE.
SWOOO

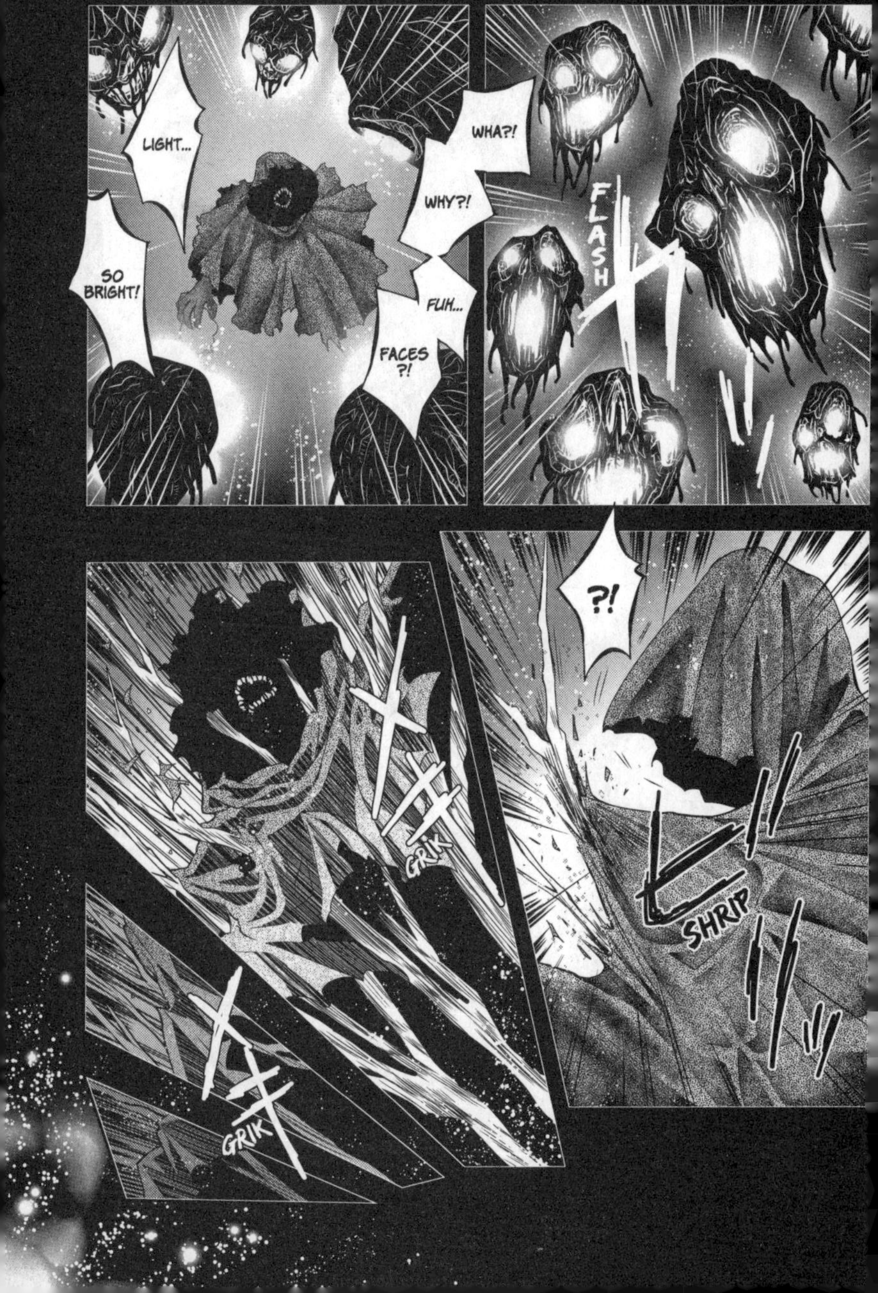
FLASH
WHA?!
WHY?!
FUH...
FACES ?!
LIGHT...
SO BRIGHT!
?!
SHRIP
GRIK
GRIK

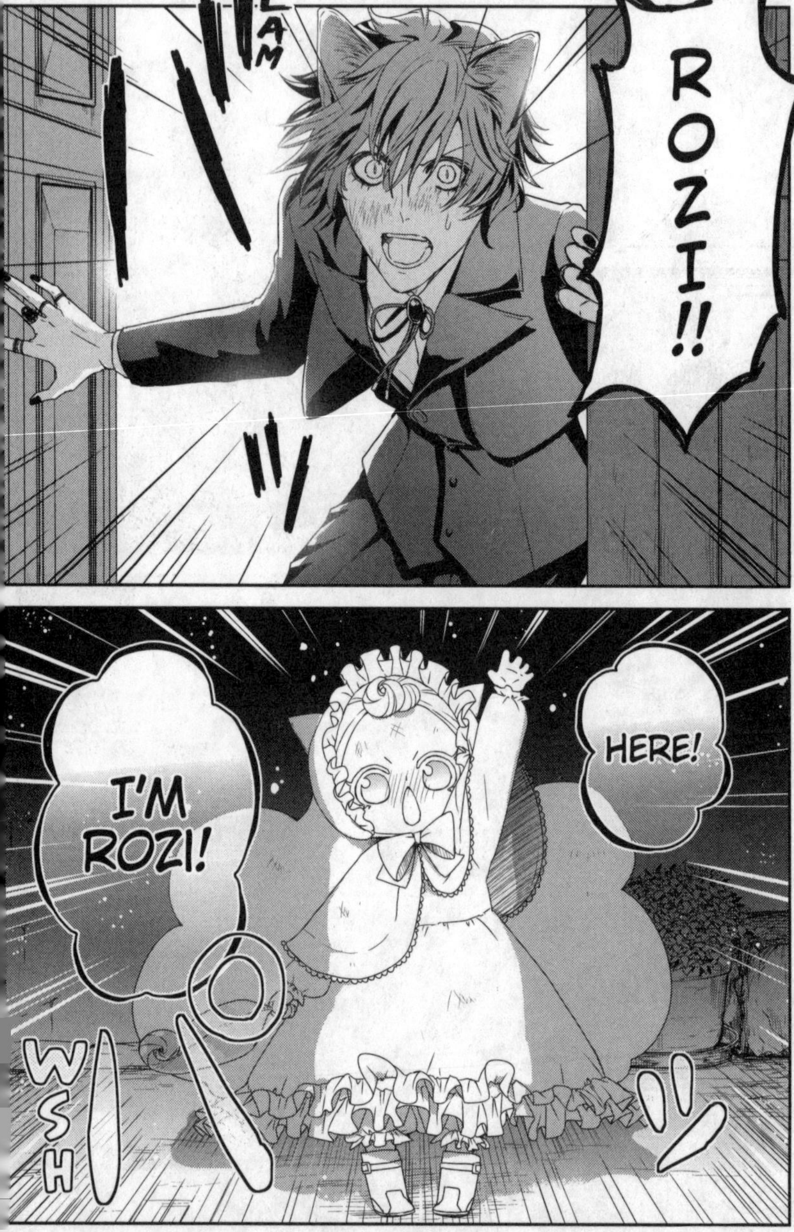

ROZI!!
SLAM
HERE!
I'M ROZI!
WSH

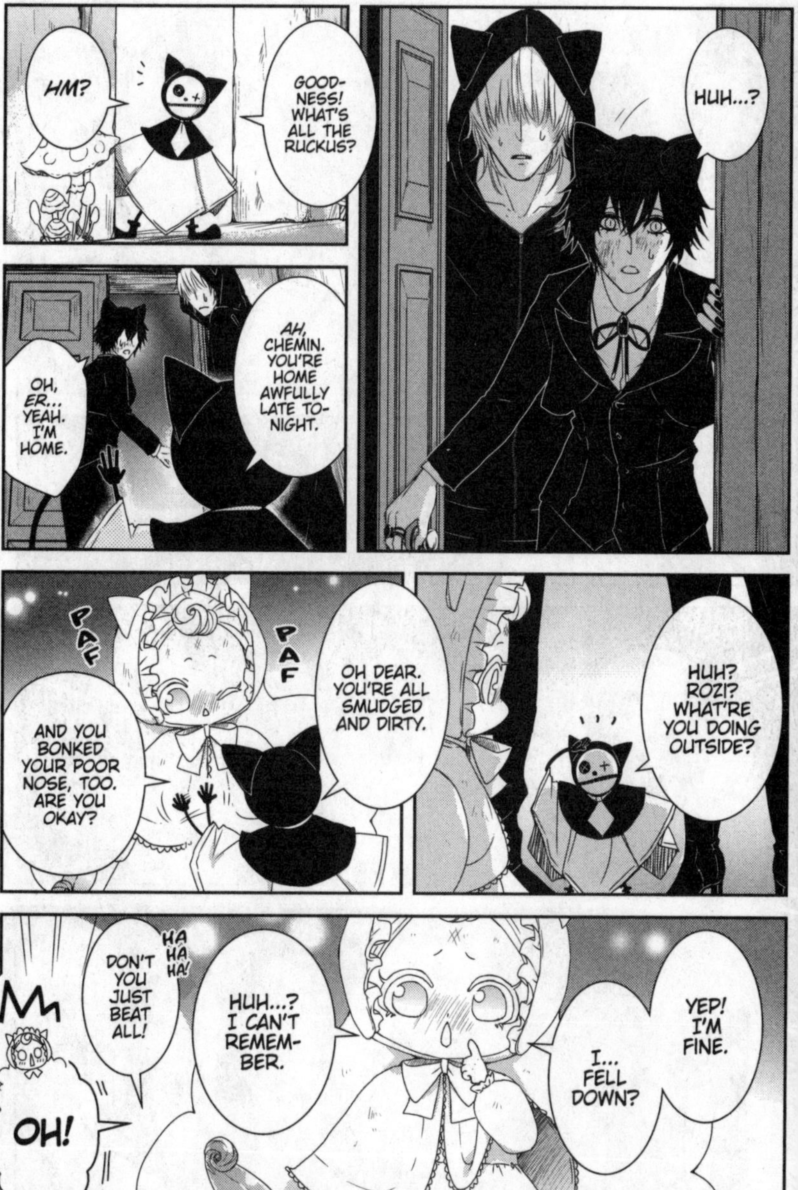
HUH...?
GOODNESS! WHAT'S ALL THE RUCKUS?
HM?
AH, CHEMIN. YOU'RE HOME AWFULLY LATE TO-NIGHT.
OH, ER... YEAH. I'M HOME.
HUH? ROZI? WHAT'RE YOU DOING OUTSIDE?
OH DEAR. YOU'RE ALL SMUDGED AND DIRTY.
PAF
PAF
AND YOU BONKED YOUR POOR NOSE, TOO. ARE YOU OKAY?
YEP! I'M FINE.
I... FELL DOWN?
HUH...? I CAN'T REMEM-BER.
HA HA HA!
DON'T YOU JUST BEAT ALL!
OH!

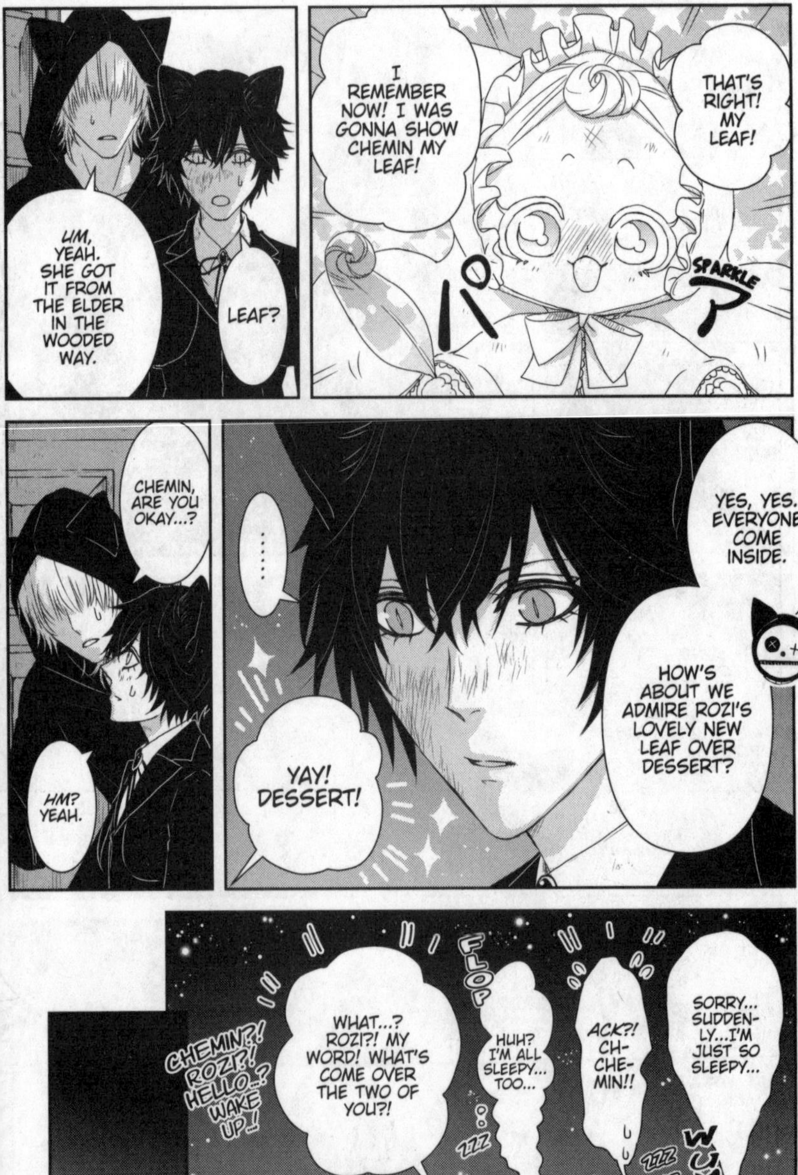
THAT'S RIGHT! MY LEAF!
I REMEMBER NOW! I WAS GONNA SHOW CHEMIN MY LEAF!
SPARKLE
LEAF?
UM, YEAH. SHE GOT IT FROM THE ELDER IN THE WOODED WAY.
YES, YES. EVERYONE COME INSIDE.
HOW'S ABOUT WE ADMIRE ROZI'S LOVELY NEW LEAF OVER DESSERT?
......
YAY! DESSERT!
CHEMIN, ARE YOU OKAY...?
HM? YEAH.
SORRY... SUDDEN-LY...I'M JUST SO SLEEPY...
WUMP
ACK?! CH-CHE-MIN!!
ZZZ ZZZ
HUH? I'M ALL SLEEPY... TOO...
FLOP
ZZZ
WHAT...? ROZI?! MY WORD! WHAT'S COME OVER THE TWO OF YOU?!
CHEMIN?! ROZI?! HELLO...? WAKE UP...!

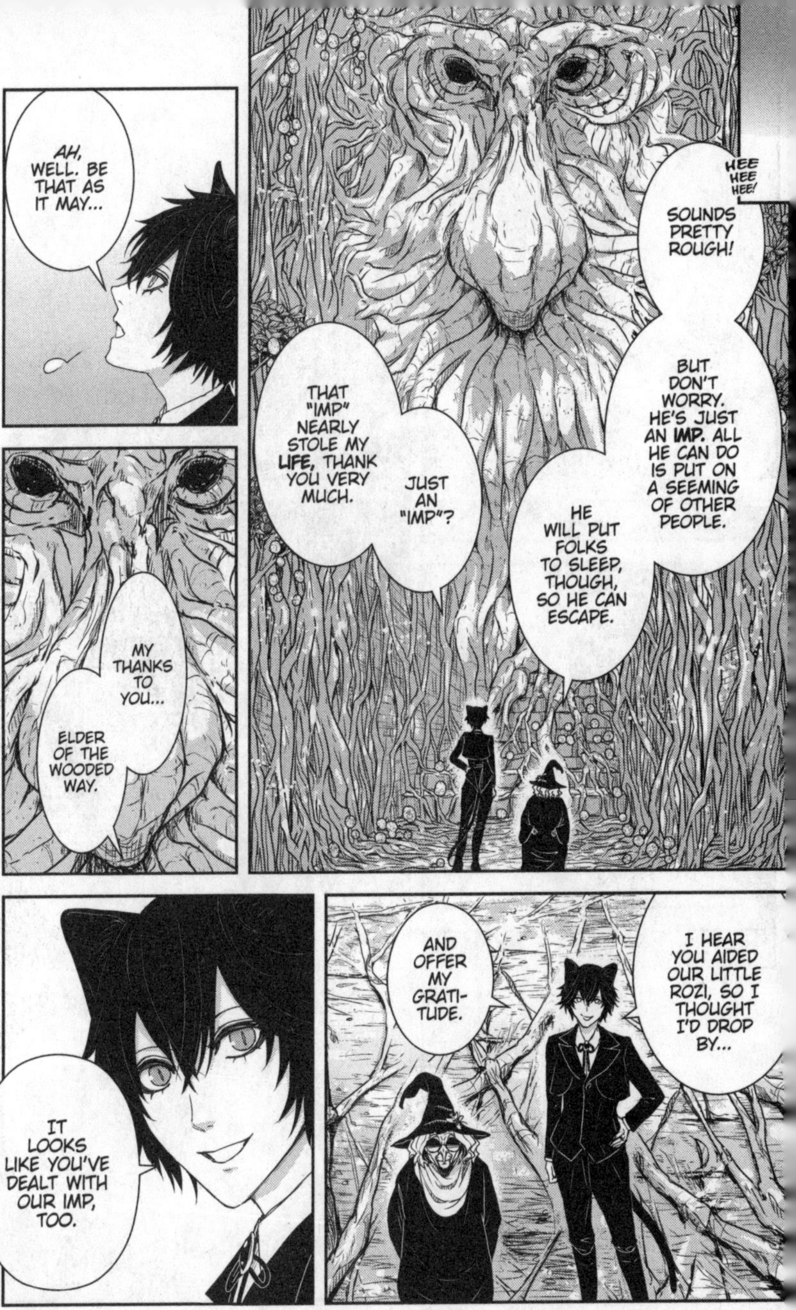
HEE HEE HEE!
SOUNDS PRETTY ROUGH!
BUT DON'T WORRY. HE'S JUST AN **IMP.** ALL HE CAN DO IS PUT ON A SEEMING OF OTHER PEOPLE.
HE WILL PUT FOLKS TO SLEEP, THOUGH, SO HE CAN ESCAPE.
JUST AN "IMP"?
THAT "IMP" NEARLY STOLE MY **LIFE,** THANK YOU VERY MUCH.
AH, WELL. BE THAT AS IT MAY...
MY THANKS TO YOU...
ELDER OF THE WOODED WAY.
I HEAR YOU AIDED OUR LITTLE ROZI, SO I THOUGHT I'D DROP BY...
AND OFFER MY GRATITUDE.
IT LOOKS LIKE YOU'VE DEALT WITH OUR IMP, TOO.

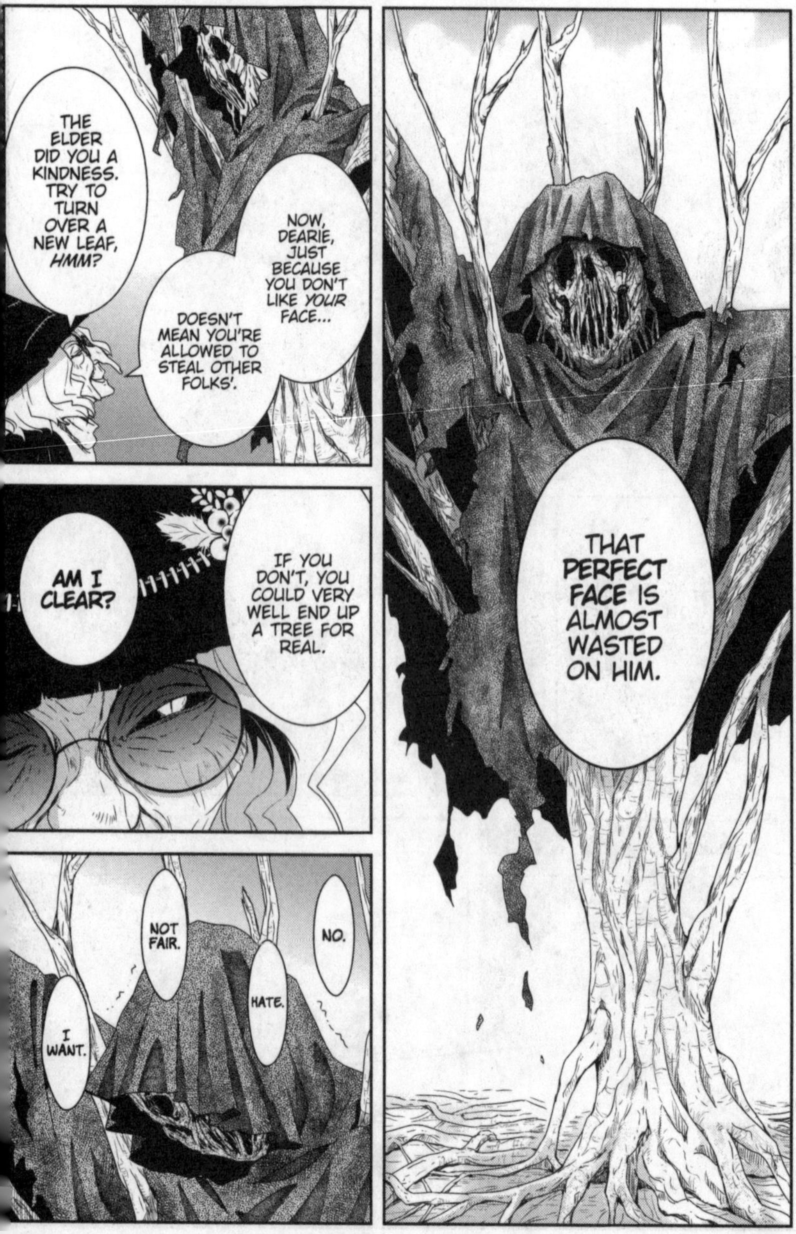
THAT PERFECT FACE IS ALMOST WASTED ON HIM.
NOW, DEARIE, JUST BECAUSE YOU DON'T LIKE *YOUR* FACE...
DOESN'T MEAN YOU'RE ALLOWED TO STEAL OTHER FOLKS'.
THE ELDER DID YOU A KINDNESS. TRY TO TURN OVER A NEW LEAF, *HMM?*
IF YOU DON'T, YOU COULD VERY WELL END UP A TREE FOR REAL.
AM I CLEAR?
NO.
NOT FAIR.
HATE.
I WANT.

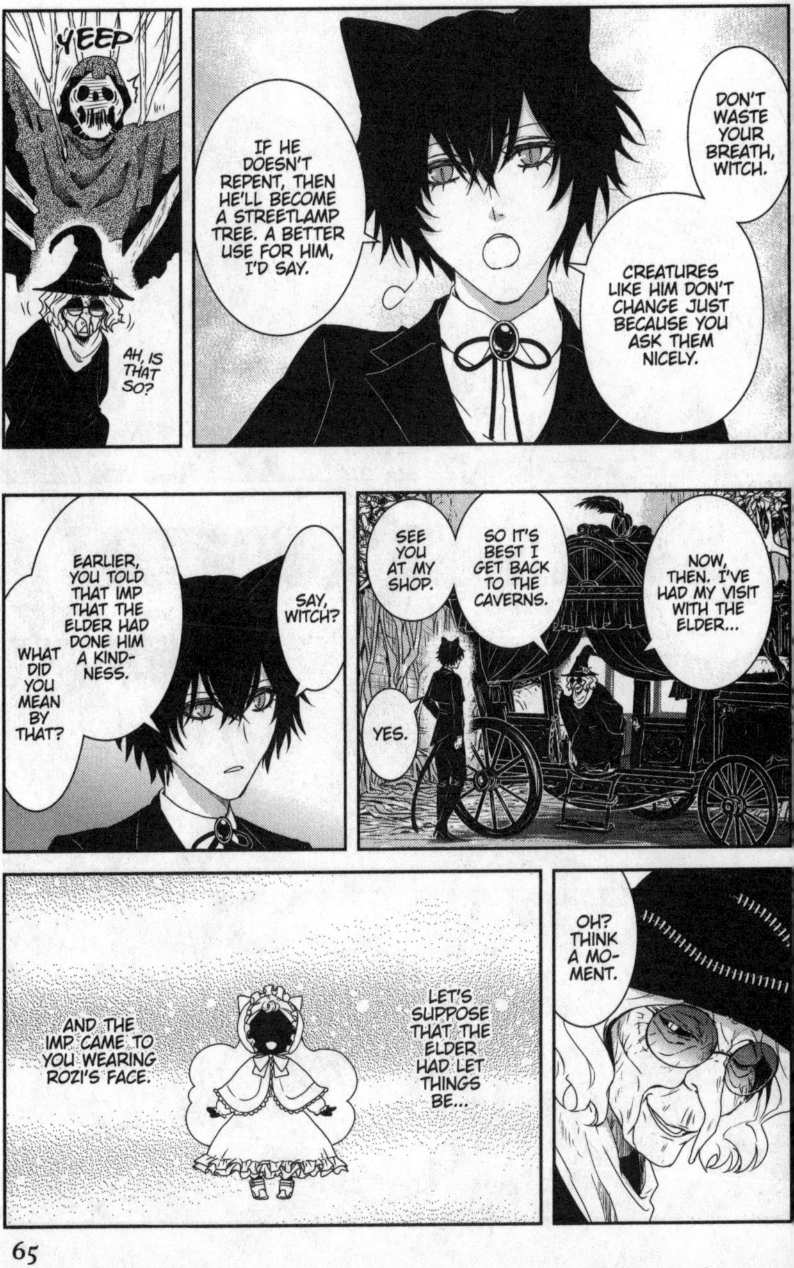
DON'T WASTE YOUR BREATH, WITCH.
CREATURES LIKE HIM DON'T CHANGE JUST BECAUSE YOU ASK THEM NICELY.
IF HE DOESN'T REPENT, THEN HE'LL BECOME A STREETLAMP TREE. A BETTER USE FOR HIM, I'D SAY.
YEEP
AH, IS THAT SO?
NOW, THEN. I'VE HAD MY VISIT WITH THE ELDER...
SO IT'S BEST I GET BACK TO THE CAVERNS.
SEE YOU AT MY SHOP.
YES.
SAY, WITCH?
EARLIER, YOU TOLD THAT IMP THAT THE ELDER HAD DONE HIM A KIND-NESS.
WHAT DID YOU MEAN BY THAT?
OH? THINK A MO-MENT.
LET'S SUPPOSE THAT THE ELDER HAD LET THINGS BE...
AND THE IMP CAME TO YOU WEARING ROZI'S FACE.

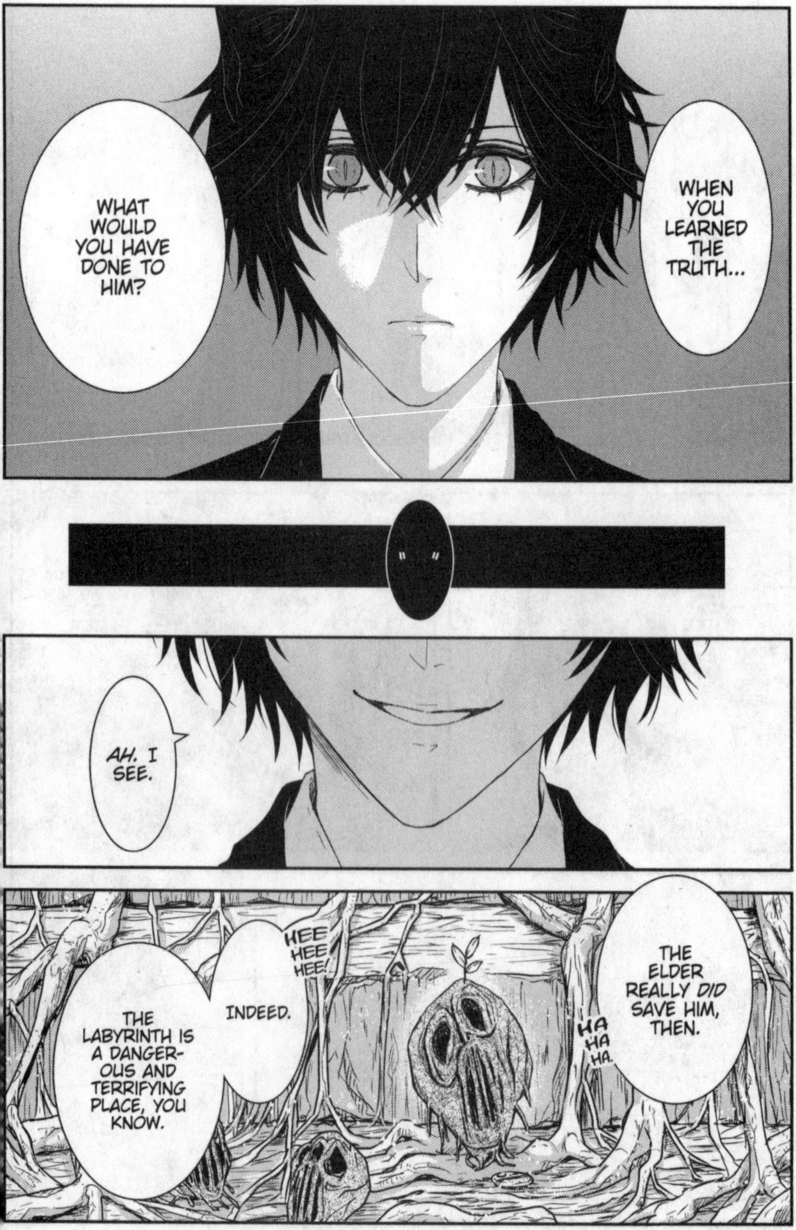
WHEN YOU LEARNED THE TRUTH...
WHAT WOULD YOU HAVE DONE TO HIM?
AH. I SEE.
THE ELDER REALLY *DID* SAVE HIM, THEN.
HA HA HA.
HEE HEE HEE!
INDEED.
THE LABYRINTH IS A DANGER-OUS AND TERRIFYING PLACE, YOU KNOW.

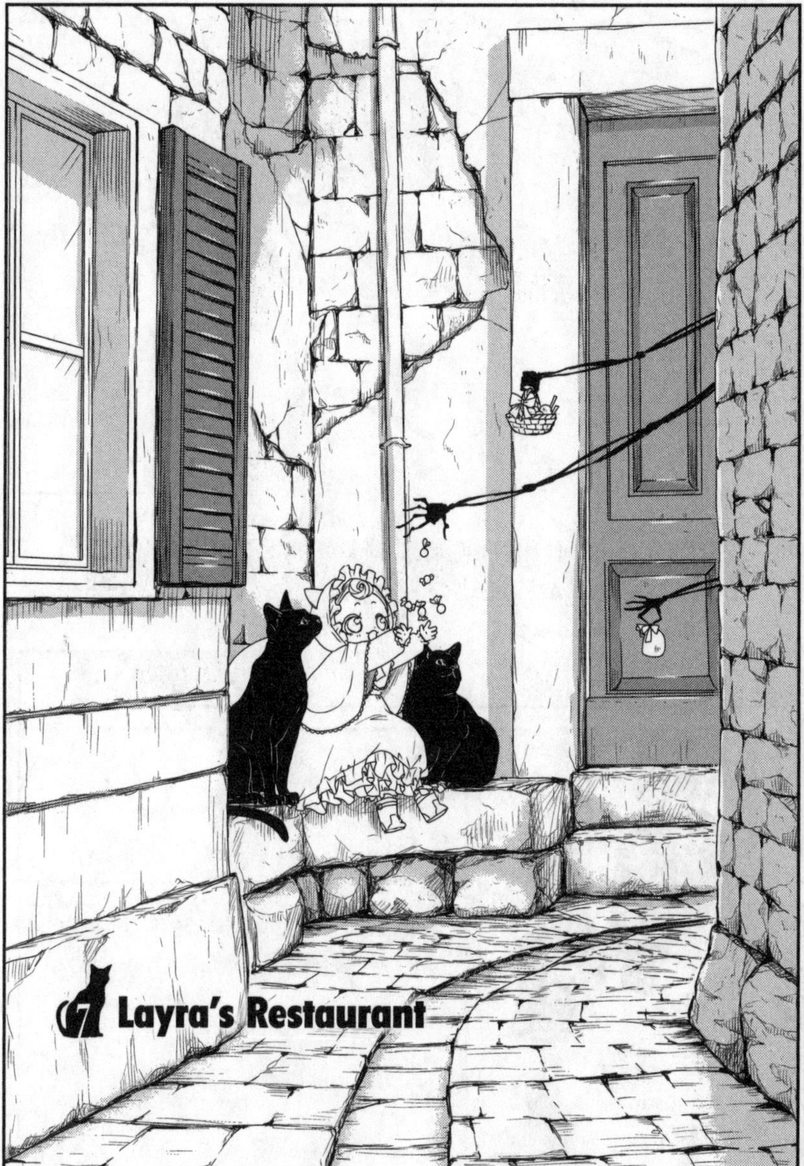
7 Layra's Restaurant

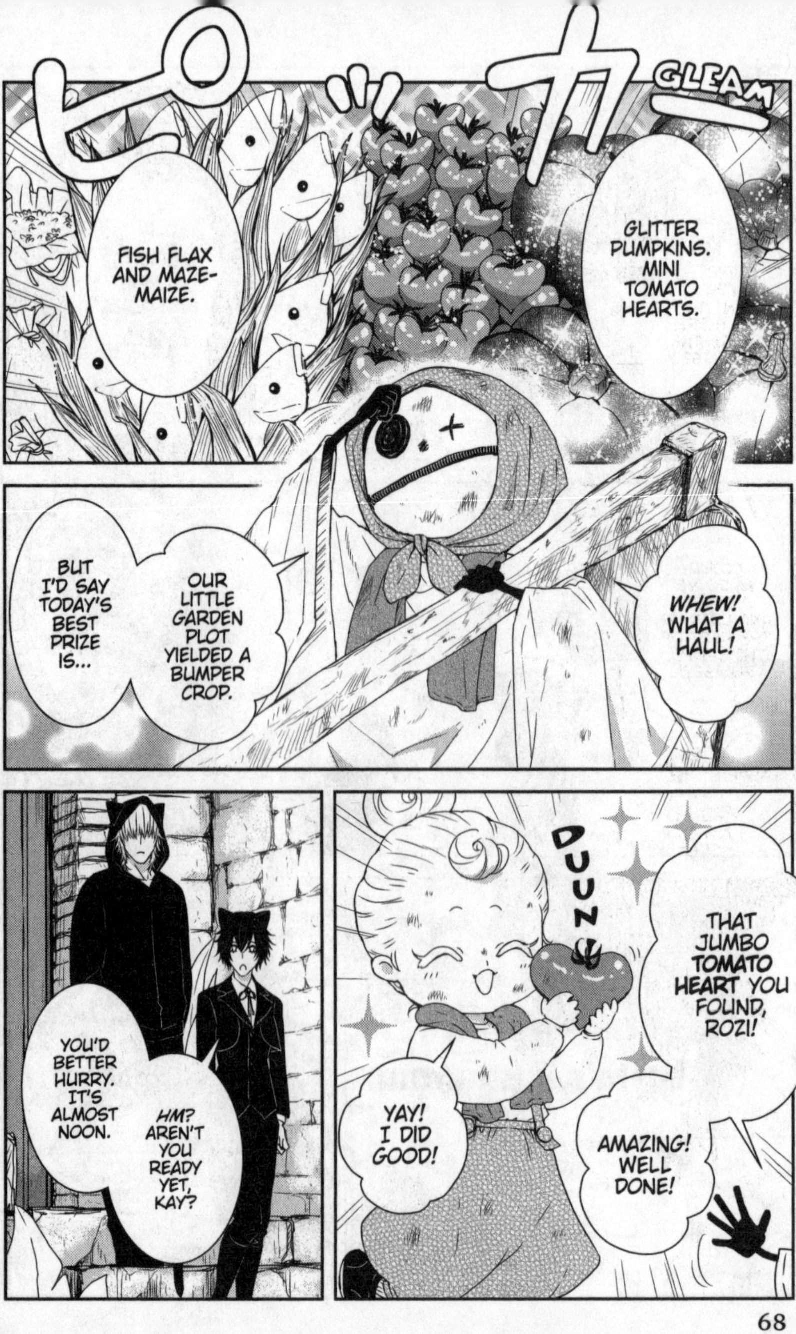
GLEAM
GLITTER PUMPKINS. MINI TOMATO HEARTS.
FISH FLAX AND MAZE-MAIZE.
WHEW! WHAT A HAUL!
OUR LITTLE GARDEN PLOT YIELDED A BUMPER CROP.
BUT I'D SAY TODAY'S BEST PRIZE IS...
DUUN
THAT JUMBO TOMATO HEART YOU FOUND, ROZI!
AMAZING! WELL DONE!
YAY! I DID GOOD!
HM? AREN'T YOU READY YET, KAY?
YOU'D BETTER HURRY. IT'S ALMOST NOON.

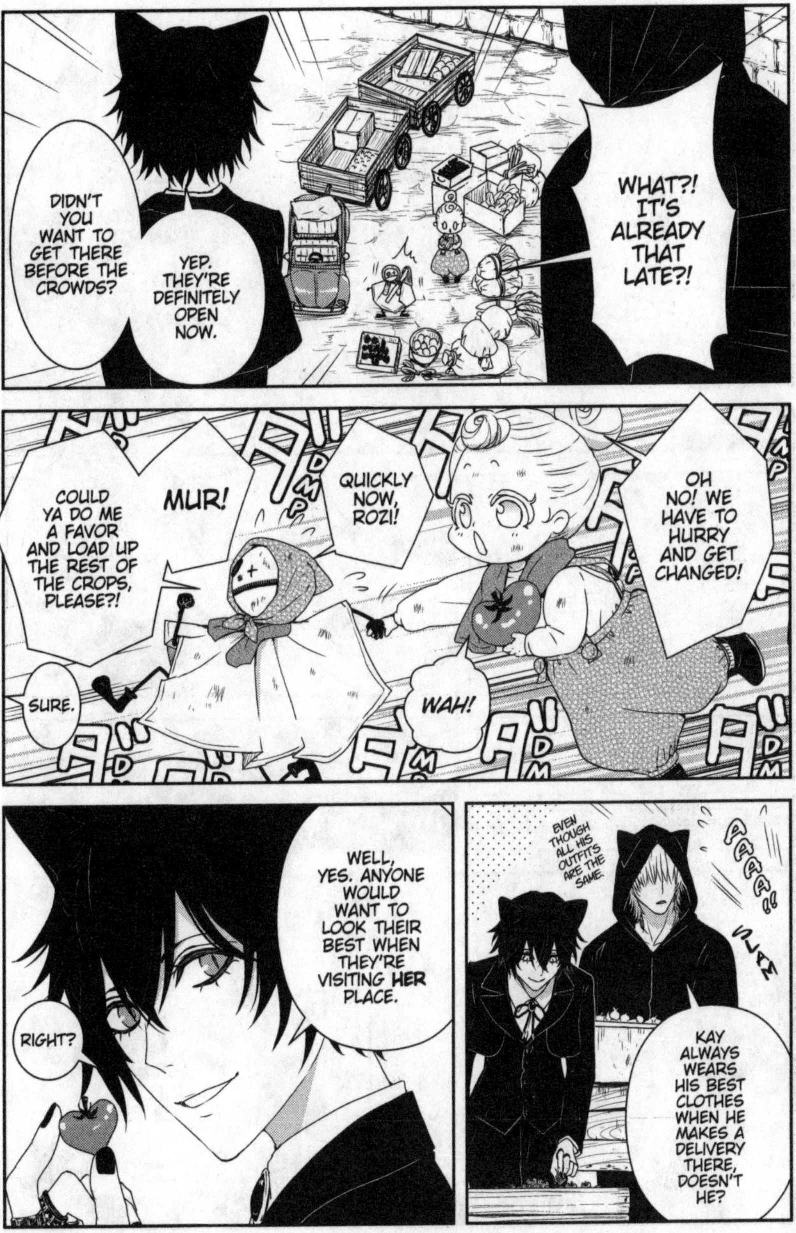
WHAT?! IT'S ALREADY THAT LATE?!
YEP. THEY'RE DEFINITELY OPEN NOW.
DIDN'T YOU WANT TO GET THERE BEFORE THE CROWDS?
OH NO! WE HAVE TO HURRY AND GET CHANGED!
QUICKLY NOW, ROZI!
WAH!
MUR!
COULD YA DO ME A FAVOR AND LOAD UP THE REST OF THE CROPS, PLEASE?!
SURE.
DMP
AAAA!!
EVEN THOUGH ALL HIS OUTFITS ARE THE SAME.
KAY ALWAYS WEARS HIS BEST CLOTHES WHEN HE MAKES A DELIVERY THERE, DOESN'T HE?
WELL, YES. ANYONE WOULD WANT TO LOOK THEIR BEST WHEN THEY'RE VISITING HER PLACE.
RIGHT?

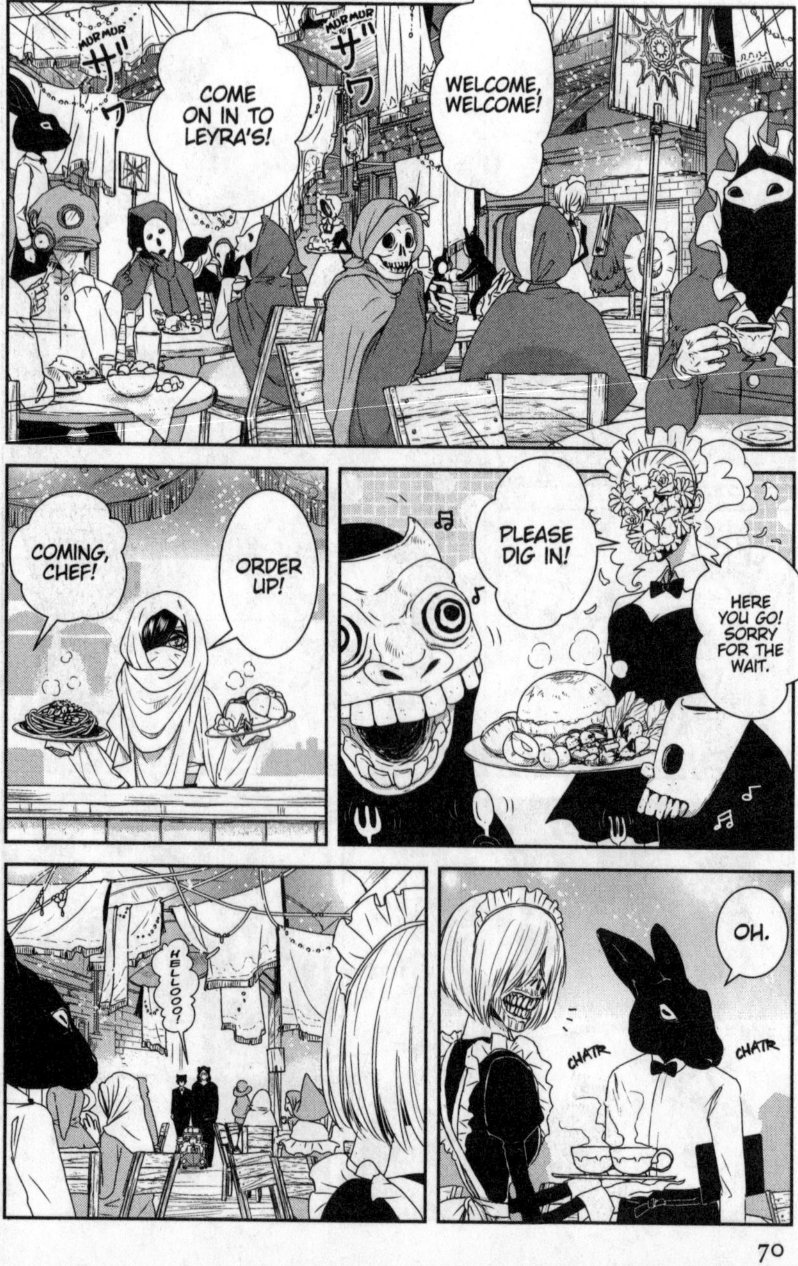

WELCOME, WELCOME!
MURMUR
ザワ
COME ON IN TO LEYRA'S!
MURMUR
ザワ
HERE YOU GO! SORRY FOR THE WAIT.
PLEASE DIG IN!
ORDER UP!
COMING, CHEF!
OH.
CHATR
CHATR
HELLOOO!

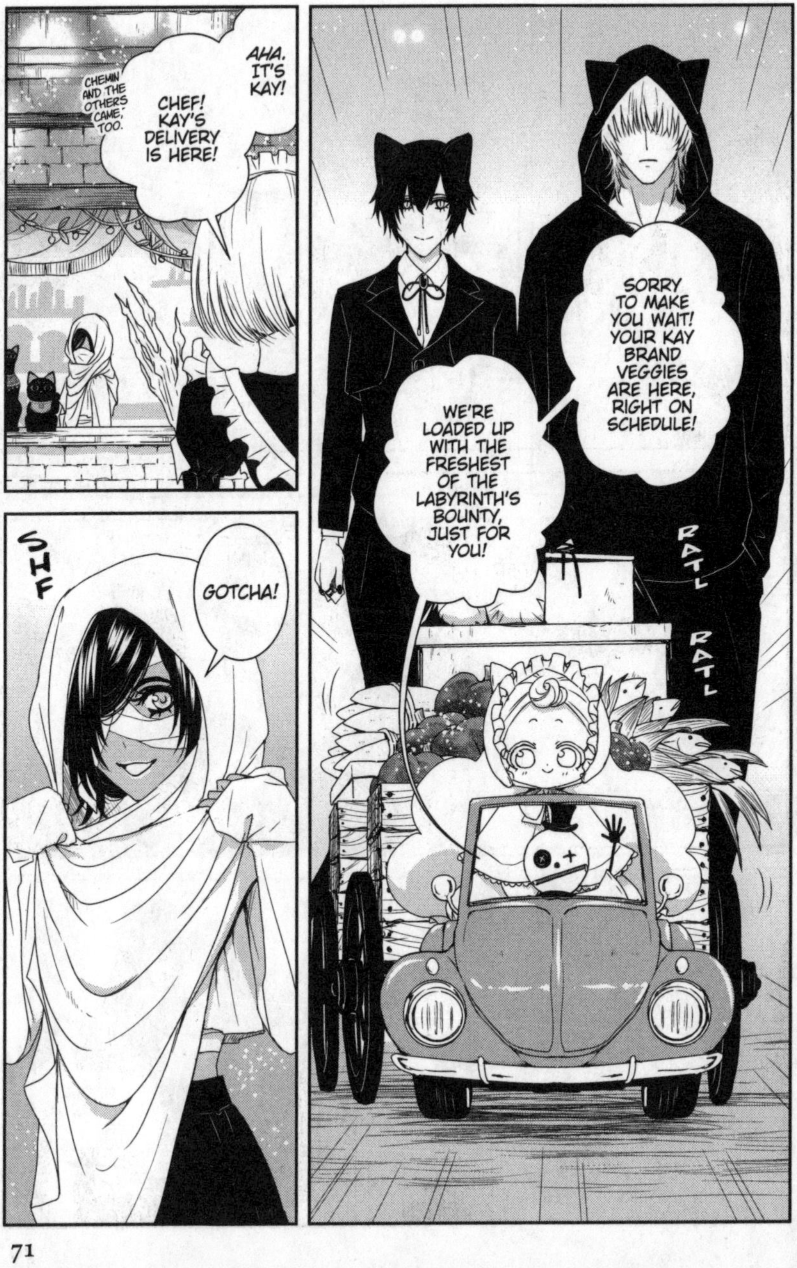
SORRY TO MAKE YOU WAIT! YOUR KAY BRAND VEGGIES ARE HERE, RIGHT ON SCHEDULE!
WE'RE LOADED UP WITH THE FRESHEST OF THE LABYRINTH'S BOUNTY, JUST FOR YOU!
RATL
RATL
AHA. IT'S KAY!
CHEF! KAY'S DELIVERY IS HERE!
CHEMIN AND THE OTHERS CAME, TOO.
SHF
GOTCHA!

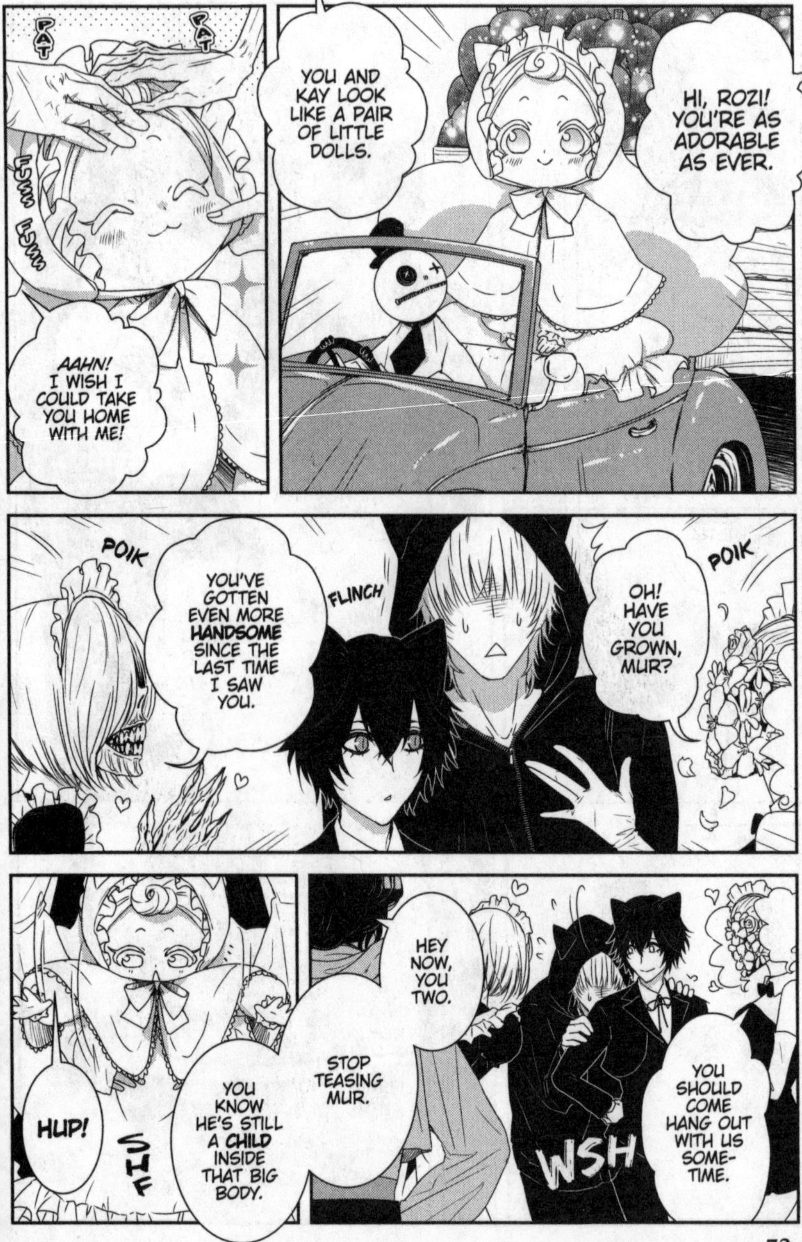
HI, ROZI! YOU'RE AS ADORABLE AS EVER.
YOU AND KAY LOOK LIKE A PAIR OF LITTLE DOLLS.
PAT
PAT
AAHN! I WISH I COULD TAKE YOU HOME WITH ME!
POIK
OH! HAVE YOU GROWN, MUR?
FLINCH
YOU'VE GOTTEN EVEN MORE HANDSOME SINCE THE LAST TIME I SAW YOU.
POIK
HEY NOW, YOU TWO.
YOU SHOULD COME HANG OUT WITH US SOME-TIME.
WSH
STOP TEASING MUR.
YOU KNOW HE'S STILL A CHILD INSIDE THAT BIG BODY.
SHF
HUP!

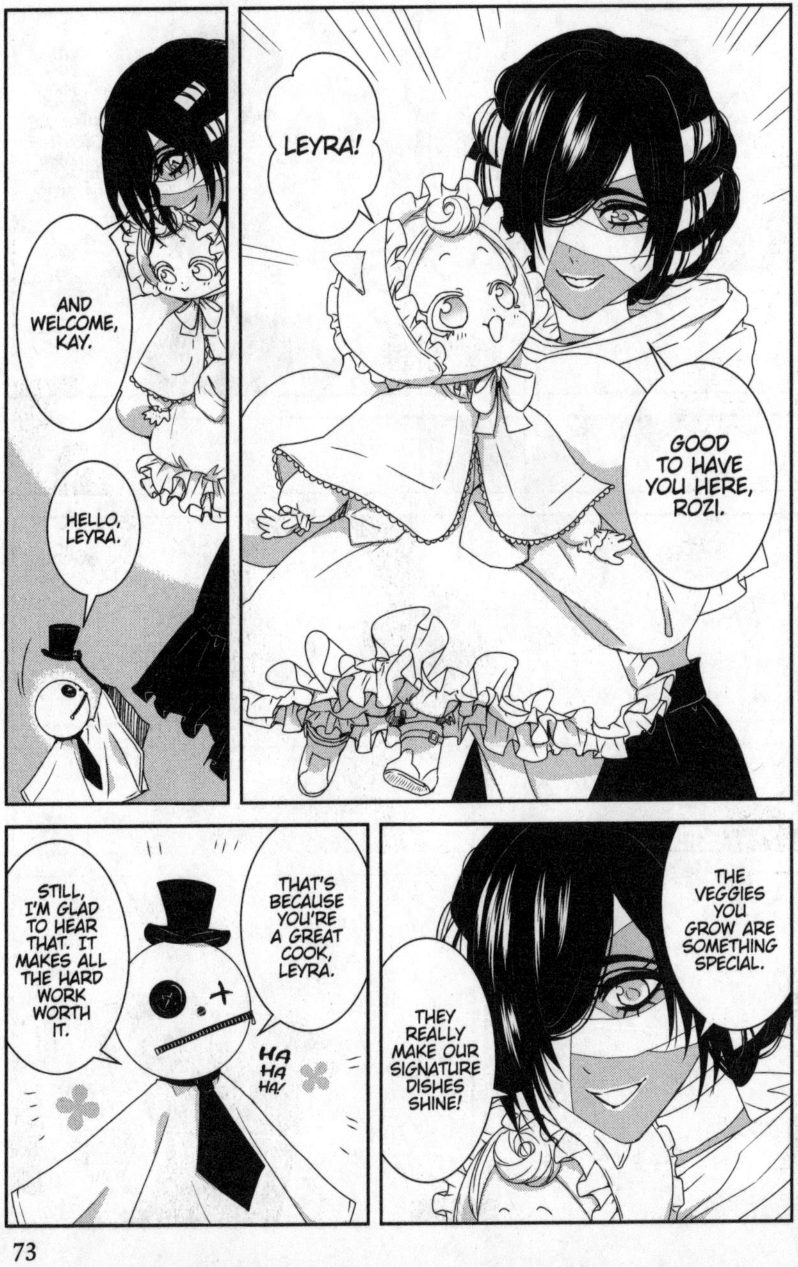
LEYRA!
GOOD TO HAVE YOU HERE, ROZI.
AND WELCOME, KAY.
HELLO, LEYRA.
THE VEGGIES YOU GROW ARE SOMETHING SPECIAL.
THEY REALLY MAKE OUR SIGNATURE DISHES SHINE!
THAT'S BECAUSE YOU'RE A GREAT COOK, LEYRA.
STILL, I'M GLAD TO HEAR THAT. IT MAKES ALL THE HARD WORK WORTH IT.
HA HA HA!

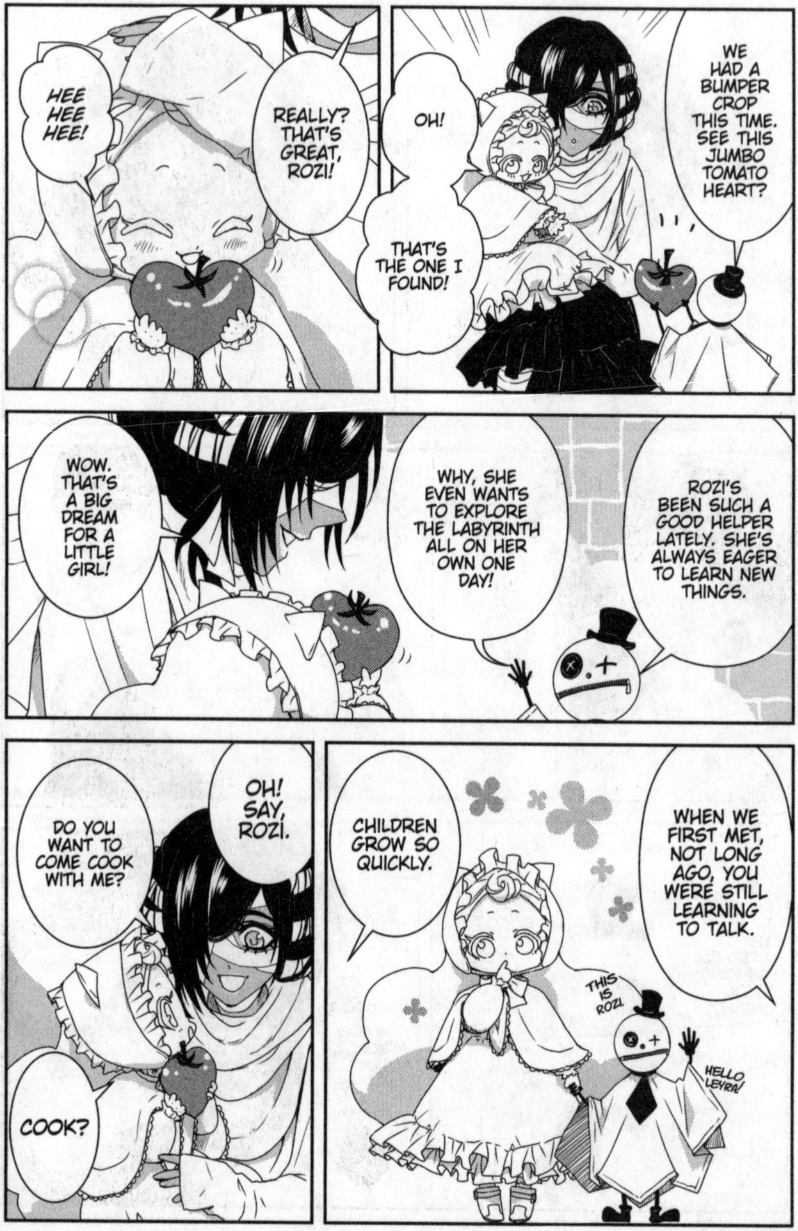
WE HAD A BUMPER CROP THIS TIME. SEE THIS JUMBO TOMATO HEART?
OH!
THAT'S THE ONE I FOUND!
REALLY? THAT'S GREAT, ROZI!
HEE HEE HEE!
ROZI'S BEEN SUCH A GOOD HELPER LATELY. SHE'S ALWAYS EAGER TO LEARN NEW THINGS.
WHY, SHE EVEN WANTS TO EXPLORE THE LABYRINTH ALL ON HER OWN ONE DAY!
WOW. THAT'S A BIG DREAM FOR A LITTLE GIRL!
WHEN WE FIRST MET, NOT LONG AGO, YOU WERE STILL LEARNING TO TALK.
CHILDREN GROW SO QUICKLY.
THIS IS ROZI.
HELLO, LEYRA!
OH! SAY, ROZI.
DO YOU WANT TO COME COOK WITH ME?
COOK?

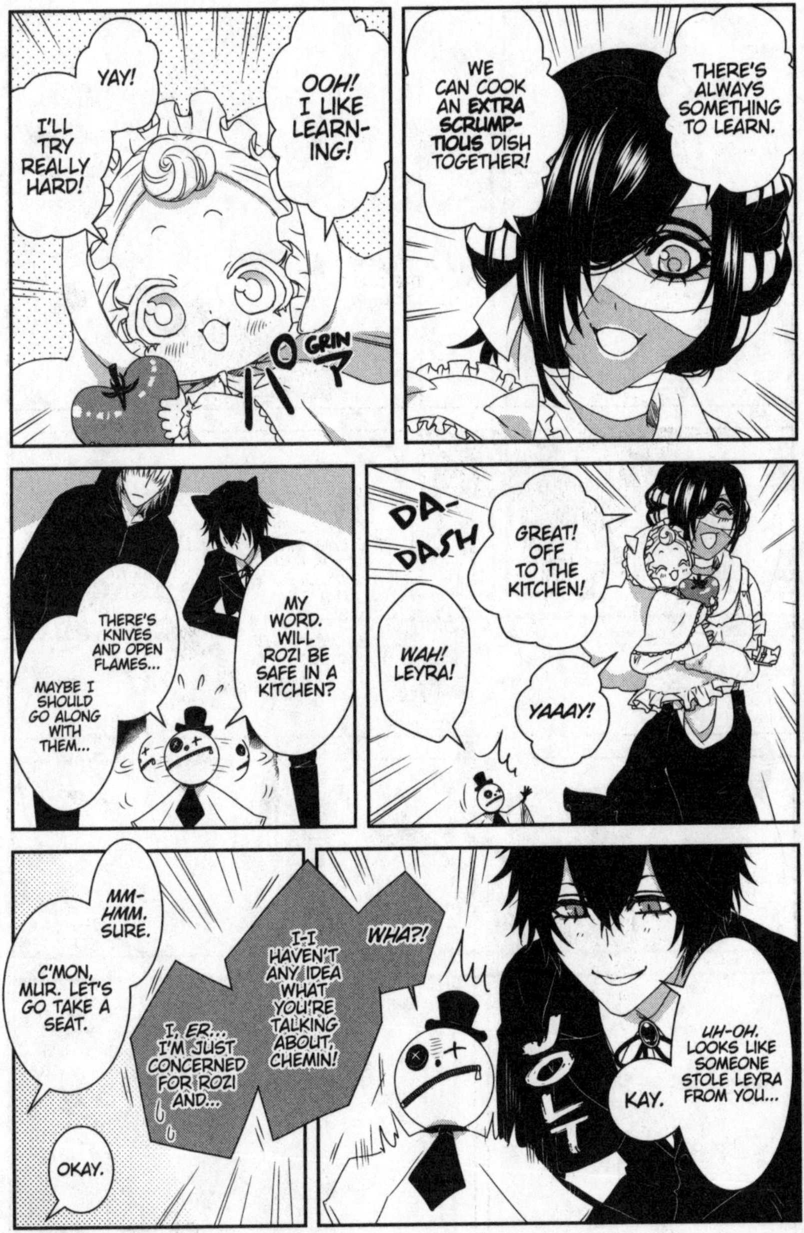
THERE'S ALWAYS SOMETHING TO LEARN.
WE CAN COOK AN EXTRA SCRUMPTIOUS DISH TOGETHER!
OOH! I LIKE LEARNING!
YAY!
I'LL TRY REALLY HARD!
GRIN
DA-DASH
GREAT! OFF TO THE KITCHEN!
YAAAY!
WAH! LEYRA!
MY WORD. WILL ROZI BE SAFE IN A KITCHEN?
THERE'S KNIVES AND OPEN FLAMES...
MAYBE I SHOULD GO ALONG WITH THEM...
UH-OH. LOOKS LIKE SOMEONE STOLE LEYRA FROM YOU...
KAY.
JOLT
WHA?!
I-I HAVEN'T ANY IDEA WHAT YOU'RE TALKING ABOUT, CHEMIN!
I, ER... I'M JUST CONCERNED FOR ROZI AND...
MM-HMM. SURE.
C'MON, MUR. LET'S GO TAKE A SEAT.
OKAY.

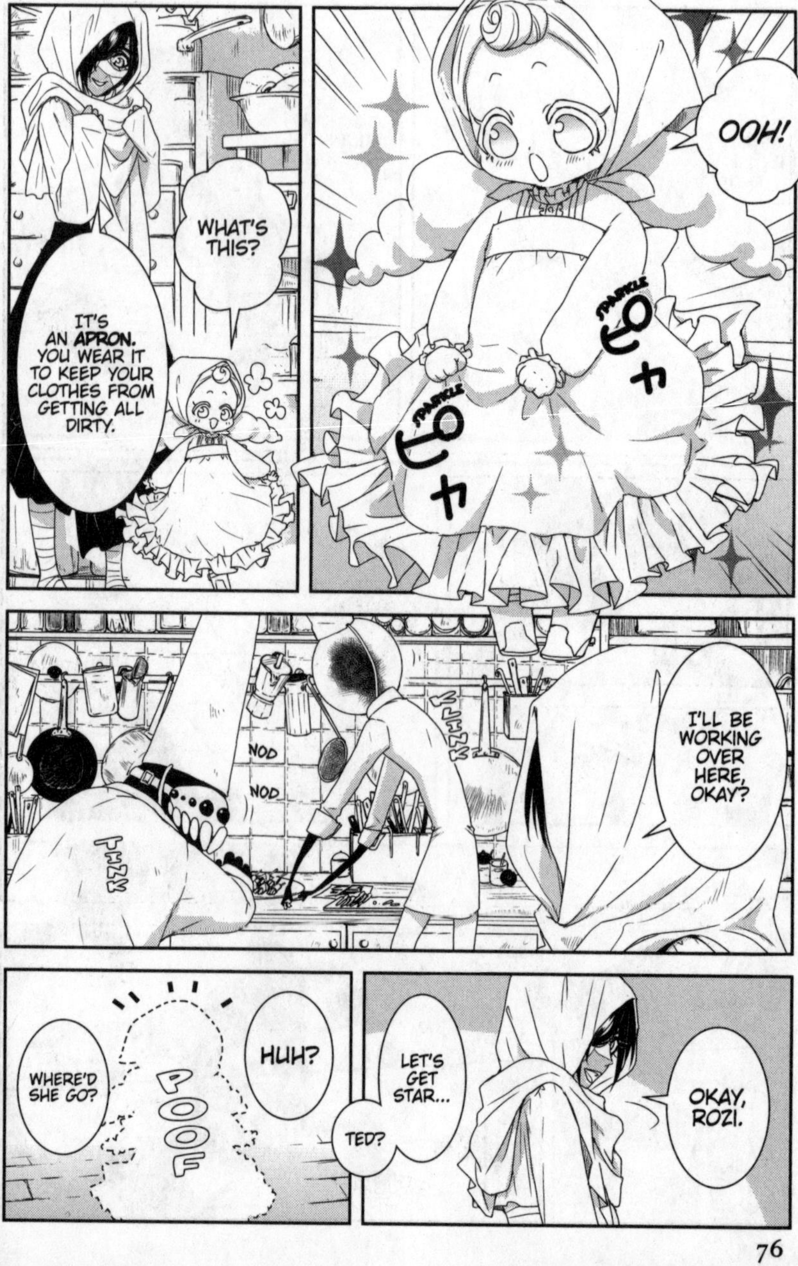
OOH!
SPARKLE
SPARKLE
WHAT'S THIS?
IT'S AN APRON. YOU WEAR IT TO KEEP YOUR CLOTHES FROM GETTING ALL DIRTY.
I'LL BE WORKING OVER HERE, OKAY?
NOD
NOD
TINK
OKAY, ROZI.
LET'S GET STAR...
TED?
HUH?
POOF
WHERE'D SHE GO?

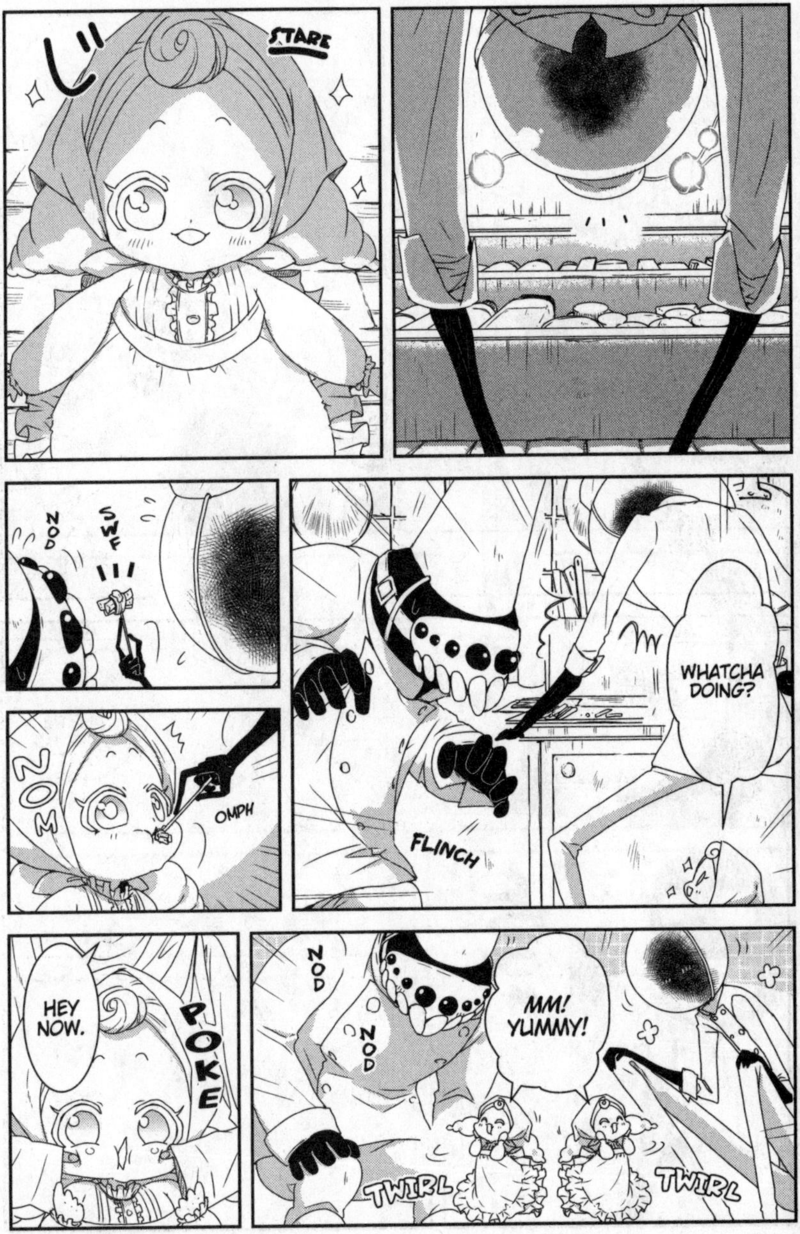

STARE
じ
WHATCHA DOING?
FLINCH
SWF
NOD
OMPH
NOM
MM! YUMMY!
NOD
NOD
TWIRL
TWIRL
POKE
HEY NOW.

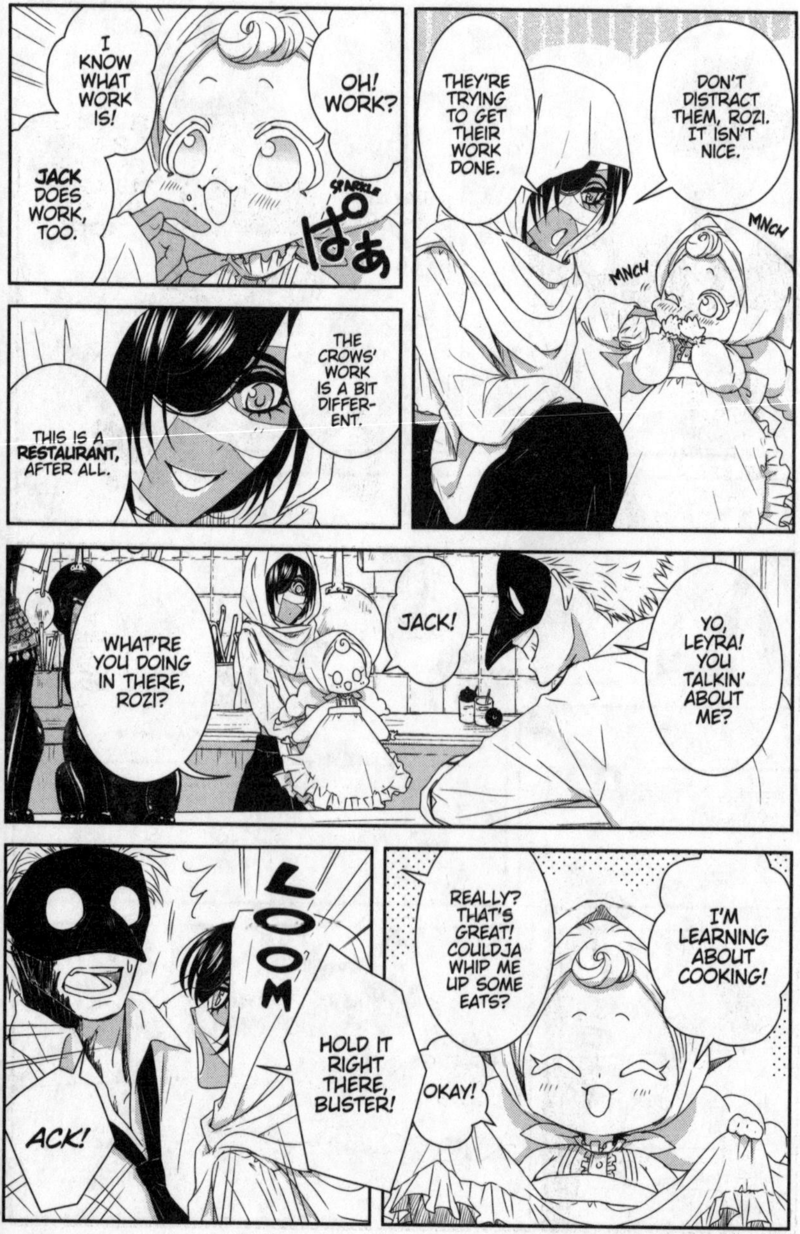
DON'T DISTRACT THEM, ROZI. IT ISN'T NICE.
THEY'RE TRYING TO GET THEIR WORK DONE.
MNCH
MNCH
OH! WORK?
I KNOW WHAT WORK IS!
JACK DOES WORK, TOO.
SPARKLE
ぱあ
THE CROWS' WORK IS A BIT DIFFER- ENT.
THIS IS A RESTAURANT, AFTER ALL.
YO, LEYRA! YOU TALKIN' ABOUT ME?
JACK!
WHAT'RE YOU DOING IN THERE, ROZI?
I'M LEARNING ABOUT COOKING!
REALLY? THAT'S GREAT! COULDJA WHIP ME UP SOME EATS?
OKAY!
LOOM
HOLD IT RIGHT THERE, BUSTER!
ACK!

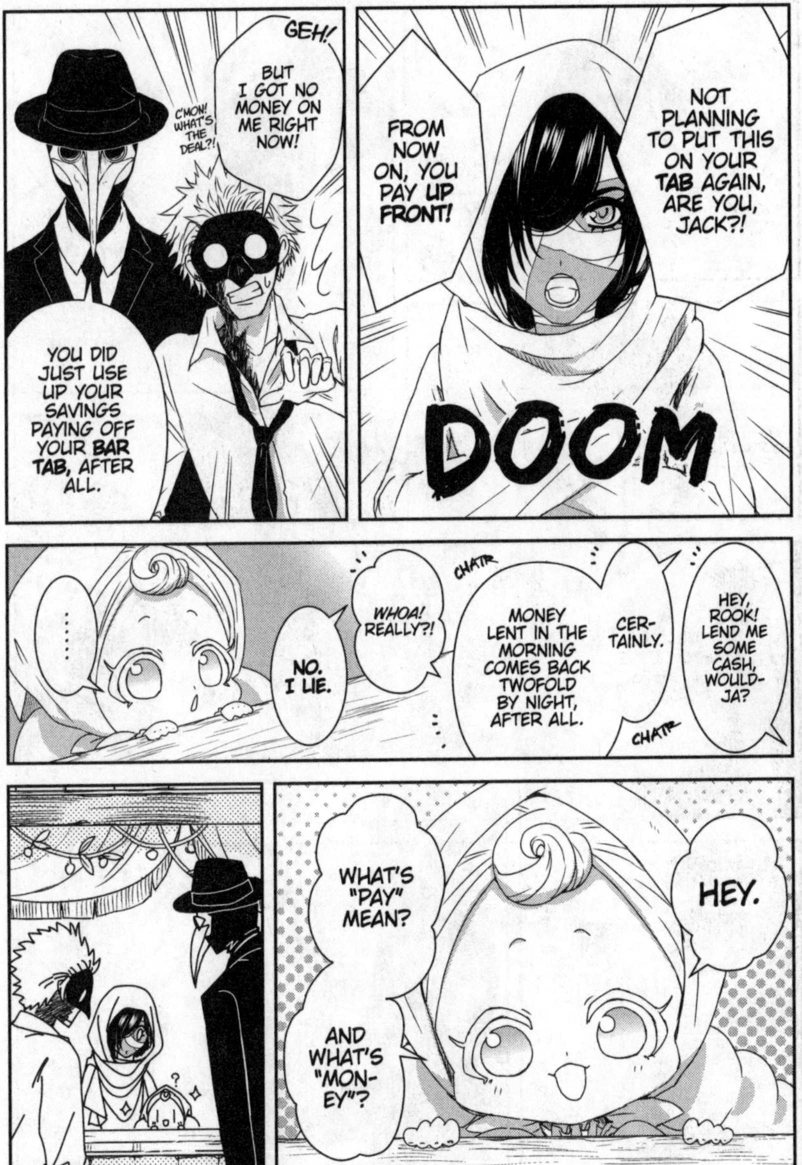
NOT PLANNING TO PUT THIS ON YOUR TAB AGAIN, ARE YOU, JACK?!
FROM NOW ON, YOU PAY UP FRONT!
DOOM
GEH!
BUT I GOT NO MONEY ON ME RIGHT NOW!
C'MON! WHAT'S THE DEAL?!
YOU DID JUST USE UP YOUR SAVINGS PAYING OFF YOUR BAR TAB, AFTER ALL.
HEY, ROOK! LEND ME SOME CASH, WOULD-JA?
CHATR
CER-TAINLY.
MONEY LENT IN THE MORNING COMES BACK TWOFOLD BY NIGHT, AFTER ALL.
CHATR
WHOA! REALLY?!
NO. I LIE.
......
HEY.
WHAT'S "PAY" MEAN?
AND WHAT'S "MON-EY"?

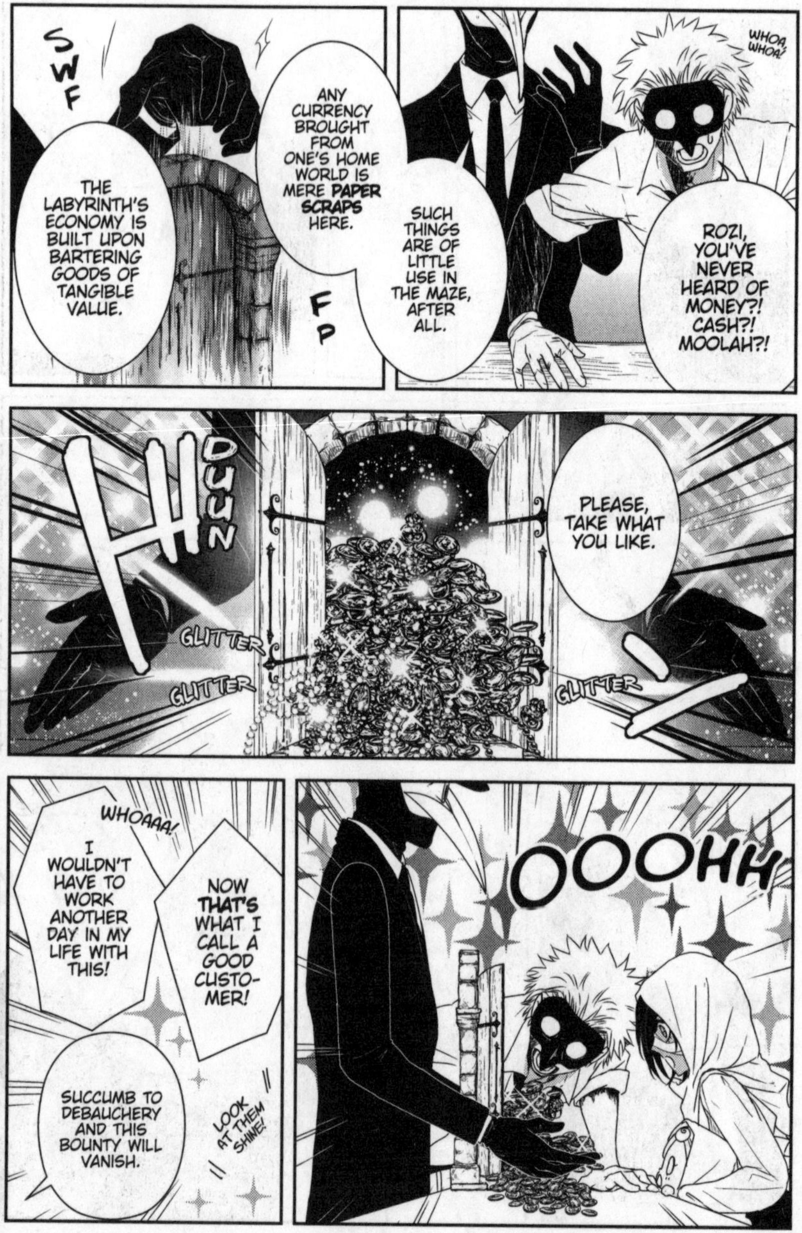
WHOA, WHOA!
ROZI, YOU'VE NEVER HEARD OF MONEY?! CASH?! MOOLAH?!
SUCH THINGS ARE OF LITTLE USE IN THE MAZE, AFTER ALL.
ANY CURRENCY BROUGHT FROM ONE'S HOME WORLD IS MERE **PAPER SCRAPS** HERE.
SWF
THE LABYRINTH'S ECONOMY IS BUILT UPON BARTERING GOODS OF TANGIBLE VALUE.
FP
PLEASE, TAKE WHAT YOU LIKE.
DUUN
GLITTER
GLITTER
GLITTER
OOOHH
LOOK AT THEM SHINE!
NOW **THAT'S** WHAT I CALL A GOOD CUSTO-MER!
WHOAAA!
I WOULDN'T HAVE TO WORK ANOTHER DAY IN MY LIFE WITH THIS!
SUCCUMB TO DEBAUCHERY AND THIS BOUNTY WILL VANISH.

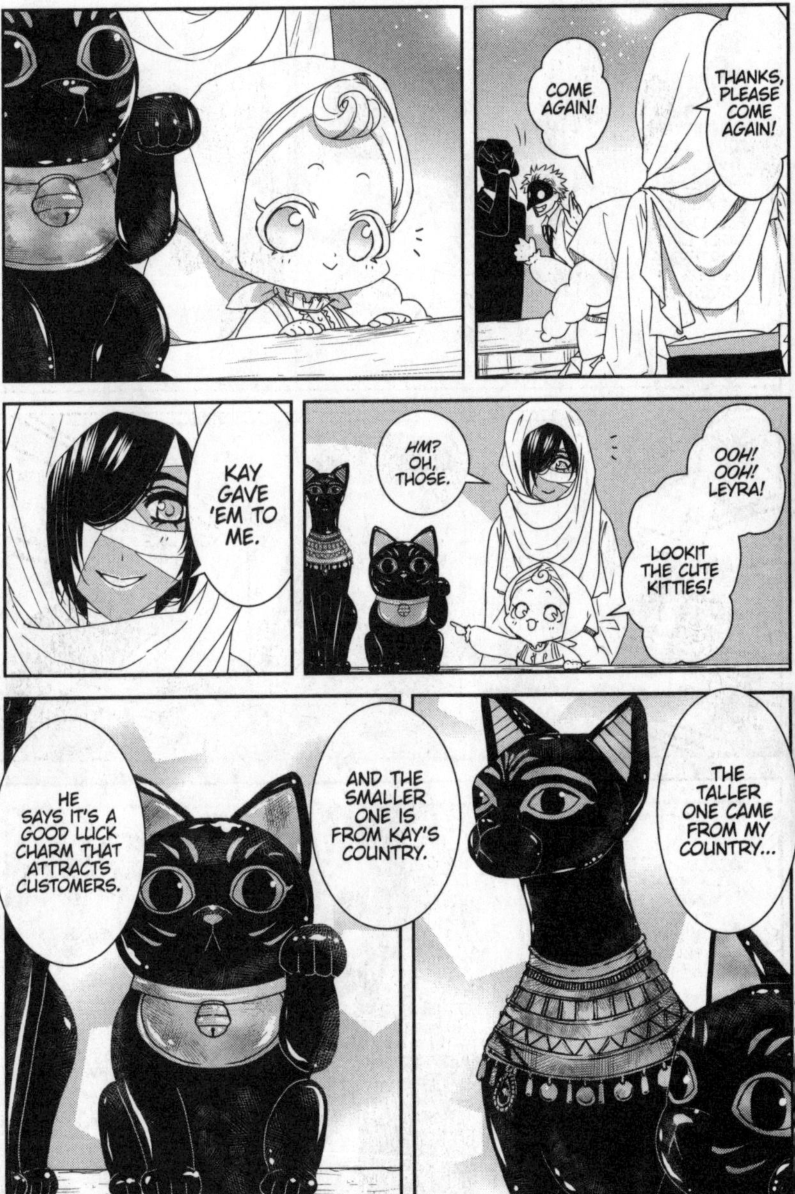
THANKS, PLEASE COME AGAIN!
COME AGAIN!
OOH! OOH! LEYRA!
LOOKIT THE CUTE KITTIES!
HM? OH, THOSE.
KAY GAVE 'EM TO ME.
THE TALLER ONE CAME FROM MY COUNTRY...
AND THE SMALLER ONE IS FROM KAY'S COUNTRY.
HE SAYS IT'S A GOOD LUCK CHARM THAT ATTRACTS CUSTOMERS.

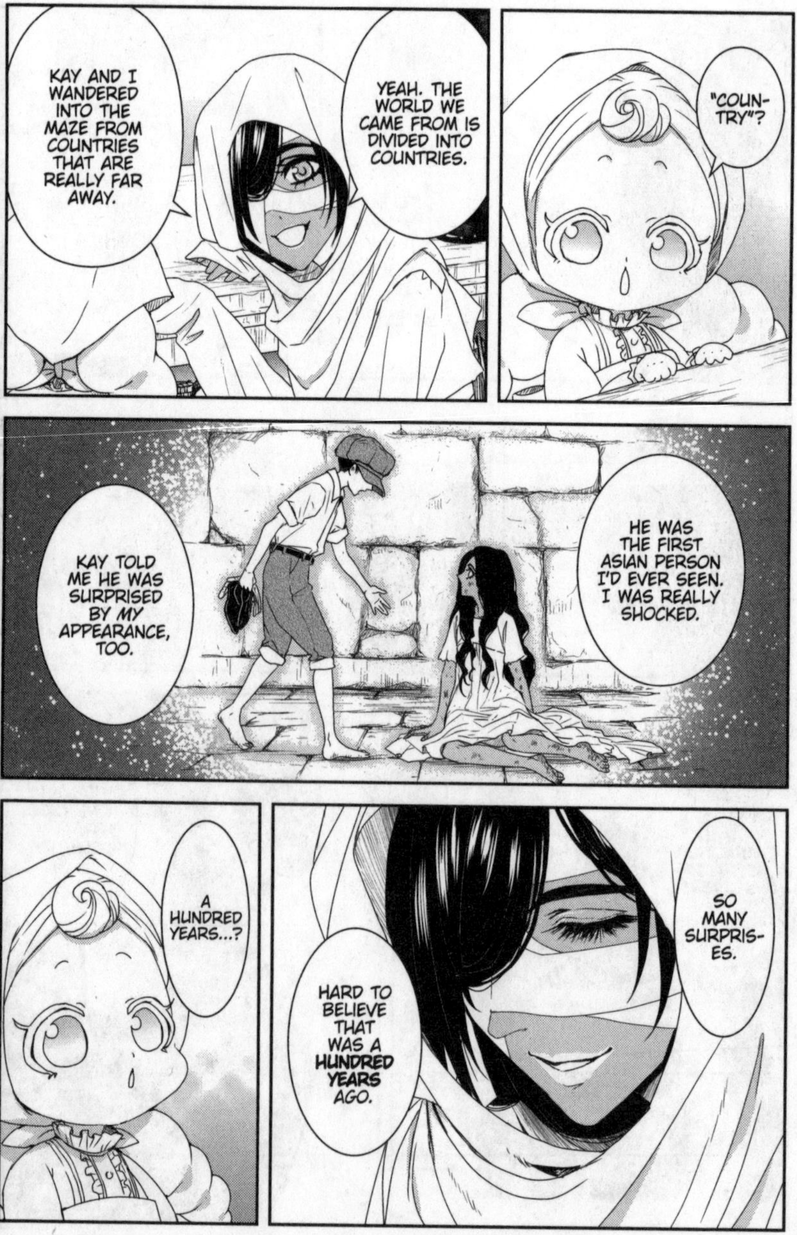
"COUN-TRY"?
YEAH. THE WORLD WE CAME FROM IS DIVIDED INTO COUNTRIES.
KAY AND I WANDERED INTO THE MAZE FROM COUNTRIES THAT ARE REALLY FAR AWAY.
HE WAS THE FIRST ASIAN PERSON I'D EVER SEEN. I WAS REALLY SHOCKED.
KAY TOLD ME HE WAS SURPRISED BY *MY* APPEARANCE, TOO.
SO MANY SURPRIS-ES.
HARD TO BELIEVE THAT WAS A **HUNDRED YEARS** AGO.
A HUNDRED YEARS...?

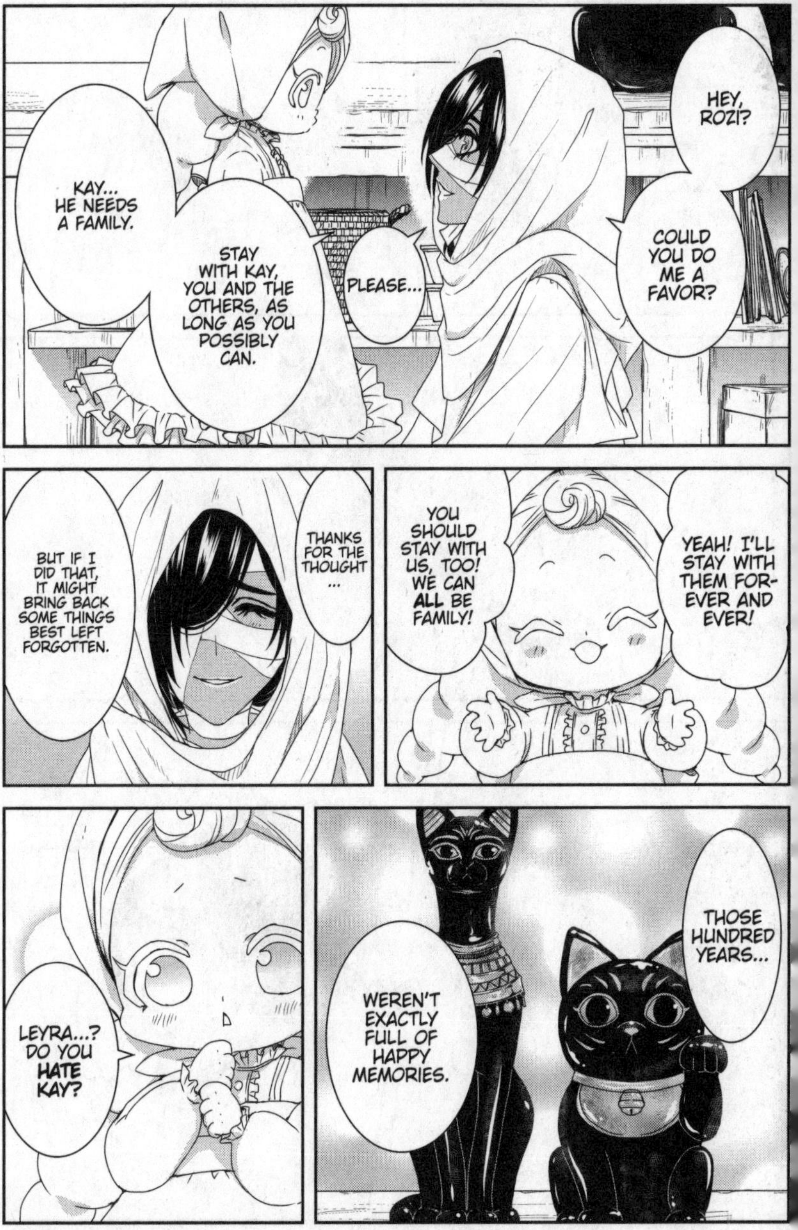
HEY, ROZI?
COULD YOU DO ME A FAVOR?
PLEASE...
STAY WITH KAY, YOU AND THE OTHERS, AS LONG AS YOU POSSIBLY CAN.
KAY... HE NEEDS A FAMILY.
YEAH! I'LL STAY WITH THEM FOR-EVER AND EVER!
YOU SHOULD STAY WITH US, TOO! WE CAN ALL BE FAMILY!
THANKS FOR THE THOUGHT...
BUT IF I DID THAT, IT MIGHT BRING BACK SOME THINGS BEST LEFT FORGOTTEN.
THOSE HUNDRED YEARS...
WEREN'T EXACTLY FULL OF HAPPY MEMORIES.
LEYRA...? DO YOU HATE KAY?

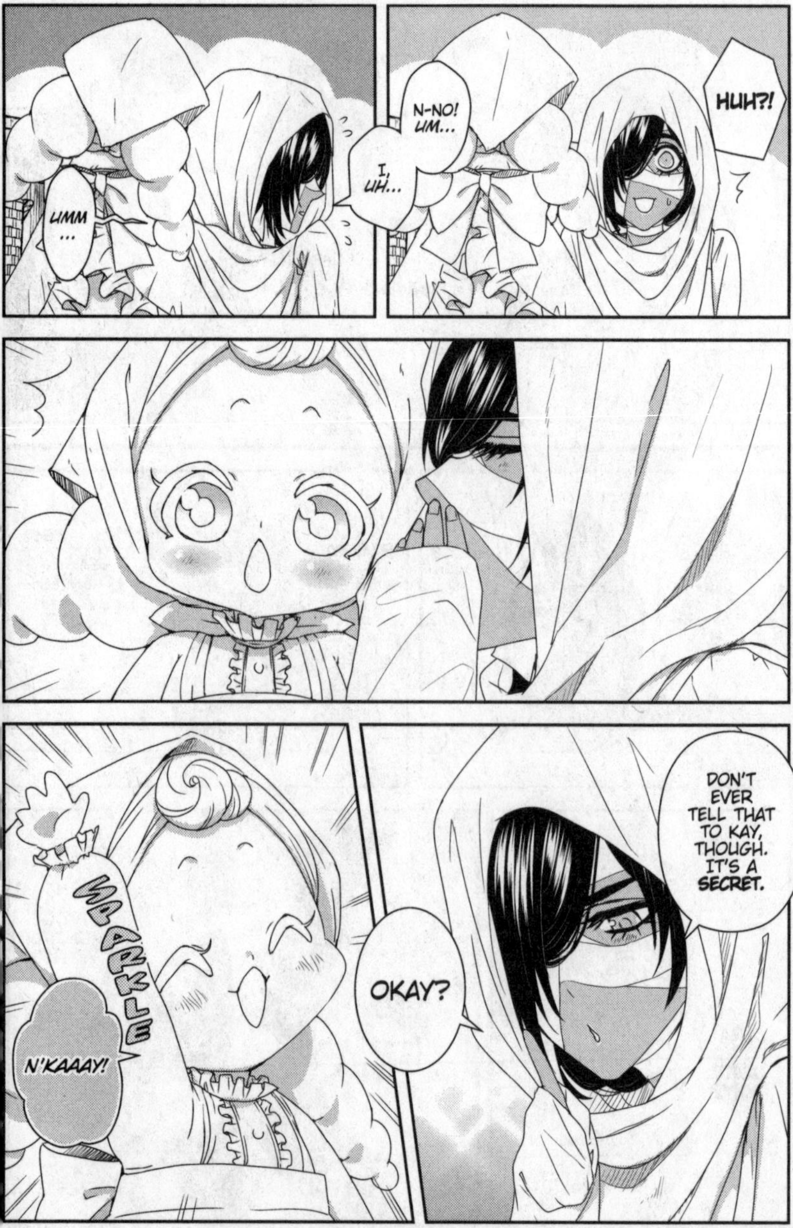
HUH?!
N-NO! UM...
I, UH...
UMM ...
DON'T EVER TELL THAT TO KAY, THOUGH. IT'S A SECRET.
OKAY?
SPARKLE
N'KAAAY!

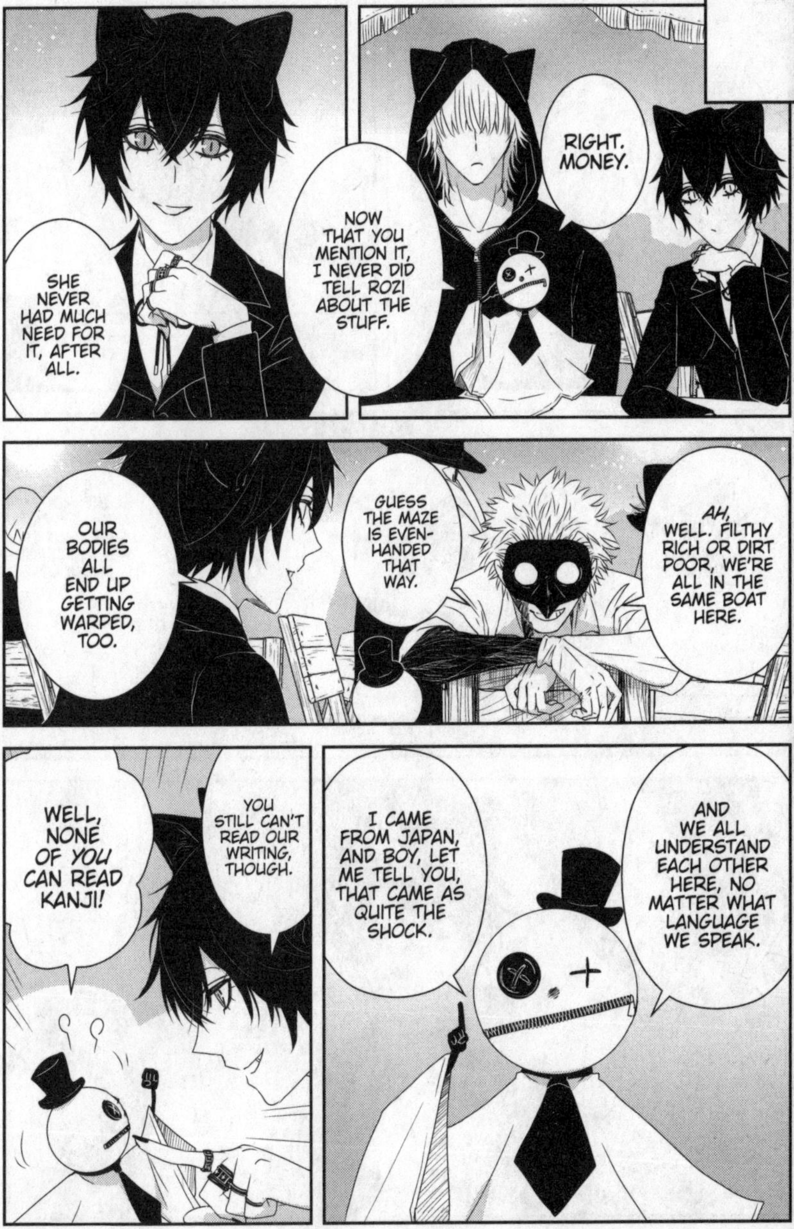
RIGHT. MONEY.
NOW THAT YOU MENTION IT, I NEVER DID TELL ROZI ABOUT THE STUFF.
SHE NEVER HAD MUCH NEED FOR IT, AFTER ALL.
AH, WELL. FILTHY RICH OR DIRT POOR, WE'RE ALL IN THE SAME BOAT HERE.
GUESS THE MAZE IS EVEN-HANDED THAT WAY.
OUR BODIES ALL END UP GETTING WARPED, TOO.
AND WE ALL UNDERSTAND EACH OTHER HERE, NO MATTER WHAT LANGUAGE WE SPEAK.
I CAME FROM JAPAN, AND BOY, LET ME TELL YOU, THAT CAME AS QUITE THE SHOCK.
YOU STILL CAN'T READ OUR WRITING, THOUGH.
WELL, NONE OF *YOU* CAN READ KANJI!

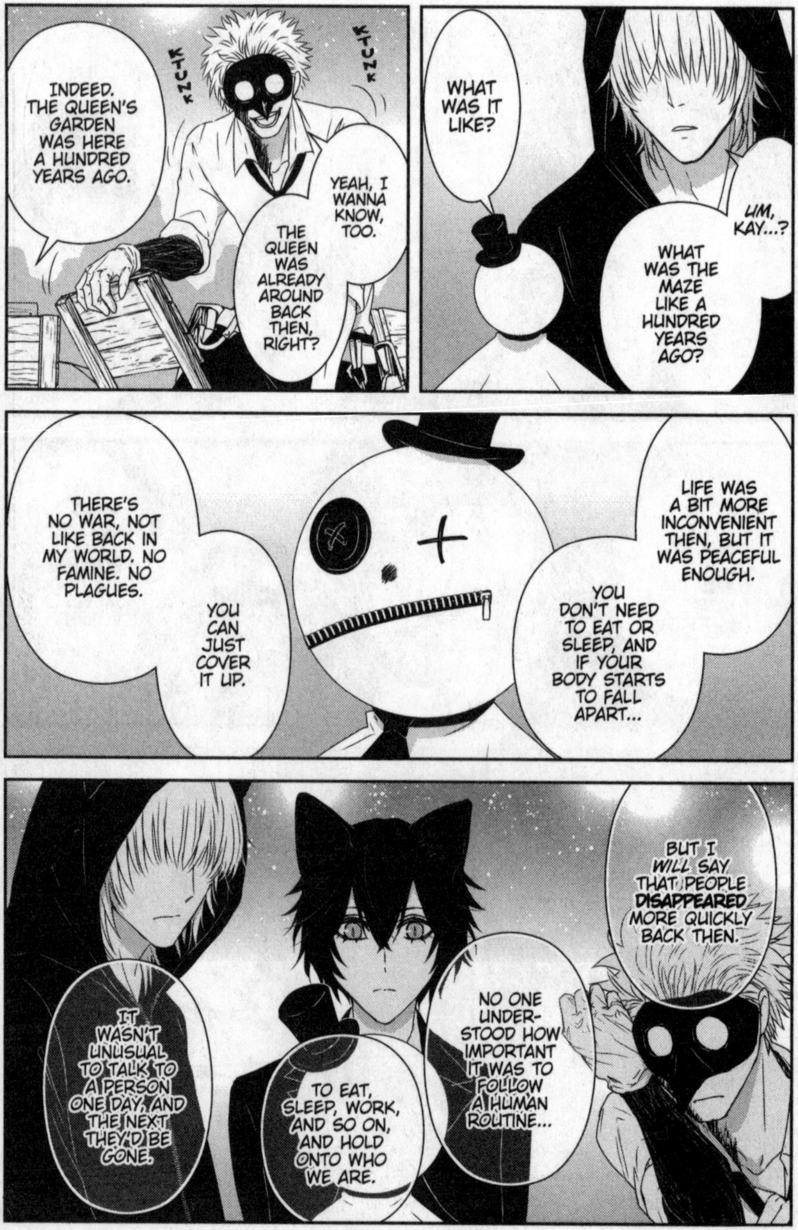
UM, KAY...?
WHAT WAS THE MAZE LIKE A HUNDRED YEARS AGO?
WHAT WAS IT LIKE?
KTUNK
KTUNK
YEAH, I WANNA KNOW, TOO.
THE QUEEN WAS ALREADY AROUND BACK THEN, RIGHT?
INDEED. THE QUEEN'S GARDEN WAS HERE A HUNDRED YEARS AGO.
LIFE WAS A BIT MORE INCONVENIENT THEN, BUT IT WAS PEACEFUL ENOUGH.
YOU DON'T NEED TO EAT OR SLEEP, AND IF YOUR BODY STARTS TO FALL APART...
YOU CAN JUST COVER IT UP.
THERE'S NO WAR, NOT LIKE BACK IN MY WORLD. NO FAMINE. NO PLAGUES.
BUT I *WILL* SAY THAT PEOPLE **DISAPPEARED** MORE QUICKLY BACK THEN.
NO ONE UNDER-STOOD HOW IMPORTANT IT WAS TO FOLLOW A HUMAN ROUTINE...
TO EAT, SLEEP, WORK, AND SO ON, AND HOLD ONTO WHO WE ARE.
IT WASN'T UNUSUAL TO TALK TO A PERSON ONE DAY, AND THE NEXT THEY'D BE GONE.

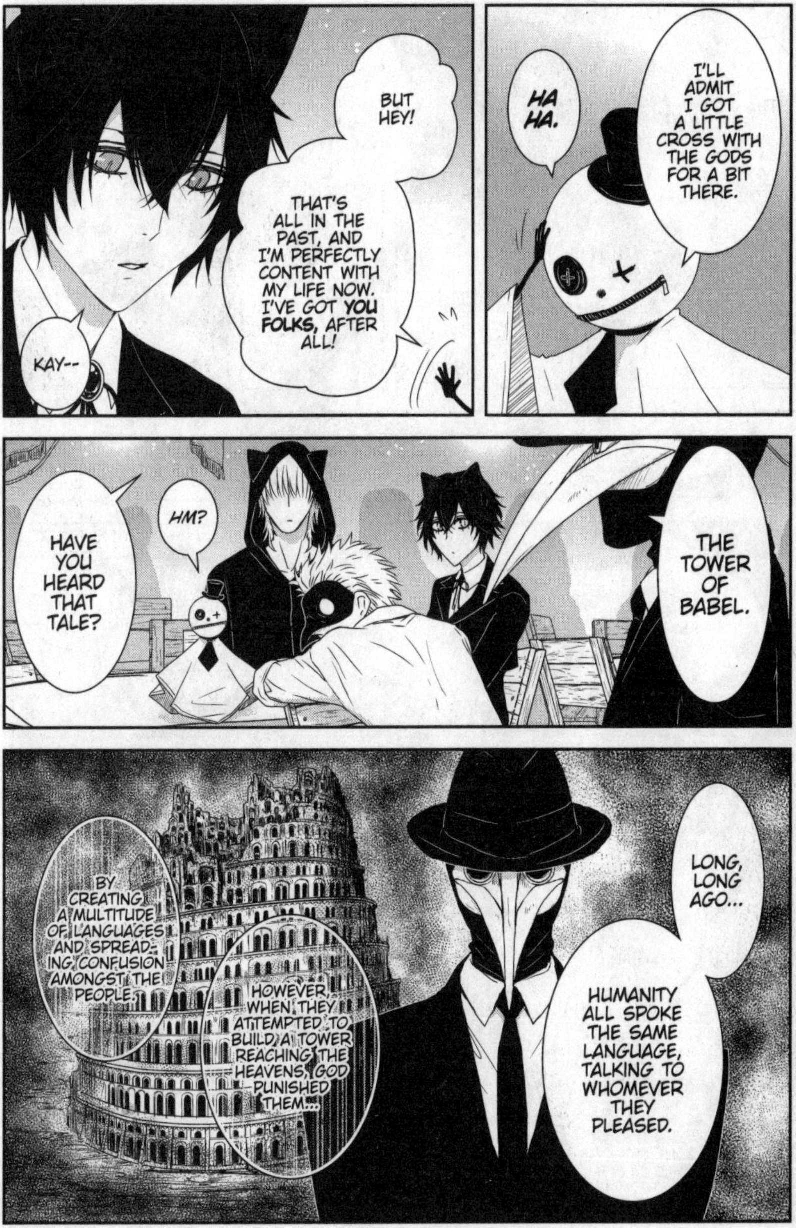
I'LL ADMIT I GOT A LITTLE CROSS WITH THE GODS FOR A BIT THERE.
HA HA.
BUT HEY!
THAT'S ALL IN THE PAST, AND I'M PERFECTLY CONTENT WITH MY LIFE NOW. I'VE GOT YOU FOLKS, AFTER ALL!
KAY--
THE TOWER OF BABEL.
HM?
HAVE YOU HEARD THAT TALE?
LONG, LONG AGO...
HUMANITY ALL SPOKE THE SAME LANGUAGE, TALKING TO WHOMEVER THEY PLEASED.
HOWEVER, WHEN THEY ATTEMPTED TO BUILD A TOWER REACHING THE HEAVENS, GOD PUNISHED THEM...
BY CREATING A MULTITUDE OF LANGUAGES AND SPREADING CONFUSION AMONGST THE PEOPLE.

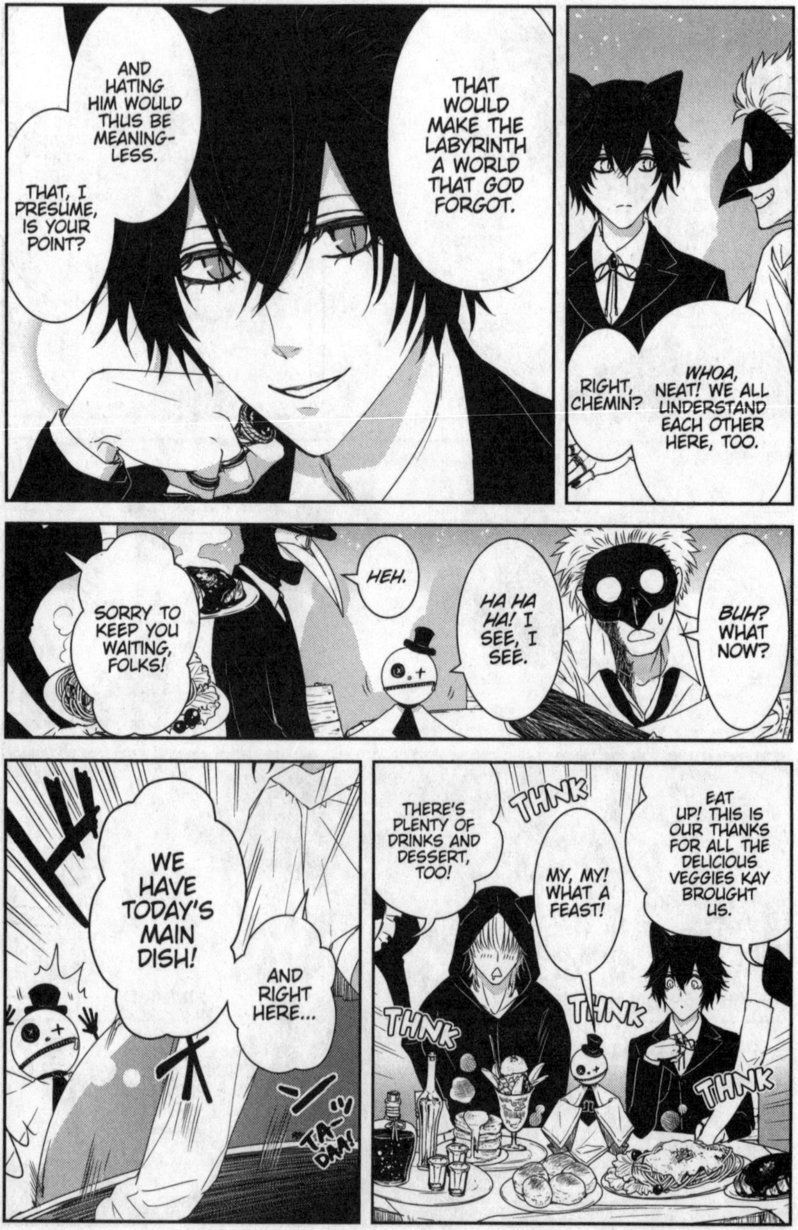
WHOA, NEAT! WE ALL UNDERSTAND EACH OTHER HERE, TOO.
RIGHT, CHEMIN?
THAT WOULD MAKE THE LABYRINTH A WORLD THAT GOD FORGOT.
AND HATING HIM WOULD THUS BE MEANING-LESS.
THAT, I PRESUME, IS YOUR POINT?
BUH? WHAT NOW?
HA HA HA! I SEE, I SEE.
HEH.
SORRY TO KEEP YOU WAITING, FOLKS!
EAT UP! THIS IS OUR THANKS FOR ALL THE DELICIOUS VEGGIES KAY BROUGHT US.
THNK
MY, MY! WHAT A FEAST!
THERE'S PLENTY OF DRINKS AND DESSERT, TOO!
THNK
THNK
THNK
WE HAVE TODAY'S MAIN DISH!
AND RIGHT HERE...
TA-DAA!

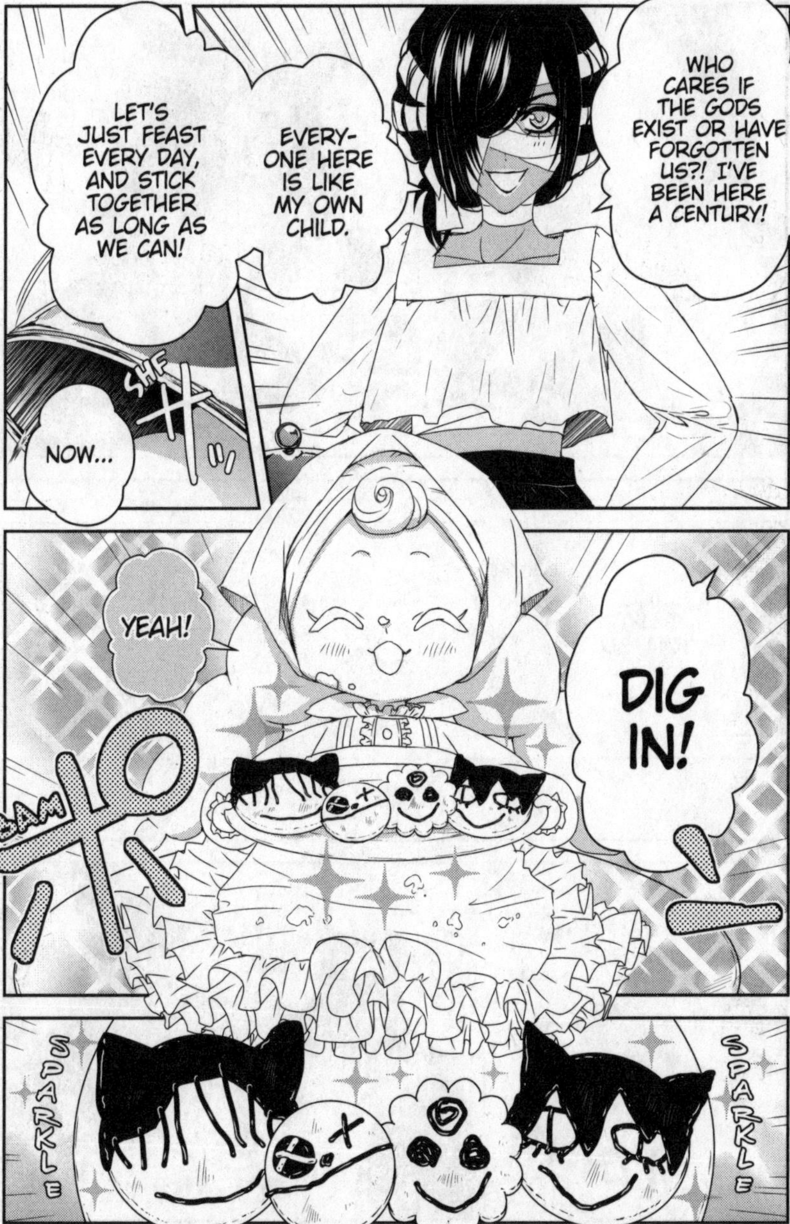
WHO CARES IF THE GODS EXIST OR HAVE FORGOTTEN US?! I'VE BEEN HERE A CENTURY!
EVERY-ONE HERE IS LIKE MY OWN CHILD.
LET'S JUST FEAST EVERY DAY, AND STICK TOGETHER AS LONG AS WE CAN!
SHF
NOW...
DIG IN!
YEAH!
BAM
SPARKLE
SPARKLE

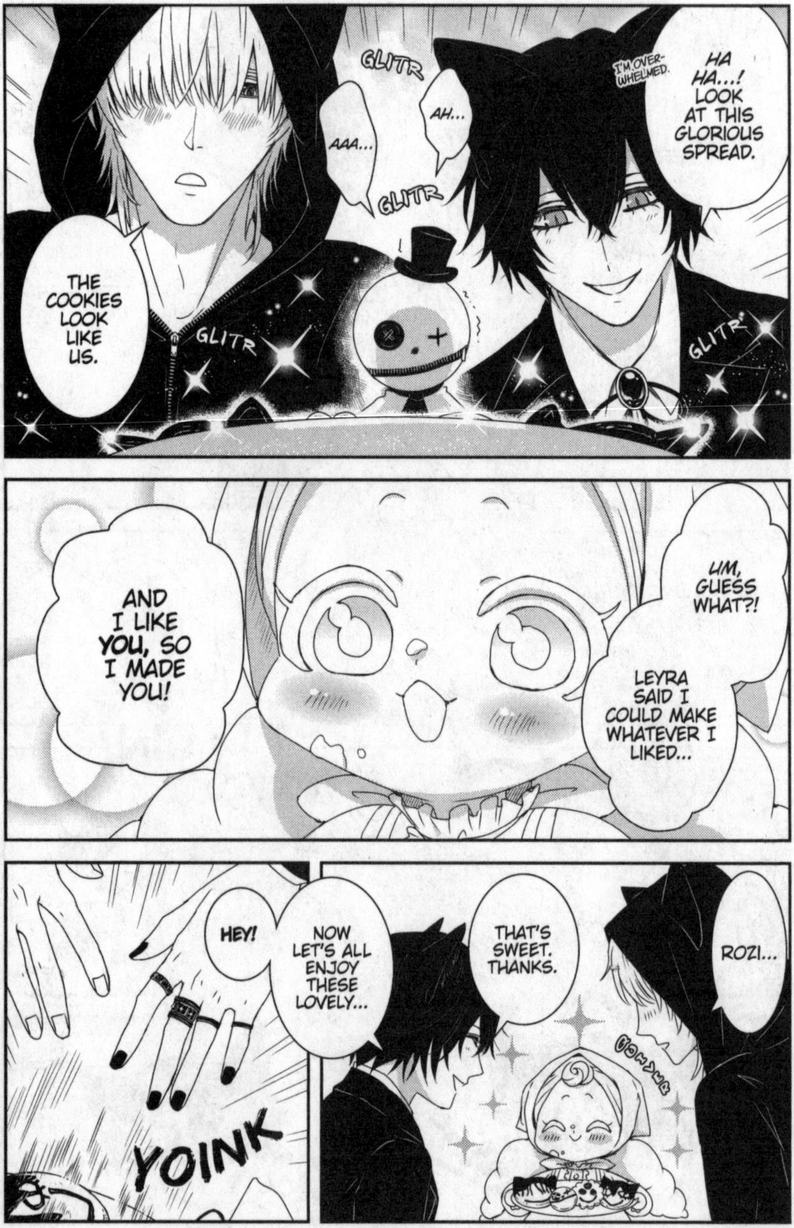
I'M OVER-WHELMED.
HA HA...! LOOK AT THIS GLORIOUS SPREAD.
GLITR
AH...
AAA...
GLITR
THE COOKIES LOOK LIKE US.
GLITR
GLITR
UM, GUESS WHAT?!
LEYRA SAID I COULD MAKE WHATEVER I LIKED...
AND I LIKE YOU, SO I MADE YOU!
ROZI...
THAT'S SWEET. THANKS.
NOW LET'S ALL ENJOY THESE LOVELY...
HEY!
YOINK

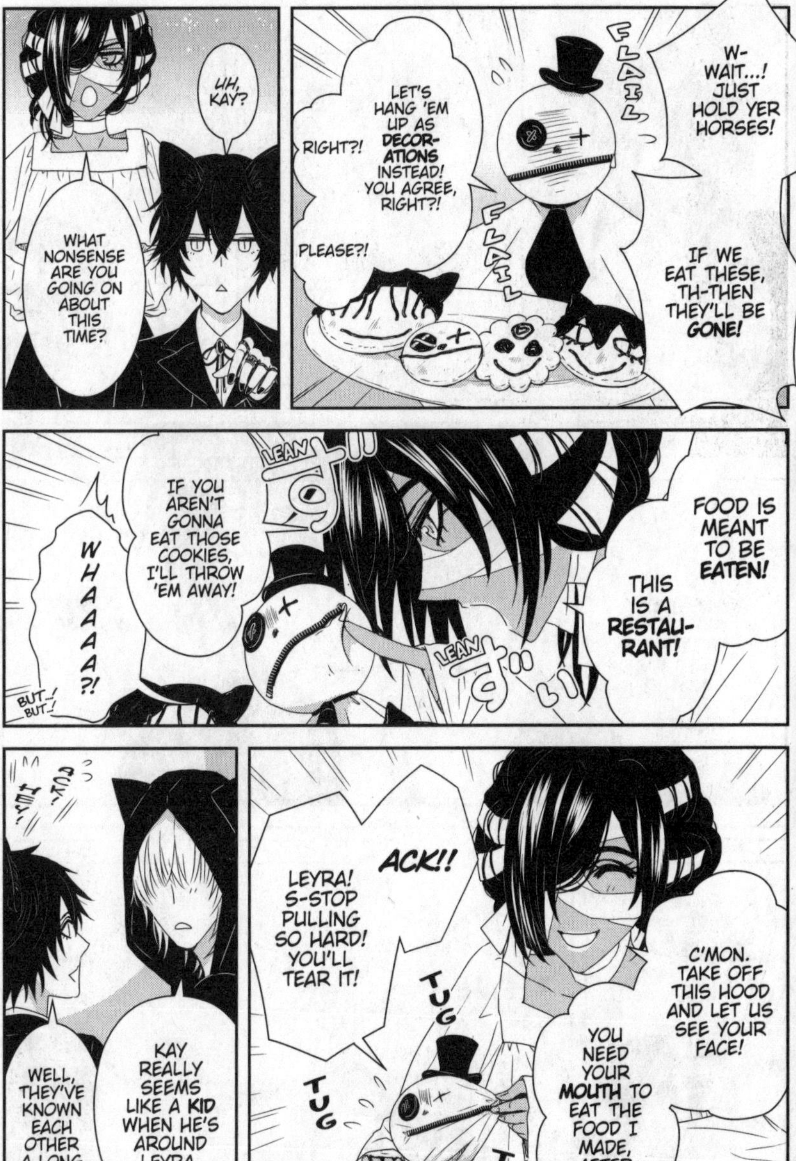
W-WAIT...! JUST HOLD YER HORSES!
FLAIL
IF WE EAT THESE, TH-THEN THEY'LL BE GONE!
LET'S HANG 'EM UP AS DECORATIONS INSTEAD! YOU AGREE, RIGHT?!
RIGHT?!
PLEASE?!
FLAIL
UH, KAY?
WHAT NONSENSE ARE YOU GOING ON ABOUT THIS TIME?
FOOD IS MEANT TO BE EATEN!
THIS IS A RESTAURANT!
LEAN
IF YOU AREN'T GONNA EAT THOSE COOKIES, I'LL THROW 'EM AWAY!
WHAAAAAA?!
BUT..! BUT..!
LEAN
C'MON. TAKE OFF THIS HOOD AND LET US SEE YOUR FACE!
ACK!!
LEYRA! S-STOP PULLING SO HARD! YOU'LL TEAR IT!
YOU NEED YOUR MOUTH TO EAT THE FOOD I MADE, AFTER ALL!
TUG
TUG
TUG
ACK! HEY!
KAY REALLY SEEMS LIKE A KID WHEN HE'S AROUND LEYRA.
WELL, THEY'VE KNOWN EACH OTHER A LONG TIME.

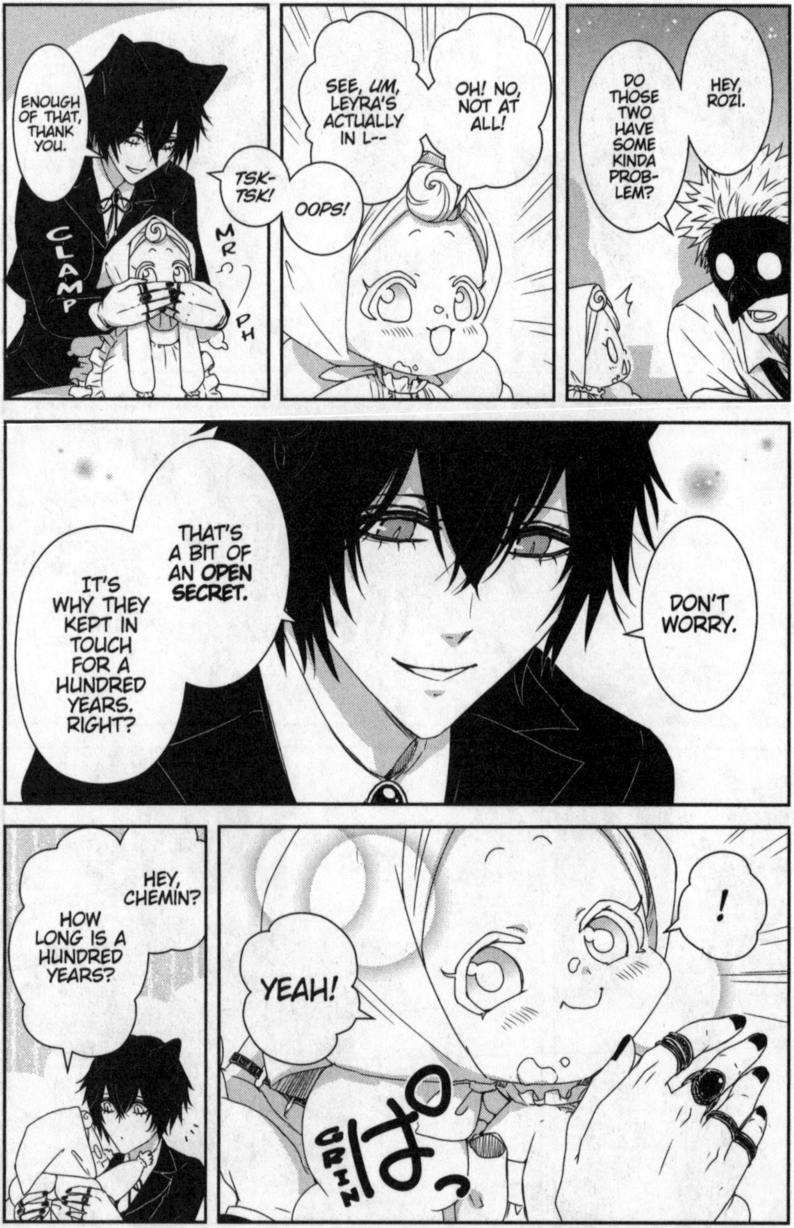
HEY, ROZI.
DO THOSE TWO HAVE SOME KINDA PROBLEM?
OH! NO, NOT AT ALL!
SEE, UM, LEYRA'S ACTUALLY IN L--
TSK-TSK!
OOPS!
ENOUGH OF THAT, THANK YOU.
MRPH
CLAMP
DON'T WORRY.
THAT'S A BIT OF AN OPEN SECRET.
IT'S WHY THEY KEPT IN TOUCH FOR A HUNDRED YEARS. RIGHT?
!
YEAH!
ぱっ
GRIN
HEY, CHEMIN?
HOW LONG IS A HUNDRED YEARS?

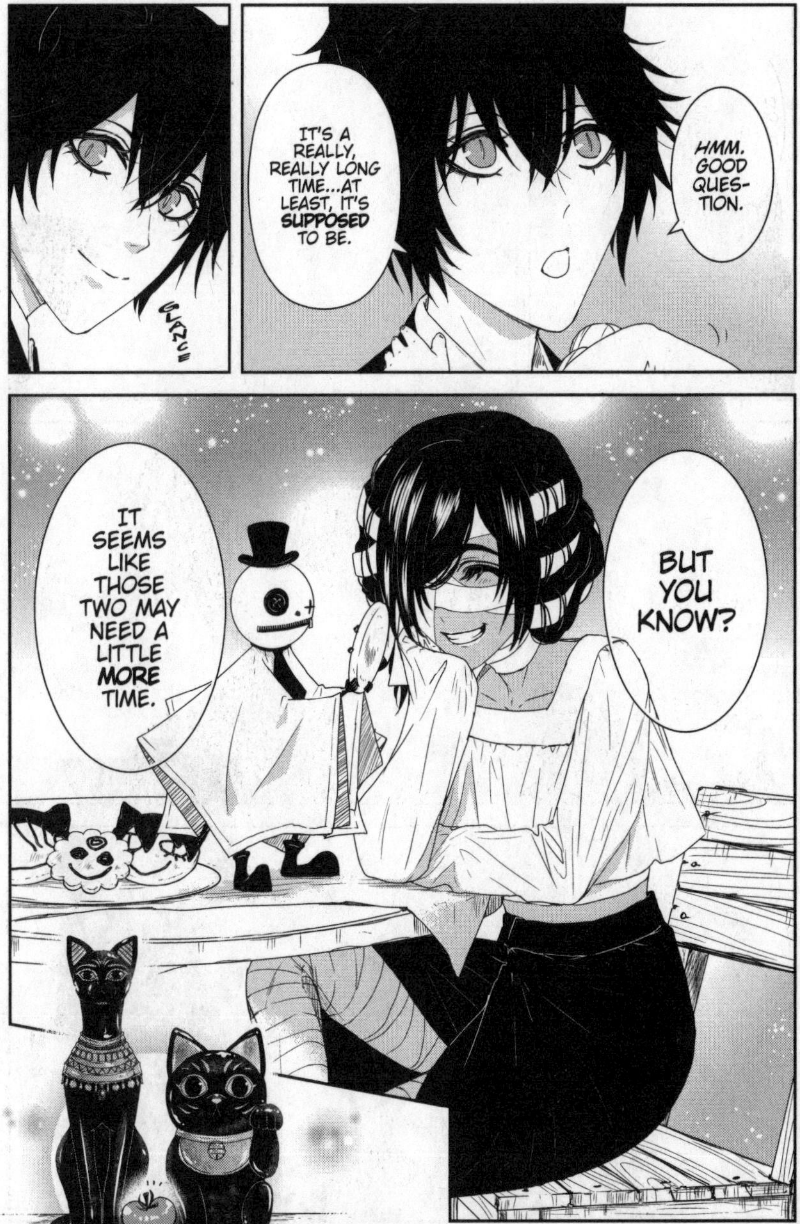
HMM. GOOD QUES-TION.
IT'S A REALLY, REALLY LONG TIME...AT LEAST, IT'S **SUPPOSED** TO BE.
GLANCE
BUT YOU KNOW?
IT SEEMS LIKE THOSE TWO MAY NEED A LITTLE **MORE** TIME.

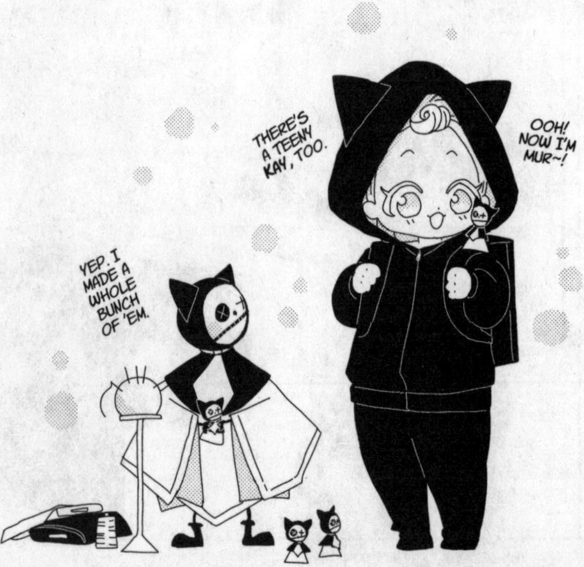
OOH! NOW I'M MUR~!
THERE'S A TEENY KAY, TOO.
YEP. I MADE A WHOLE BUNCH OF 'EM.

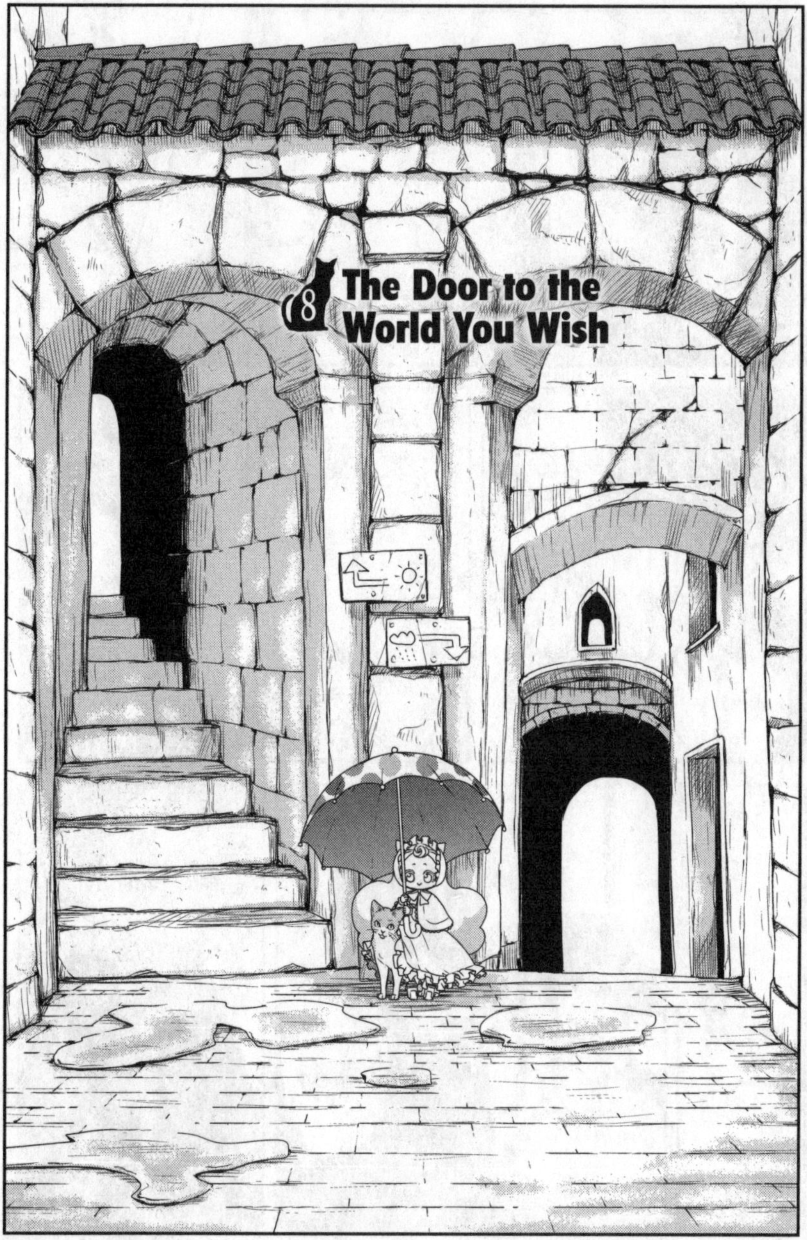
8
The Door to the World You Wish

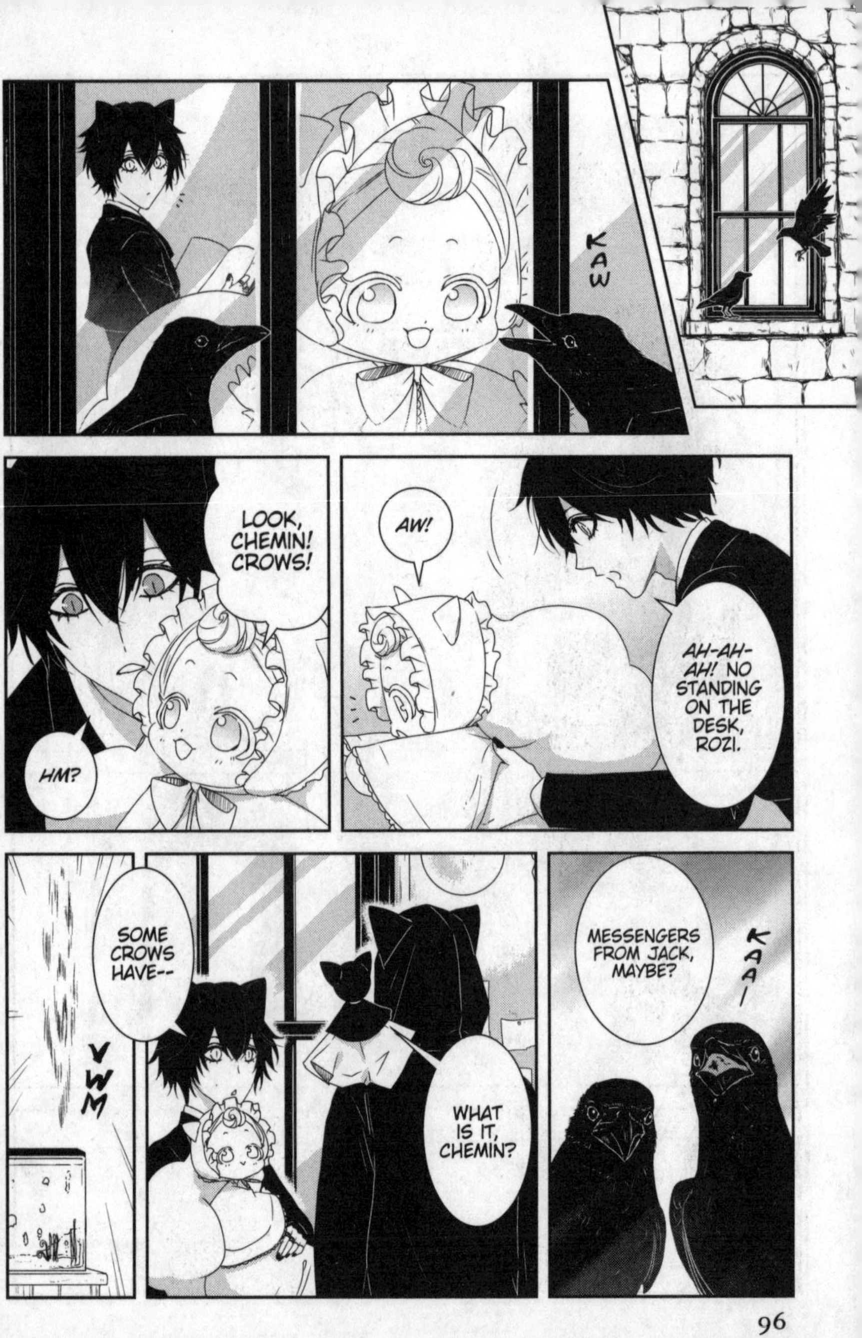
KAW
AW!
AH-AH-AH! NO STANDING ON THE DESK, ROZI.
LOOK, CHEMIN! CROWS!
HM?
MESSENGERS FROM JACK, MAYBE?
KAA
SOME CROWS HAVE--
WHAT IS IT, CHEMIN?
VWM

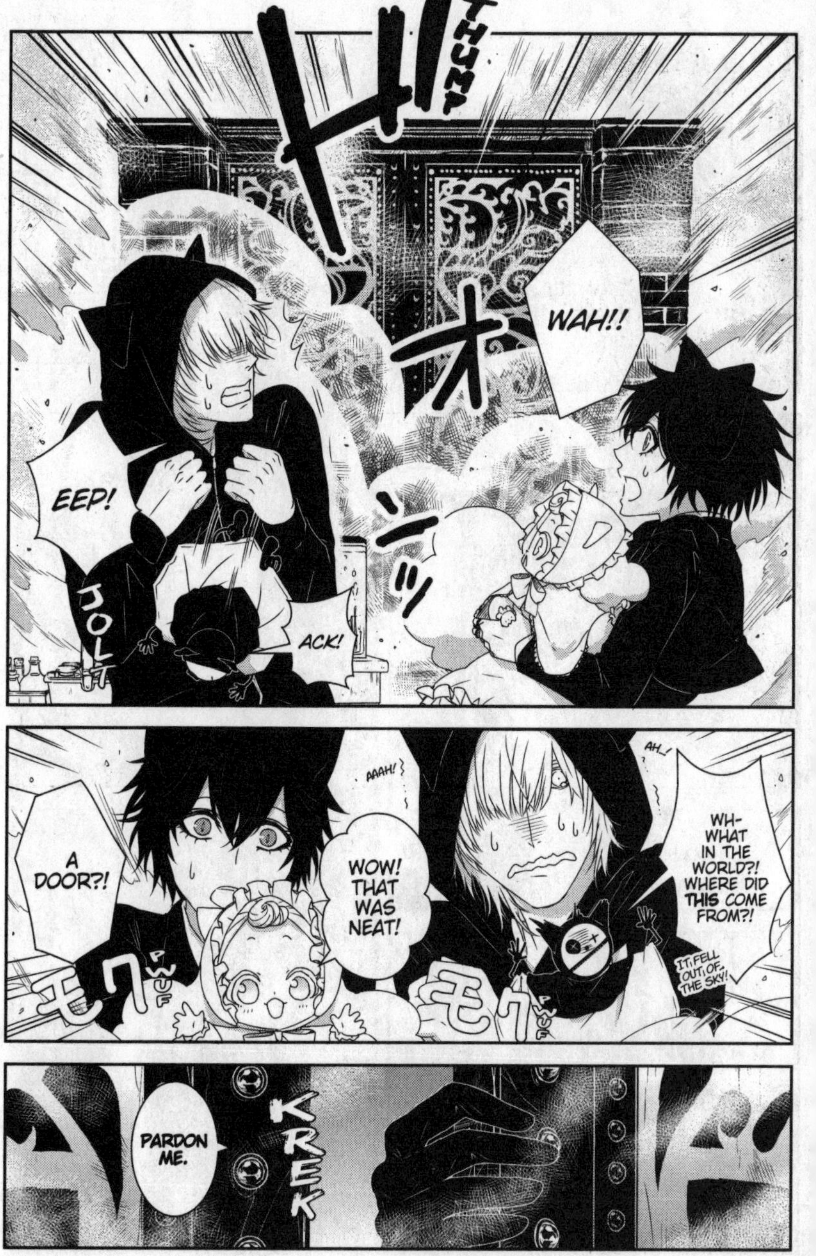
THUMP
WAH!!
EEP!
ACK!
JOLT
AH..!
WH-WHAT IN THE WORLD?! WHERE DID THIS COME FROM?!
IT FELL OUT OF THE SKY!
PWUF
WOW! THAT WAS NEAT!
AAAH!
A DOOR?!
PWUF
KREK
PARDON ME.

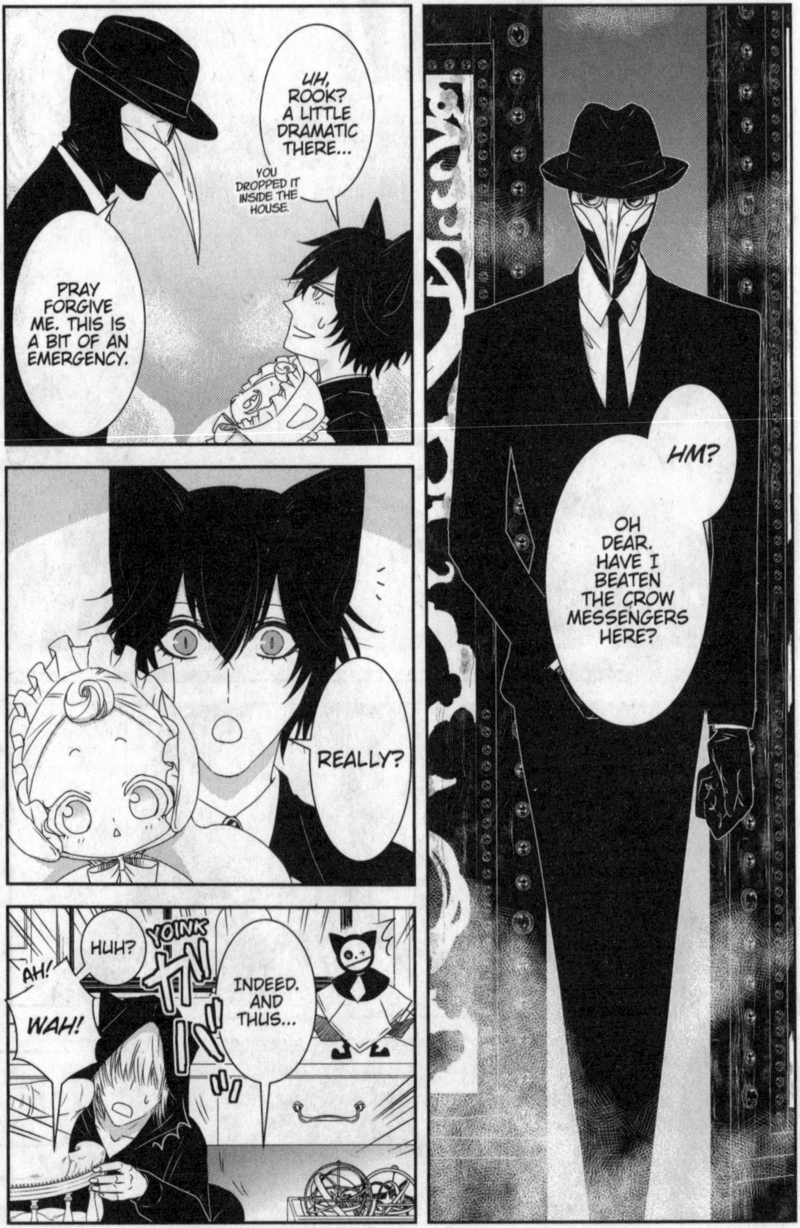
HM?
OH DEAR. HAVE I BEATEN THE CROW MESSENGERS HERE?
UH, ROOK? A LITTLE DRAMATIC THERE...
YOU DROPPED IT INSIDE THE HOUSE.
PRAY FORGIVE ME. THIS IS A BIT OF AN EMERGENCY.
REALLY?
YOINK
INDEED. AND THUS...
HUH?
AH!
WAH!

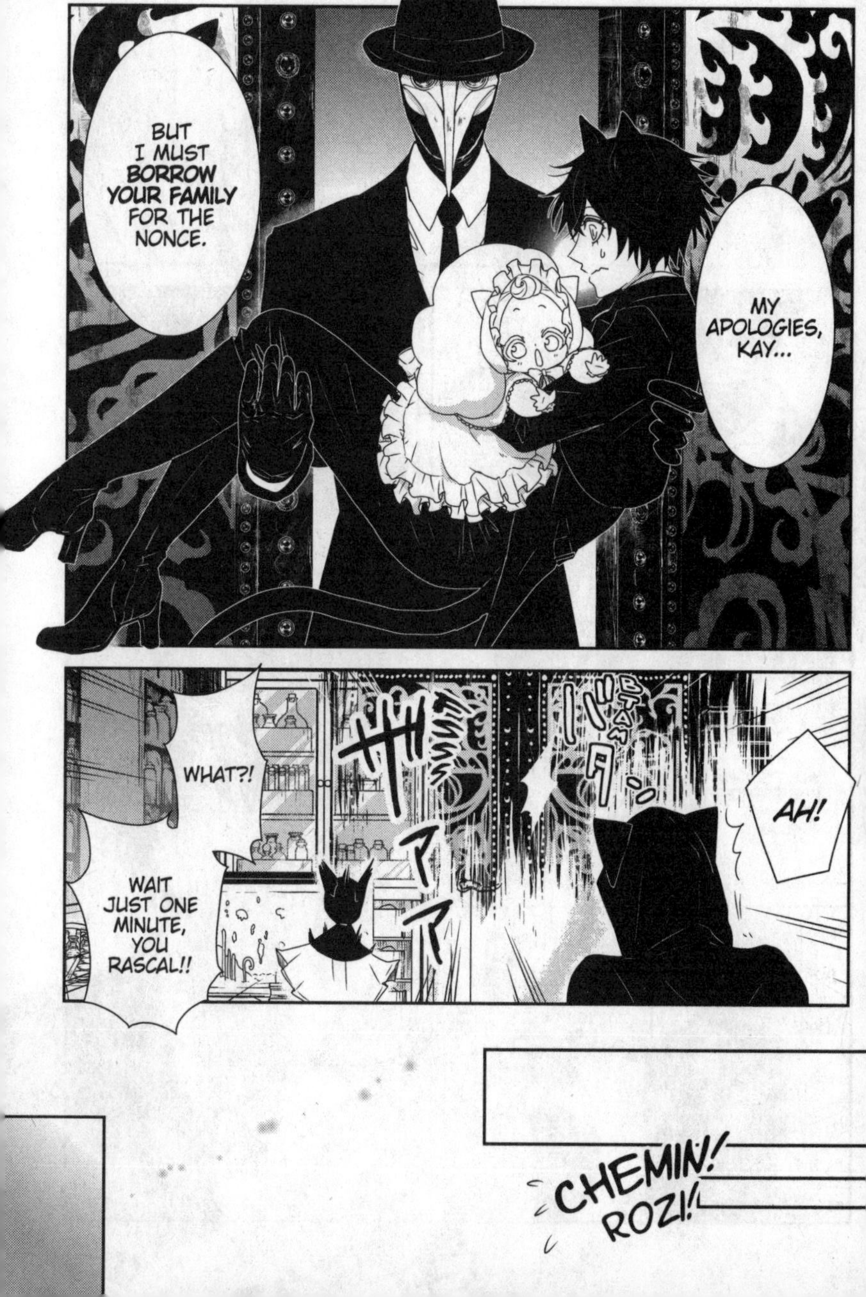
MY APOLOGIES, KAY...
BUT I MUST BORROW YOUR FAMILY FOR THE NONCE.
AH!
BTAM
WHAT?!
WAIT JUST ONE MINUTE, YOU RASCAL!!
CHEMIN! ROZI!

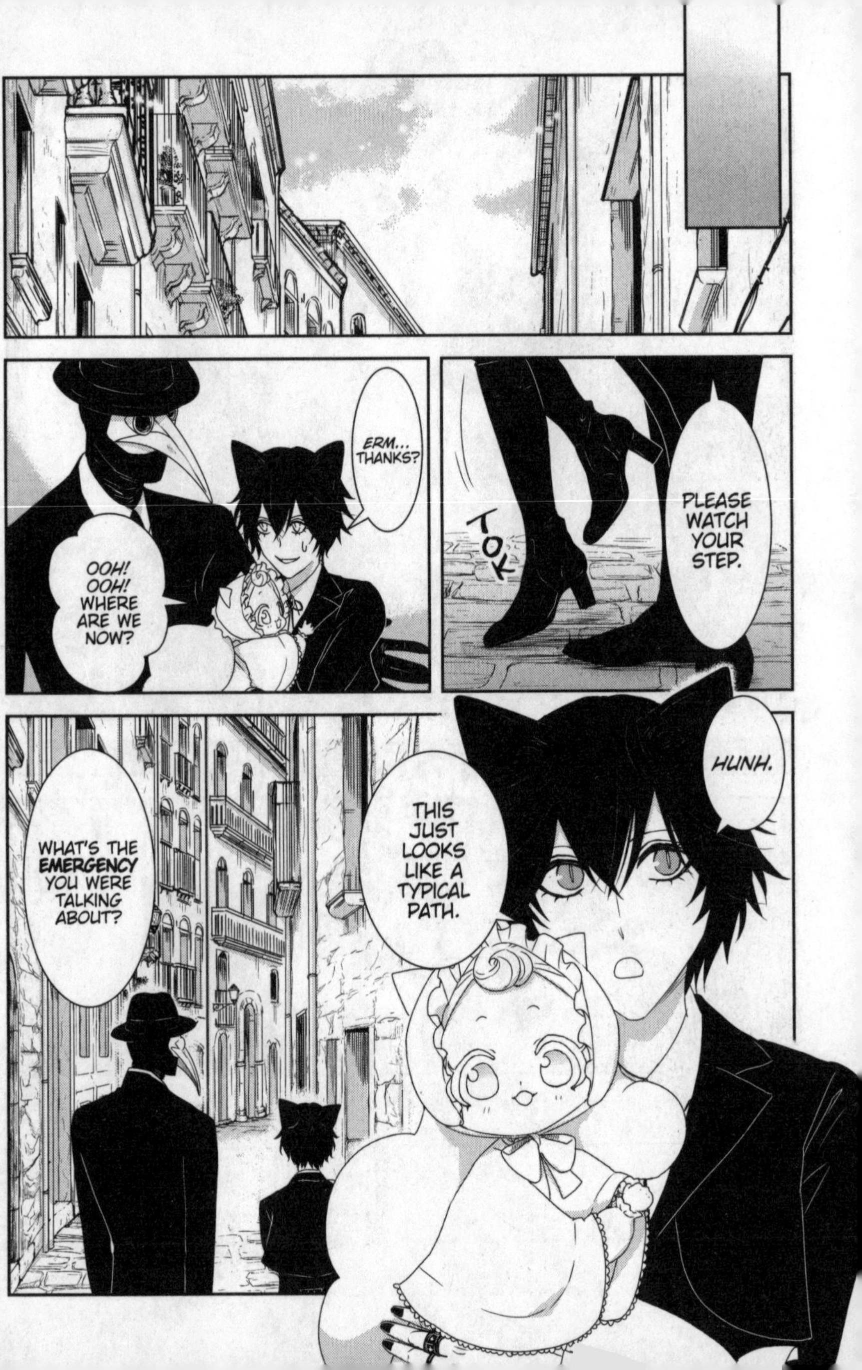
PLEASE WATCH YOUR STEP.
TOK
ERM... THANKS?
OOH! OOH! WHERE ARE WE NOW?
HUNH.
THIS JUST LOOKS LIKE A TYPICAL PATH.
WHAT'S THE EMERGENCY YOU WERE TALKING ABOUT?

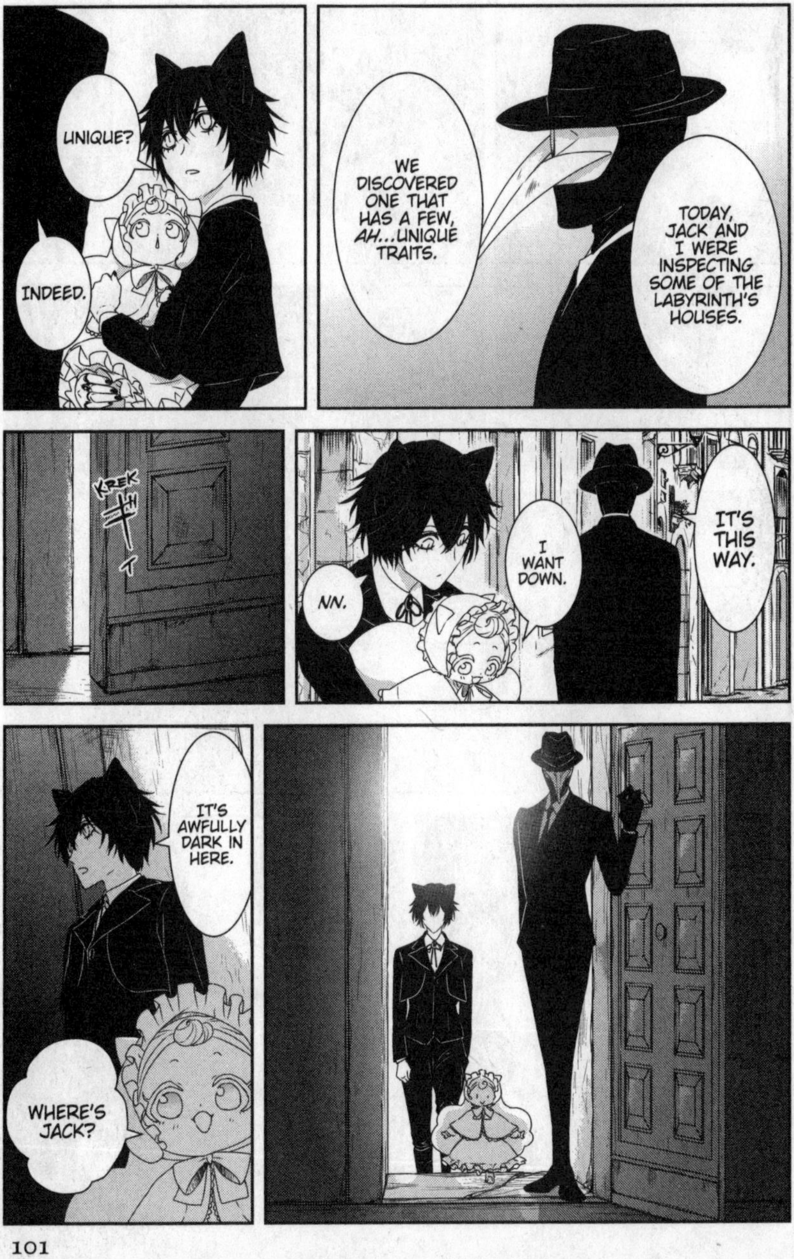
TODAY, JACK AND I WERE INSPECTING SOME OF THE LABYRINTH'S HOUSES.
WE DISCOVERED ONE THAT HAS A FEW, *AH*...UNIQUE TRAITS.
UNIQUE?
INDEED.
IT'S THIS WAY.
I WANT DOWN.
NN.
KREK
IT'S AWFULLY DARK IN HERE.
WHERE'S JACK?

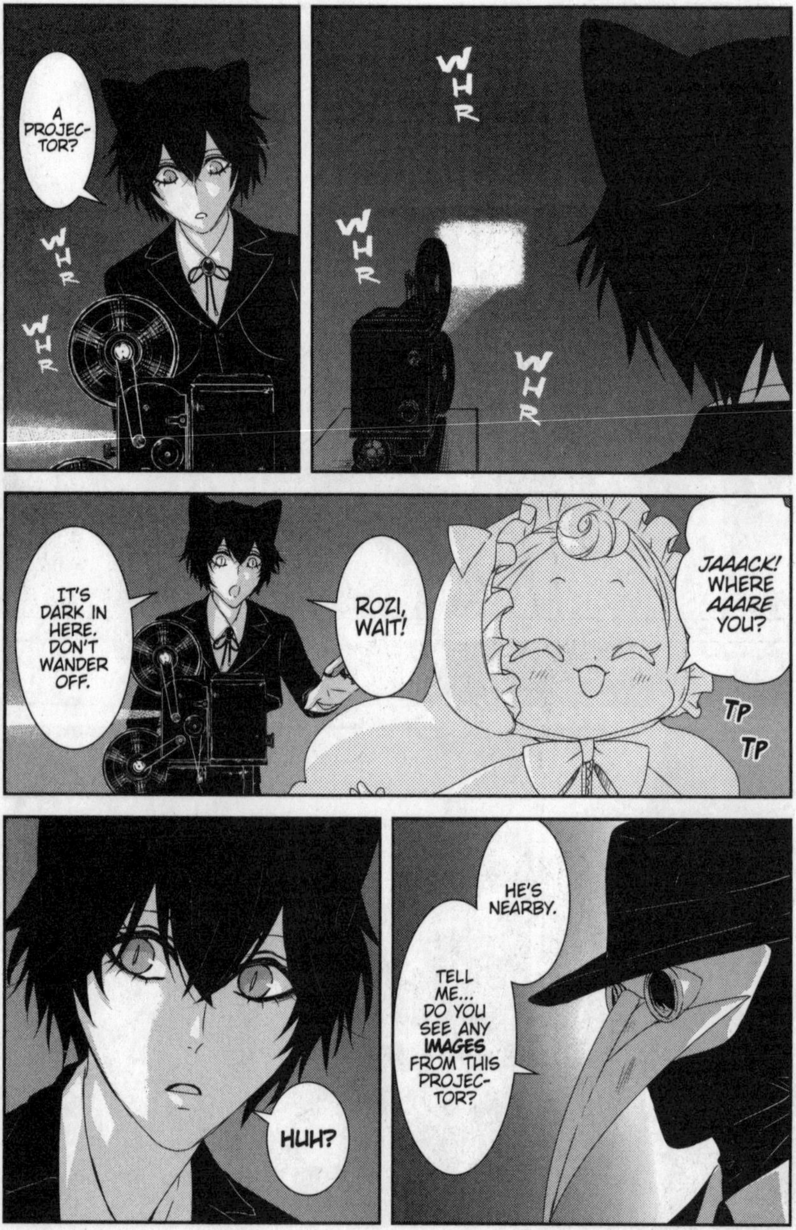
WHR
WHR
WHR
A PROJECTOR?
WHR
WHR
JAAACK! WHERE AAARE YOU?
TP TP
ROZI, WAIT!
IT'S DARK IN HERE. DON'T WANDER OFF.
HE'S NEARBY.
TELL ME... DO YOU SEE ANY IMAGES FROM THIS PROJECTOR?
HUH?

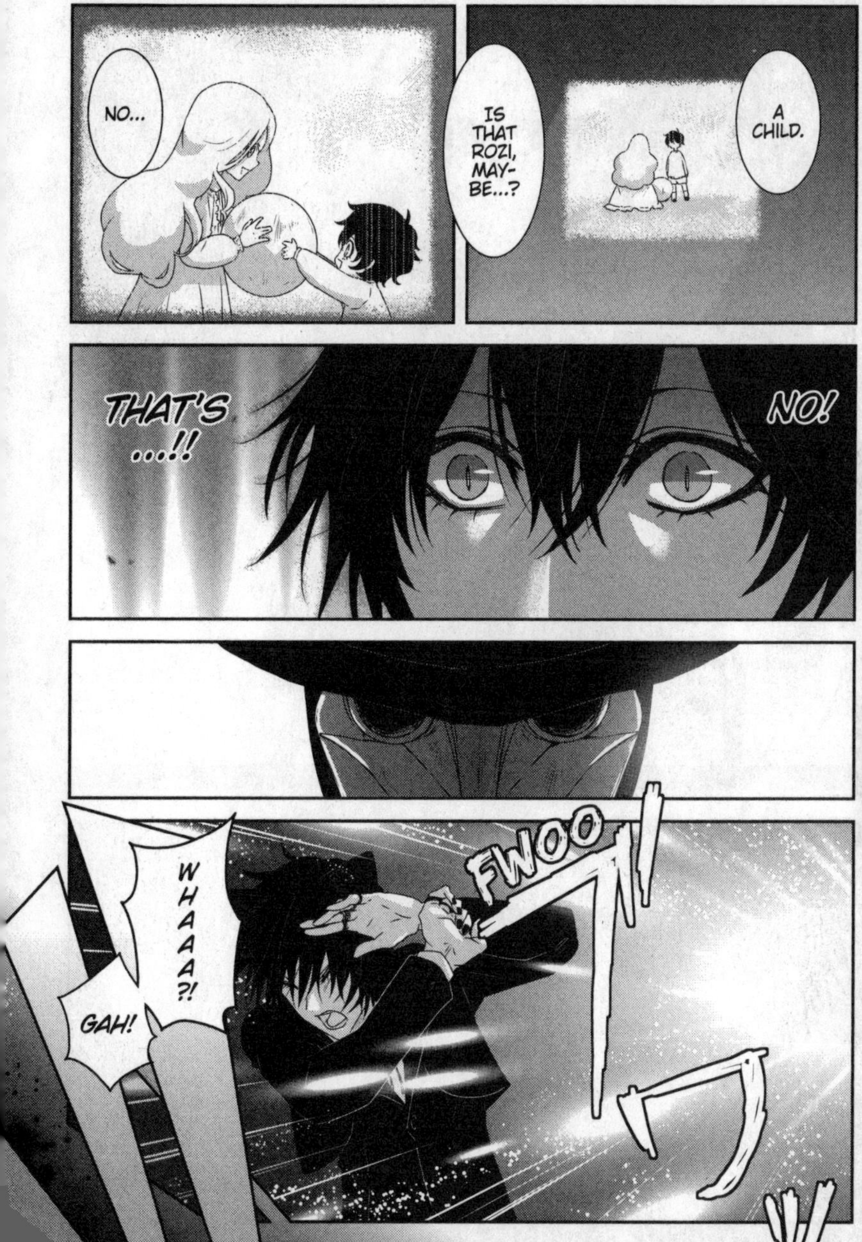
A CHILD.
IS THAT ROZI, MAY-BE...?
NO...
NO!
THAT'S ...!!
FWOO
WHAAAA?!
GAH!

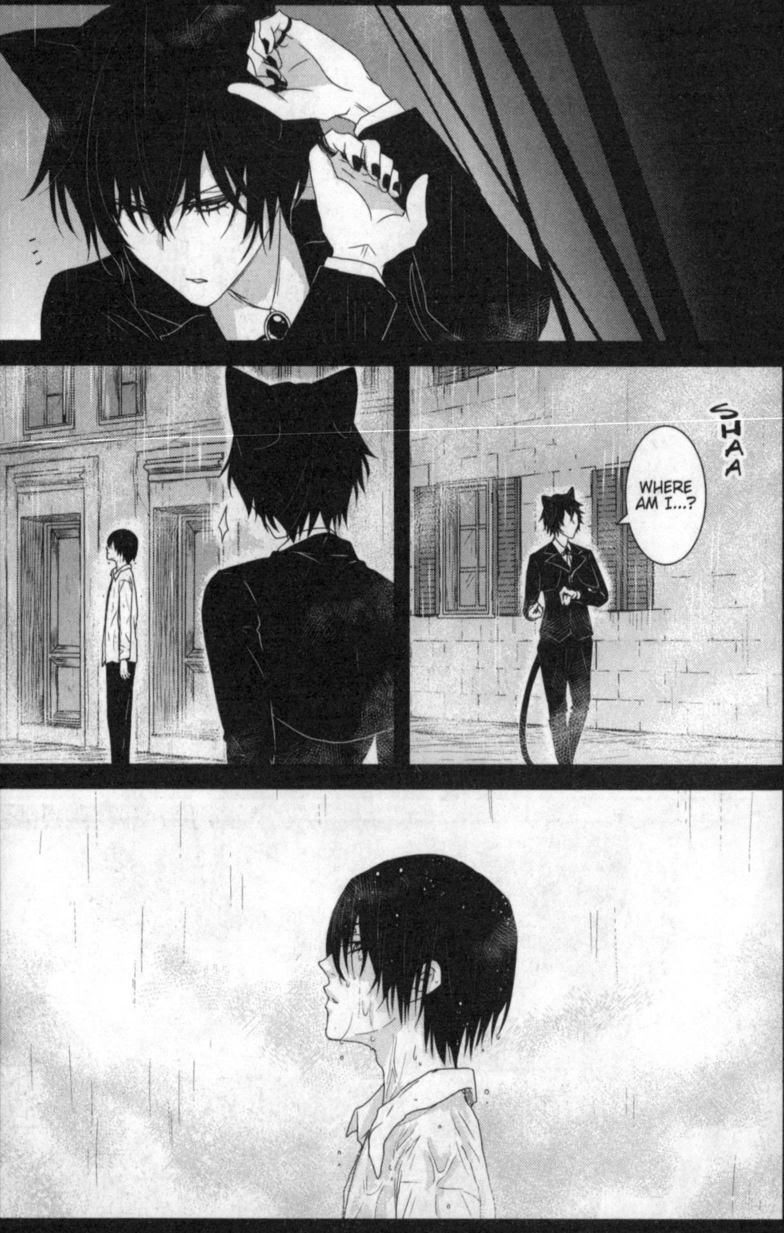
SHAA
WHERE AM I...?

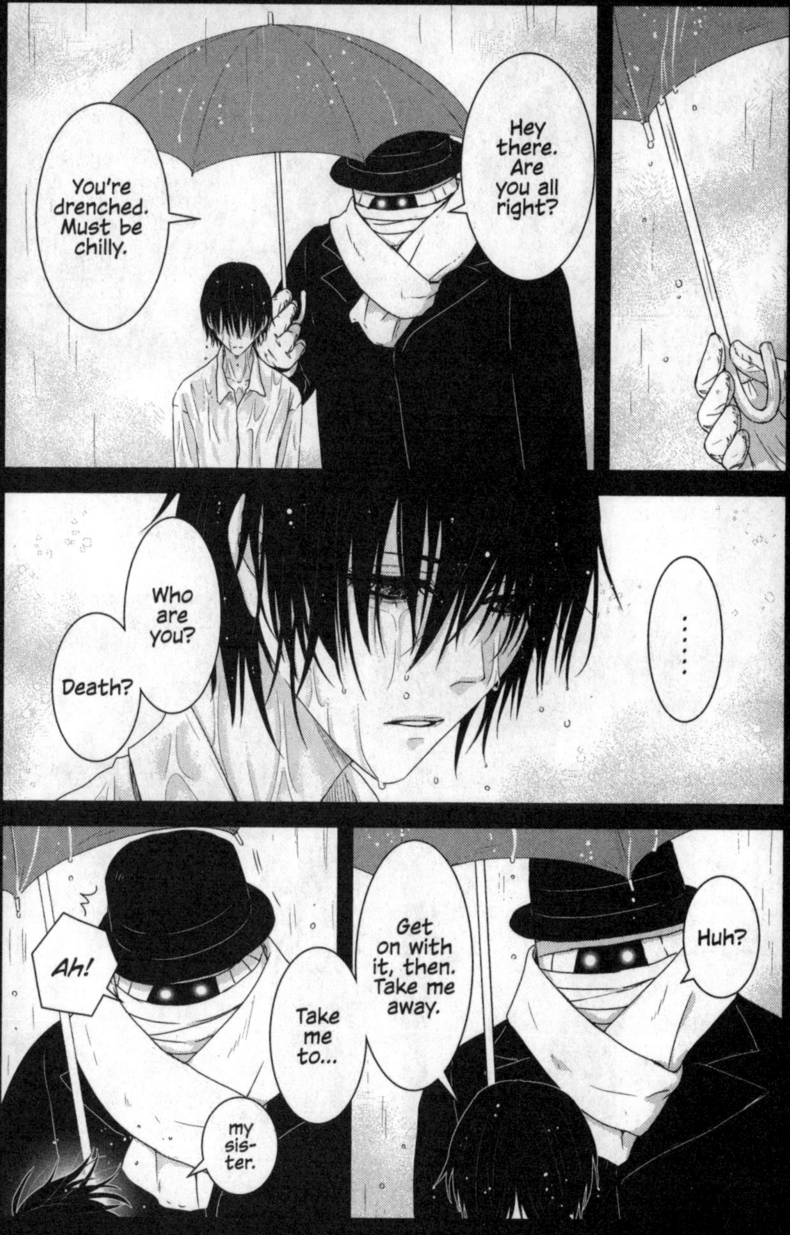
Hey there. Are you all right?
You're drenched. Must be chilly.
……
Who are you?
Death?
Huh?
Get on with it, then. Take me away.
Ah!
Take me to...
my sis-ter.

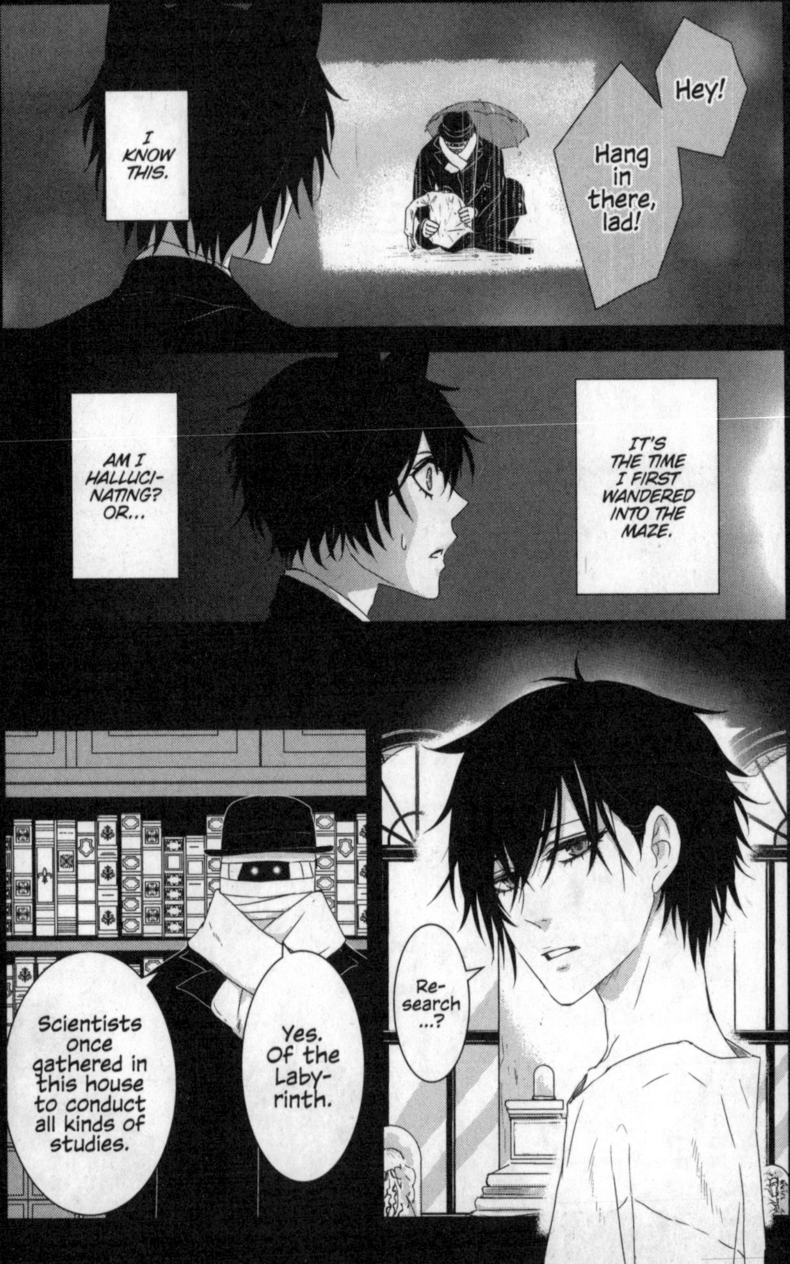
Hey!
Hang in there, lad!
I KNOW THIS.
IT'S THE TIME I FIRST WANDERED INTO THE MAZE.
AM I HALLUCI-NATING? OR...
Re-search ...?
Yes. Of the Laby-rinth.
Scientists once gathered in this house to conduct all kinds of studies.

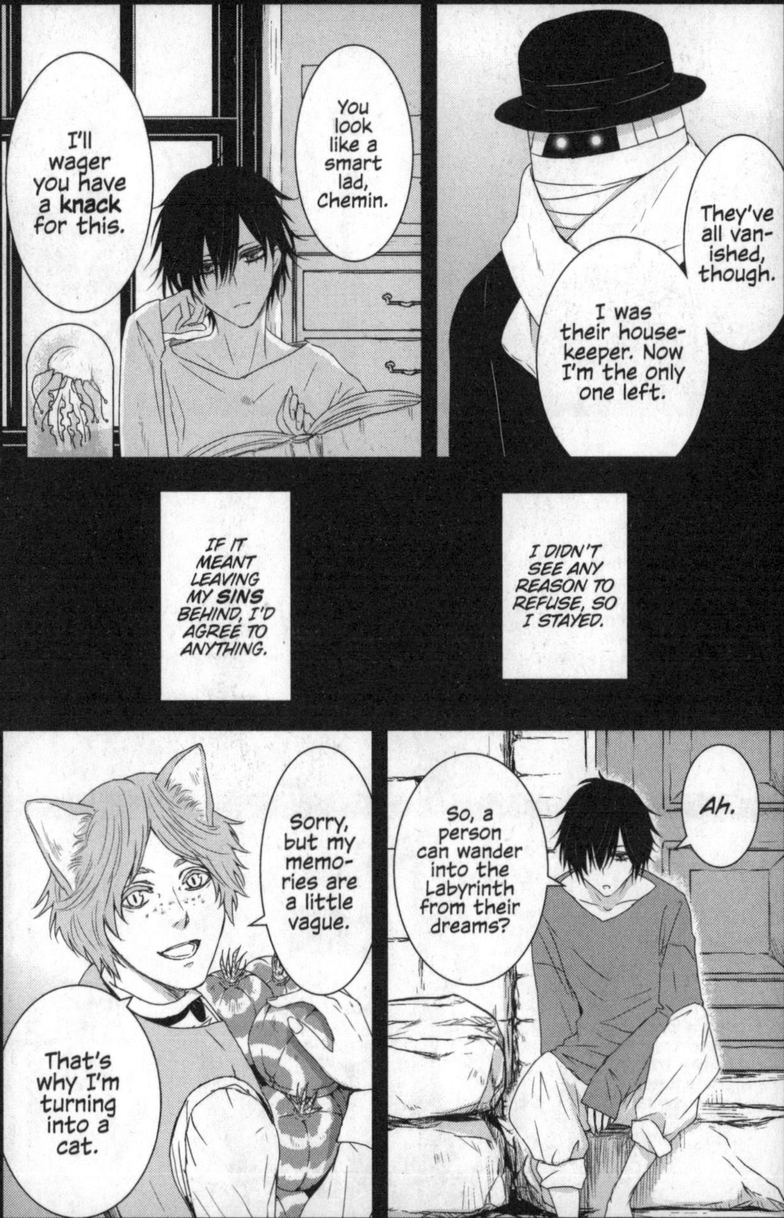
They've all vanished, though.
I was their housekeeper. Now I'm the only one left.
You look like a smart lad, Chemin.
I'll wager you have a **knack** for this.
I DIDN'T SEE ANY REASON TO REFUSE, SO I STAYED.
IF IT MEANT LEAVING MY **SINS** BEHIND, I'D AGREE TO ANYTHING.
Ah.
So, a person can wander into the Labyrinth from their dreams?
Sorry, but my memories are a little vague.
That's why I'm turning into a cat.

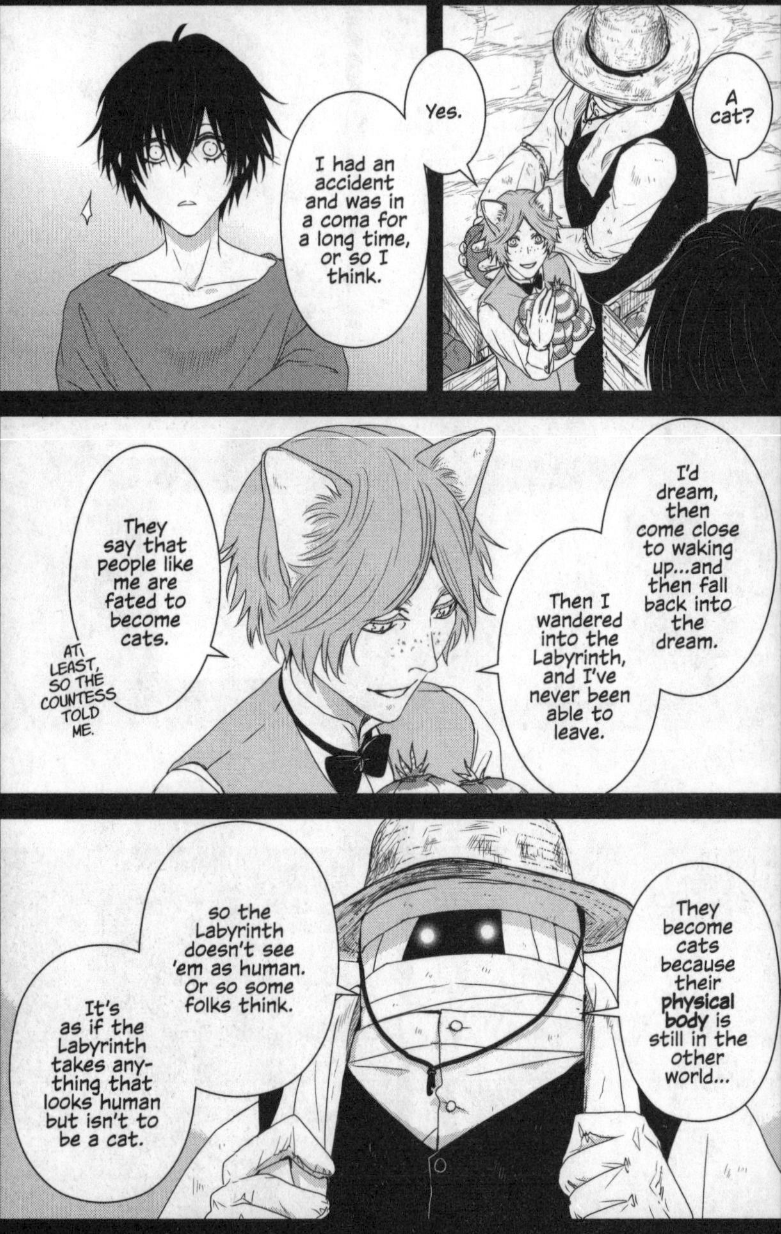
A cat?
Yes.
I had an accident and was in a coma for a long time, or so I think.
I'd dream, then come close to waking up...and then fall back into the dream.
Then I wandered into the Labyrinth, and I've never been able to leave.
They say that people like me are fated to become cats.
AT LEAST, SO THE COUNTESS TOLD ME.
They become cats because their **physical body** is still in the other world...
so the Labyrinth doesn't see 'em as human. Or so some folks think.
It's as if the Labyrinth takes any-thing that looks human but isn't to be a cat.

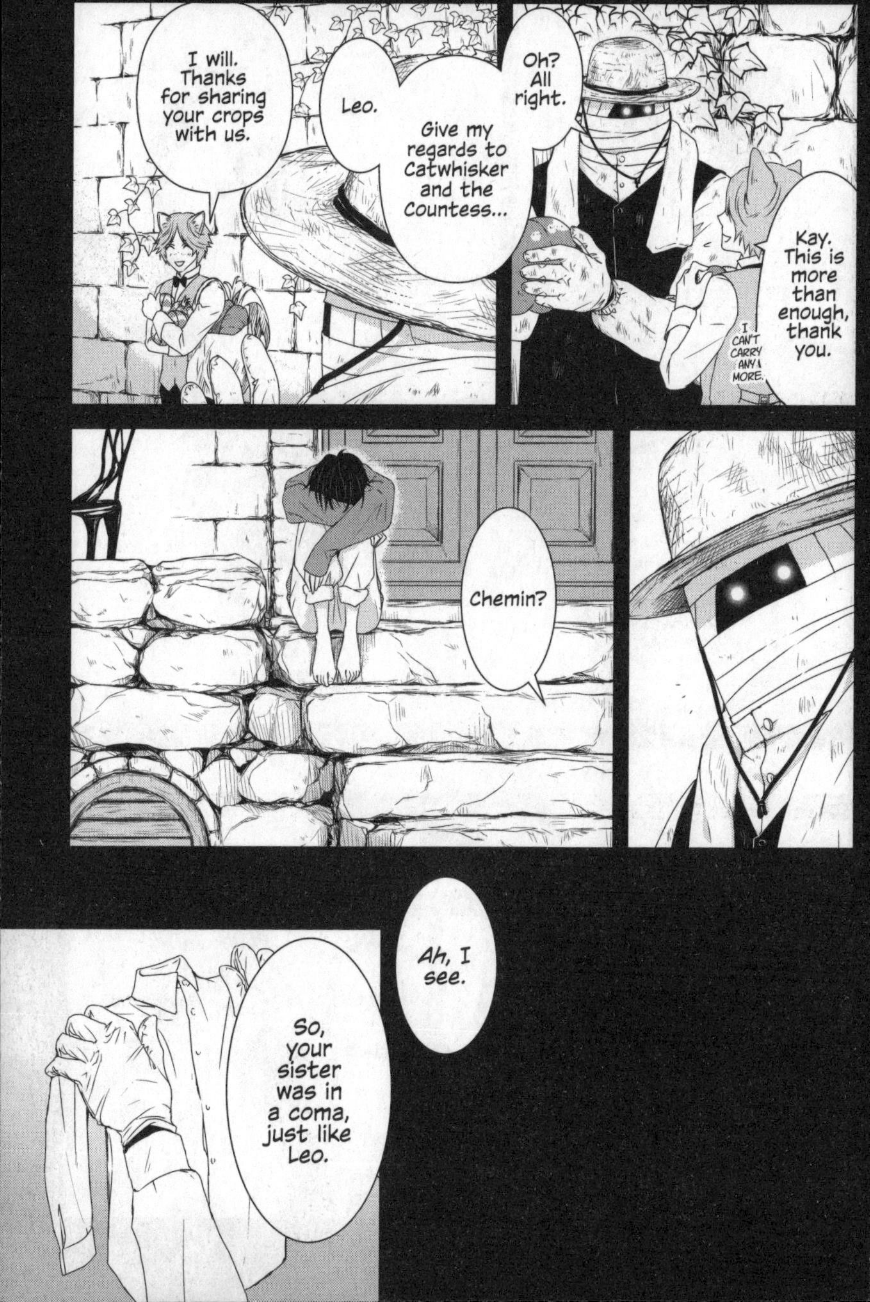
Kay. This is more than enough, thank you.
I CAN'T CARRY ANY MORE.
Oh? All right.
Leo.
Give my regards to Catwhisker and the Countess...
I will. Thanks for sharing your crops with us.
Chemin?
Ah, I see.
So, your sister was in a coma, just like Leo.

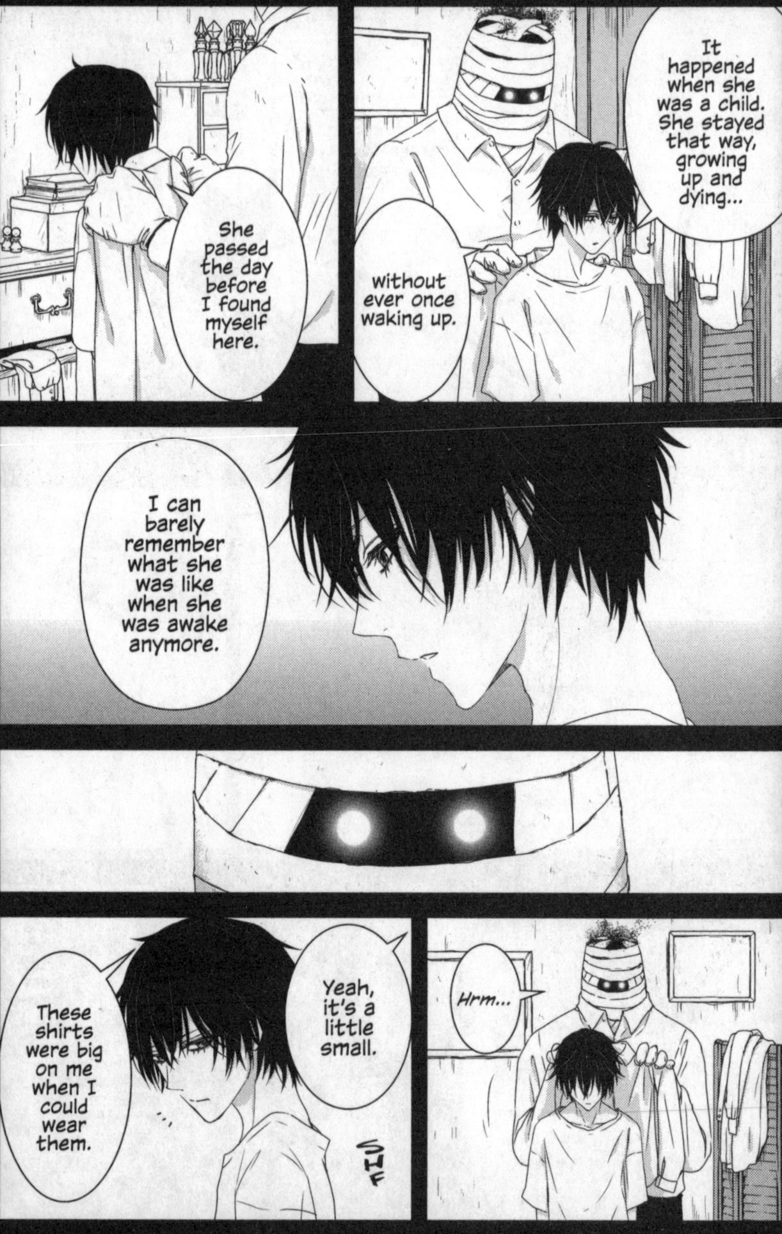
It happened when she was a child. She stayed that way, growing up and dying...
without ever once waking up.
She passed the day before I found myself here.
I can barely remember what she was like when she was awake anymore.
Hrm...
Yeah, it's a little small.
These shirts were big on me when I could wear them.
...
SHF

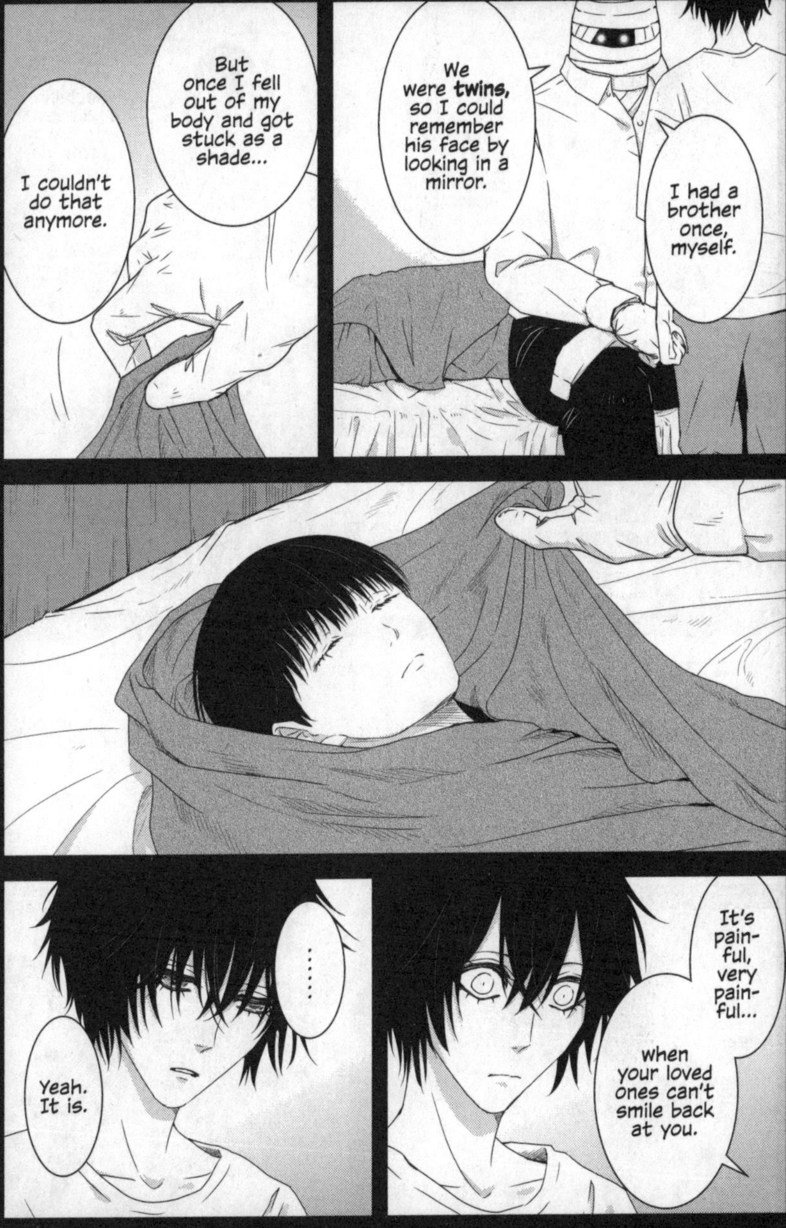

I had a brother once, myself.
We were **twins,** so I could remember his face by looking in a mirror.
But once I fell out of my body and got stuck as a shade...
I couldn't do that anymore.
It's painful, very painful...
when your loved ones can't smile back at you.
......
Yeah. It is.

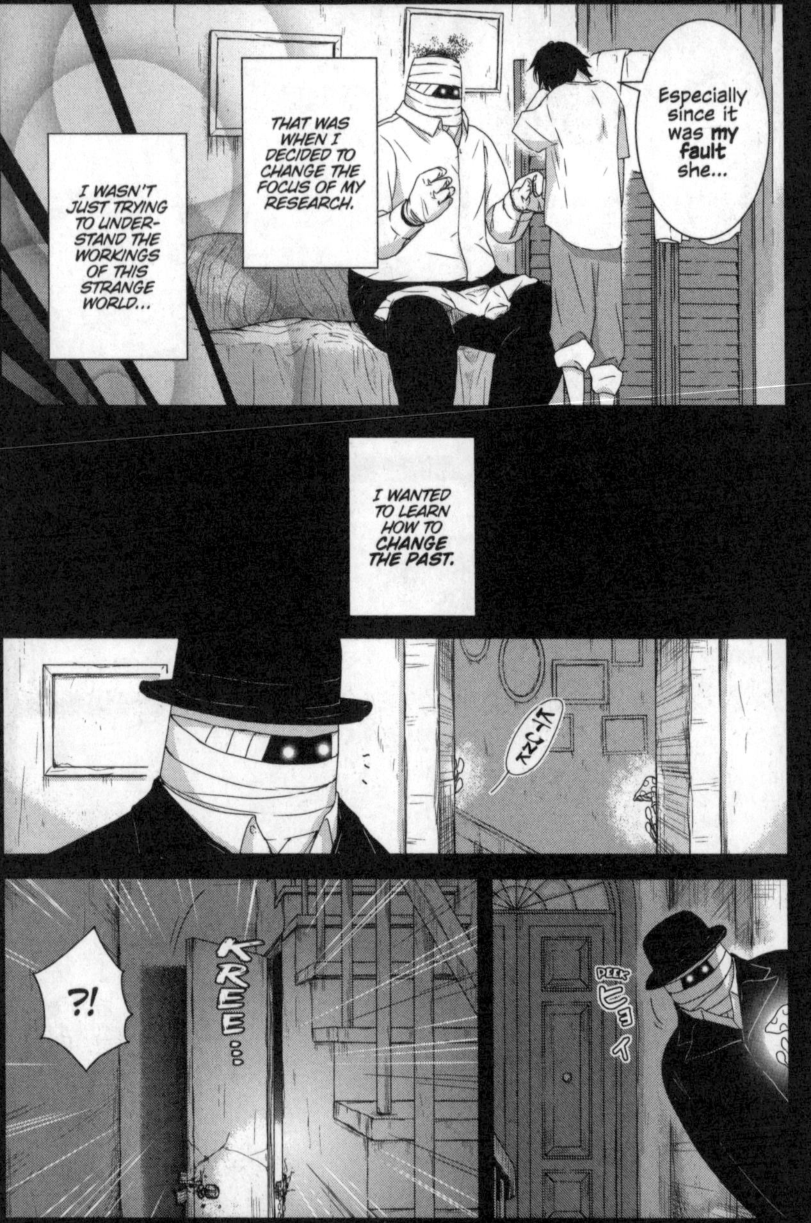

Especially since it was **my fault** she...
THAT WAS WHEN I DECIDED TO CHANGE THE FOCUS OF MY RESEARCH.
I WASN'T JUST TRYING TO UNDERSTAND THE WORKINGS OF THIS STRANGE WORLD...
I WANTED TO LEARN HOW TO CHANGE THE PAST.
PEEK
ヒョイ
KREE...
?!

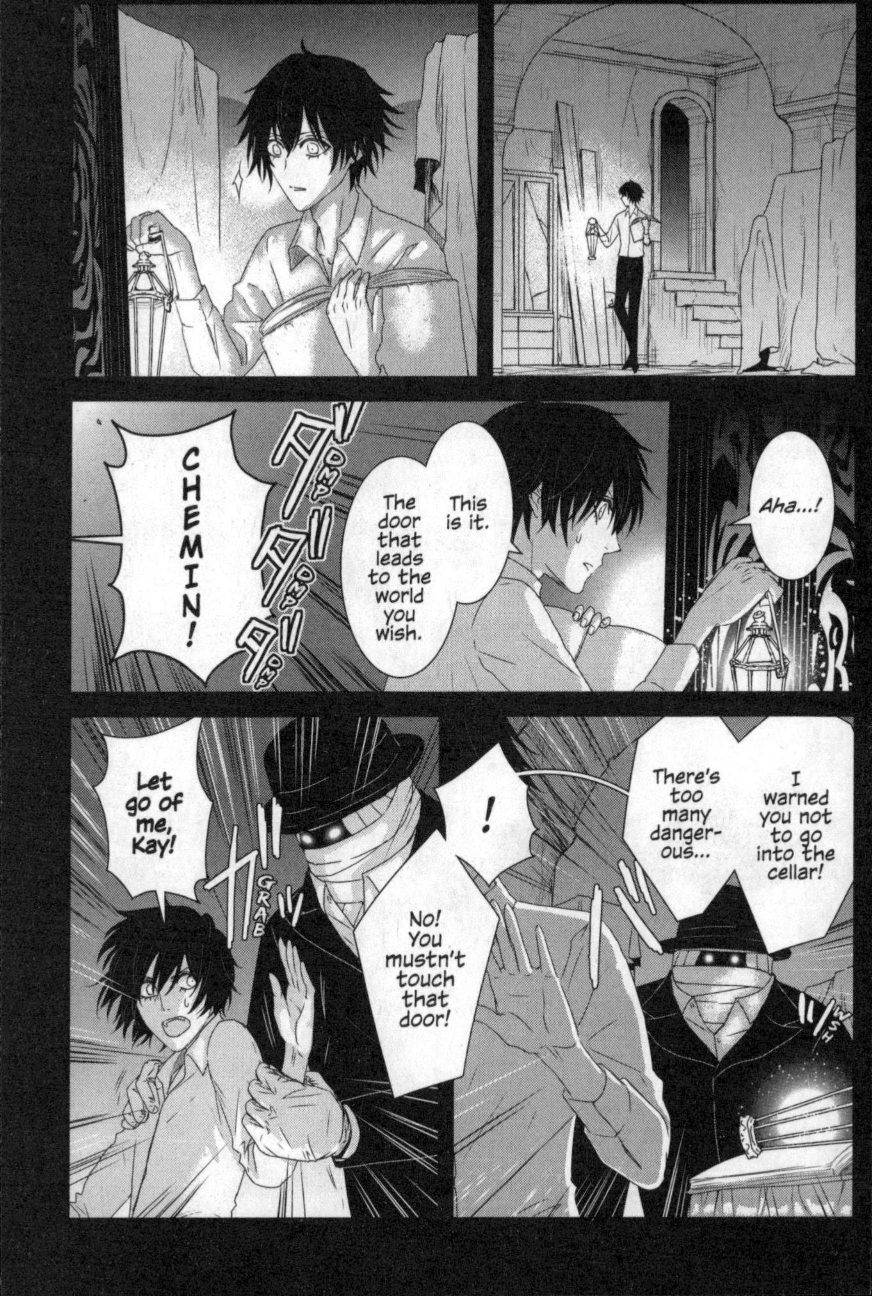
Aha...!
This is it.
The door that leads to the world you wish.
DOMP DOMP DOMP
CHEMIN!
I warned you not to go into the cellar!
There's too many danger-ous...
WSH
!
No! You mustn't touch that door!
GRAB
Let go of me, Kay!

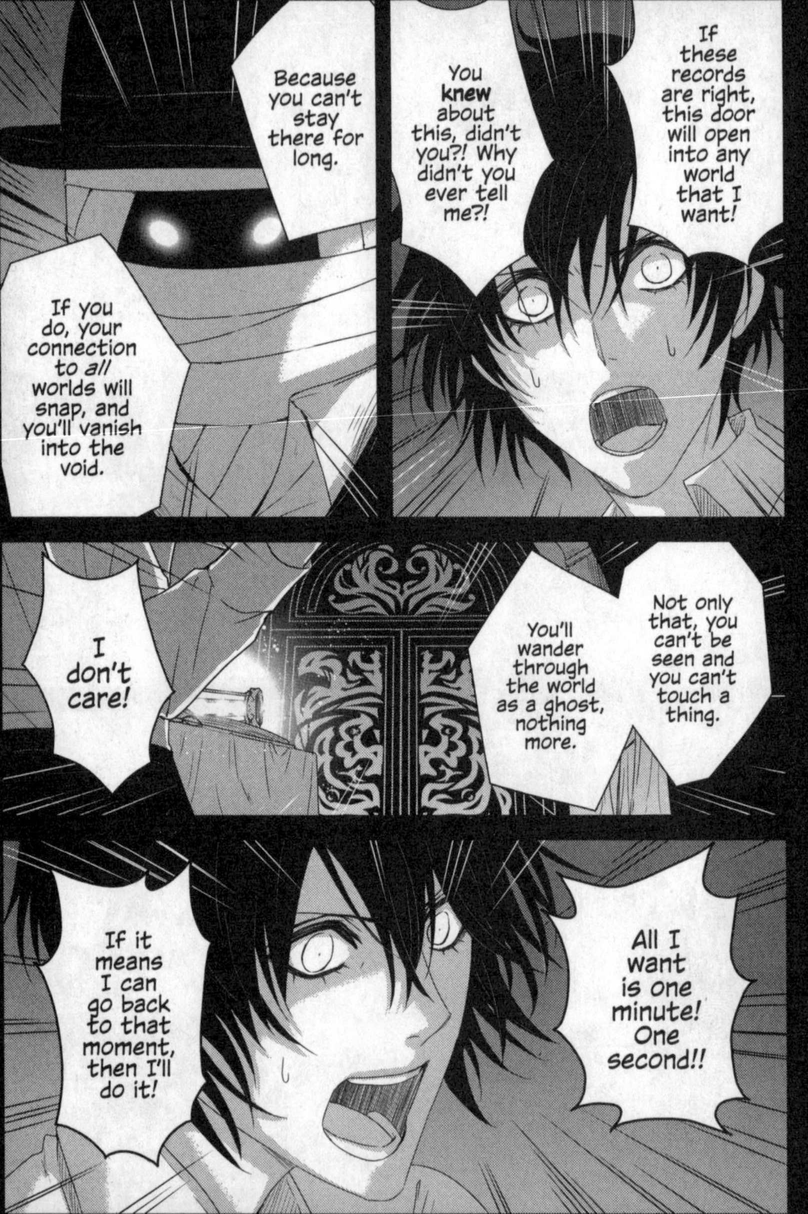
If these records are right, this door will open into any world that I want!
You **knew** about this, didn't you?! Why didn't you ever tell me?!
Because you can't stay there for long.
If you do, your connection to *all* worlds will snap, and you'll vanish into the void.
Not only that, you can't be seen and you can't touch a thing.
You'll wander through the world as a ghost, nothing more.
I don't care!
All I want is one minute! One second!!
If it means I can go back to that moment, then I'll do it!

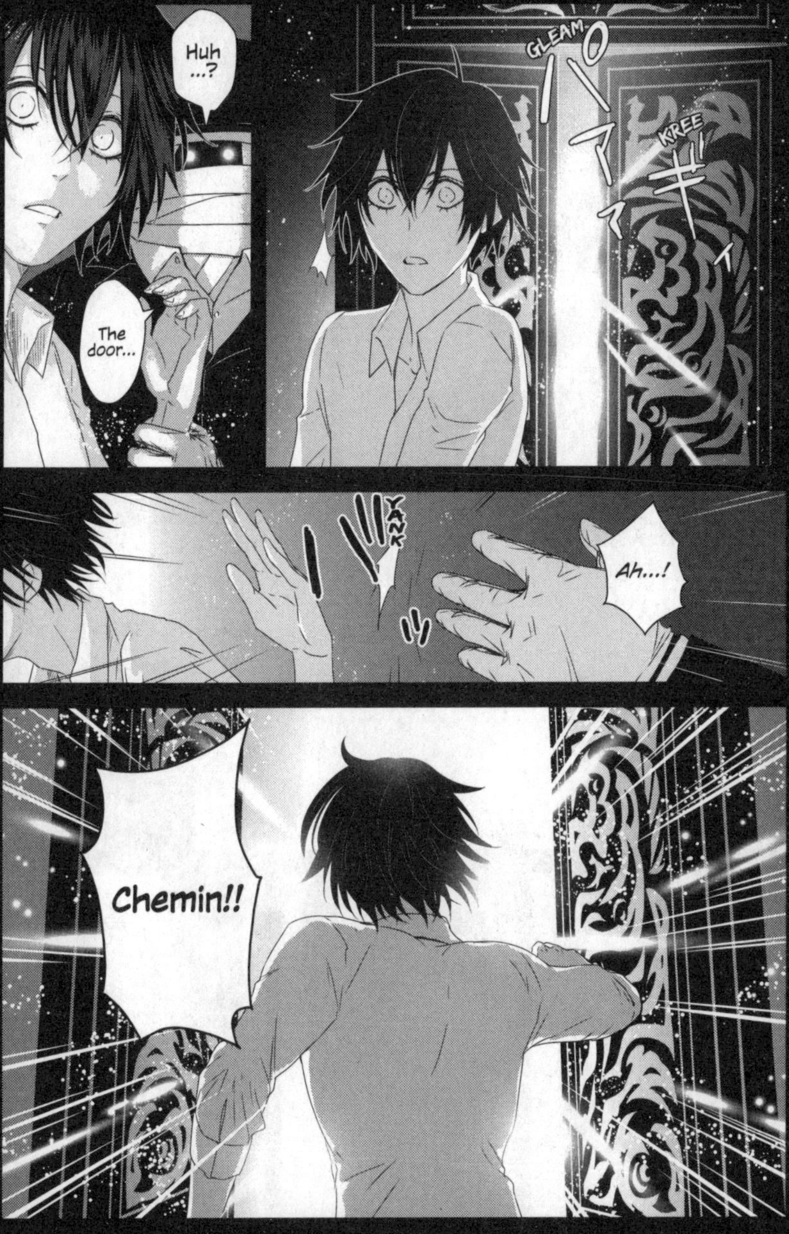
GLEAM
KREE
Huh ...?
The door...
Ah...!
YANK
Chemin!!

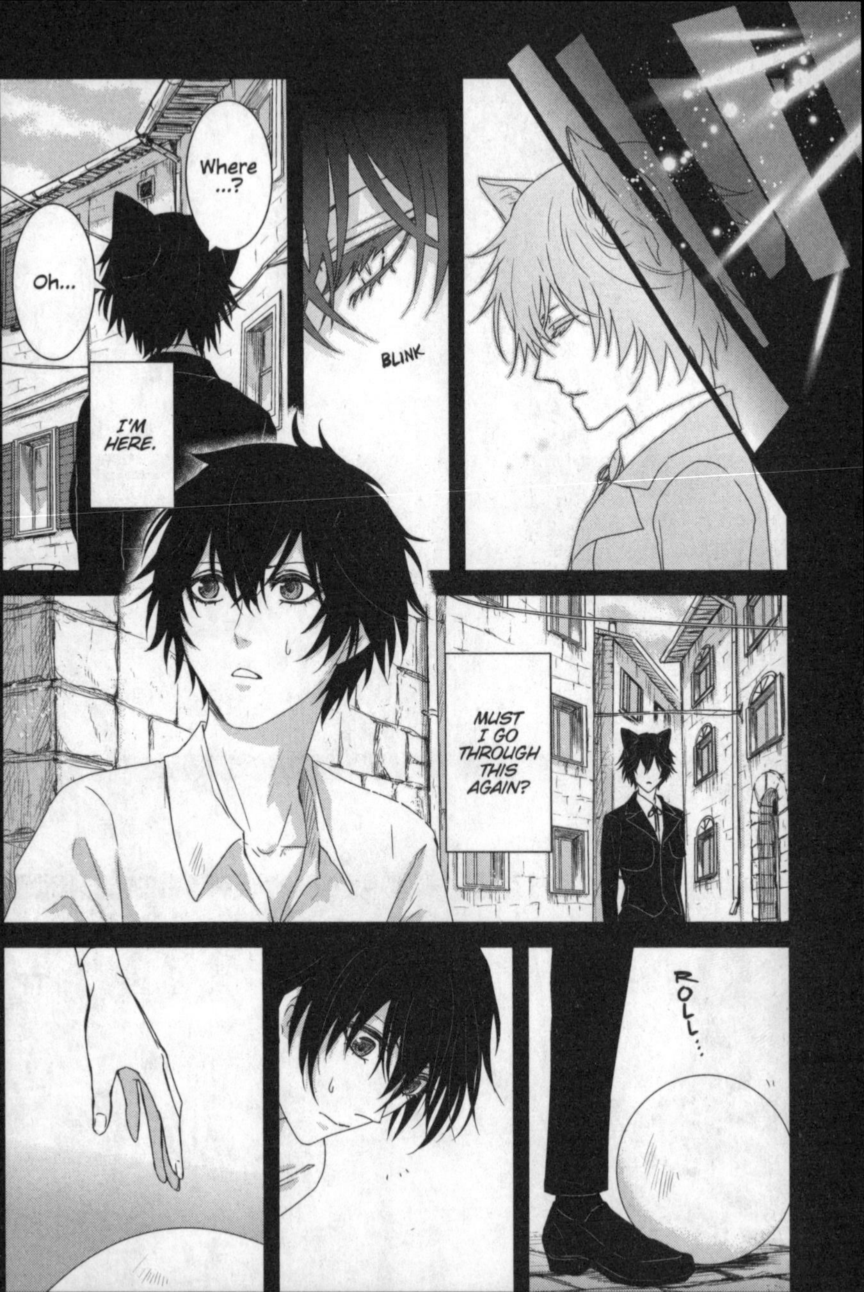
BLINK
Where ...?
Oh...
I'M HERE.
MUST I GO THROUGH THIS AGAIN?
ROLL...

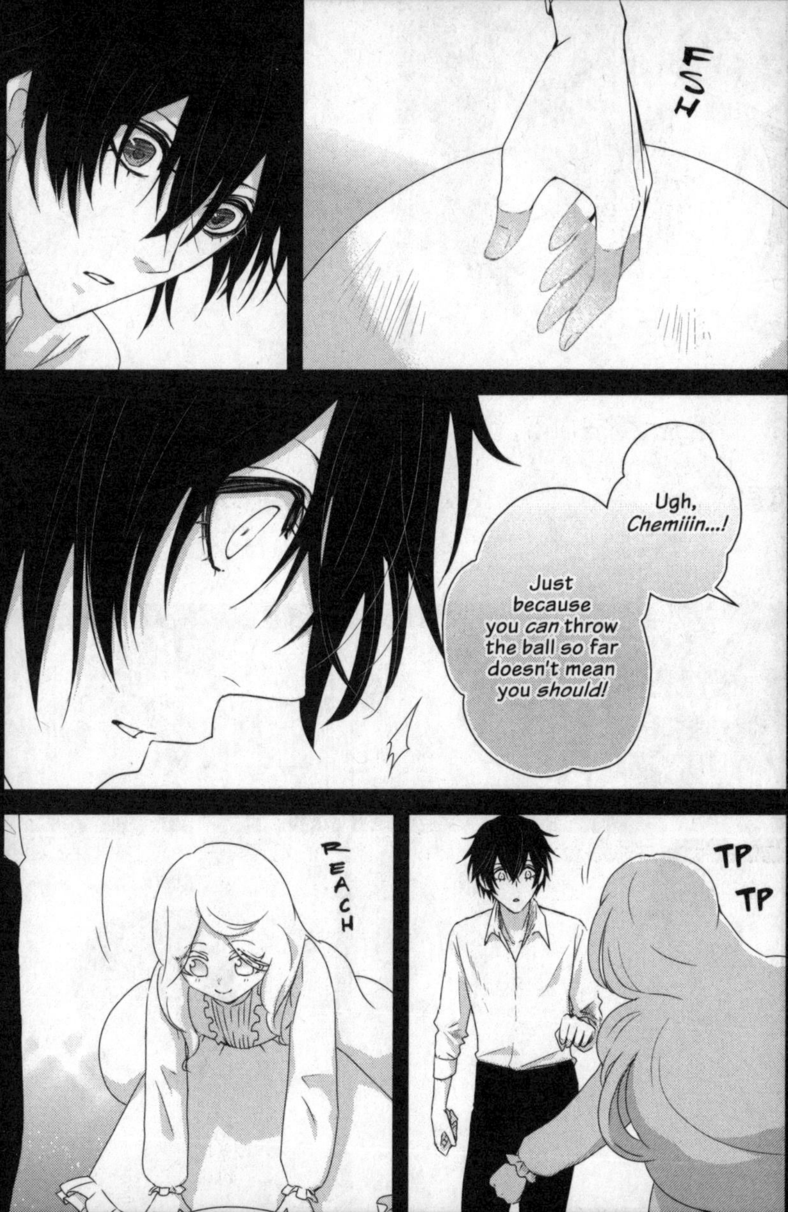
FSH
Ugh, Chemiiin...!
Just because you *can* throw the ball so far doesn't mean you *should!*
TP
TP
REACH

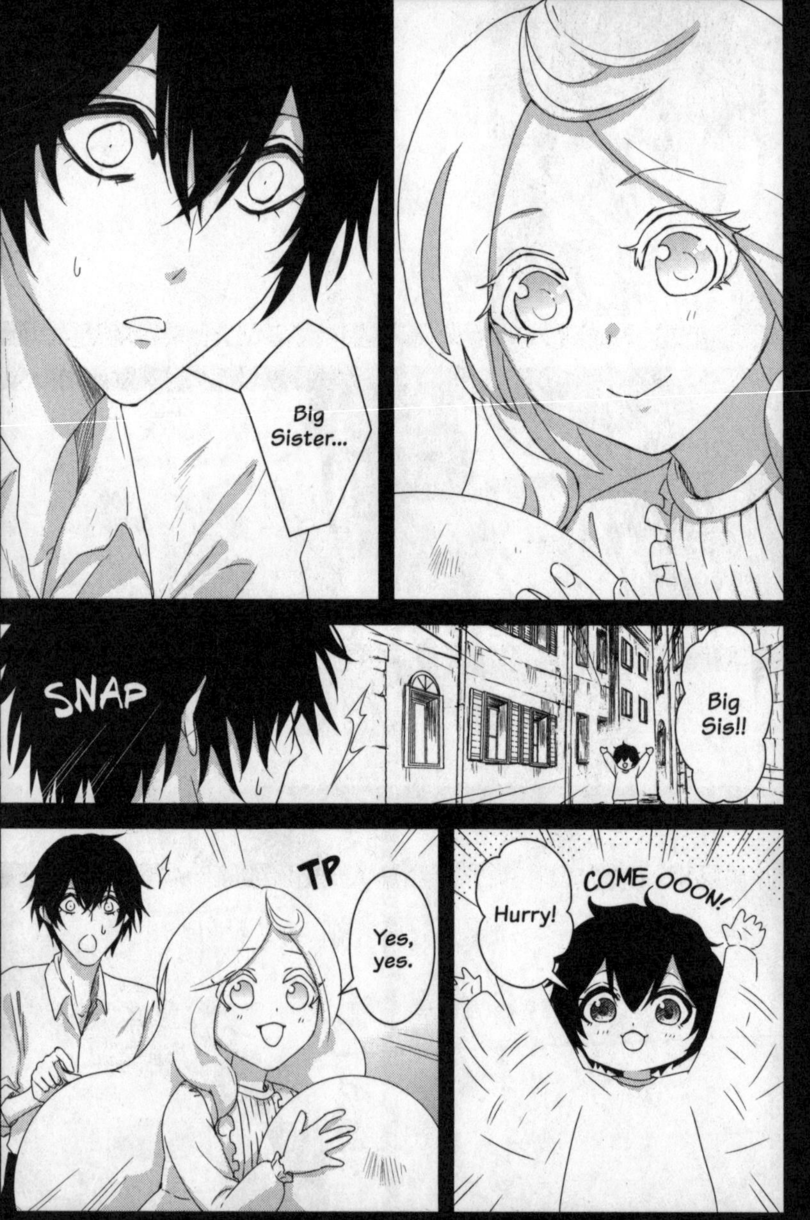
Big Sister...
Big Sis!!
SNAP
COME OOON!
Hurry!
TP
Yes, yes.

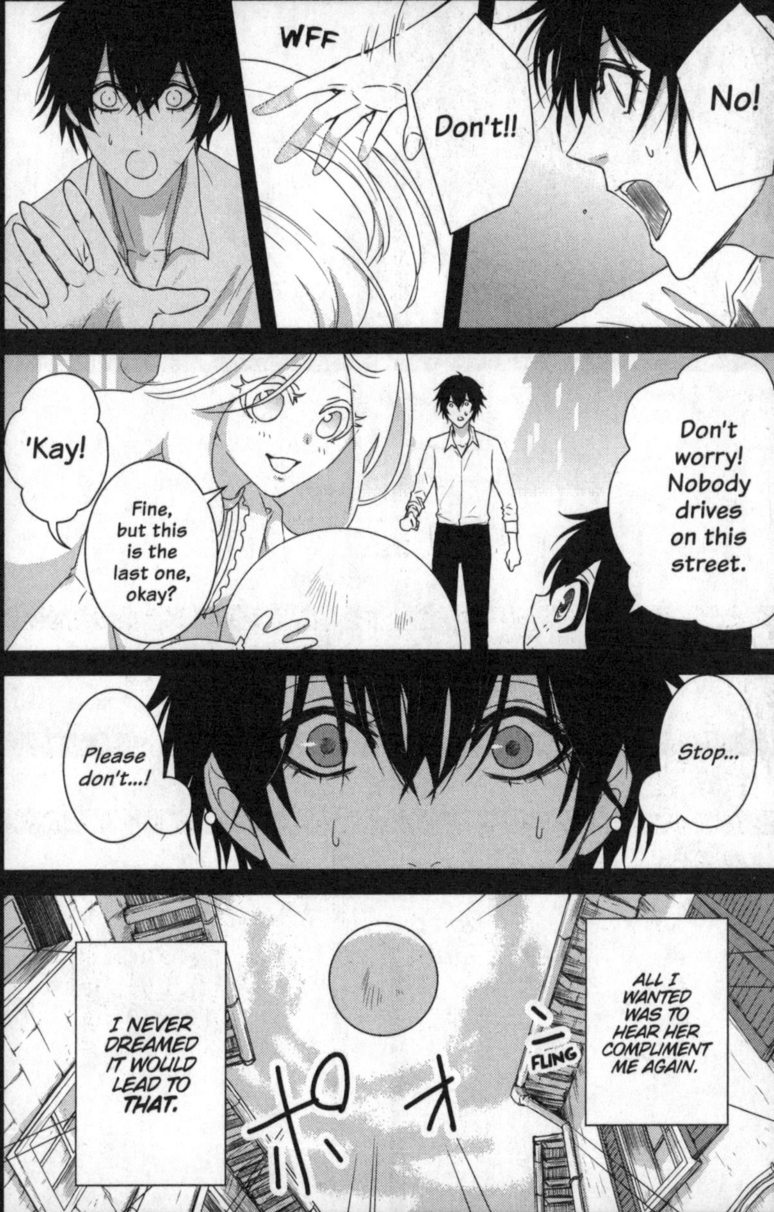
No!
Don't!!
WFF
Don't worry! Nobody drives on this street.
Fine, but this is the last one, okay?
'Kay!
Stop...
Please don't...!
ALL I WANTED WAS TO HEAR HER COMPLIMENT ME AGAIN.
FLING
I NEVER DREAMED IT WOULD LEAD TO THAT.

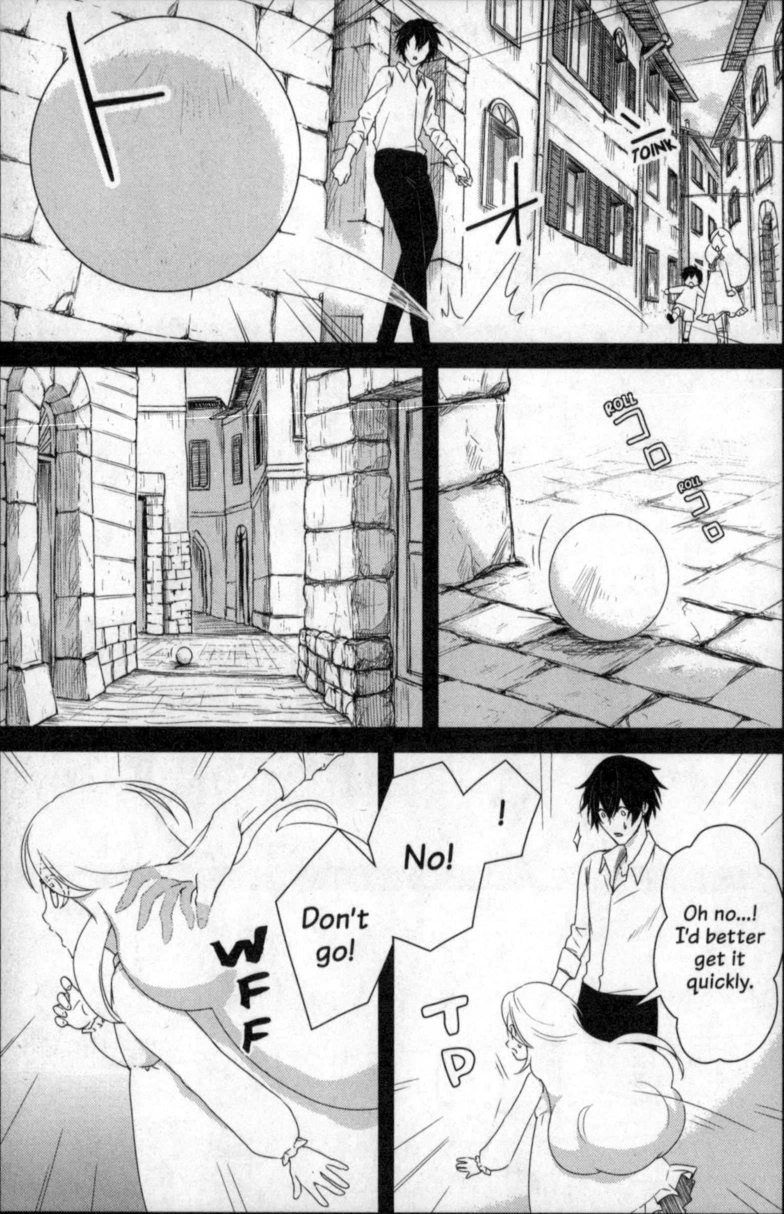
TOINK
ROLL
コロ
ROLL
コロ
!
Oh no...! I'd better get it quickly.
TP
No!
Don't go!
WFF

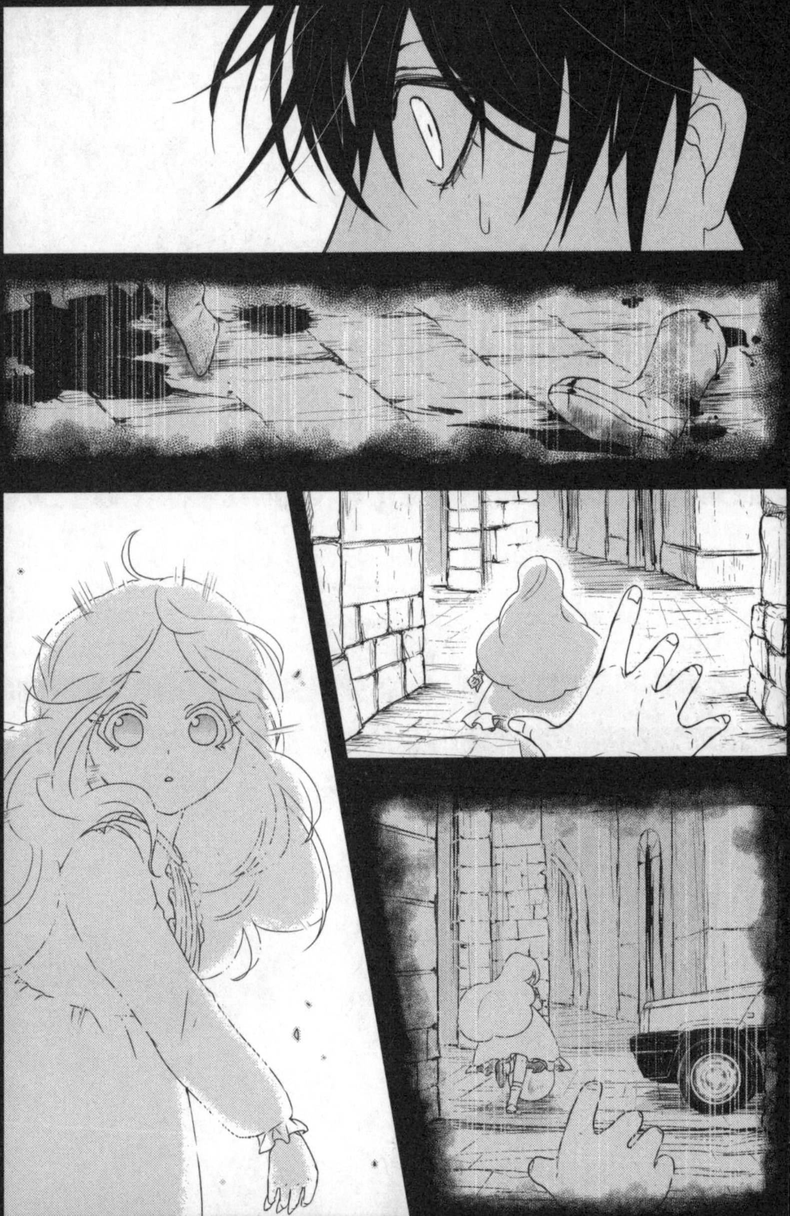

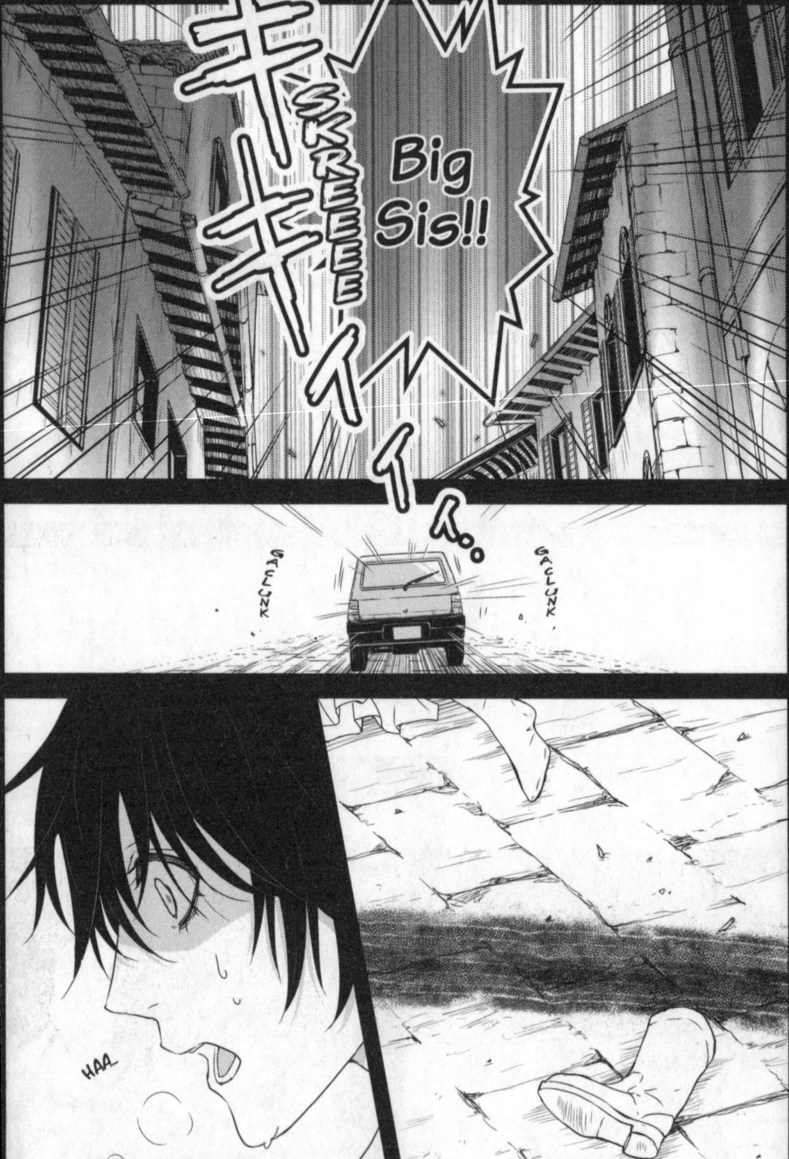
SKREEEE
Big Sis!!
GACLUNK
GACLUNK
HAA...

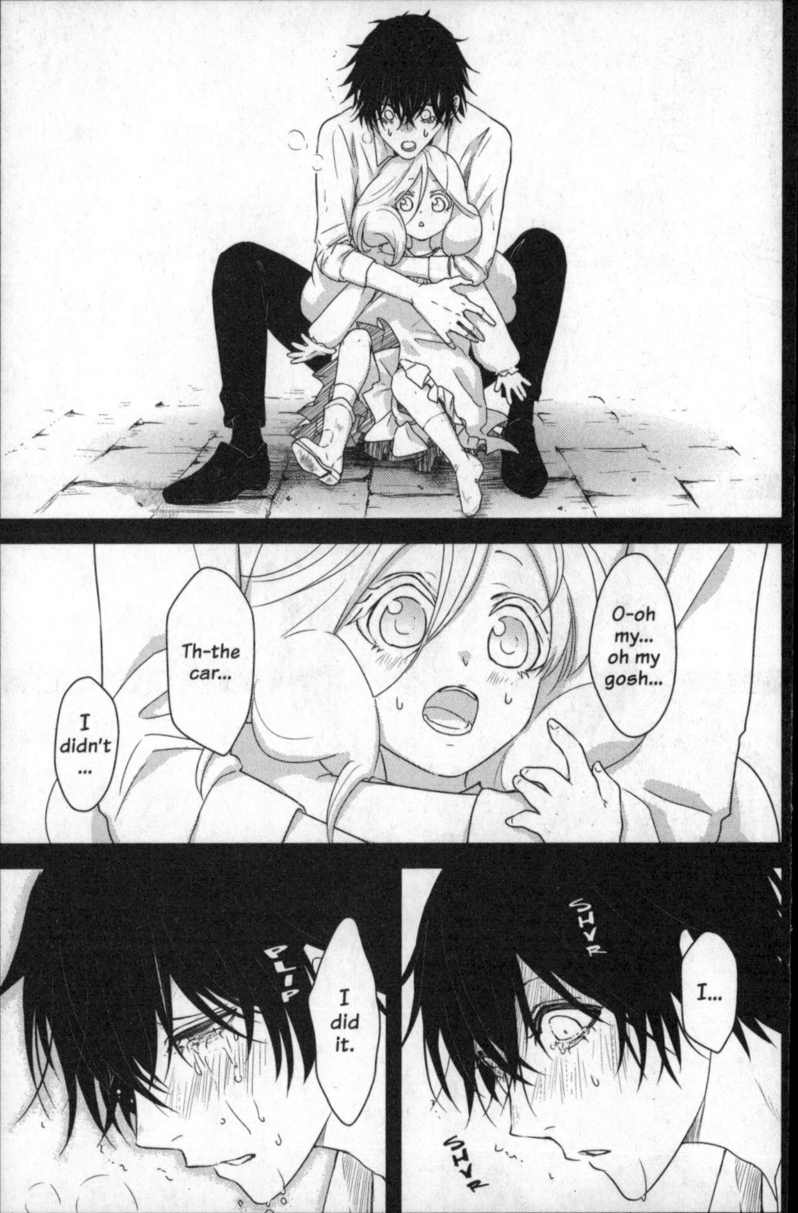
O-oh my... oh my gosh...
Th-the car...
I didn't ...
SHVR
I...
SHVR
PLIP
I did it.

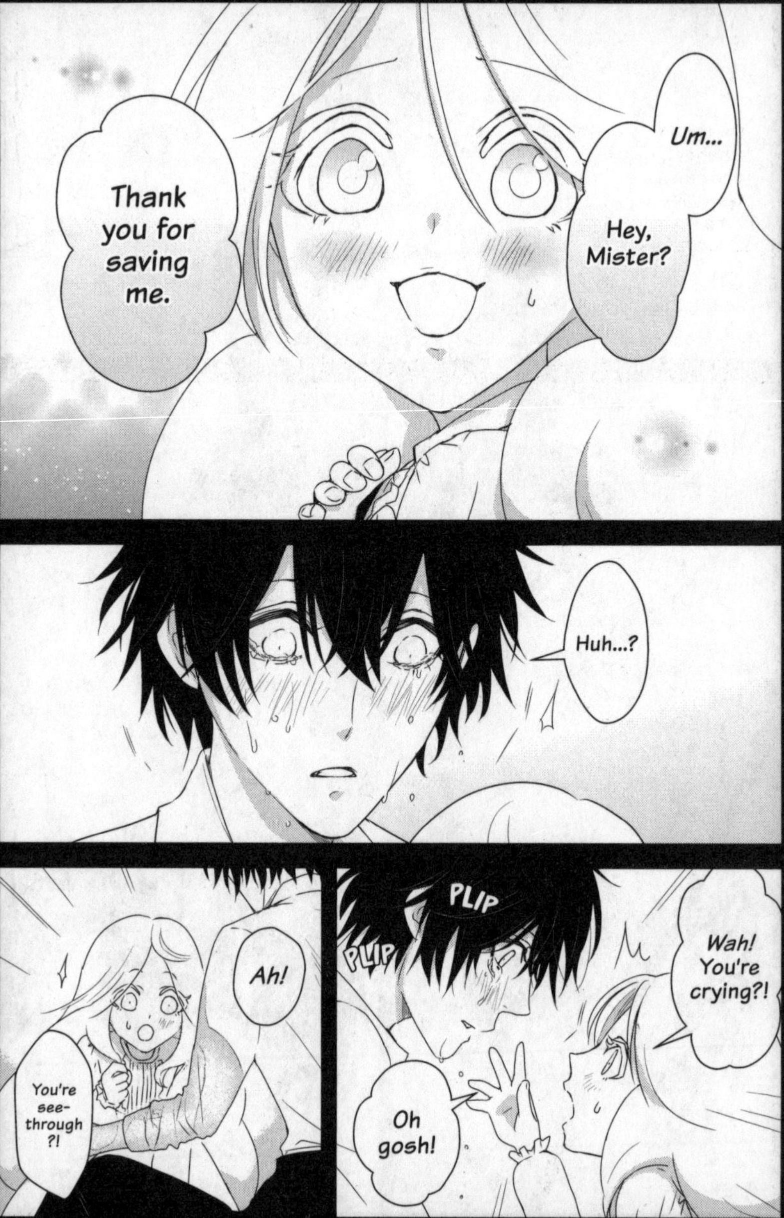
Um...
Hey, Mister?
Thank you for saving me.
Huh...?
PLIP
PLIP
Wah! You're crying?!
Oh gosh!
Ah!
You're see-through?!

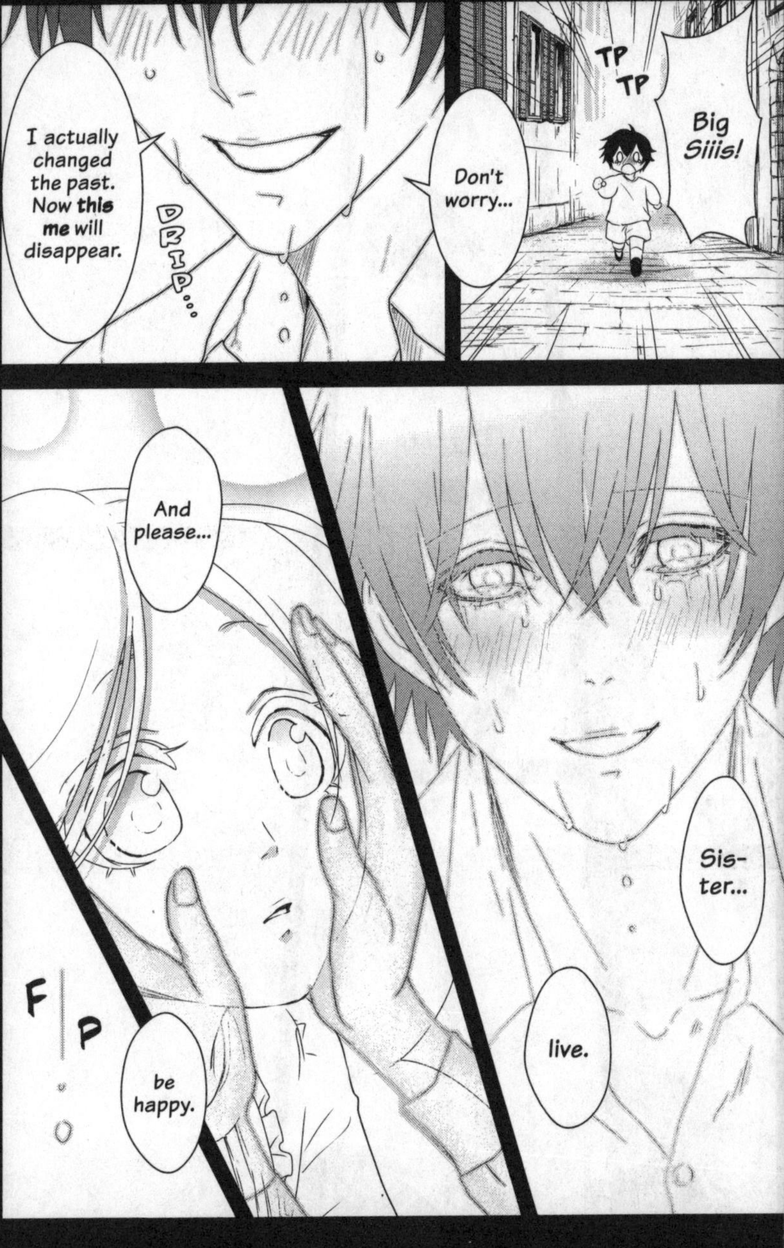
Big Siiis!
TP TP
Don't worry...
I actually changed the past. Now this me will disappear.
DRIP...
Sis-ter...
live.
And please...
be happy.
FP

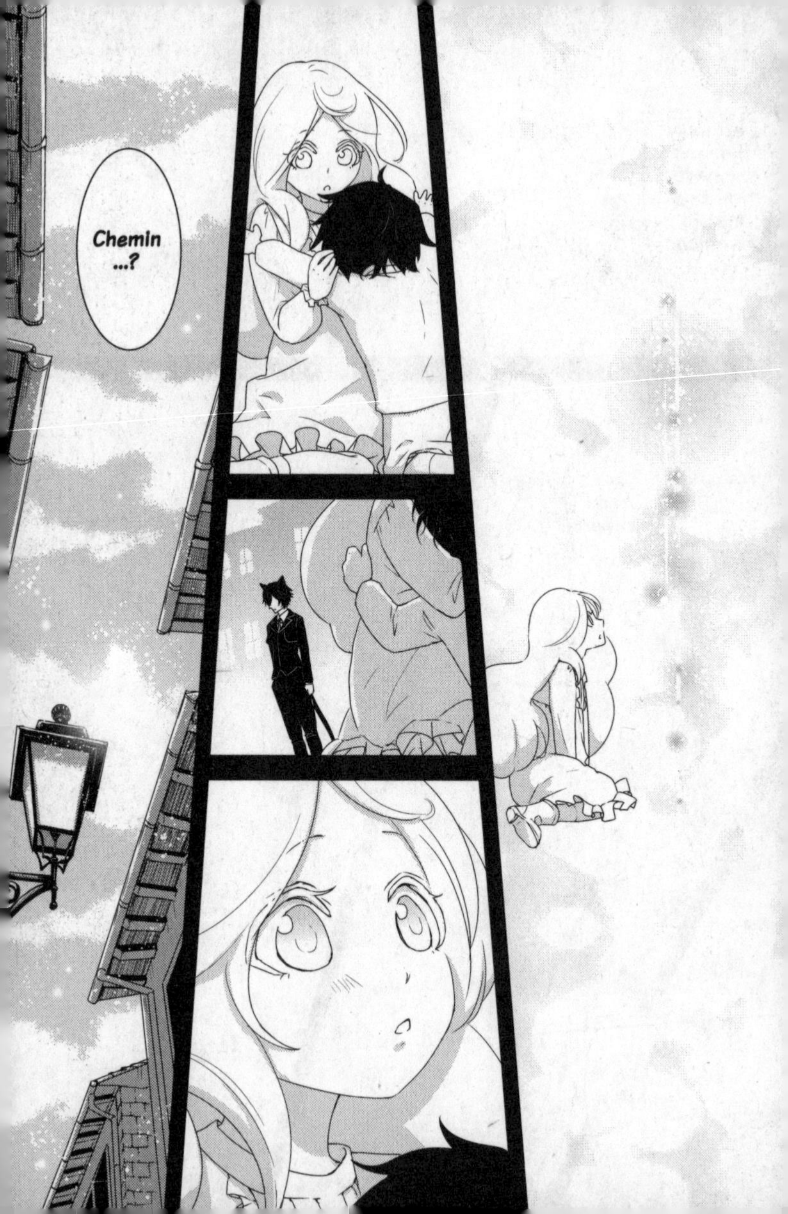
Chemin
...?

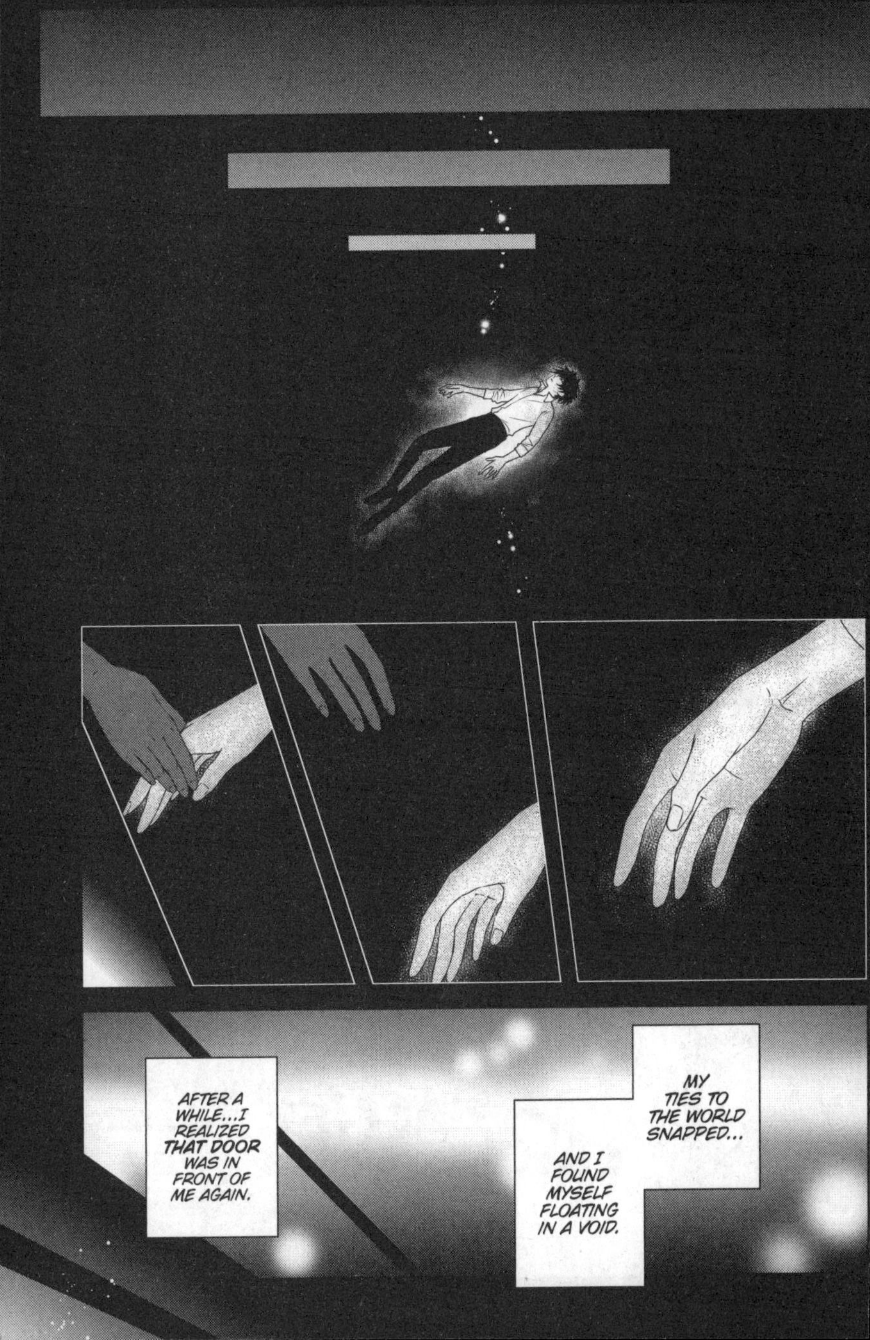
MY TIES TO THE WORLD SNAPPED...
AND I FOUND MYSELF FLOATING IN A VOID.
AFTER A WHILE...I REALIZED THAT DOOR WAS IN FRONT OF ME AGAIN.

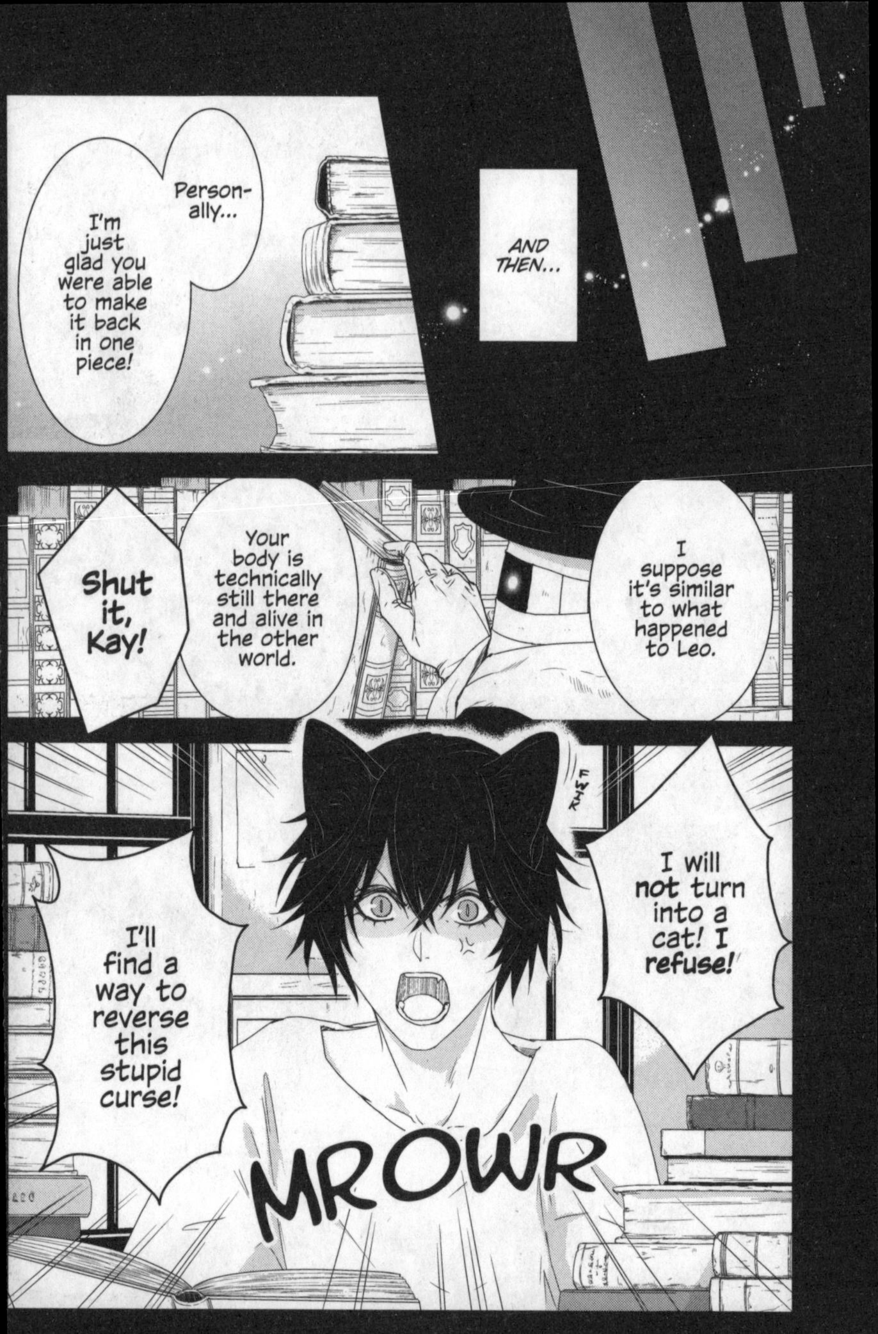
AND THEN...
Personally... I'm just glad you were able to make it back in one piece!
I suppose it's similar to what happened to Leo.
Your body is technically still there and alive in the other world.
Shut it, Kay!
I will not turn into a cat! I refuse!
I'll find a way to reverse this stupid curse!
MROWR

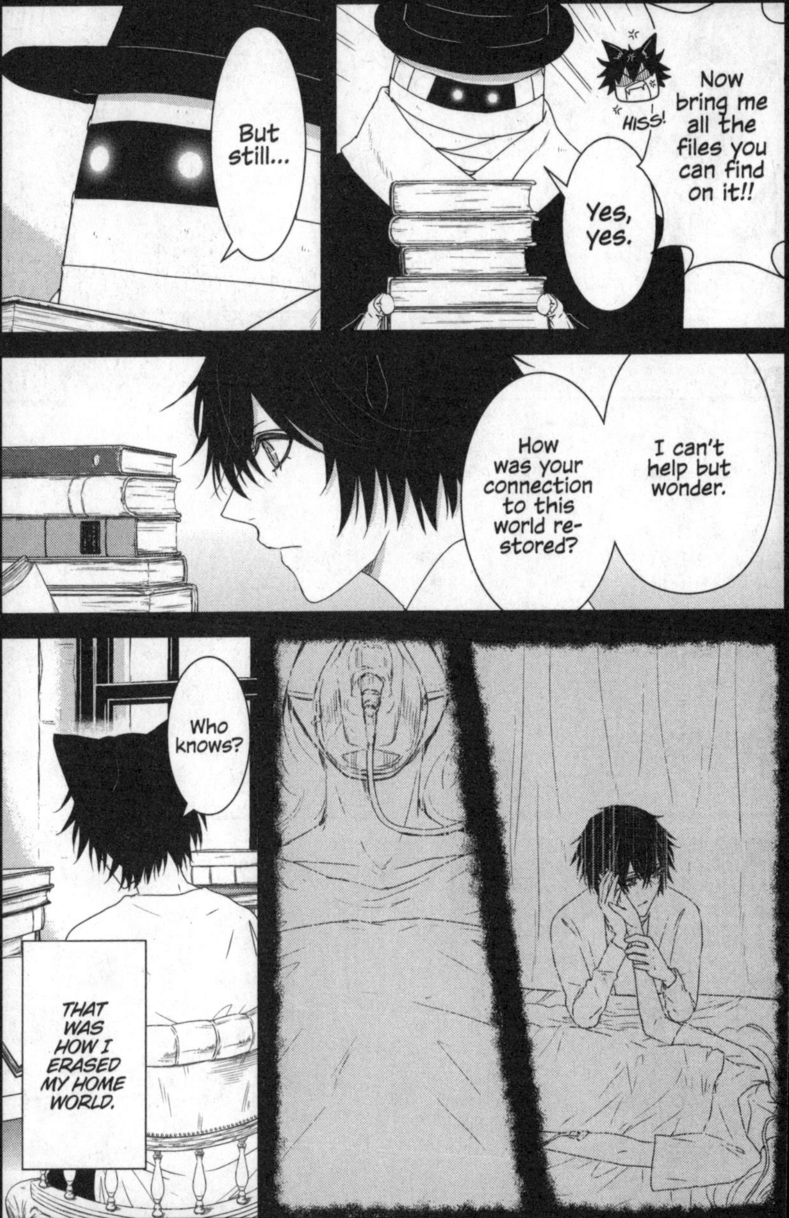
Now bring me all the files you can find on it!!
HISS!
Yes, yes.
But still...
I can't help but wonder.
How was your connection to this world re-stored?
Who knows?
THAT WAS HOW I ERASED MY HOME WORLD.

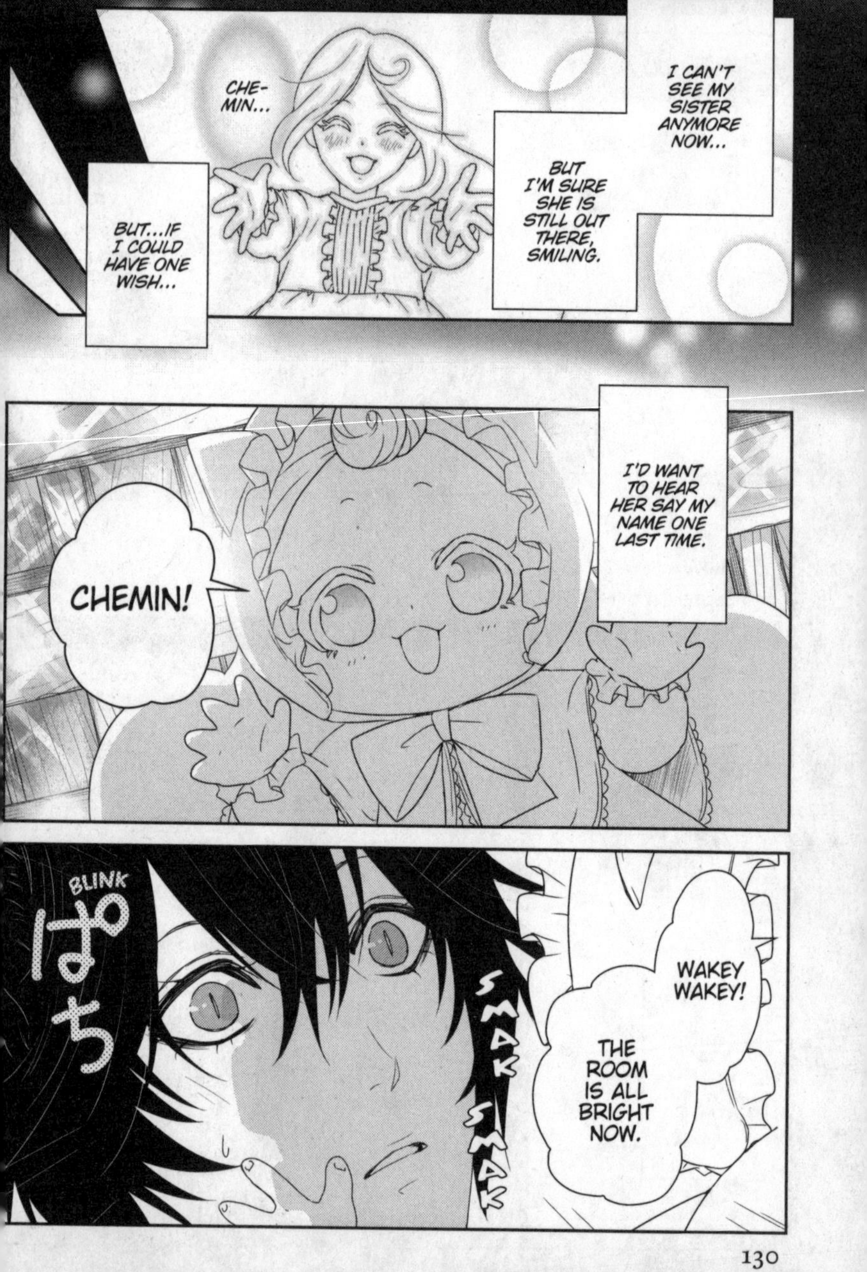
I CAN'T SEE MY SISTER ANYMORE NOW...
BUT I'M SURE SHE IS STILL OUT THERE, SMILING.
CHE-MIN...
BUT...IF I COULD HAVE ONE WISH...
I'D WANT TO HEAR HER SAY MY NAME ONE LAST TIME.
CHEMIN!
WAKEY WAKEY!
THE ROOM IS ALL BRIGHT NOW.
SMAK SMAK
BLINK
ぱち

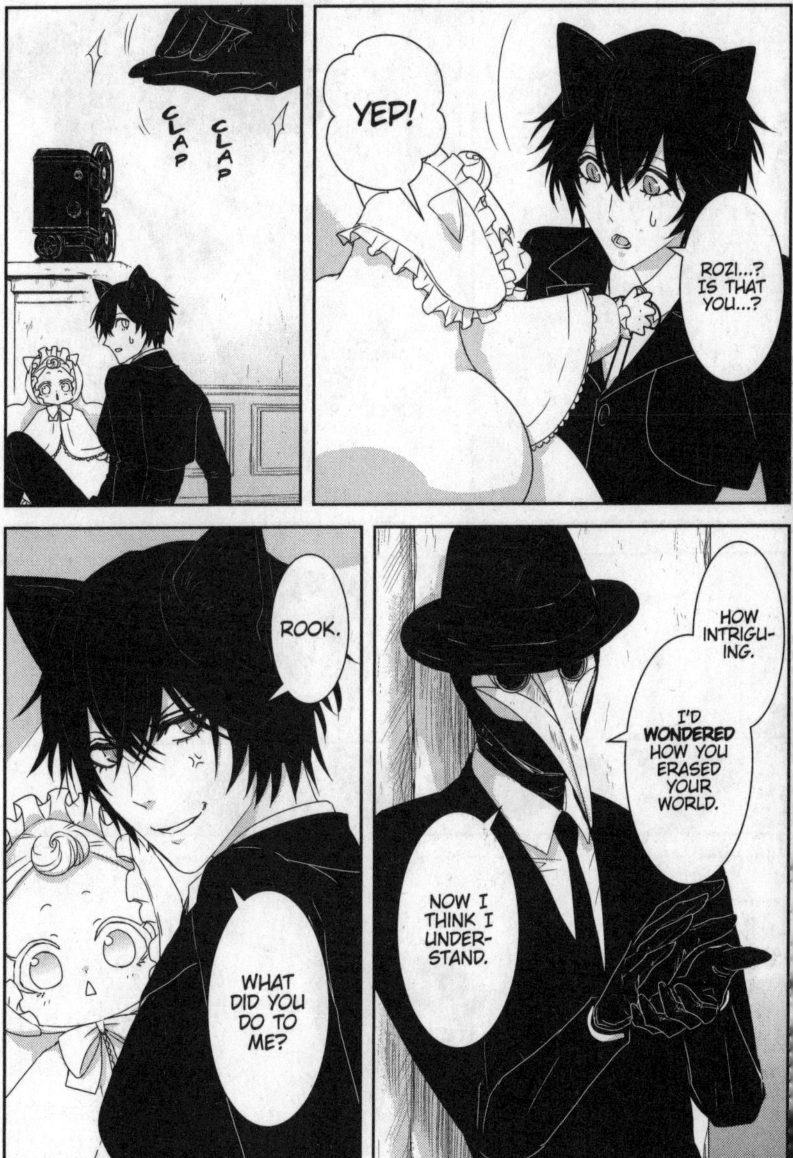
ROZI...? IS THAT YOU...?
YEP!
CLAP CLAP
HOW INTRIGUING.
I'D **WONDERED** HOW YOU ERASED YOUR WORLD.
NOW I THINK I UNDERSTAND.
ROOK.
WHAT DID YOU DO TO ME?

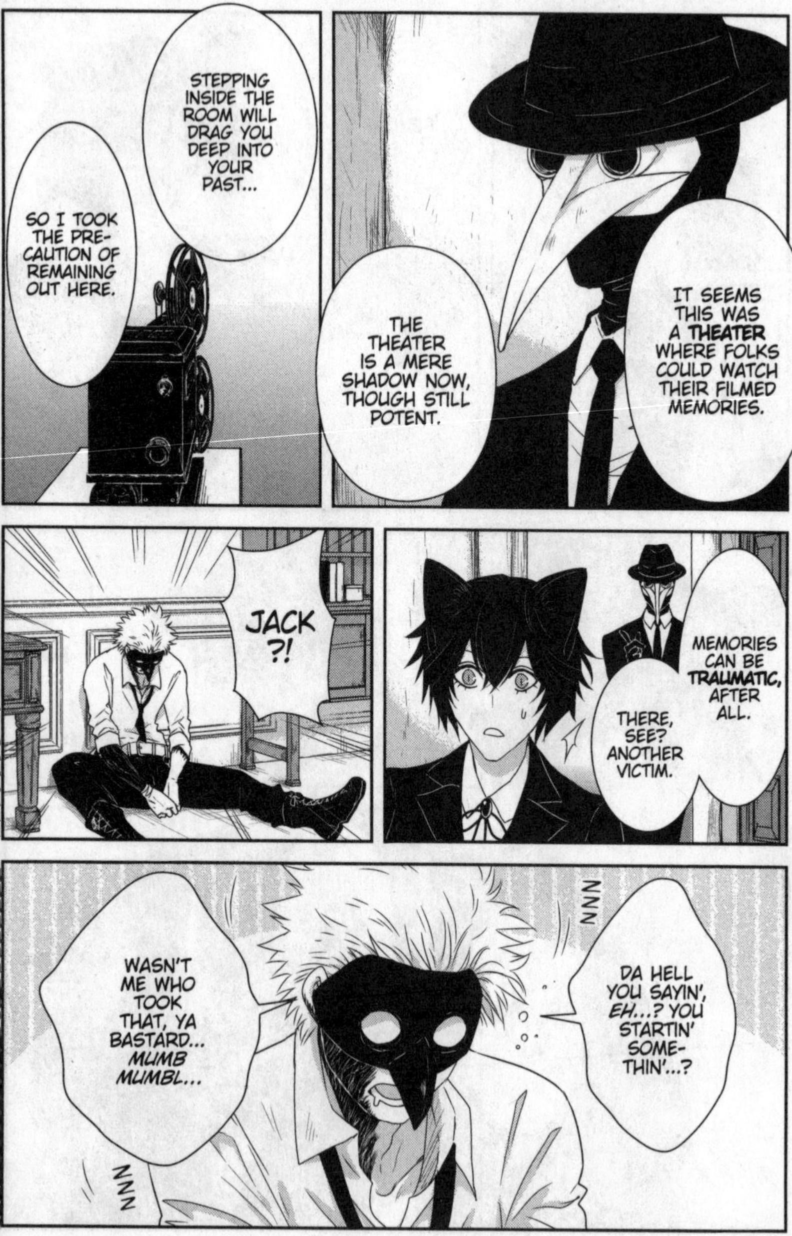
IT SEEMS THIS WAS A **THEATER** WHERE FOLKS COULD WATCH THEIR FILMED MEMORIES.
THE THEATER IS A MERE SHADOW NOW, THOUGH STILL POTENT.
STEPPING INSIDE THE ROOM WILL DRAG YOU DEEP INTO YOUR PAST...
SO I TOOK THE PRE-CAUTION OF REMAINING OUT HERE.
MEMORIES CAN BE **TRAUMATIC,** AFTER ALL.
THERE, SEE? ANOTHER VICTIM.
JACK ?!
NNN
DA HELL YOU SAYIN', *EH...?* YOU STARTIN' SOME-THIN'...?
WASN'T ME WHO TOOK THAT, YA BASTARD... *MUMB MUMBL...*
NNN

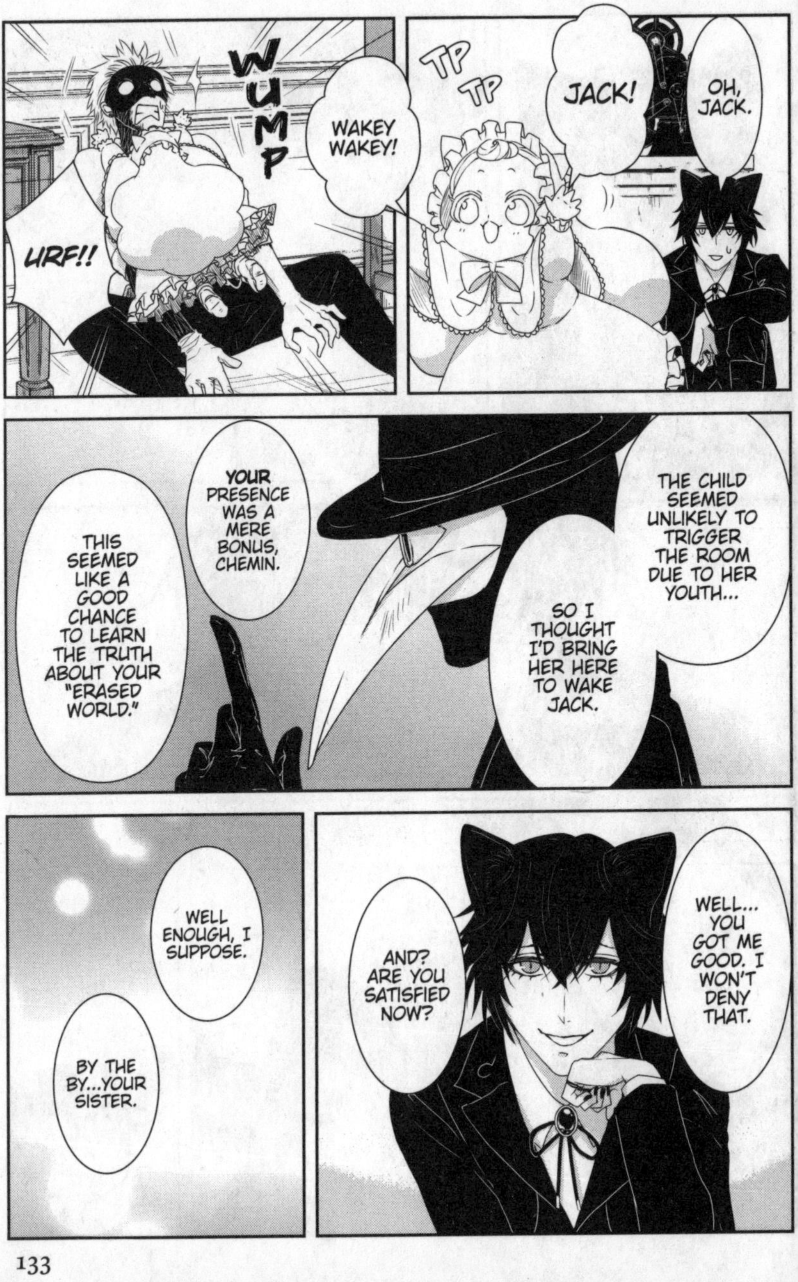
OH, JACK.
JACK!
TP TP
WAKEY WAKEY!
WUMP
URF!!
THE CHILD SEEMED UNLIKELY TO TRIGGER THE ROOM DUE TO HER YOUTH...
SO I THOUGHT I'D BRING HER HERE TO WAKE JACK.
YOUR PRESENCE WAS A MERE BONUS, CHEMIN.
THIS SEEMED LIKE A GOOD CHANCE TO LEARN THE TRUTH ABOUT YOUR "ERASED WORLD."
WELL... YOU GOT ME GOOD. I WON'T DENY THAT.
AND? ARE YOU SATISFIED NOW?
WELL ENOUGH, I SUPPOSE.
BY THE BY...YOUR SISTER.

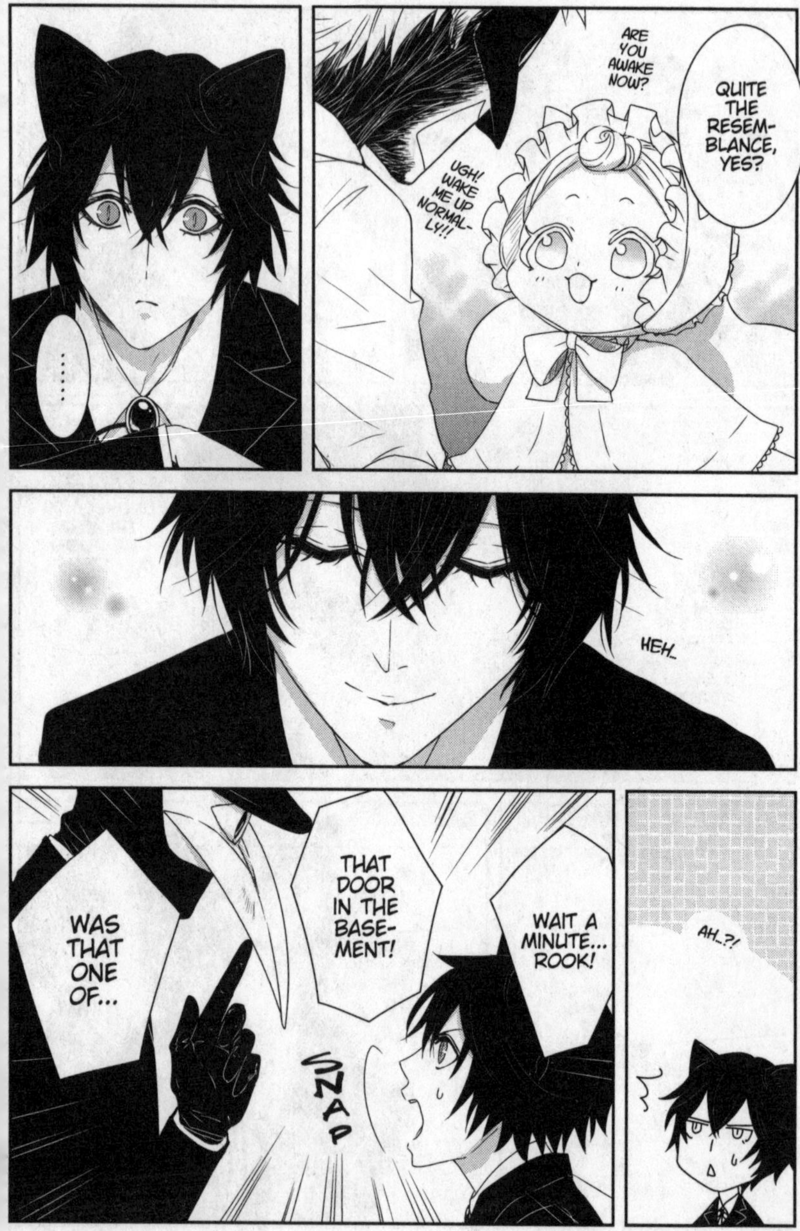
QUITE THE RESEM- BLANCE, YES?
ARE YOU AWAKE NOW?
UGH! WAKE ME UP NORMAL- LY!!
......
HEH...
AH...?!
WAIT A MINUTE... ROOK!
THAT DOOR IN THE BASE- MENT!
WAS THAT ONE OF...
SNAP

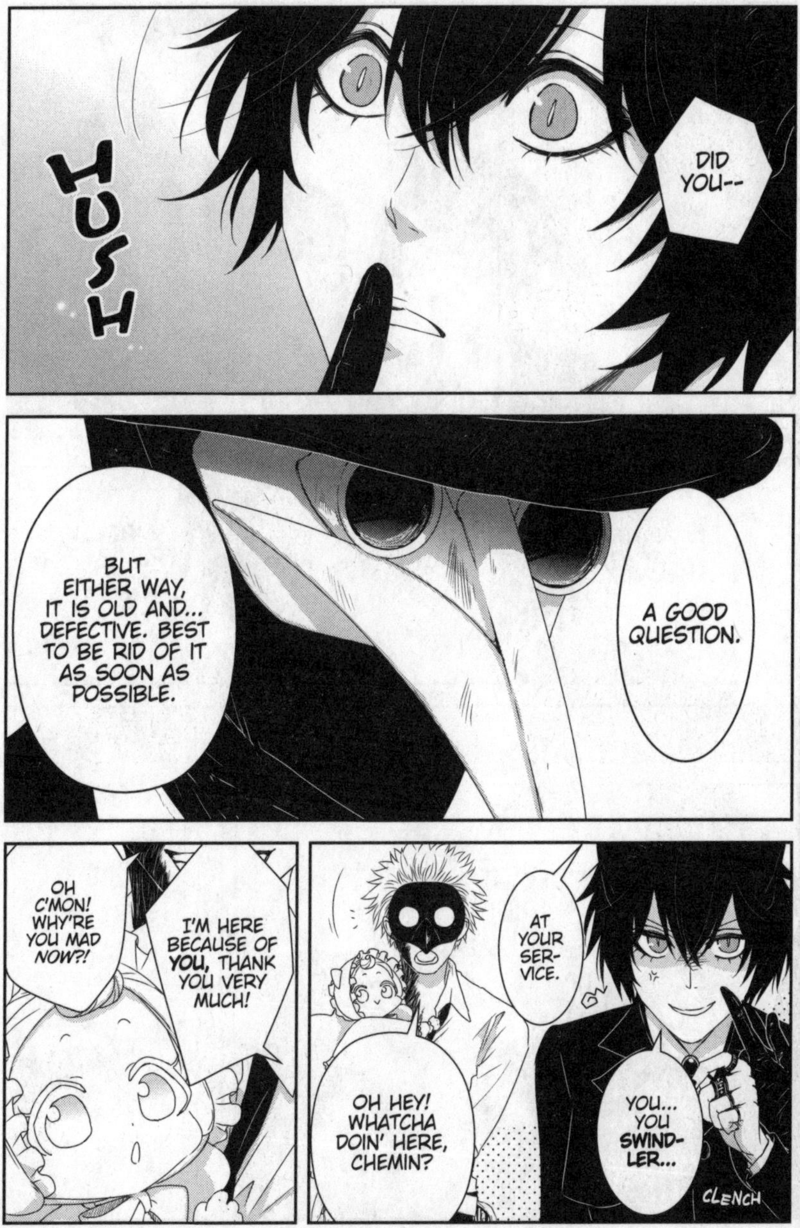
DID YOU--
HUSH
A GOOD QUESTION.
BUT EITHER WAY, IT IS OLD AND... DEFECTIVE. BEST TO BE RID OF IT AS SOON AS POSSIBLE.
AT YOUR SER-VICE.
YOU... YOU SWINDLER...
CLENCH
OH HEY! WHATCHA DOIN' HERE, CHEMIN?
I'M HERE BECAUSE OF **YOU**, THANK YOU VERY MUCH!
OH C'MON! WHY'RE YOU MAD NOW?!

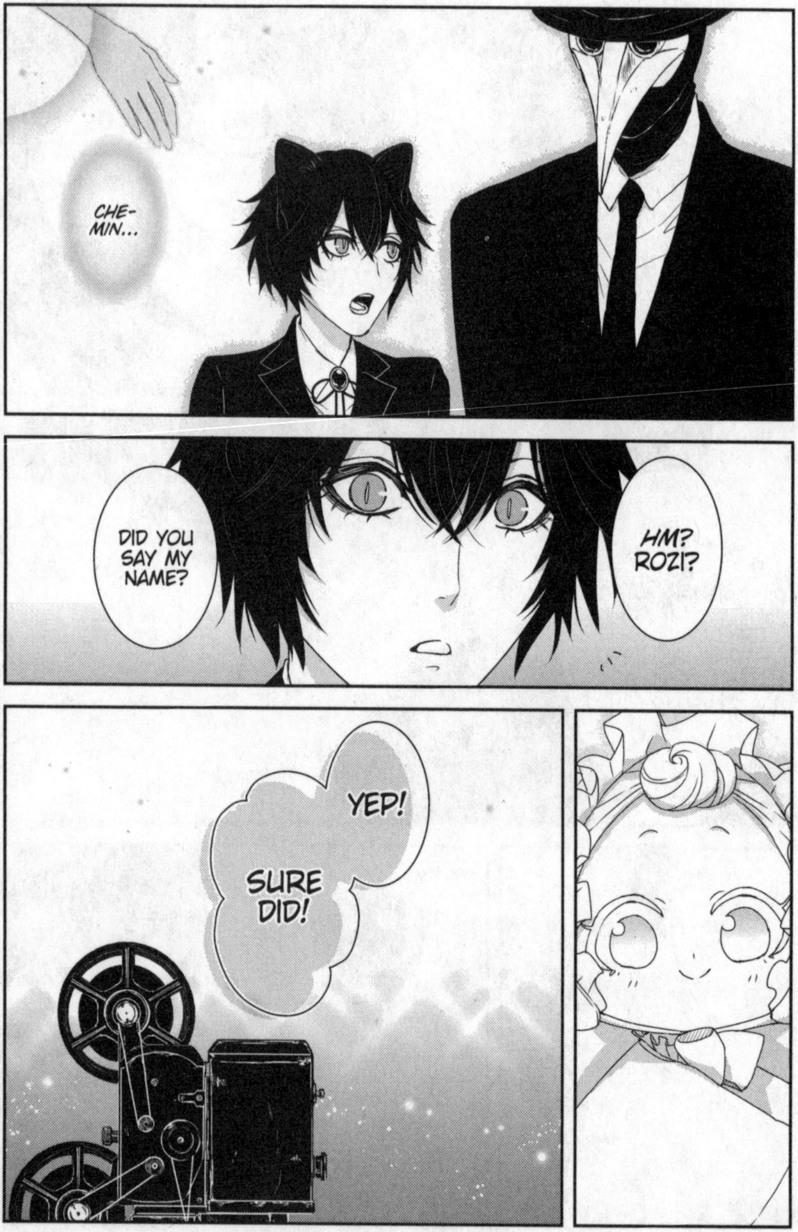
CHE-MIN...
HM? ROZI?
DID YOU SAY MY NAME?
YEP!
SURE DID!

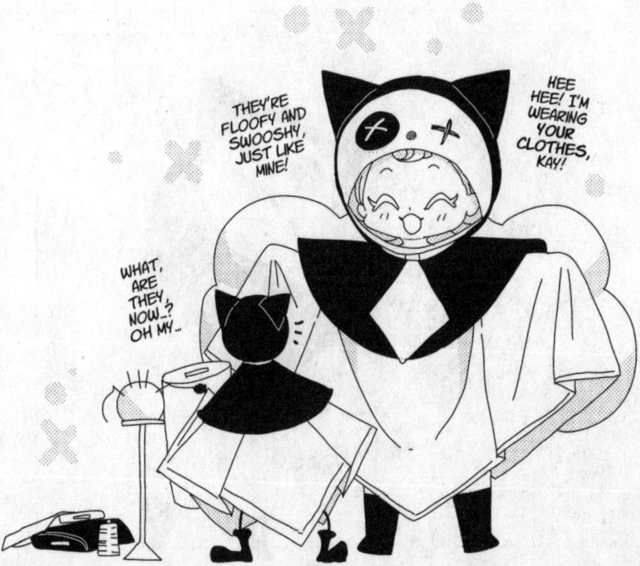
HEE HEE! I'M WEARING YOUR CLOTHES, KAY!
THEY'RE FLOOFY AND SWOOSHY, JUST LIKE MINE!
WHAT, ARE THEY, NOW...? OH MY...

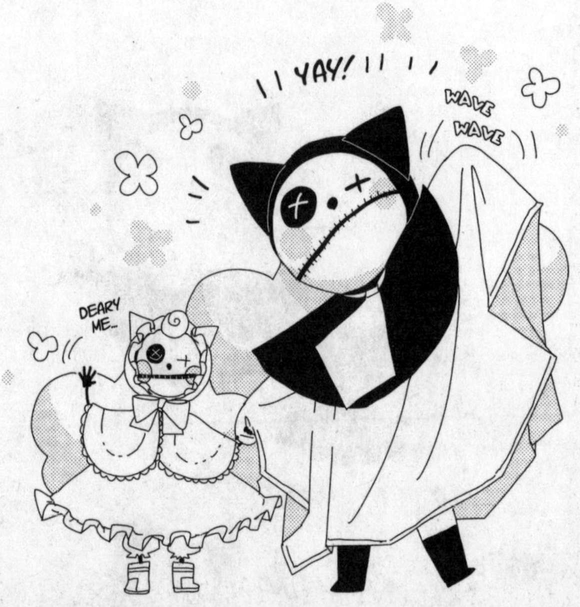
YAY!
WAVE WAVE
DEARY ME...

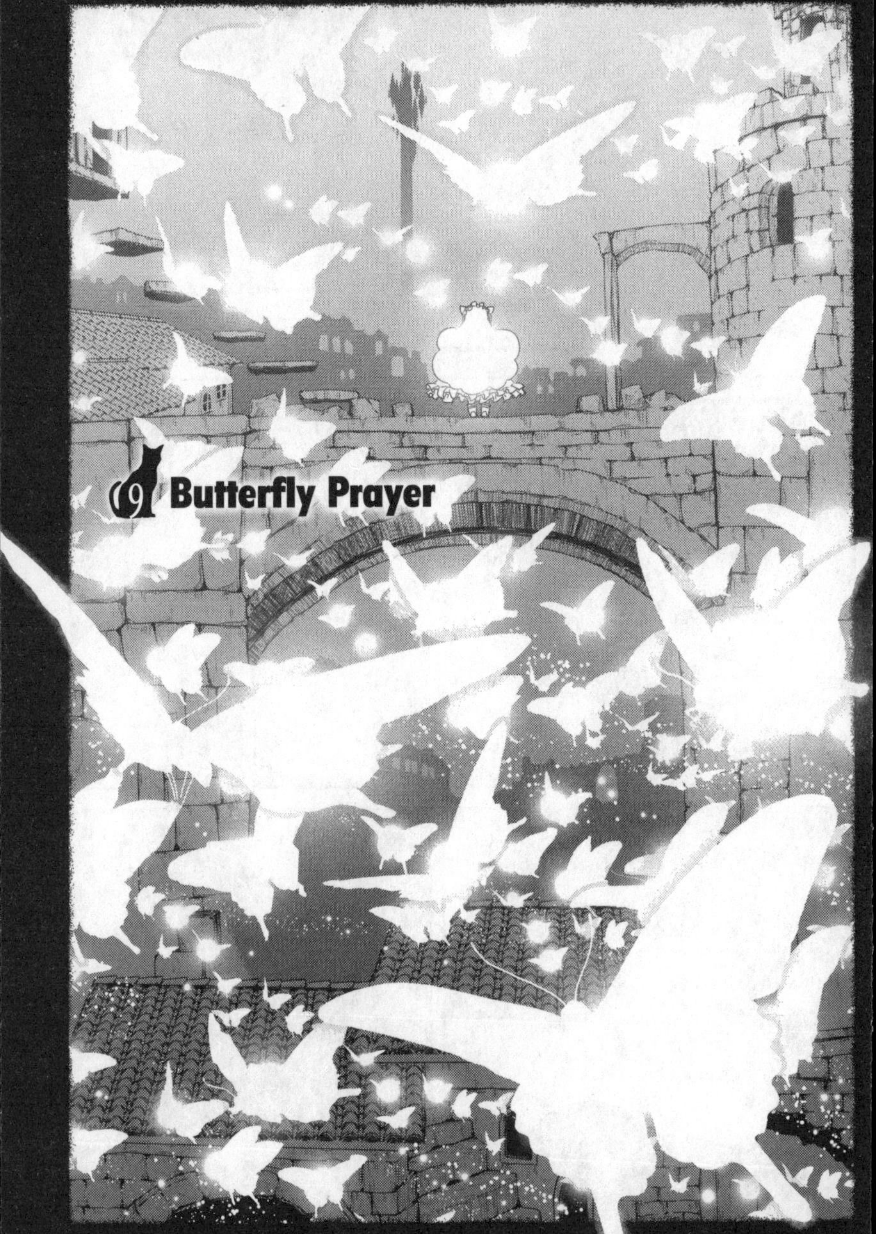
9 Butterfly Prayer

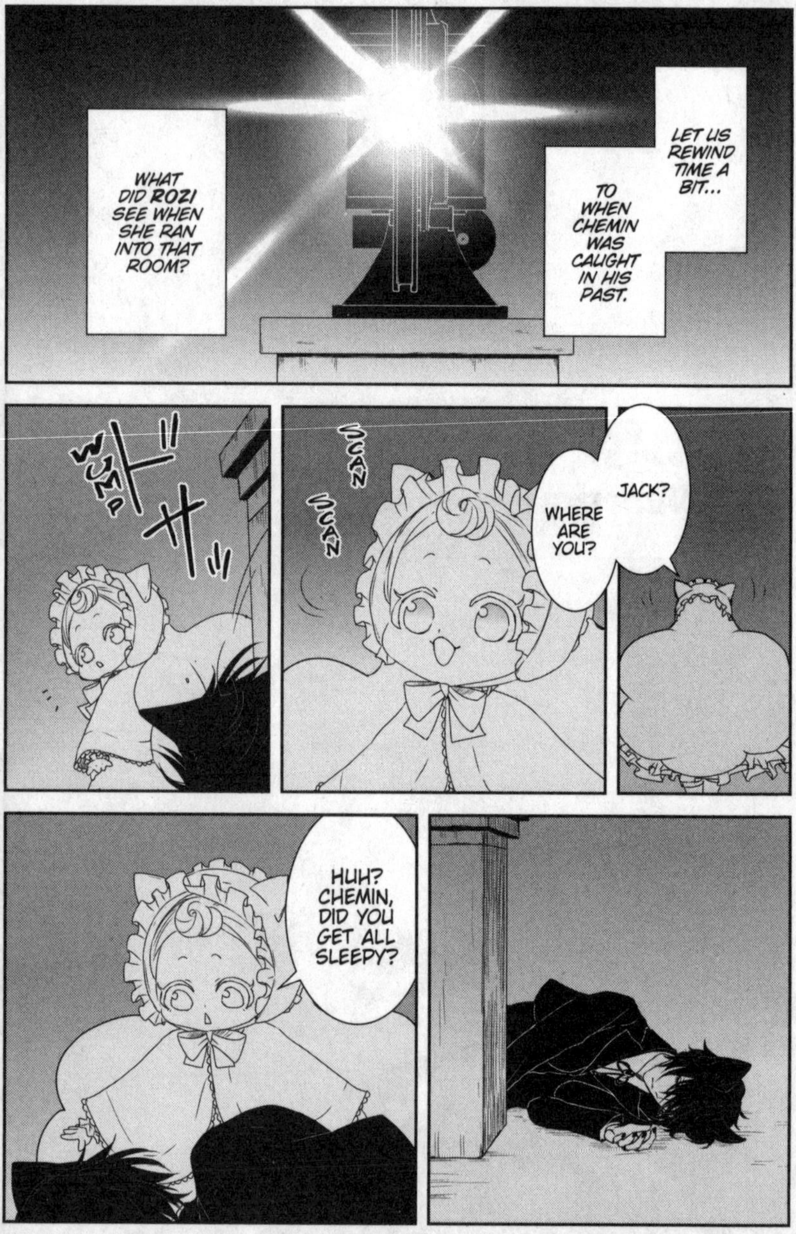
LET US REWIND TIME A BIT...
TO WHEN CHEMIN WAS CAUGHT IN HIS PAST.
WHAT DID ROZI SEE WHEN SHE RAN INTO THAT ROOM?
JACK?
WHERE ARE YOU?
SCAN
SCAN
WUMP
HUH? CHEMIN, DID YOU GET ALL SLEEPY?

OME...
FWIF
HUH?
WANT TO GO HOME.
WANT TO GO BACK.
BACK TO MY WORLD...
BACK TO MY REAL FORM.
SHIMMER

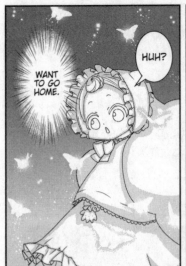

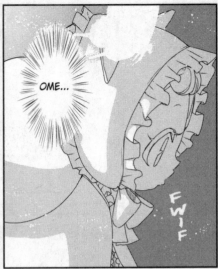

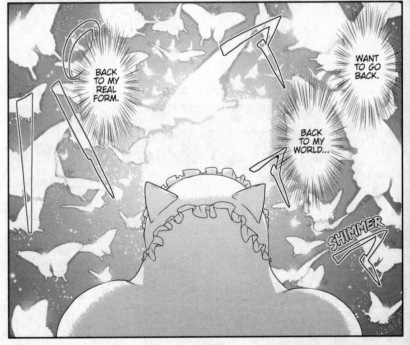

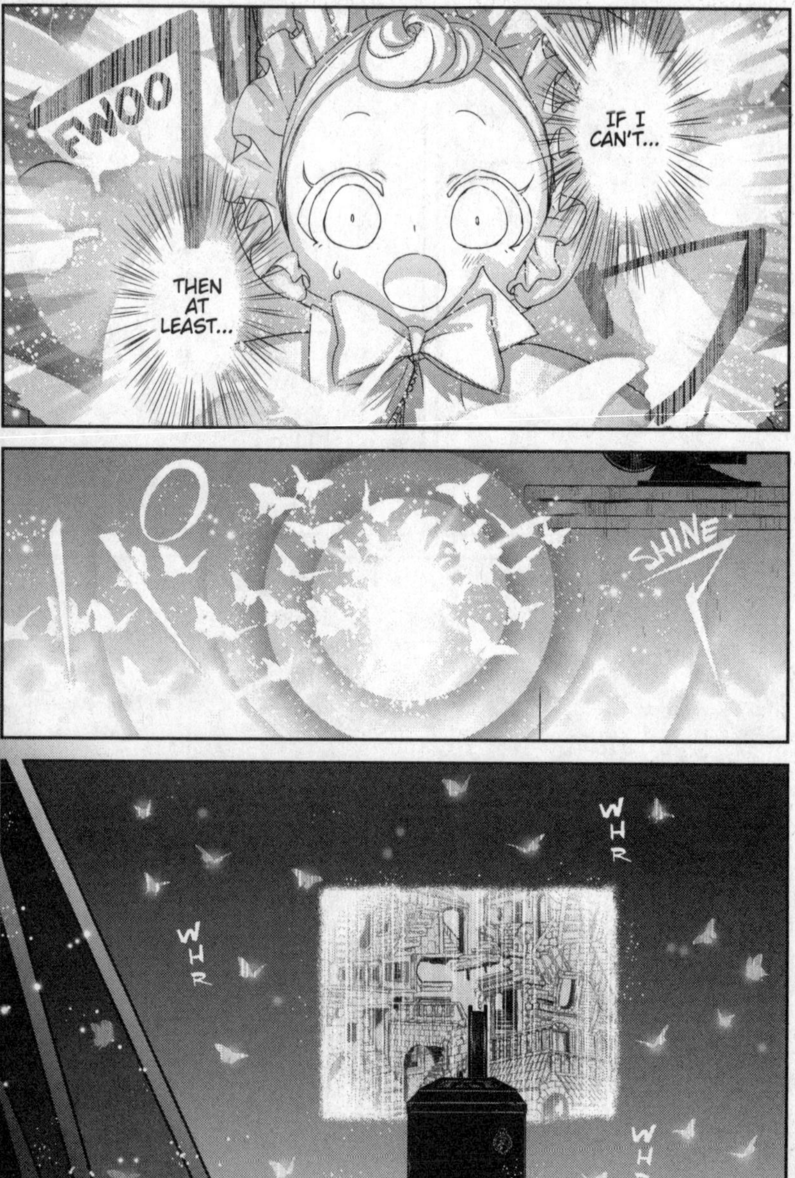
IF I CAN'T...
FWOO
THEN AT LEAST...
SHINE
WHR
WHR
WHR

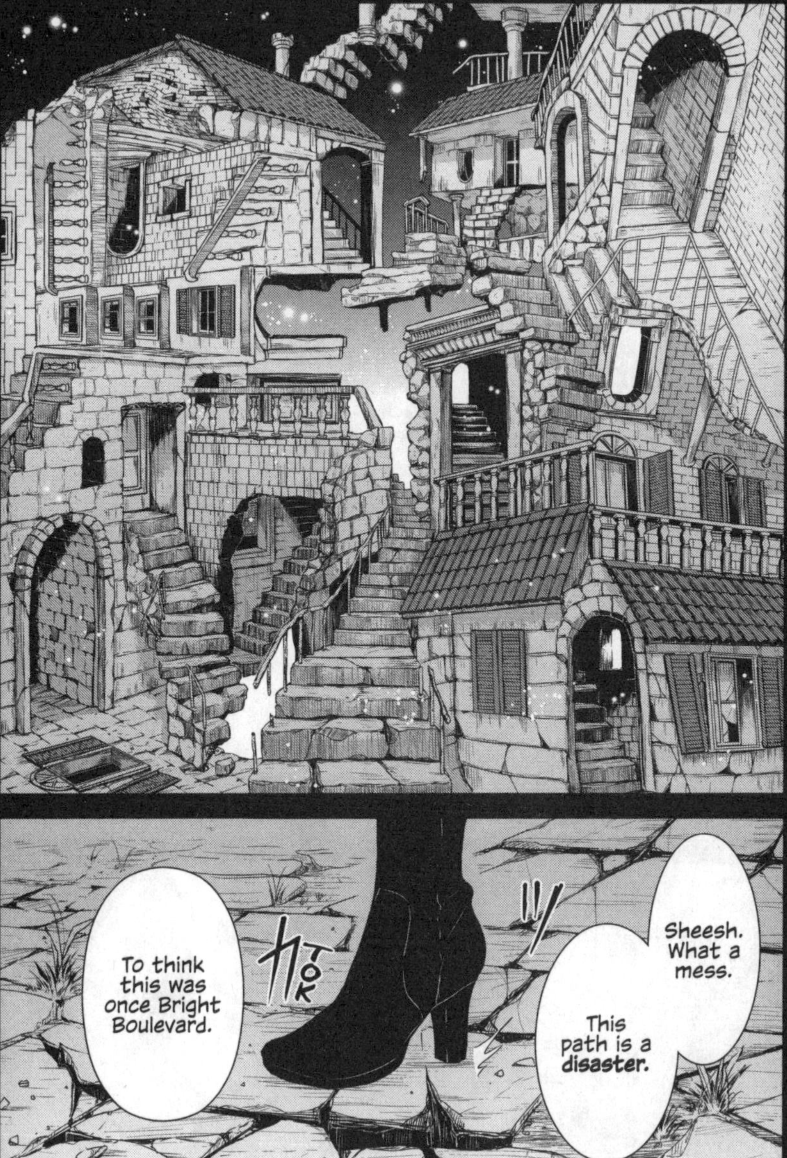
Sheesh. What a mess.
This path is a disaster.
TOK
To think this was once Bright Boulevard.

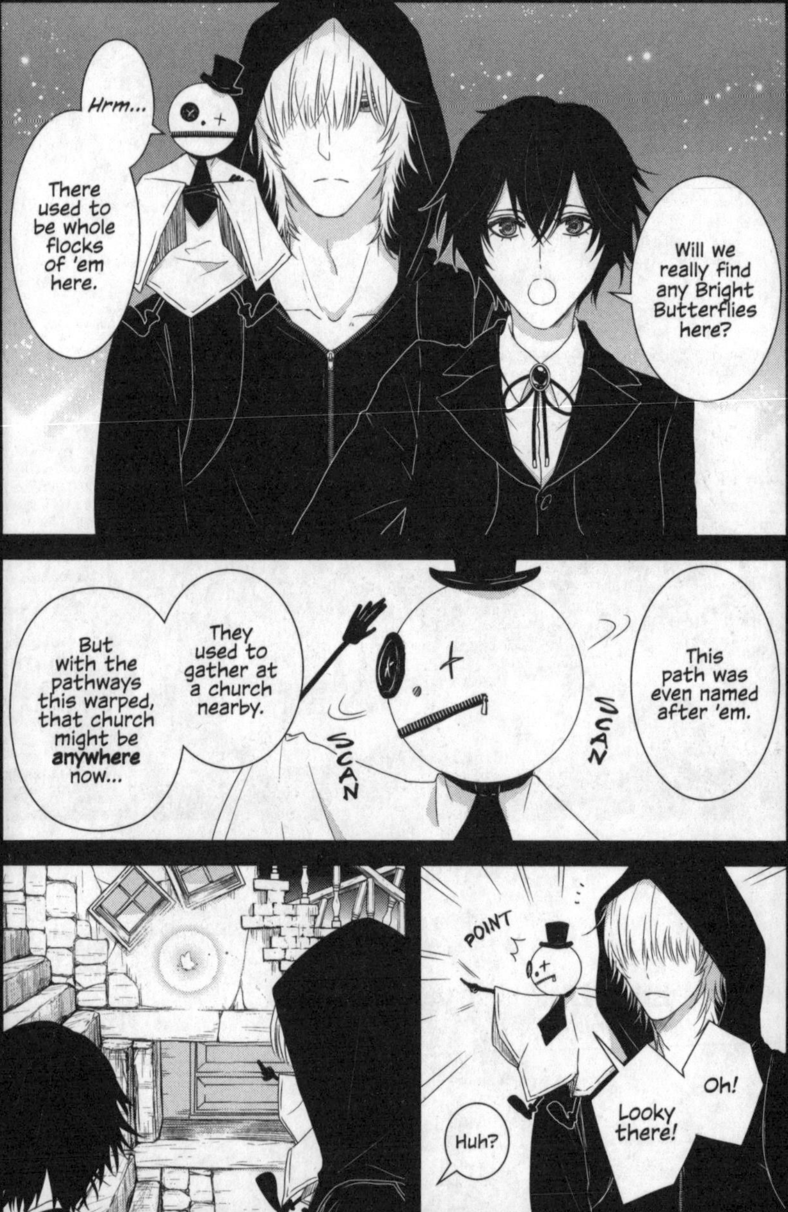
Will we really find any Bright Butterflies here?
Hrm...
There used to be whole flocks of 'em here.
This path was even named after 'em.
SCAN
SCAN
They used to gather at a church nearby.
But with the pathways this warped, that church might be **anywhere** now...
POINT
Oh!
Looky there!
Huh?

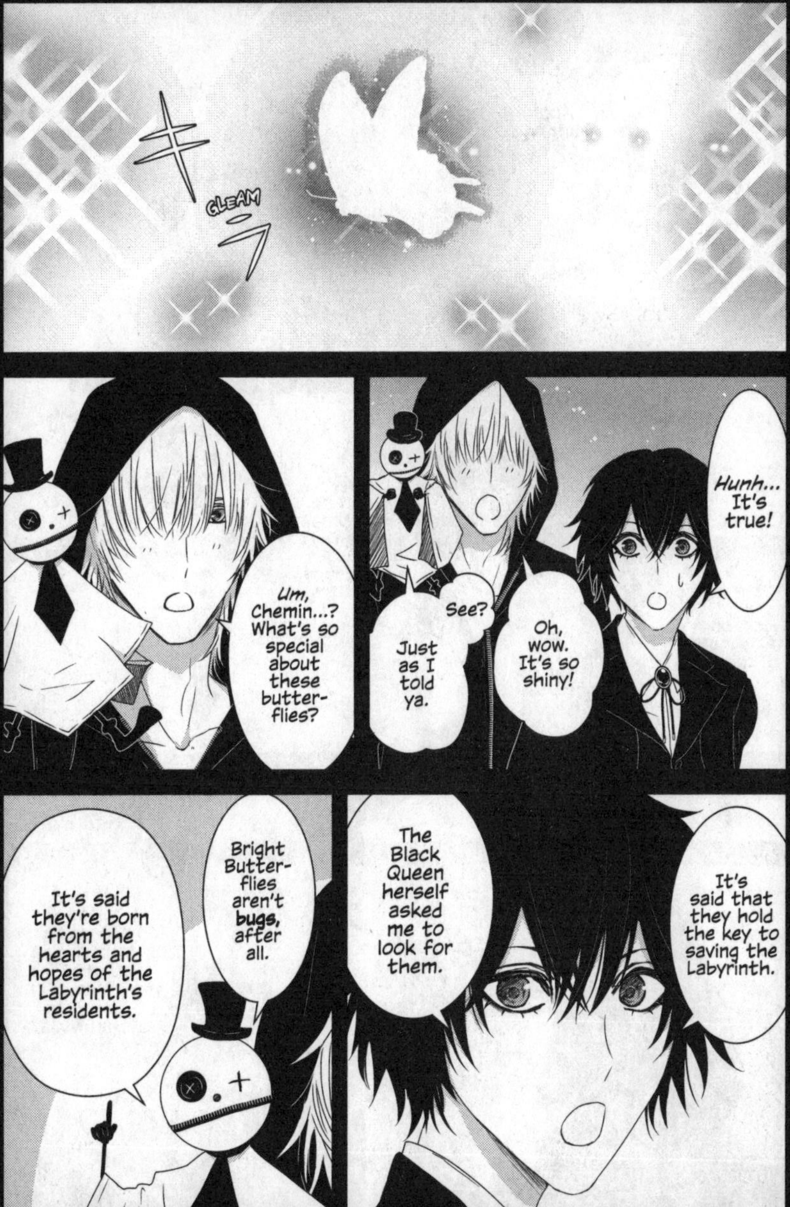
GLEAM
Hunh... It's true!
See?
Just as I told ya.
Oh, wow. It's so shiny!
Um, Chemin...? What's so special about these butterflies?
It's said that they hold the key to saving the Labyrinth.
The Black Queen herself asked me to look for them.
Bright Butterflies aren't **bugs**, after all.
It's said they're born from the hearts and hopes of the Labyrinth's residents.

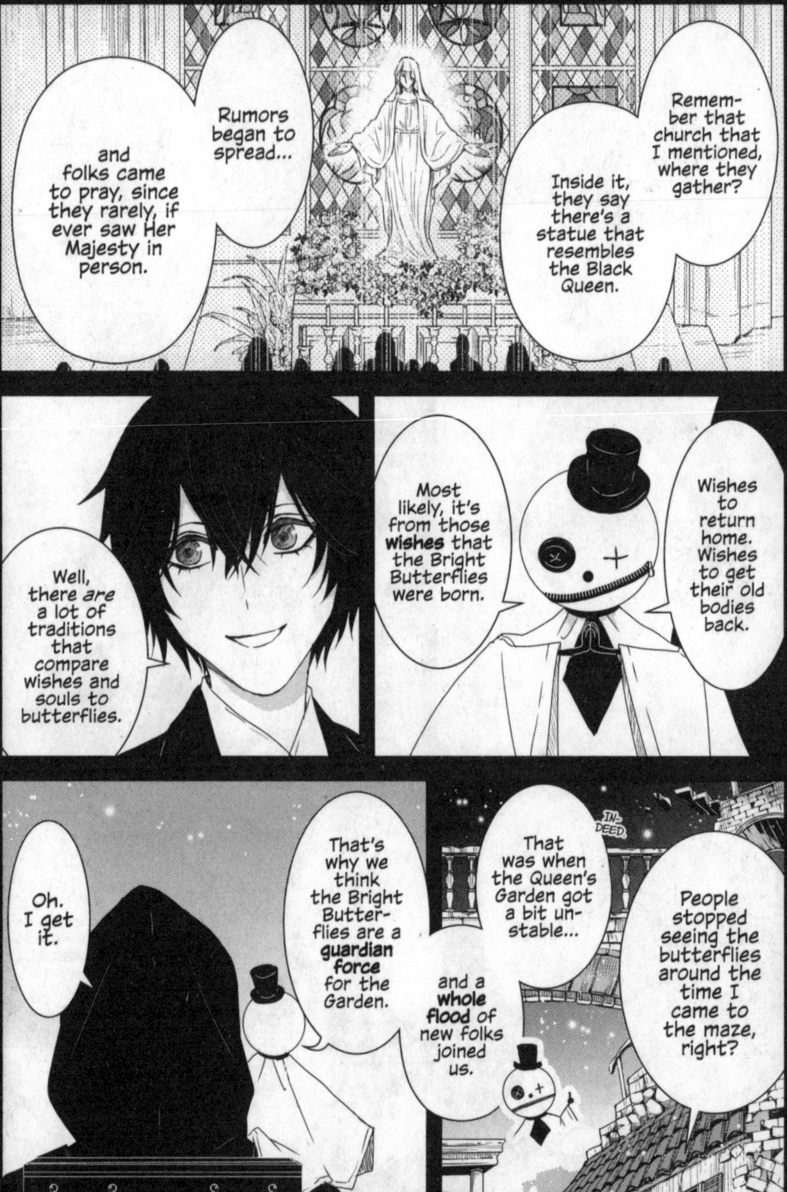
Remember that church that I mentioned, where they gather?
Inside it, they say there's a statue that resembles the Black Queen.
Rumors began to spread...
and folks came to pray, since they rarely, if ever saw Her Majesty in person.
Wishes to return home. Wishes to get their old bodies back.
Most likely, it's from those **wishes** that the Bright Butterflies were born.
Well, there *are* a lot of traditions that compare wishes and souls to butterflies.
People stopped seeing the butterflies around the time I came to the maze, right?
IN-DEED.
That was when the Queen's Garden got a bit unstable...
and a **whole flood** of new folks joined us.
That's why we think the Bright Butterflies are a **guardian force** for the Garden.
Oh. I get it.

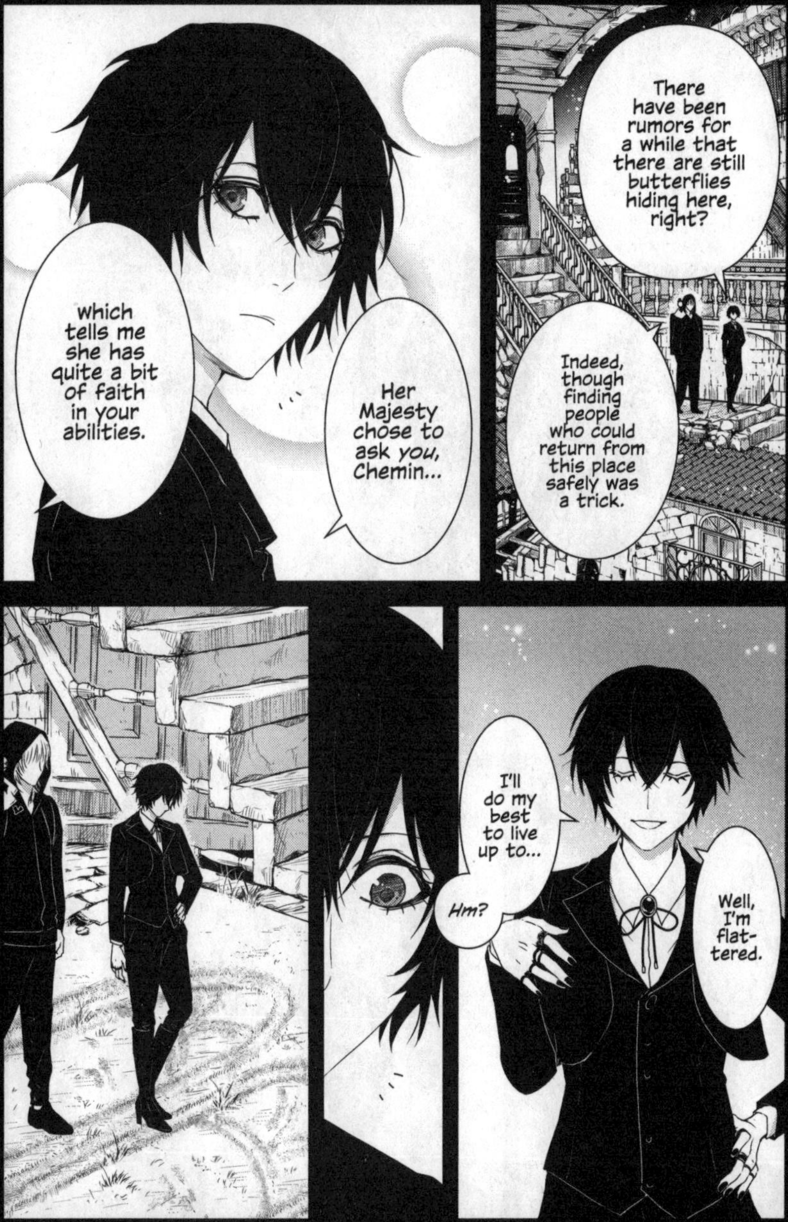
There have been rumors for a while that there are still butterflies hiding here, right?
Indeed, though finding people who could return from this place safely was a trick.
Her Majesty chose to ask *you*, Chemin...
which tells me she has quite a bit of faith in your abilities.
Well, I'm flat-tered.
I'll do my best to live up to...
Hm?

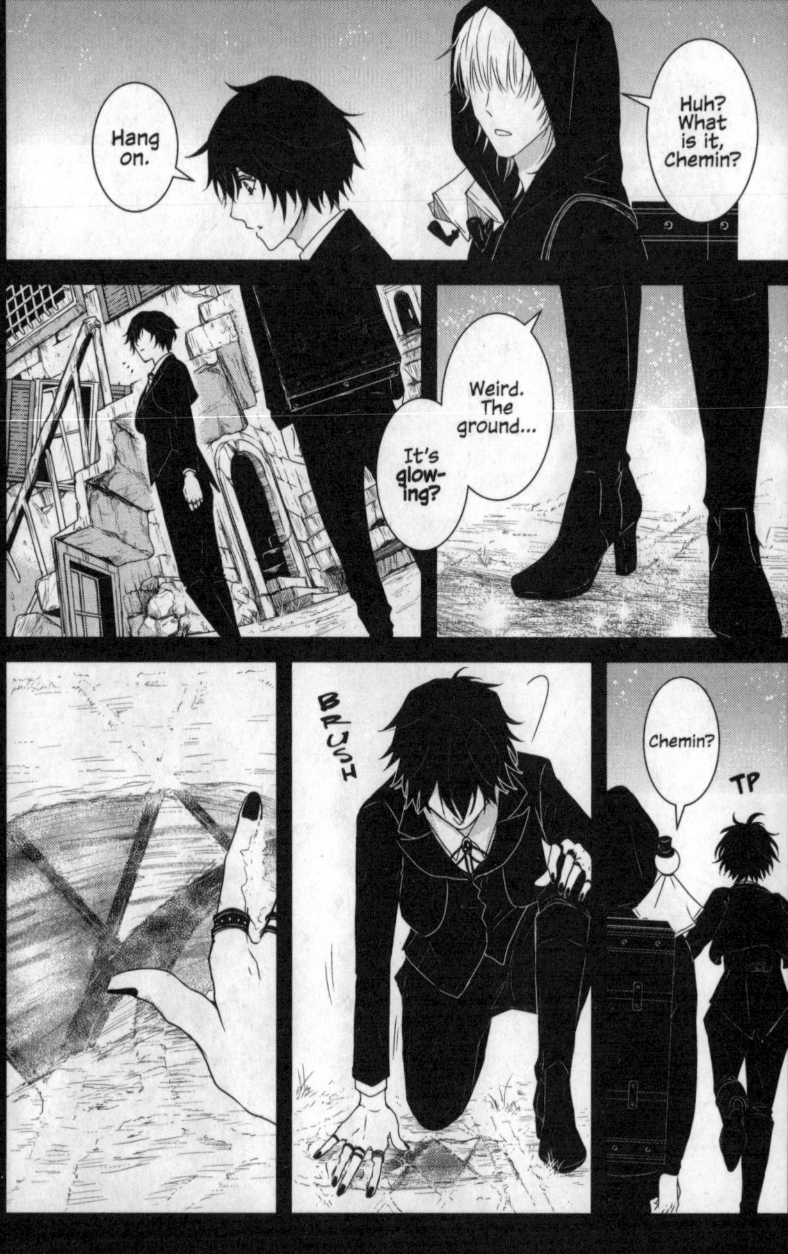
Huh? What is it, Chemin?
Hang on.
Weird. The ground...
It's glow-ing?
Chemin?
TP
BRUSH

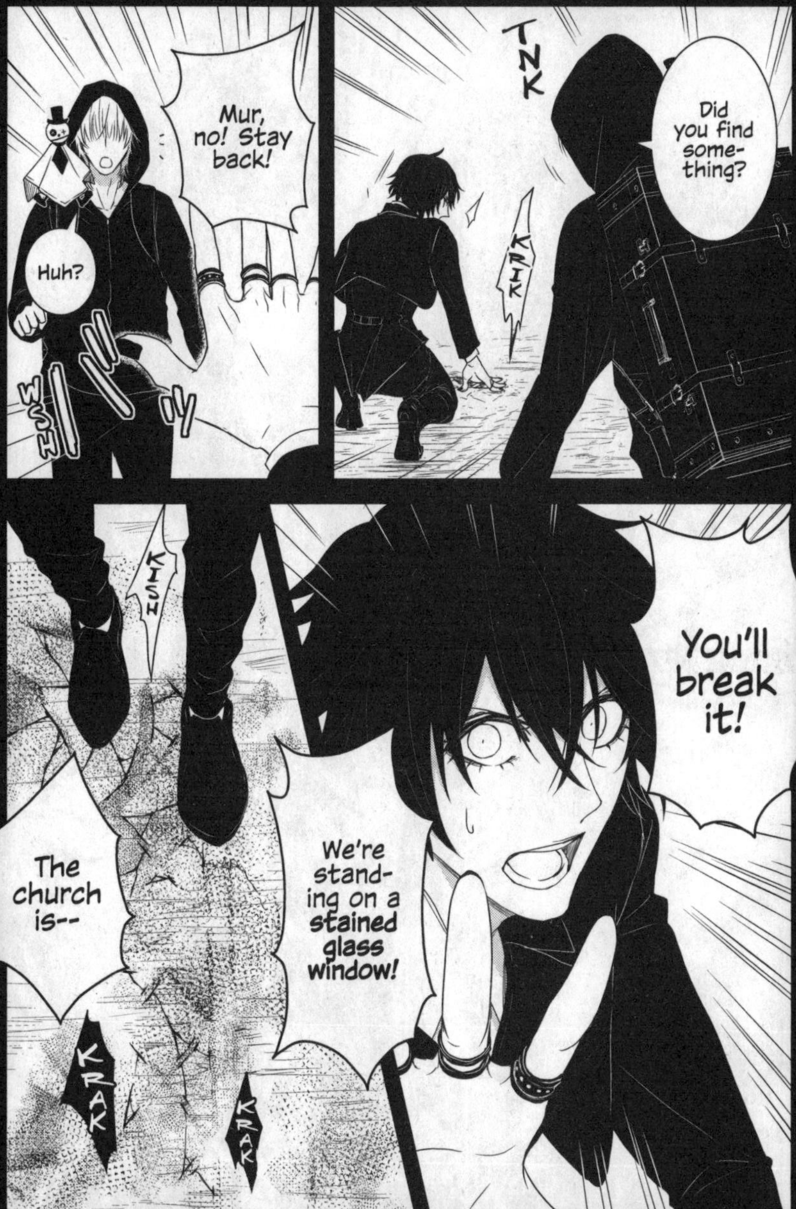
Did you find something?
TNK
KRIK
Mur, no! Stay back!
Huh?
WSH
You'll break it!
We're standing on a stained glass window!
KISH
The church is--
KRAK
KRAK

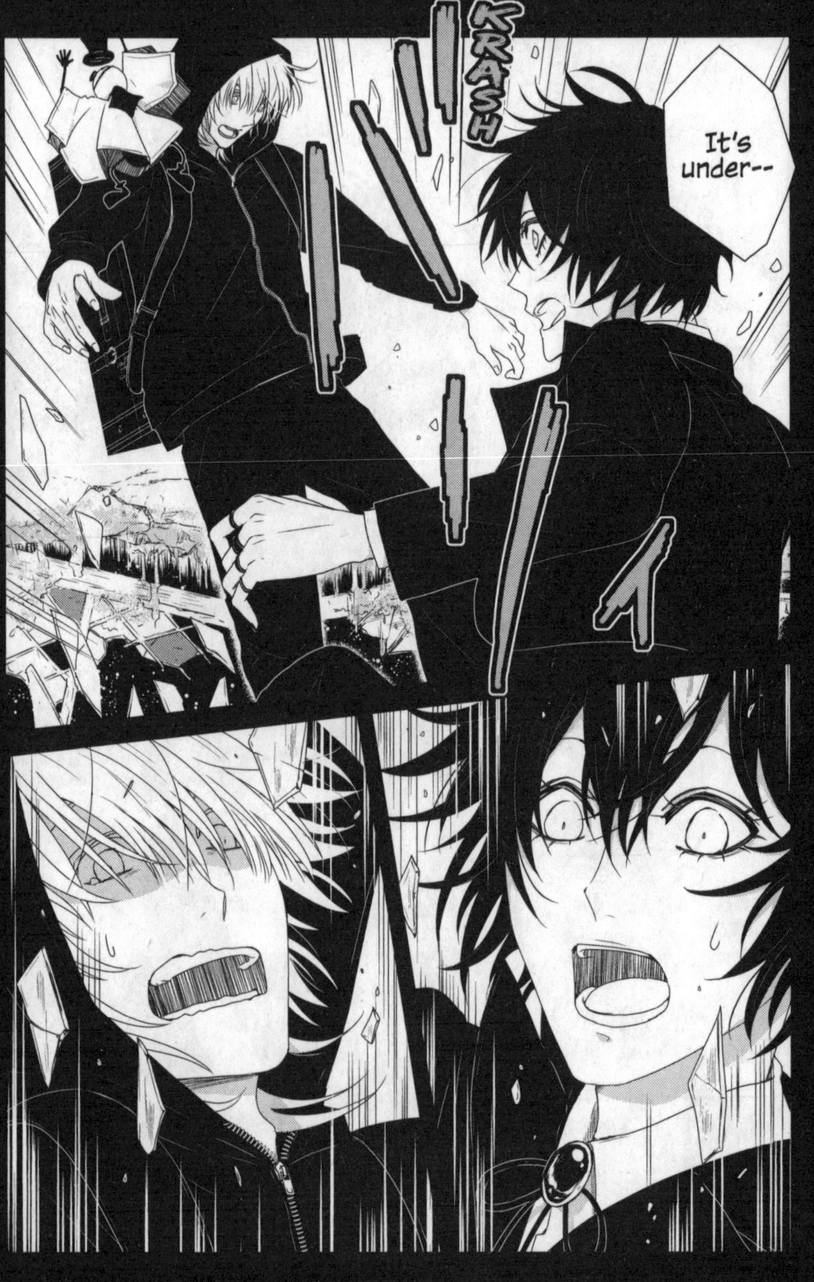
It's under--
KRASH

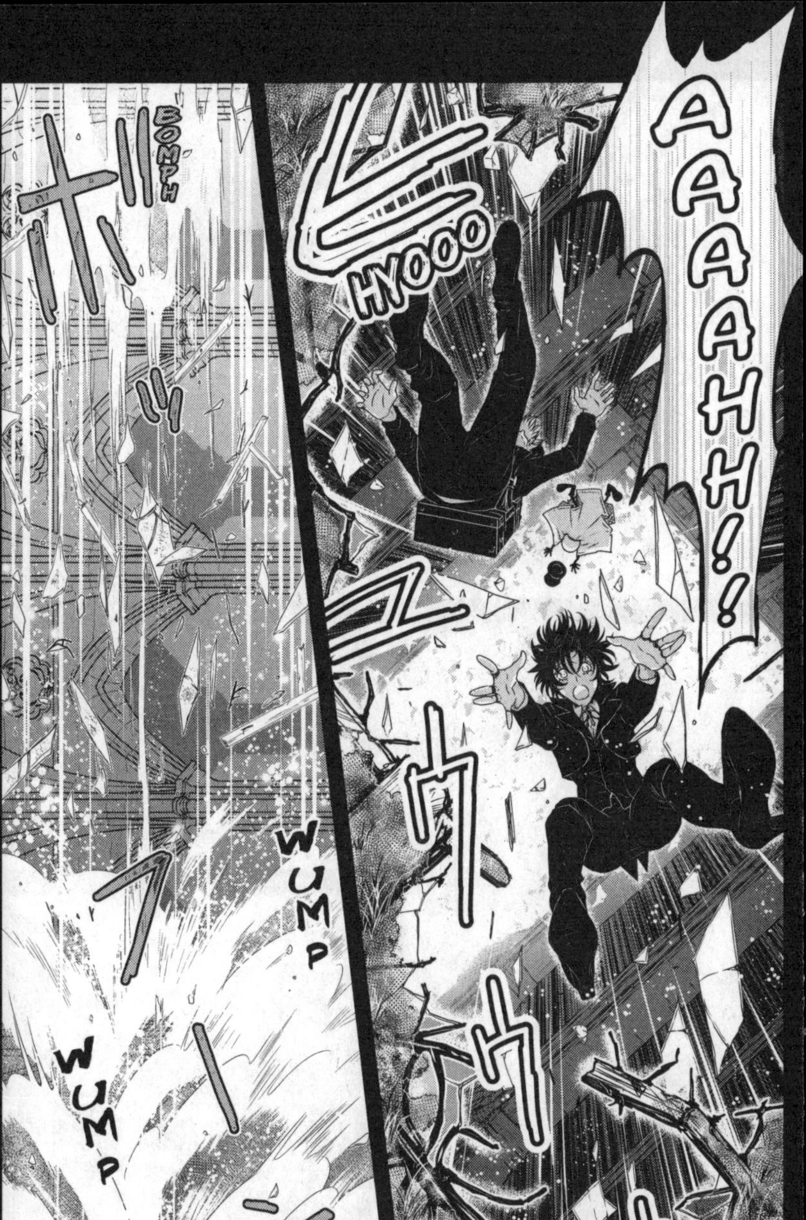
AAAAHH!!
HYOOO
BOMPH
WUMP
WUMP

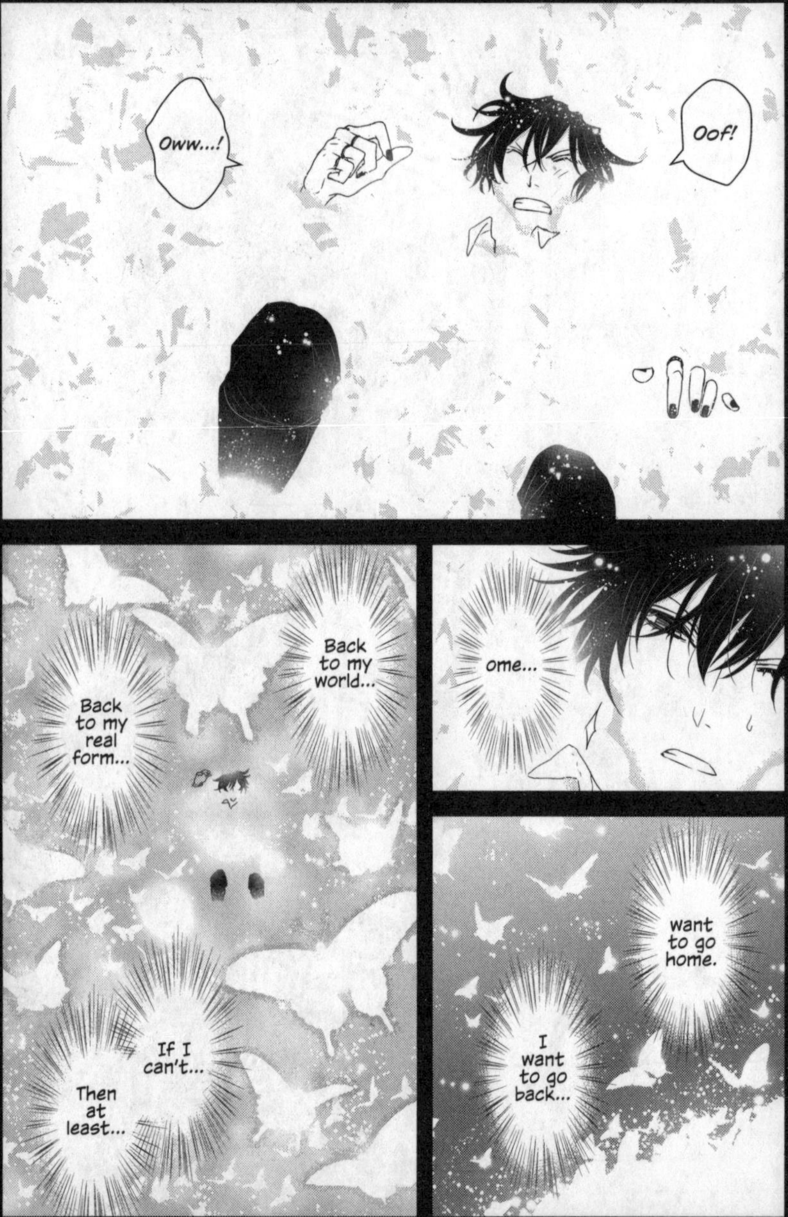

Oof!
Oww...!
ome...
want to go home.
I want to go back...
Back to my world...
Back to my real form...
If I can't...
Then at least...

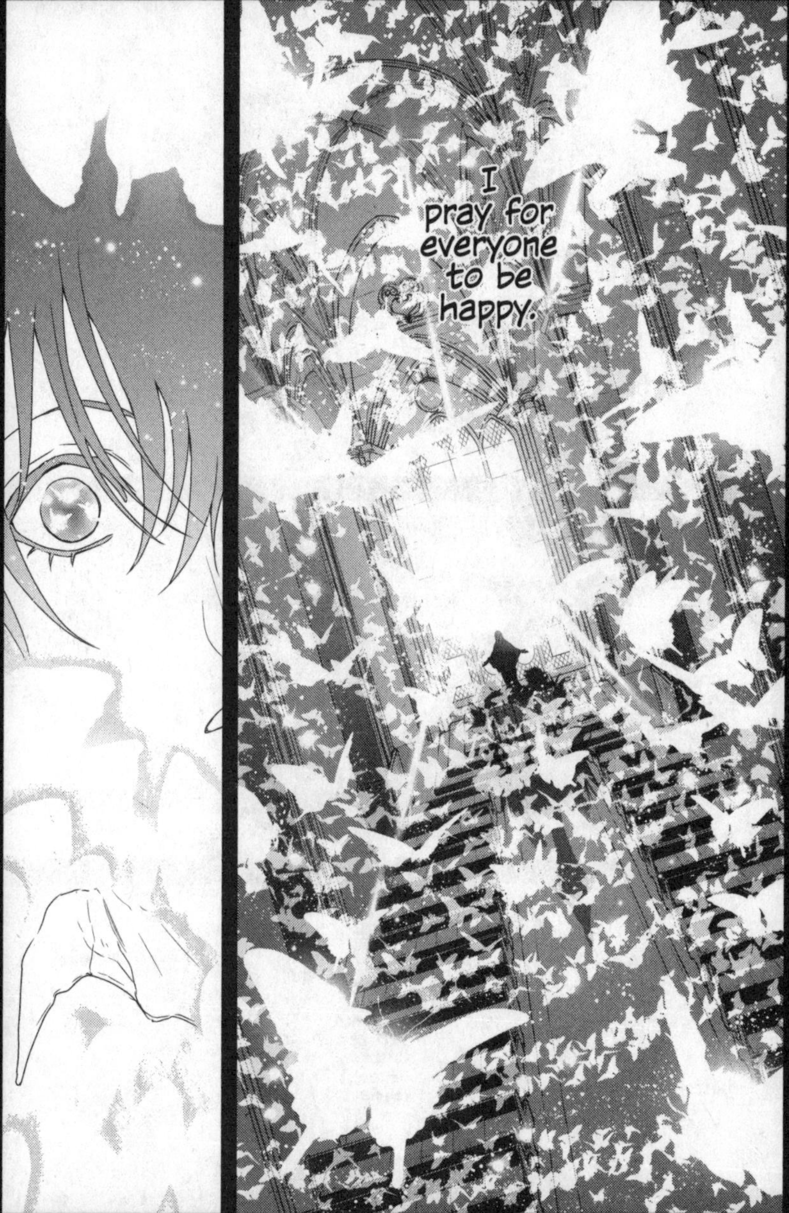
I pray for everyone to be happy.

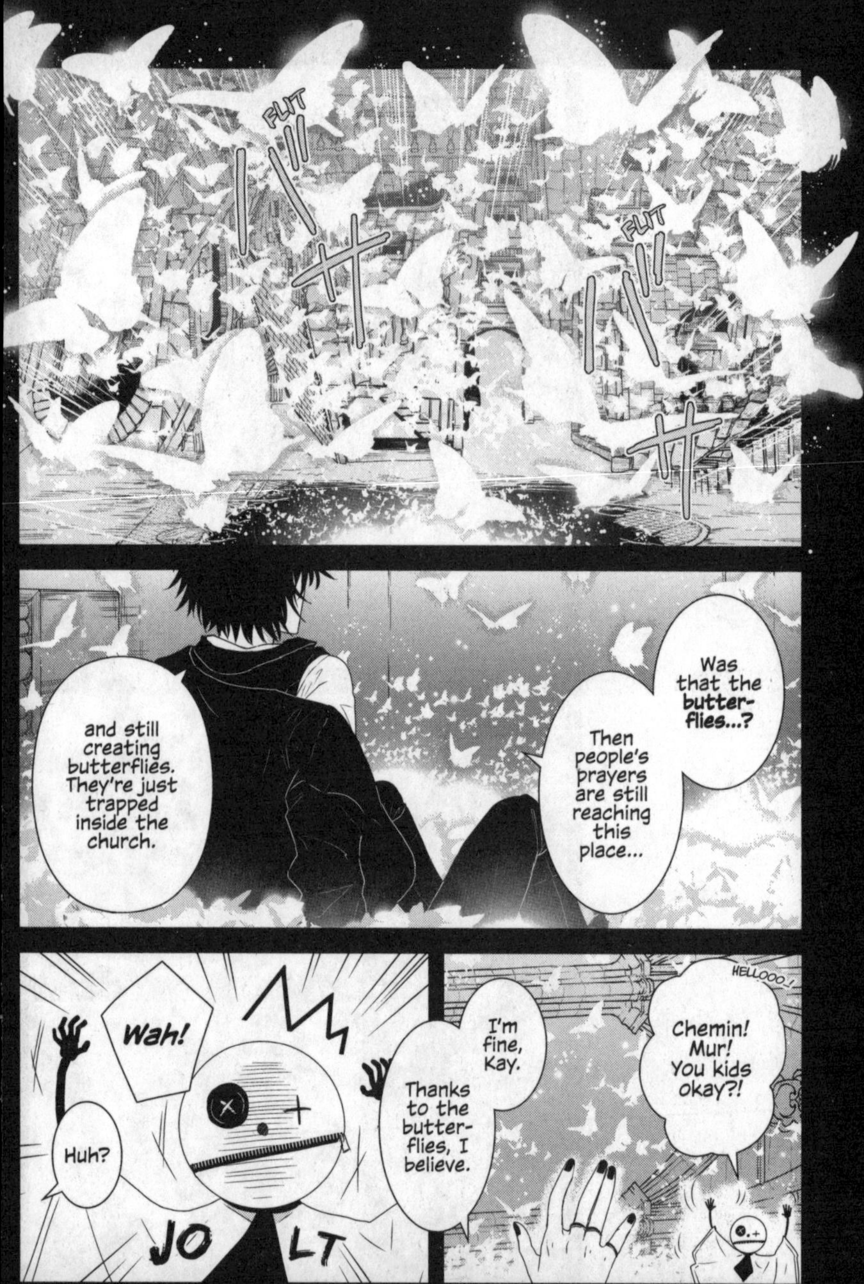
FLIT
FLIT
Was that the butterflies...?
Then people's prayers are still reaching this place...
and still creating butterflies. They're just trapped inside the church.
HELLOOO..!
Chemin! Mur! You kids okay?!
I'm fine, Kay.
Thanks to the butterflies, I believe.
Wah!
Huh?
JOLT

Your ears. They're, ah...

AND YOUR EYES, TOO.

Erm... Chemin?

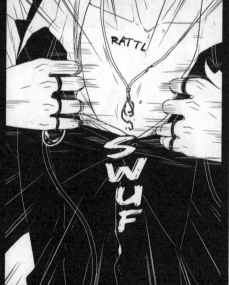

RATTL

SWUF

My ears?

HUH...? THEY'RE GONE.

TUG

BLANCH

PAF PAF

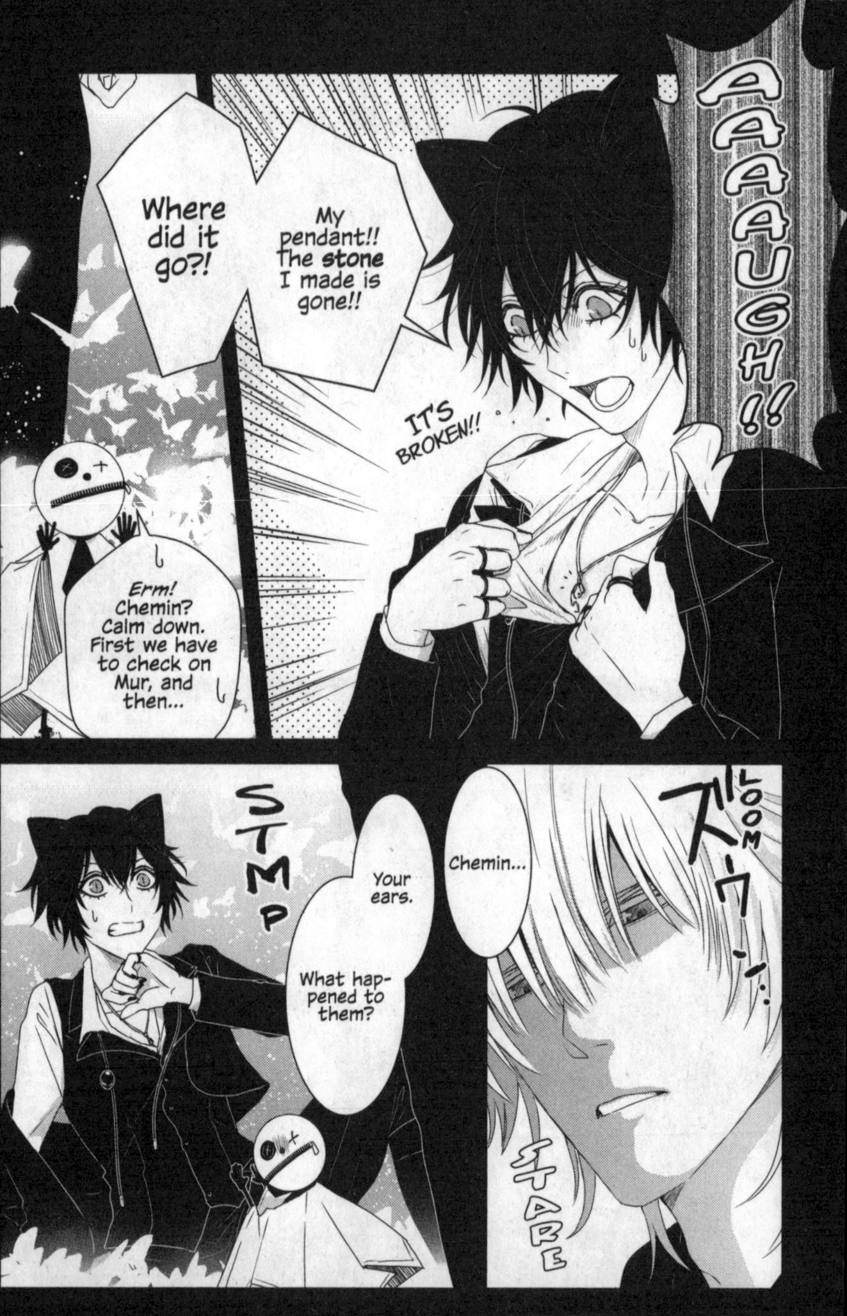
AAAAUGH!!
My pendant!! The stone I made is gone!!
Where did it go?!
IT'S BROKEN!!
Erm! Chemin? Calm down. First we have to check on Mur, and then...
LOOM
Chemin...
STARE
STMP
Your ears.
What hap-pened to them?

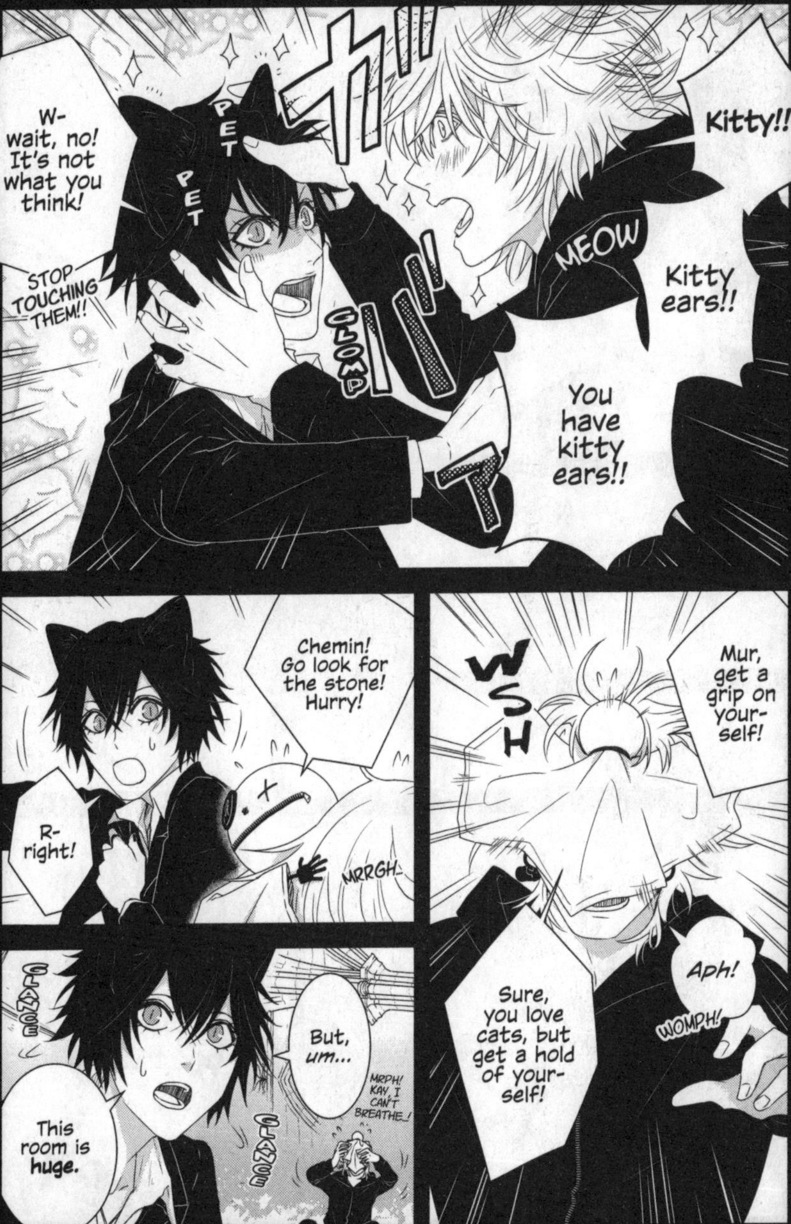
Kitty!!
Kitty ears!!
You have kitty ears!!
MEOW
GLOMP
PET
PET
W-wait, no! It's not what you think!
STOP TOUCHING THEM!!
Mur, get a grip on your-self!
WSH
Aph!
WOMPH!
Sure, you love cats, but get a hold of your-self!
Chemin! Go look for the stone! Hurry!
MRRGH...
R-right!
GLANCE
But, um...
MRPH! KAY, I CAN'T BREATHE...!
GLANCE
This room is **huge**.

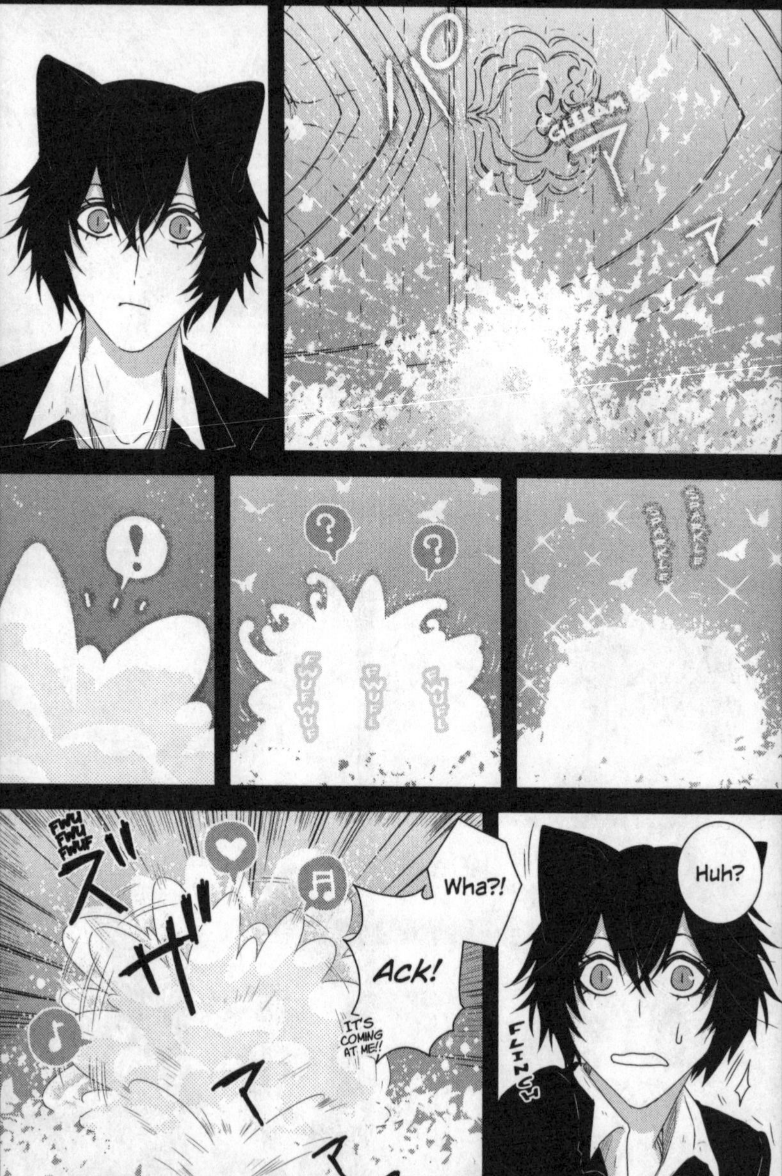
GEEAM
SPARKLE
SPARKLE
FWUF
FWUF
FWUFWUF
Huh?
FLINCH
Wha?!
Ack!
IT'S COMING AT ME!!
FWU FWU FWUF

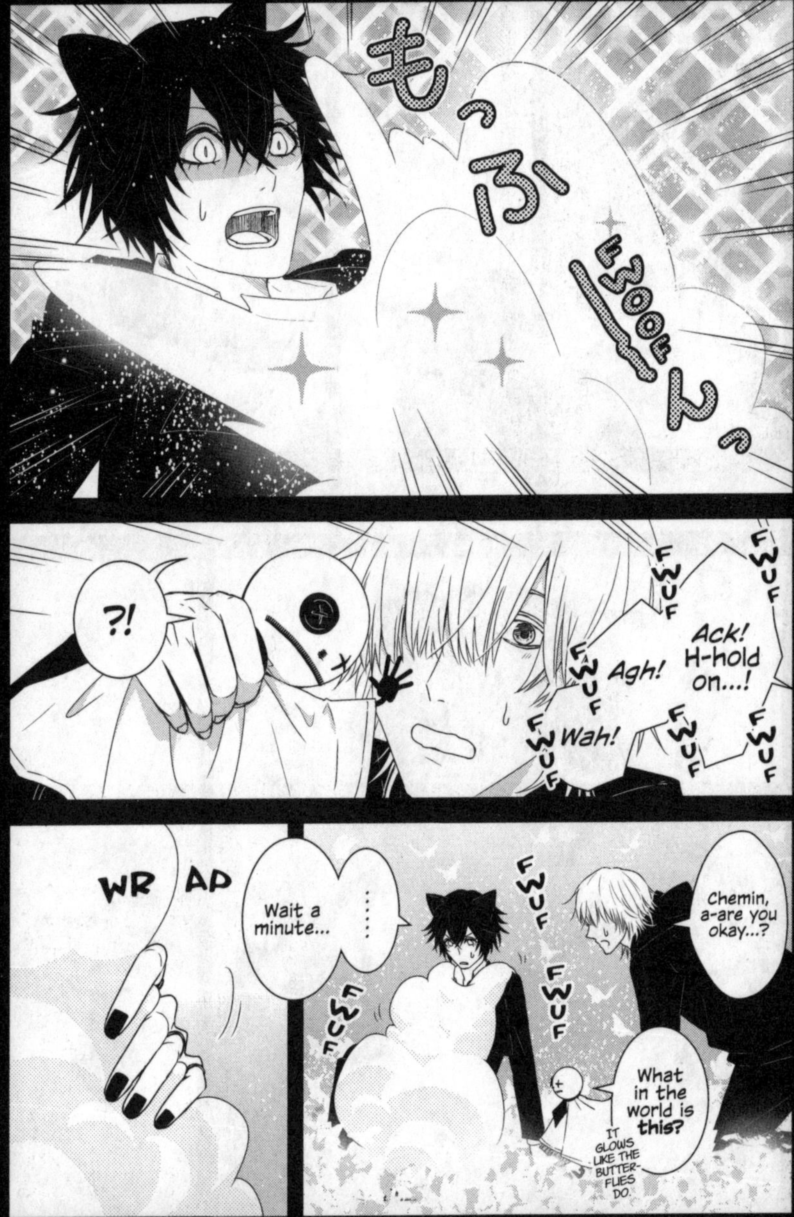
もっふ〜ん
FWOOF
FWUF
FWUF
Ack! H-hold on...!
Agh!
FWUF
FWUF
FWUF
Wah!
FWUF
?!
Chemin, a-are you okay...?
FWUF
FWUF
What in the world is this?
IT GLOWS LIKE THE BUTTER-FLIES DO.
Wait a minute...
......
WR AP

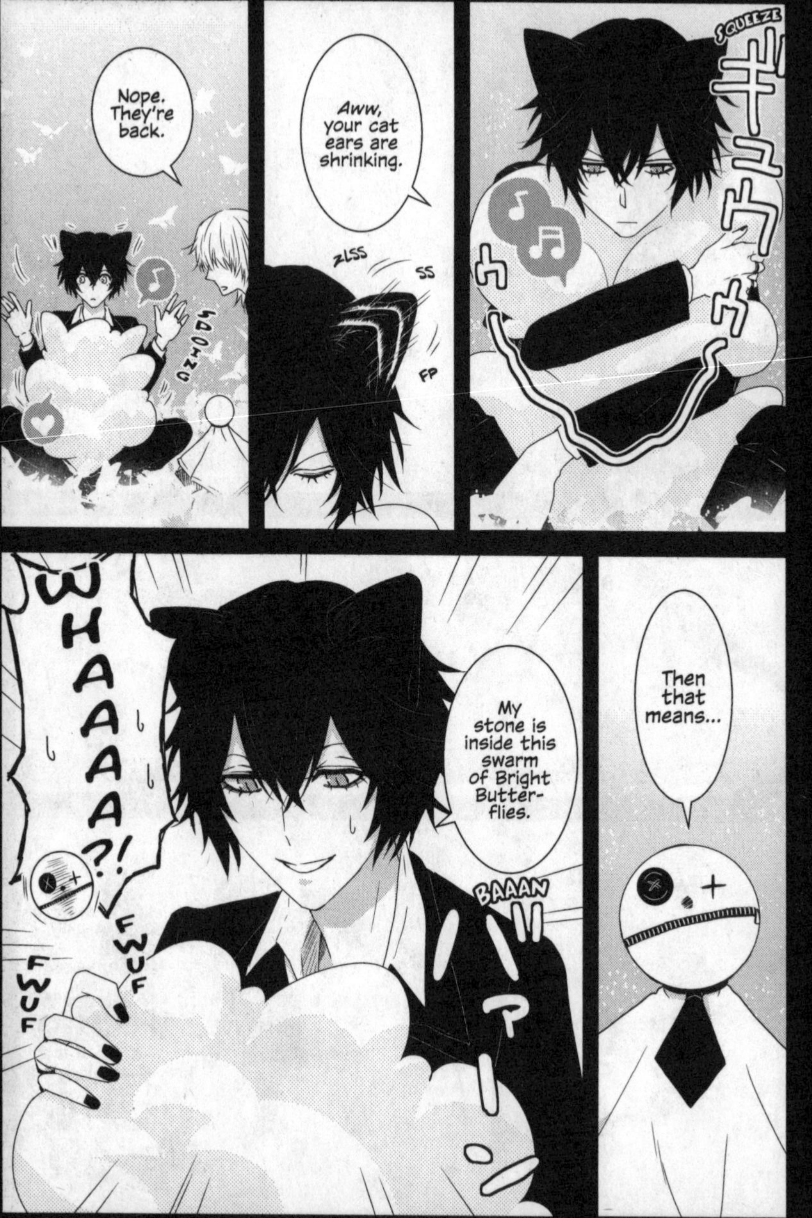
SQUEEZE
Aww, your cat ears are shrinking.
ZLSS
SS
FP
Nope. They're back.
SDOING
Then that means...
My stone is inside this swarm of Bright Butterflies.
BAAAN
WHAAAAA?!
FWUF
FWUF

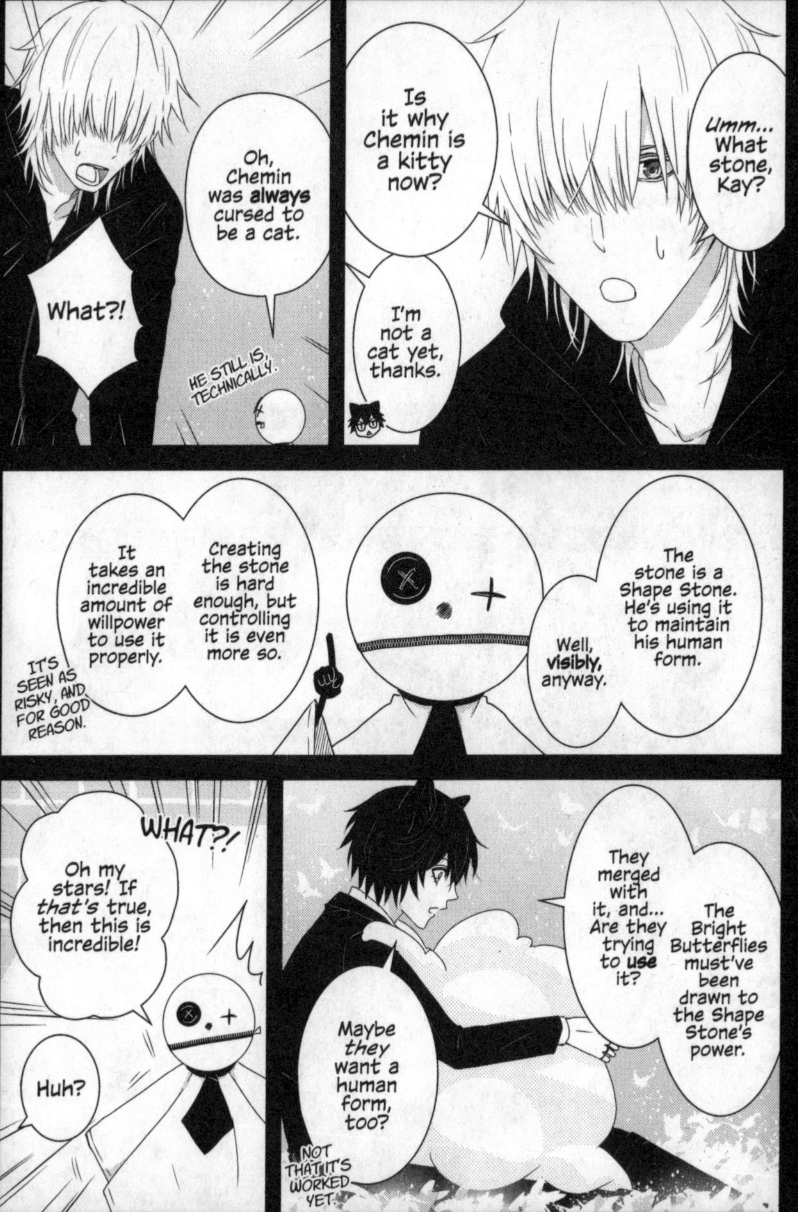
Umm... What stone, Kay?
Is it why Chemin is a kitty now?
I'm not a cat yet, thanks.
Oh, Chemin was **always** cursed to be a cat.
What?!
HE STILL IS, TECHNICALLY.
The stone is a Shape Stone. He's using it to maintain his human form.
Well, **visibly,** anyway.
Creating the stone is hard enough, but controlling it is even more so.
It takes an incredible amount of willpower to use it properly.
IT'S SEEN AS RISKY, AND FOR GOOD REASON.
The Bright Butterflies must've been drawn to the Shape Stone's power.
They merged with it, and... Are they trying to **use** it?
Maybe *they* want a human form, too?
NOT THAT IT'S WORKED YET.
WHAT?!
Oh my stars! If *that*'s true, then this is incredible!
Huh?

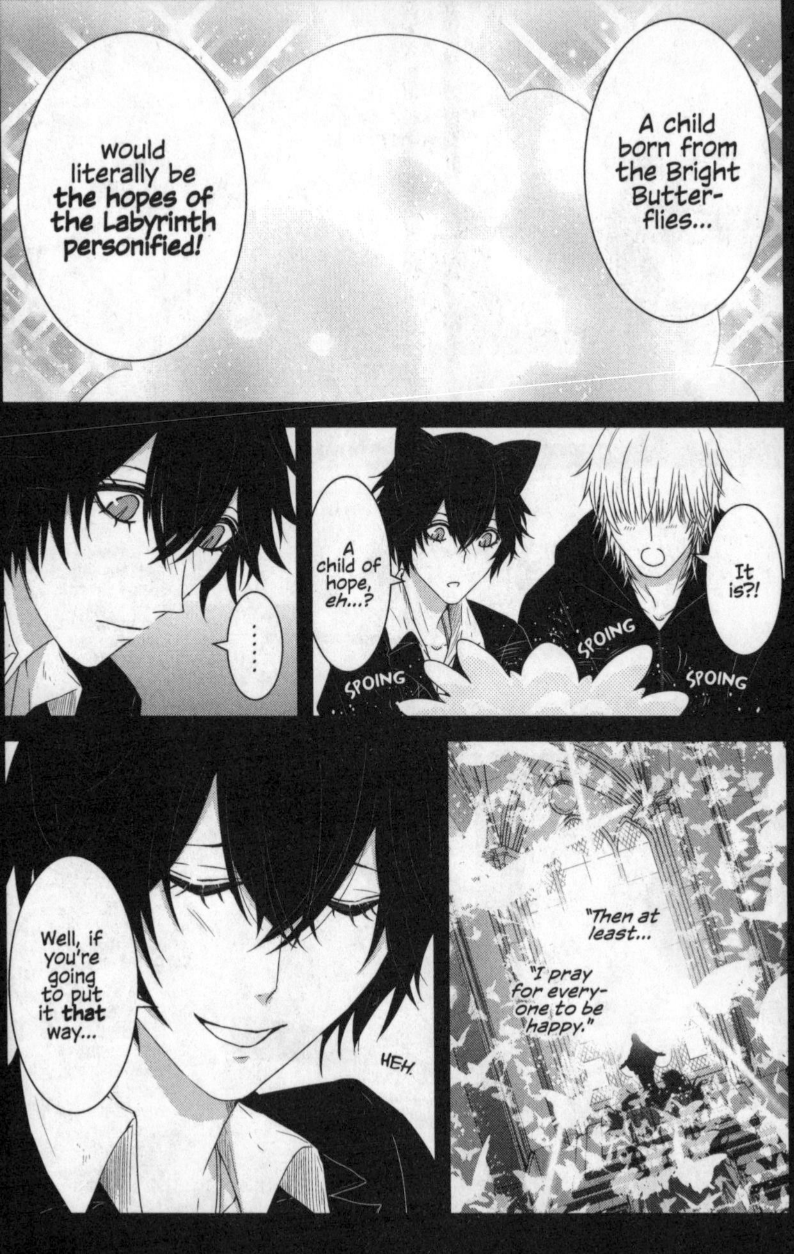
A child born from the Bright Butter-flies...
would literally be the hopes of the Labyrinth personified!
It is?!
SPOING
SPOING
SPOING
A child of hope, eh...?
......
"Then at least...
"I pray for every-one to be happy."
Well, if you're going to put it that way...
HEH.

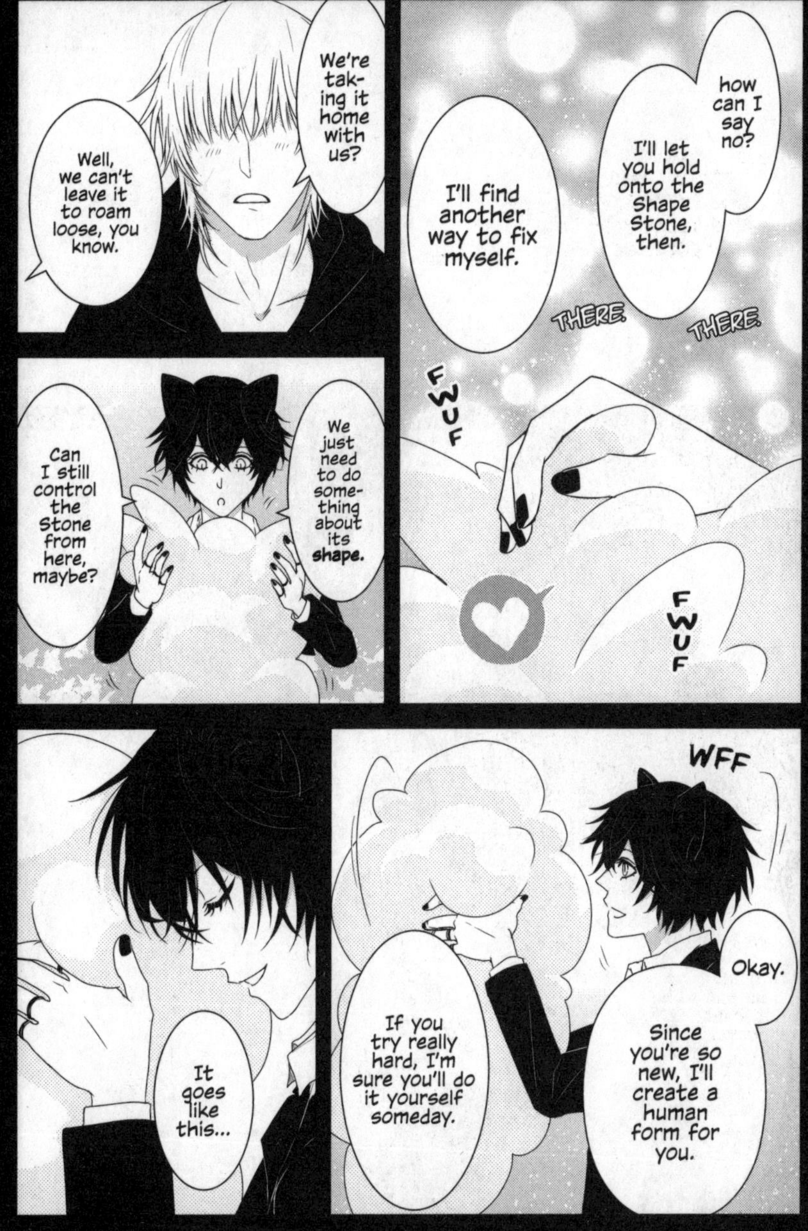
how can I say no?
I'll let you hold onto the Shape Stone, then.
I'll find another way to fix myself.
THERE.
THERE.
FWUF
FWUF
We're tak-ing it home with us?
Well, we can't leave it to roam loose, you know.
We just need to do some-thing about its **shape.**
Can I still control the Stone from here, maybe?
WFF
Okay.
Since you're so new, I'll create a human form for you.
If you try really hard, I'm sure you'll do it yourself someday.
It goes like this...

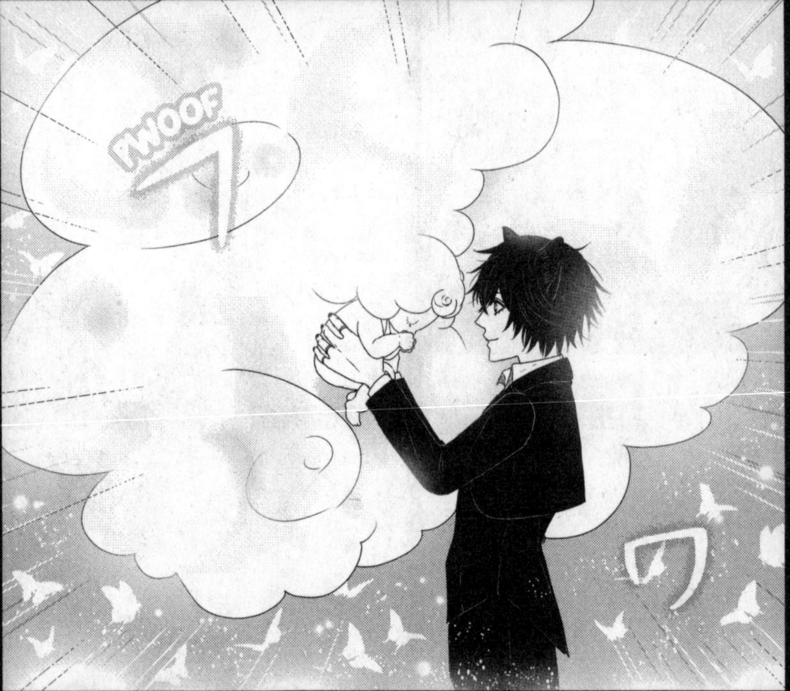
PWOOF
フ
ワ
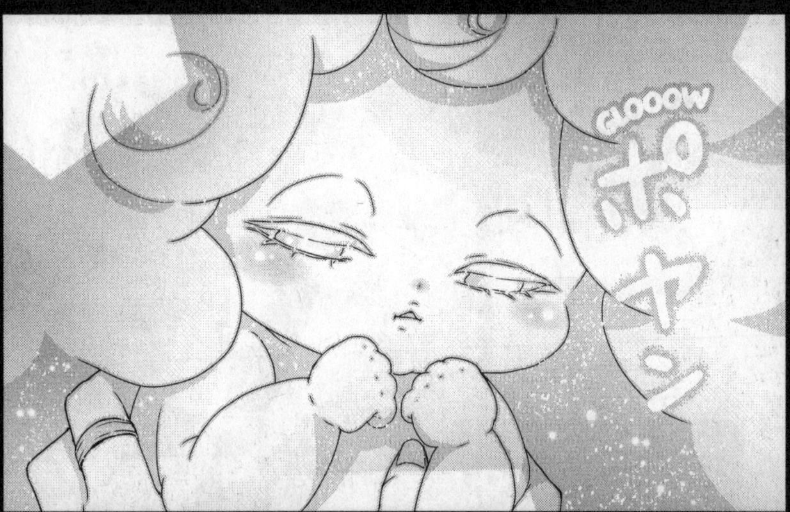
GLOOOW
ポヤン

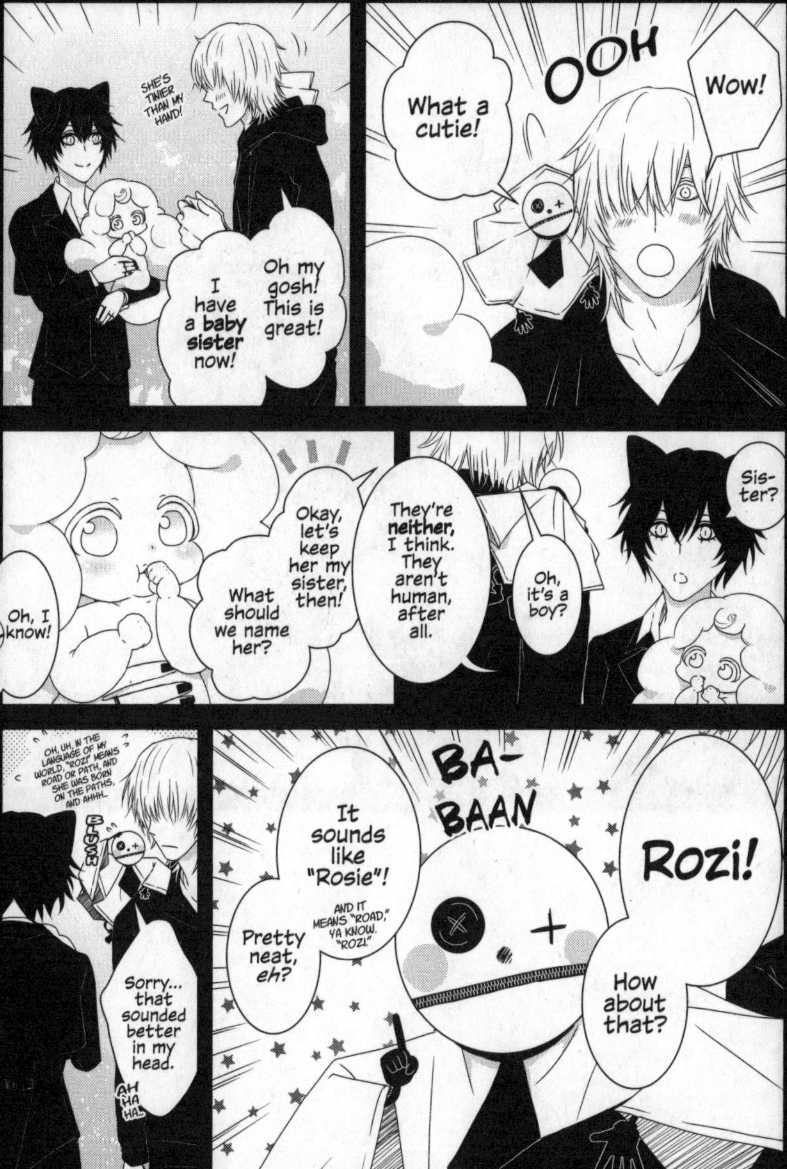
Wow!
OOH
What a cutie!
Oh my gosh! This is great!
I have a baby sister now!
SHE'S TINIER THAN MY HAND!
Sis-ter?
Oh, it's a boy?
They're neither, I think. They aren't human, after all.
Okay, let's keep her my sister, then!
What should we name her?
Oh, I know!
Rozi!
BA-BAAN
It sounds like "Rosie"!
How about that?
AND IT MEANS "ROAD," YA KNOW. "ROZI."
Pretty neat, eh?
OH, UH, IN THE LANGUAGE OF MY WORLD, "ROZI" MEANS ROAD OR PATH, AND SHE WAS BORN ON THE PATHS, AND AHHH...
BLUSH
Sorry... that sounded better in my head.
AH HA HA

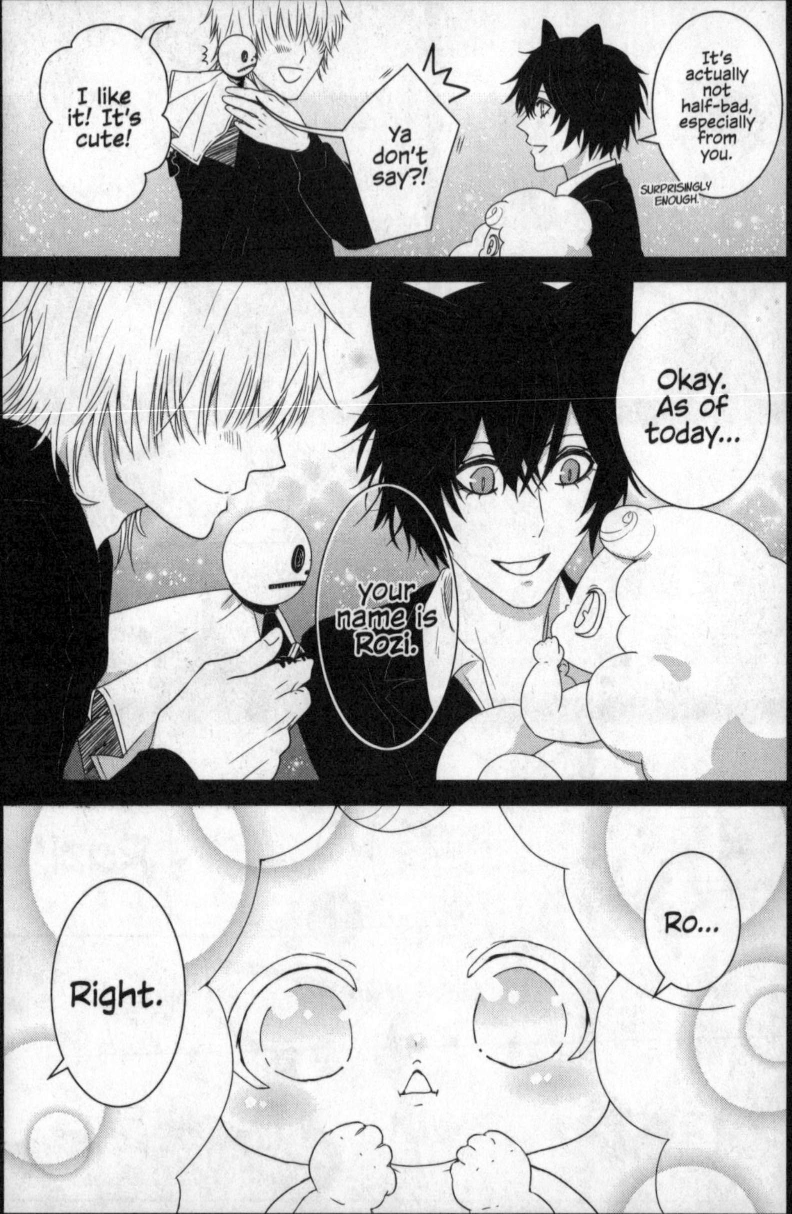
It's actually not half-bad, especially from you.
SURPRISINGLY ENOUGH.
Ya don't say?!
I like it! It's cute!
Okay. As of today...
your name is Rozi.
Ro...
Right.

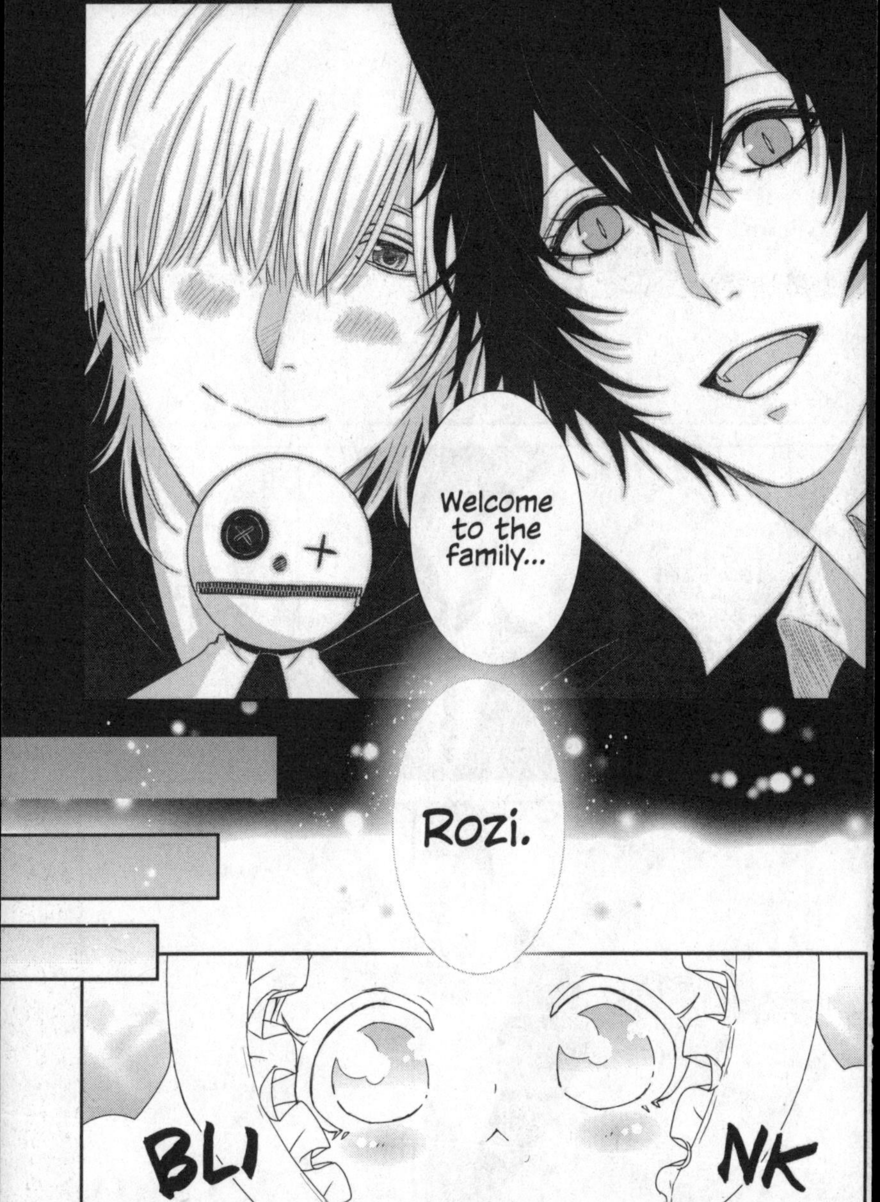
Welcome to the family...
Rozi.
BLI
NK

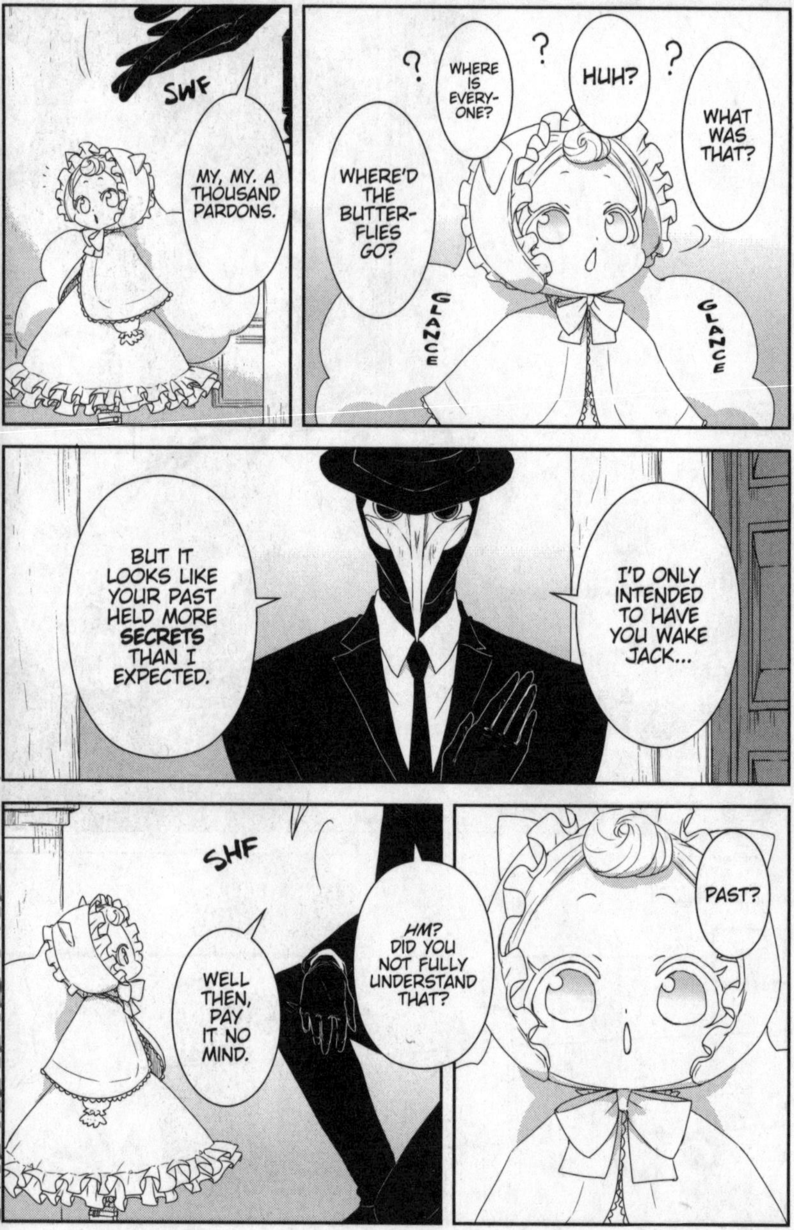
WHAT WAS THAT?
?
HUH?
?
WHERE IS EVERY-ONE?
?
WHERE'D THE BUTTER-FLIES GO?
GLANCE
GLANCE
SWF
MY, MY. A THOUSAND PARDONS.
I'D ONLY INTENDED TO HAVE YOU WAKE JACK...
BUT IT LOOKS LIKE YOUR PAST HELD MORE SECRETS THAN I EXPECTED.
PAST?
HM? DID YOU NOT FULLY UNDERSTAND THAT?
SHF
WELL THEN, PAY IT NO MIND.

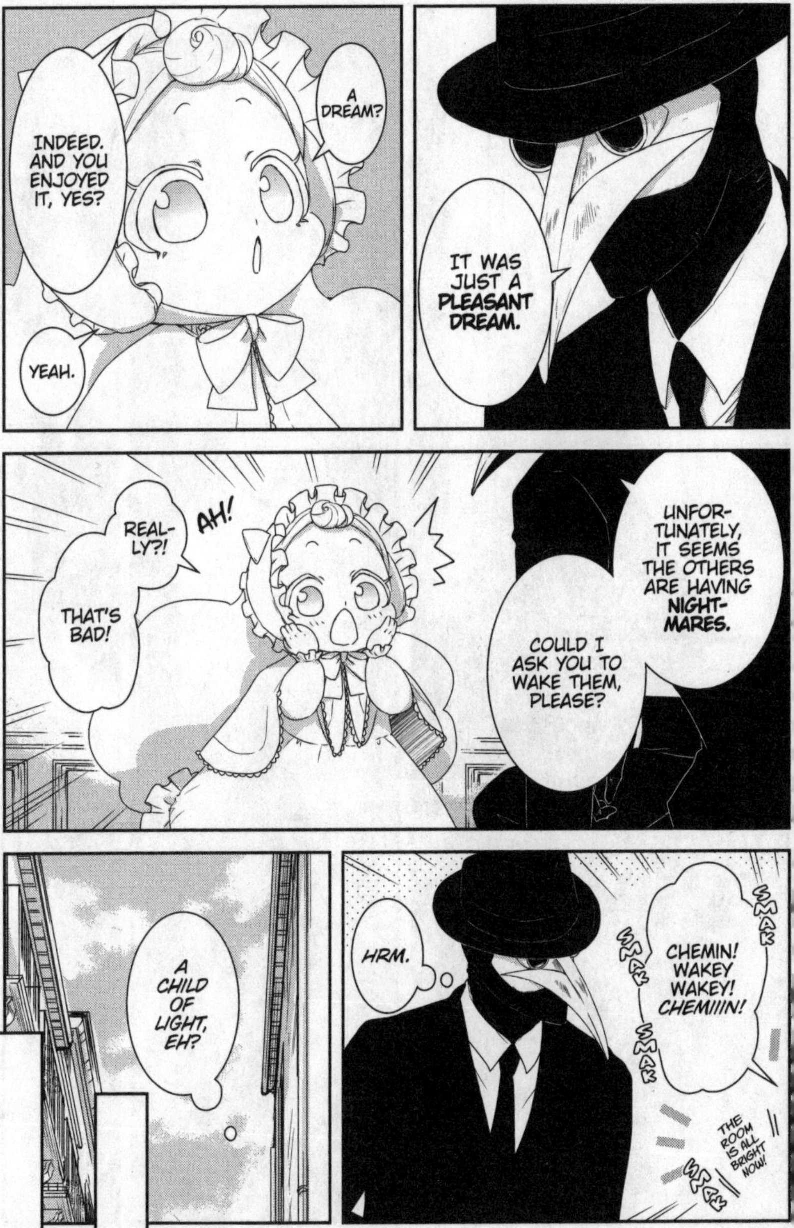
IT WAS JUST A PLEASANT DREAM.
A DREAM?
INDEED. AND YOU ENJOYED IT, YES?
YEAH.
UNFOR-TUNATELY, IT SEEMS THE OTHERS ARE HAVING NIGHT-MARES.
COULD I ASK YOU TO WAKE THEM, PLEASE?
AH!
REAL-LY?!
THAT'S BAD!
SMAK
CHEMIN! WAKEY WAKEY! CHEMIIIN!
SMAK
SMAK
SMAK
THE ROOM IS ALL BRIGHT NOW!
HRM.
A CHILD OF LIGHT, EH?

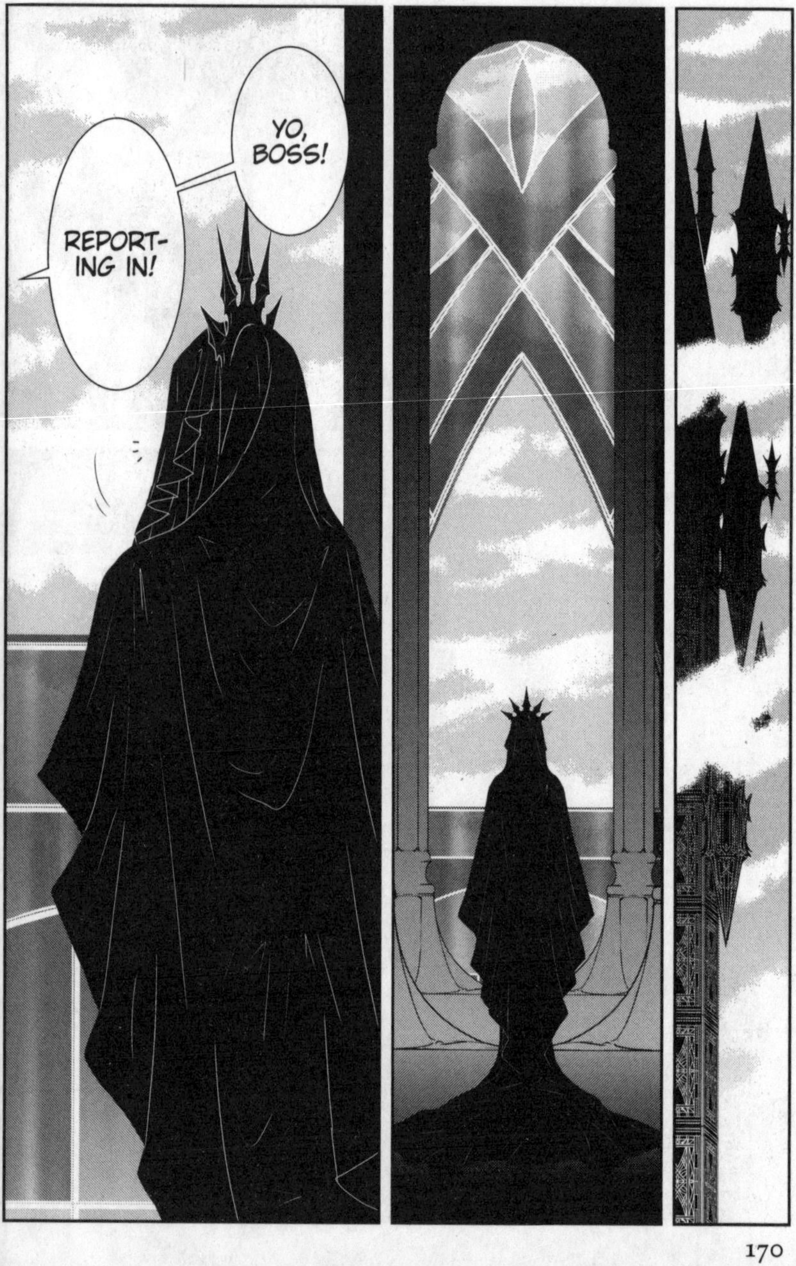
YO, BOSS!
REPORT-ING IN!

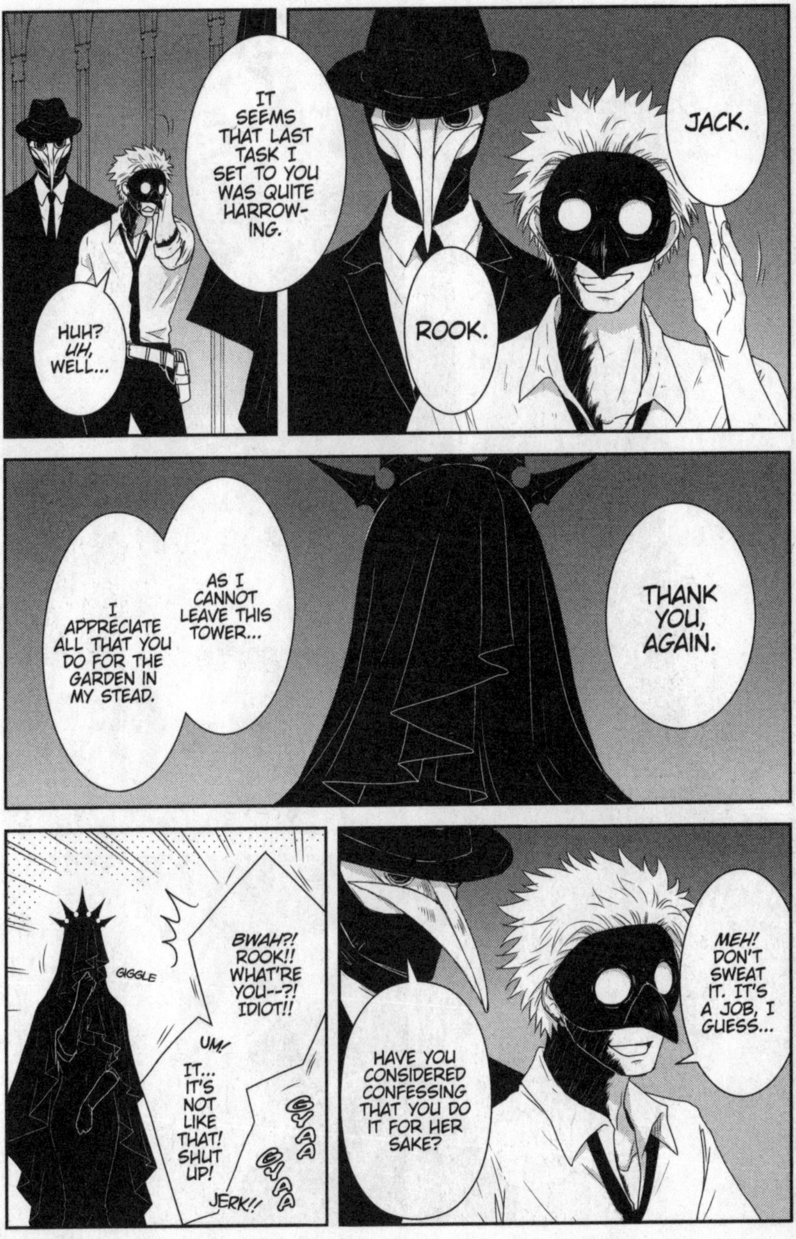
JACK.
ROOK.
IT SEEMS THAT LAST TASK I SET TO YOU WAS QUITE HARROW-ING.
HUH? UH, WELL...
THANK YOU, AGAIN.
AS I CANNOT LEAVE THIS TOWER...
I APPRECIATE ALL THAT YOU DO FOR THE GARDEN IN MY STEAD.
MEH! DON'T SWEAT IT. IT'S A JOB, I GUESS...
HAVE YOU CONSIDERED CONFESSING THAT YOU DO IT FOR HER SAKE?
BWAH?! ROOK!! WHAT'RE YOU--?! IDIOT!!
UM! IT... IT'S NOT LIKE THAT! SHUT UP!
JERK!!
GYAA
GYAA
GYAA
GIGGLE

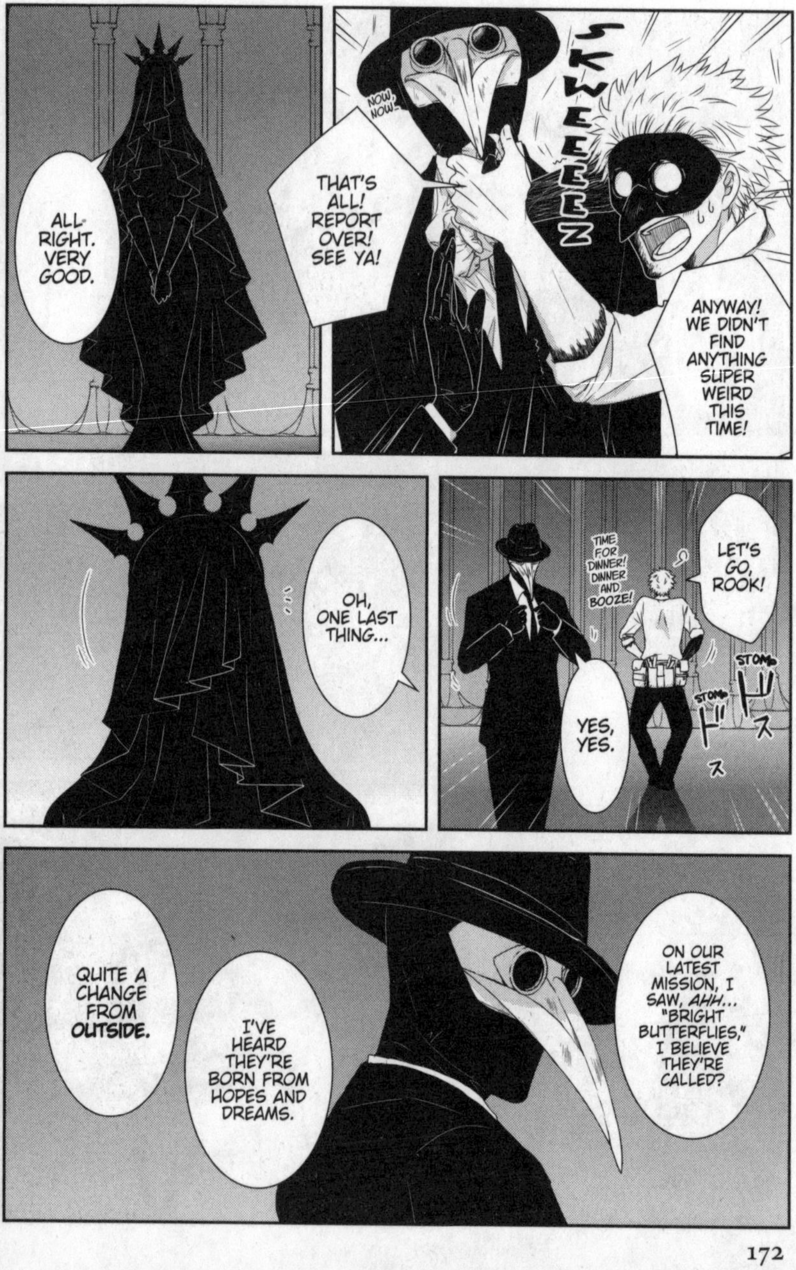
ANYWAY! WE DIDN'T FIND ANYTHING SUPER WEIRD THIS TIME!
SKWEEEZ
NOW, NOW!
THAT'S ALL! REPORT OVER! SEE YA!
ALL RIGHT. VERY GOOD.
LET'S GO, ROOK!
TIME FOR DINNER! DINNER AND BOOZE!
STOMP ドス
STOMP ドス
YES, YES.
OH, ONE LAST THING...
ON OUR LATEST MISSION, I SAW, *AHH*... "BRIGHT BUTTERFLIES," I BELIEVE THEY'RE CALLED?
I'VE HEARD THEY'RE BORN FROM HOPES AND DREAMS.
QUITE A CHANGE FROM **OUTSIDE.**

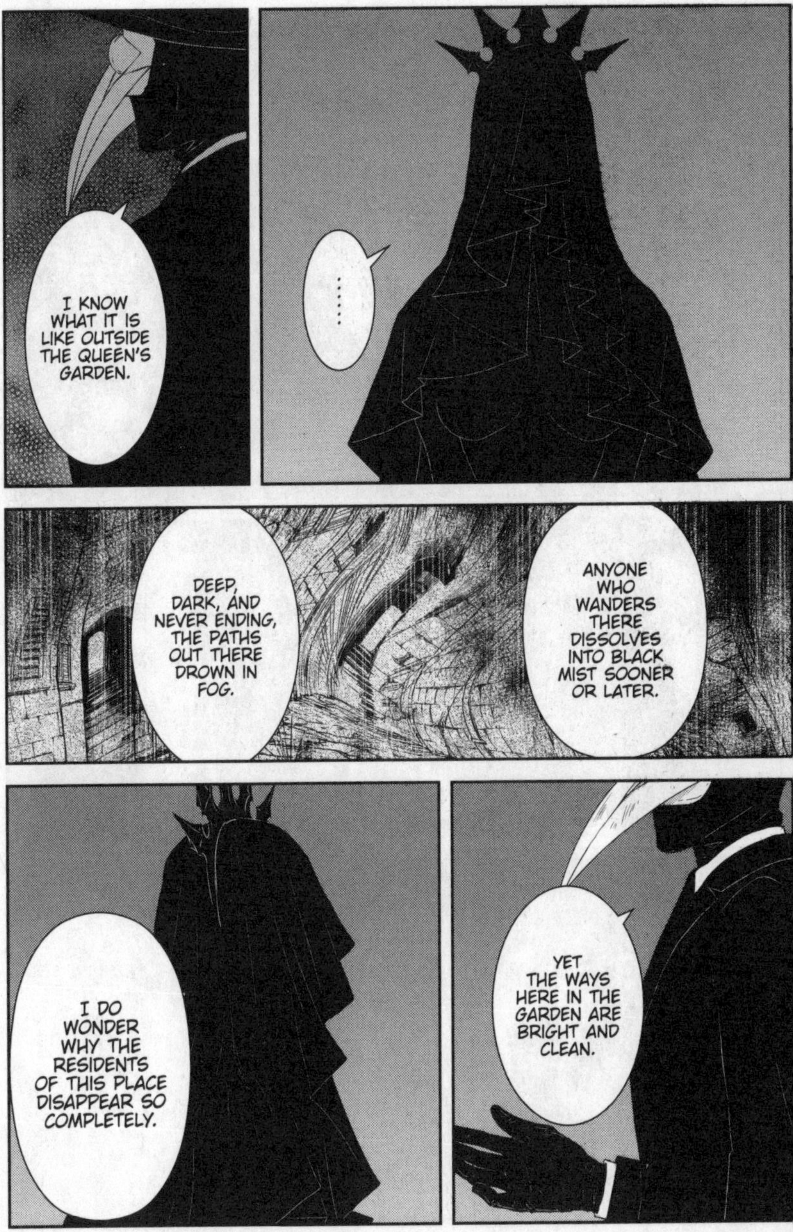
I KNOW WHAT IT IS LIKE OUTSIDE THE QUEEN'S GARDEN.
......
DEEP, DARK, AND NEVER ENDING, THE PATHS OUT THERE DROWN IN FOG.
ANYONE WHO WANDERS THERE DISSOLVES INTO BLACK MIST SOONER OR LATER.
I DO WONDER WHY THE RESIDENTS OF THIS PLACE DISAPPEAR SO COMPLETELY.
YET THE WAYS HERE IN THE GARDEN ARE BRIGHT AND CLEAN.

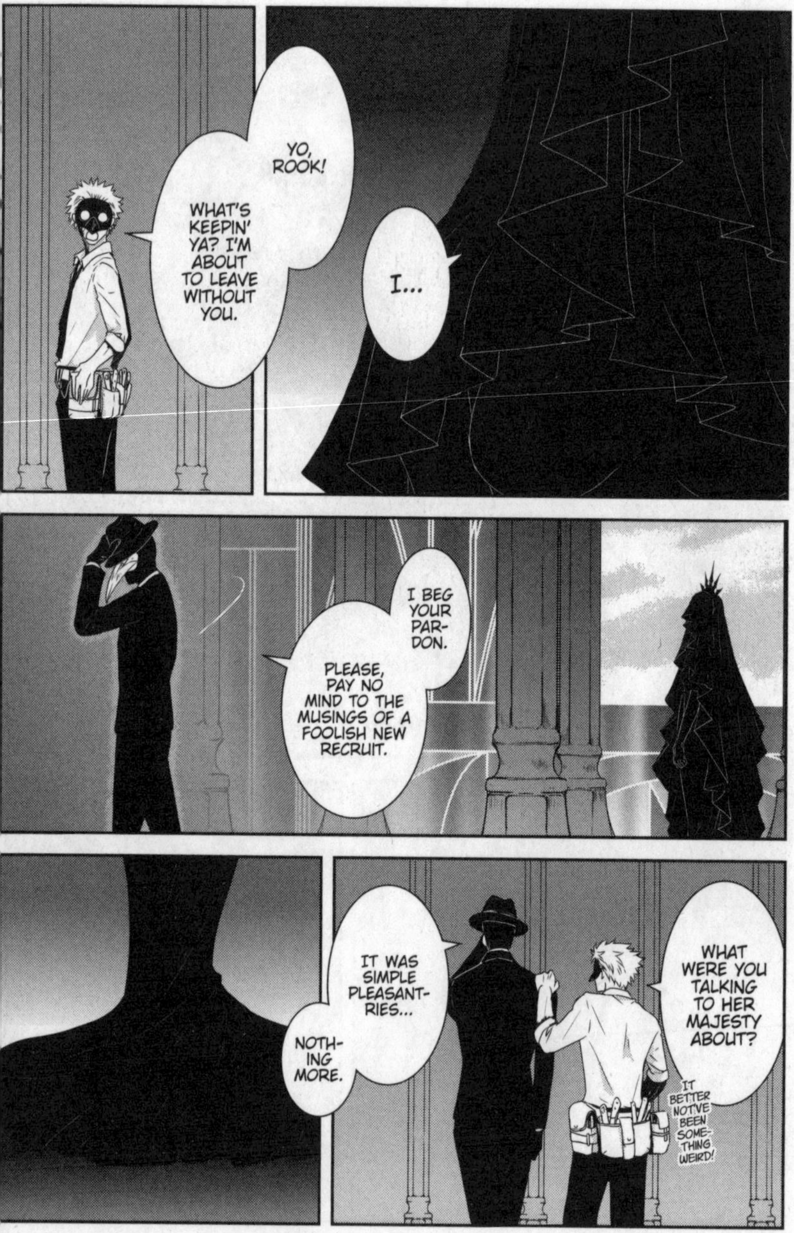
I...
YO, ROOK!
WHAT'S KEEPIN' YA? I'M ABOUT TO LEAVE WITHOUT YOU.
I BEG YOUR PARDON.
PLEASE, PAY NO MIND TO THE MUSINGS OF A FOOLISH NEW RECRUIT.
WHAT WERE YOU TALKING TO HER MAJESTY ABOUT?
IT BETTER NOT'VE BEEN SOMETHING WEIRD!
IT WAS SIMPLE PLEASANTRIES...
NOTHING MORE.

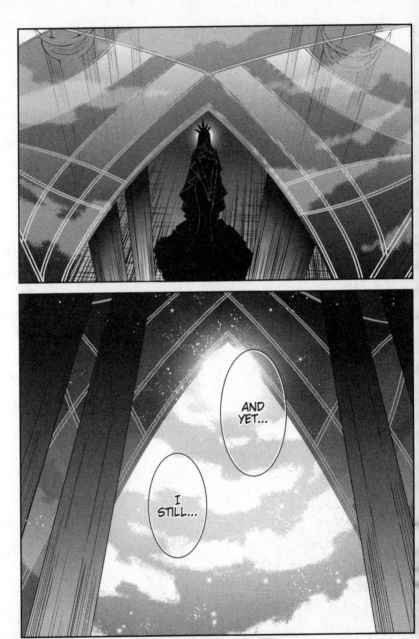

Rozi in the Labyrinth 2 **END**

TO BE CONTINUED
IN VOLUME THREE!

SEVEN SEAS ENTERTAINMENT PRESENTS

ROZI in the Labyrinth

story and art by SHIYA TOTSUKI

VOLUME 2

TRANSLATION
Adrienne Beck

LETTERING AND RETOUCH
Jennifer Skarupa

COVER DESIGN
Hanase Qi
(LOGO) George Panella

PROOFREADER
Danielle King

EDITOR
Shanti Whitesides

PREPRESS TECHNICIAN
Rhiannon Rasmussen-Silverstein

PRODUCTION ASSOCIATE
Christa Miesner

PRODUCTION MANAGER
Lissa Pattillo

MANAGING EDITOR
Julie Davis

ASSOCIATE PUBLISHER
Adam Arnold

PUBLISHER
Jason DeAngelis

ROZI IN THE LABYRINTH VOL. 2
©Shiya Totsuki 2020
All rights reserved.
Originally published in Japan in 2020 by MAG Garden Corporation, TOKYO.
English translation rights arranged through TOHAN CORPORATION, Tokyo.

Seven Seas press and purchase enquiries can be sent to Marketing Manager Lianne Sentar at press@gomanga.com. Information regarding the distribution and purchase of digital editions is available from Digital Manager CK Russell at digital@gomanga.com.

Seven Seas and the Seven Seas logo are trademarks of Seven Seas Entertainment. All rights reserved.

ISBN: 978-1-64827-933-1

Printed in Canada

First Printing: August 2021

10 9 8 7 6 5 4 3 2 1

FOLLOW US ONLINE: *www.sevenseasentertainment.com*

READING DIRECTIONS

This book reads from *right to left*, Japanese style. If this is your first time reading manga, you start reading from the top right panel on each page and take it from there. If you get lost, just follow the numbered diagram here. It may seem backwards at first, but you'll get the hang of it! Have fun!!

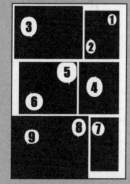

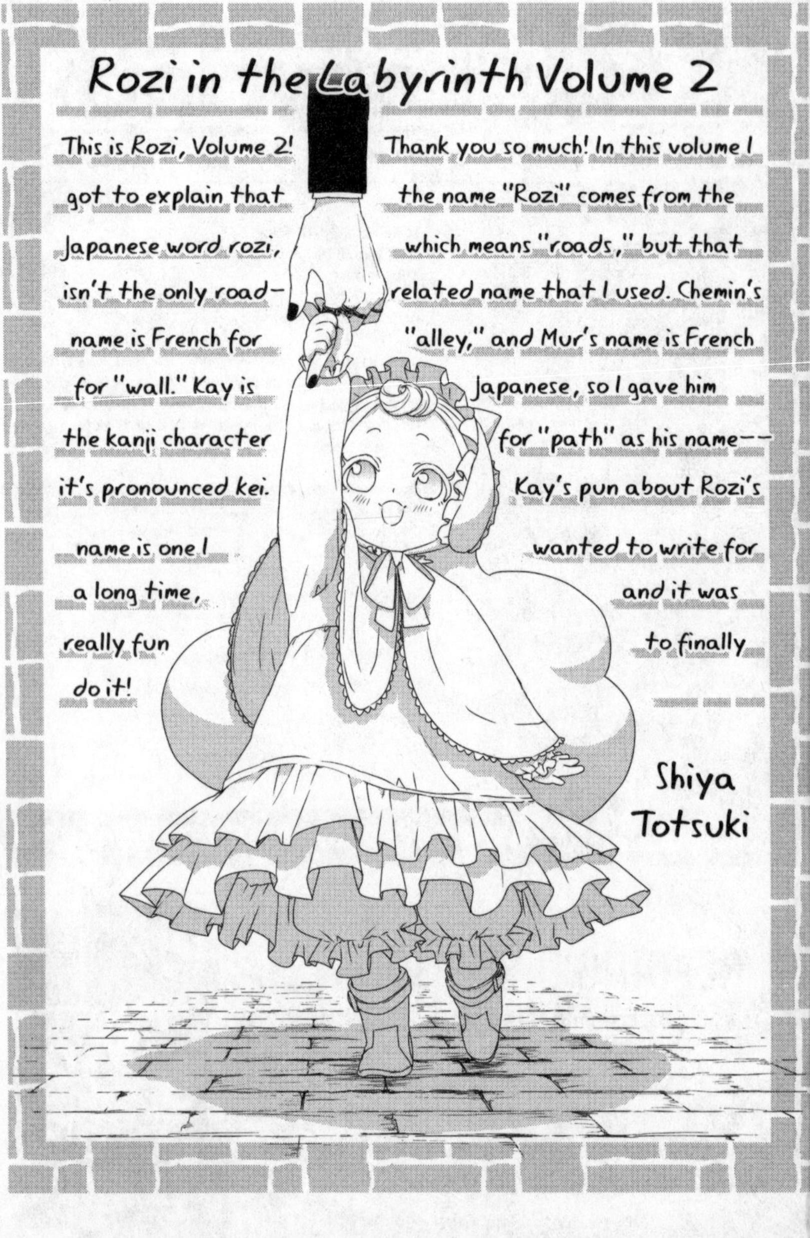

Rozi in the Labyrinth Volume 2

This is Rozi, Volume 2! Thank you so much! In this volume I got to explain that the name "Rozi" comes from the Japanese word rozi, which means "roads," but that isn't the only road-related name that I used. Chemin's name is French for "alley," and Mur's name is French for "wall." Kay is Japanese, so I gave him the kanji character for "path" as his name--it's pronounced kei. Kay's pun about Rozi's name is one I wanted to write for a long time, and it was really fun to finally do it!

Shiya Totsuki